Memoirs to My Women

Memoirs to My Women

Randall Lee

Copyright © 2010 by Randall Lee.

Library of Congress Control Number: 2010903237
ISBN: Hardcover   978-1-4500-5810-0
              Softcover   978-1-4500-5809-4
              Ebook   978-1-4500-5811-7

All rights reserved. No part of this book may be reproduced or transmitted in any form or by any means, electronic or mechanical, including photocopying, recording, or by any information storage and retrieval system, without permission in writing from the copyright owner.

This is a work of fiction. Names, characters, places and incidents either are the product of the author's imagination or are used fictitiously, and any resemblance to any actual persons, living or dead, events, or locales is entirely coincidental.

This book was printed in the United States of America.

To order additional copies of this book, contact:
Xlibris Corporation
1-888-795-4274
www.Xlibris.com
Orders@Xlibris.com
72133

PREFACE

Behind every good man is a woman. This is an old adage but I am not fortunate enough to know who said it. I am assuming that he or she was referring to people from all walks of life and not just limited to the most famous and most successful. My own progression through various stages of maturity and evolution of mind were directly affected by the women I associated with. Although consistently plagued with levels of regression while my stability factors wreaked havoc with any direct path to the full reaches of maturity, the development of my soul did not deviate from its search for spiritual growth.

Without the women who influenced my life, I would never have developed the understanding needed to become the man I am today. My writing of these memoirs to my women is a direct testimony and acknowledgment of their value and a way to express eternal indebtedness to those who dedicated their time to me in my relentless search for happiness. From the most trivial moments to the most sublime.

To share my thoughts on the written page is to bear heart and tribute to those whom I have hurt in my transgressions and to affirm my proclamation of my true love to all those connected. To develop the path to universal soul through the stepping-stones of relationships is too profound, and perhaps it explains my struggle to remove the context of moral issues that has enveloped me in remorse.

The morality of mankind is the foundation of any search, but it is the variation of interaction with others that lay the steps to form the stairway to the whole understanding. The goal of the inner self is to develop in such a manner as to complete a path of enlightenment, but it must rely on the connections of human relations to achieve proper fulfillment.

To those of you whom I do not mention, it is not that my experiences with you were of any less value, but that your contributions were of such similarity and brevity that only minute additives were affixed to the formula of my progression. I might not have found my dreams and inspirations completed during my time on this planet and will be remembered by only few. But when I finally reach the cosmos and take my experiences and pure emotions with me, I may find I have learned more than one could expect to know.

CHAPTER 1

Jill:

You were my first. First of the ones to enter my revolving door of conflicting emotions and meandering paths in my quest to finding an understanding of my existence. An understanding to my search for a purpose in life that sent me spiraling in such lost senses of directions. It projected me into a journey of repeated processes that not until much later in life was I able to clearly decipher a meaning to. I know that is a strong accusation to hurl at a nine-year-old girl whose main purpose in life at that time was to get straight As in a fourth-grade class. It was of no fault of your own, but you were the beginning of my downhill tumble into depression.

I had become infatuated with you since the start of the school year. I had no idea about what I was feeling nor did I at that primitive age ever begin to fathom the meaning of that strange throbbing in my heart. And I had no intentions of sharing this sensation nor would I be asking advice from anyone. There was a shyness in me that was so strangling that in my first year of public school, I couldn't get myself to raise my hand to go to the bathroom for fear of drawing attention. This paved the way to a rough road of some embarrassing moments for as we all know, you can only hold the pressure of a bladder for certain lengths of time, and then something has to give. I had more than a few accidents that first year. Luckily I was part of a small class, and only my teacher and possibly a fellow student or two knew why I spent a lot of time at my desk with my legs crossed and had an unusual habit of walking with my backpack in front of me. To this day, through self-administered but regimental grade-school training, my daily constitution happens with punctuality at the first rise of the sun. I only share this with you to explain how shy I actually was and what it had taken for me to do what I did on Valentine's Day.

If you can recall, I rarely talked, and I was a complete mess on the odd occasion when I had to stand up in front of the class. Public speaking was not in the cards for me. I would shake all over, and eye contact was at something on the floor by my shoes that no one else could see. I did not stutter, but nonetheless, the words never came out complete and never quite right. The closest I would ever come to stuttering came later in life when I found certain advantages in alcohol and, with abundant usage, would repeat myself. The discovery of alcohol also created an unfortunate reliance on its effects to alleviate the disadvantages of chronic shyness. Fortitude in a bottle.

You might not have known how difficult it was for me to approach you nor could you be aware of that gnawing urge in my heart to do so. And at my seasoned age of nine years, I had no comprehension of what was going on inside me. All I did know for sure was that it was an obsessive feeling that ruled my thinking processes. So to be able to concentrate on my schoolwork, I tried to bury my feelings in the concealment of my shyness, subconsciously knowing I couldn't act on them anyway. Somehow I was able to file it away under "things to be dealt with later." My first lesson in procrastination did nothing, however, to alleviate the fact that I thought of you every day. At the front of my file drawer of thought, right in the immediate forefront, was you, marching right past all other thoughts. Little did I know that this inability to control such thoughts from smothering all others, including practicality, was a precursor to what may be labeled as emotionally challenged. In that I mean I was discovering that my emotional levels were already a challenge to keep them in perspective. I had heard of the definition of puppy love but disregarded it. This was something more. But worse, this was the beginning of a path to that intertwined infatuation, lust, yearning, adoration, endearment into one big package that was defined by love. If I had recognized the innocence and the frivolity of this so-called puppy love, I may have been able to have steered my emotional development in safer directions. I do have you to thank to keep it under wraps until my high school years. With your help, I laid the mortar for the concrete wall that went up. That was where I withdrew for a long time, in the comforts of my inner world, a great complement to my shyness. All this over a Valentine's Day card.

Valentine's Day, by definition, is a way to demonstrate one's inner feelings toward another. I also thought it was an opportunity to find a discreet way to show these feelings in what seemed to be a mandatory practice on that particular day. The more my small mind weighed the tradition of that day and found balance in my thinking of a way to finally approach you to alleviate the gnawing inside me, the more an idea came about how to get around my shyness.

The following Monday was Valentine's Day, and the Saturday before that, I was on the routine excursion with my mother as country folk heading into town for their weekly supplies. My shyness did not exclude my mother, but I was at least comfortable enough to ask her for things. I asked her if she could help me find something for Valentine's Day. Unaware of what I was really asking, she was quick to find a package of those sappy small cardboard cutouts that kids pass out to their classmates. With great difficulty, even after planning the request, committing thought to action, I asked my mother if I could have one a bit bigger. Her immediate reply was that one out of the package would be sufficient for the teacher. If I had been older then, I would have recognized then some of the roots of my shyness. Talking to my parents at any emotional levels was not something that was done. Even before school, hugging had stopped. So the normal reaction for me would have been to say "Never mind," and I would go crawling back into my shell. But that day, I summoned up an unusual act of courage. I blurted out it was for a girl in my class. My mother was quick to laugh, and I shrank even smaller than I felt. She gave me a quick remark about puppy love that went through my ears like silent wind. I wasn't a puppy, and this was a deeper feeling than I had toward our Labrador chained to his doghouse in the backyard.

We were of modest means, tightly budgeted. Although my mother was quite lax on showing affection, she wasn't completely heartless either. Maybe she was thinking of a crush she had back in her youth, but in any event, she gave me permission to pick out any card I wanted. I remember that small flutter like a flock of butterflies tickling the inside of my abdomen, and I recognized it as joy. To grant me such a favor warmed me. I picked out the biggest flamboyant and brightest card in the store. It had a huge red velvet heart on the front, and the card itself would never fit in my backpack. It would have worked wonders for me attached to the front of my pants a few grades back. My mother frowned at me at first, hesitated, and then motioned for me to put it into the shopping cart. Later at the till, I understood what that frown meant, for there would be no candy treats for me that day.

I do not remember what the card read inside, only that the declaration of love was clearly defined. It also included the word *love* in the best cursive writing I could muster, just above my signature as a measure of my own proclamation. The rest of the weekend I spent reading, looking over at my treasured card in between chapters. Reading was my escape from the world, completely engrossed with the life of the characters on the page, drawn into the very vision of the story before me. There were strict rules about television in my house, where I was only allowed an hour a day. On the weekends, this was usually wasted on a morning cartoon. I distinctly remember reading Jules Verne's *Mysterious Island* that weekend while the excitement of such an adventure was the only thing that kept my nerves in check. It had been a very long weekend as I prepared myself for the big day.

Monday morning did come, and there was a big lump in my throat that made my cereal hard to swallow. You sat four rows away from me, and with the proper alignment of the kids in between us, I was able to look at you without you being aware of it. Although I was an A student, I spent more time recently doing just that, instead of looking at the teacher. Once in a while, you would catch me; and when our eyes met, you would give me a smile. It washed me with invisible warmth, like being sprayed in spring sunlight. That day you didn't look over at all while I couldn't stop looking.

A few minutes after our first recess, the moment of truth arrived. The teacher announced that it was now time to pass around any Valentine cards that we might have. In a whirlpool of frenzied kids and sliding desks, the teacher had stood with her back against the chalkboard and assessed any risk of colliding children from a vantage point out of her own harm's way. I remember weaving in and out of the other kids' paths and, in no organized fashion, placed my cardboard cutouts to the corresponding desks of my classmates. How we did this in such riotous fashion and not get some cards to the wrong desk was a mystery to me. I did not have to give any thought about where your desk was. But the huge card that I managed somehow to conceal so far was still in my desk drawer and had to be retrieved. When I pulled it out, it was slightly crumpled along the edges, from me forcing it in among the rest of my school supplies. Traffic in the classroom was still heavy, and I almost tripped once jostling through the others with no advantages of lane restrictions. I had lost sight of you, and I was somewhat relieved that you were not at your desk when I laid the card on it. We were given a few minutes to read the cards before the start of an arithmetic lesson. I shuffled through the scattered mess of cards in front of me, looking only for yours and not finding it at first. Just as I found the cute picture of a kitten with your name under it and before I could read your name over and over again, I could hear a ruckus from your side of the classroom. I glanced over at you just in time to see you balance my card on the top of your desk and open it.

A touch of horror rushed through me, for the unseen consequence of my card drawing the attention of everyone else in the class, which was soon apparent to me, would happen like a ripple effect. The blood was already rushing to my head, my face turning to the color of the heart on the card. I could hear the kids sitting beside you asking who it was from. Their need to know became loud demands and expanded the curiosity to the whole class. I watched your lips move as you read my name out loud, and although I know you didn't shout it out, it seemed to echo throughout the room. You looked over at me, and there was no smile. It was more of a look of disgust, and even then, I could not register the fact that I had centered you out, that you might be just as embarrassed as I was. Your look represented only rejection.

The room began to fade away in front of me, turning into a gray hue like the fog of discarded dreams one tries to retrieve. I could still hear my name, but no one was calling me. I drew back into the comforts of my inner shell but could still hear the cacophony of giggles bouncing off the four walls, surrounding me, piercing my eardrums at first, and then siphoning off into the remains of a fading but steady buzz. Through the drone, I could hear comments meant for ridicule and tormenting teases, but I could not make the words register in my mind. I could only feel the sting, and I withdrew even further. It was my only means of escape. I do not remember math class. I do remember the kindness of the teacher when I asked to remain inside when lunch break came. My legs felt rubbery, and I am not sure if I would have made it to the school yard if she had forced me. The day did finally pass. They always do.

When I got home that night, after a lengthy stay in the bathroom and a few bird-pickings off my supper plate by the insistence of my mother, I closed the door to my bedroom, my only real haven. I stayed there until morning. Inside the sanctuary of my room, I let the pain seep through and eventually out. You hadn't done anything wrong, but I felt that you had. Should you have blurted out my name? You were only dealing with your own embarrassment and the pressure of your peers. When I go back to looking through the mist of that day, I can remember that you had turned your own shade of red. So in retrospect, any damage to my self-esteem that day can only be blamed on me. But it certainly didn't feel that way at the time.

Did it change the way I felt about you? Not in the slightest. Once the following days added enough distance to subside the shock of that day, the gnawing infatuation I had for you gained back its strength. I went through four more years with that relentless yearning for you. Despite that, we never spoke a word to each other. I remained in my shell where I was reasonably comfortable. But grade 8 made me realize how depressed this existence was making me. Grade 8 was also the introduction to the term *going steady*. Everyone, it seemed, was paired up and would show some form of affection in the school yard. In a small school, everyone knows everyone, so it was no secret how introverted I was. I felt very left out of this boy-girl school yard game, the holding of hands, quiet walks by themselves, and some so bold as to kiss. I watched you hold hands with someone else, and what should have been devastation to me was only numbness. I had crawled deep enough inside myself to show signs of indifference, but it was only a side effect of my withdrawal. My mind still raced with the thoughts of being with you. I had wondered if you remembered my signal to you about how I felt back in grade 4. If you did, I was sure as you held hands with another that you would never tell me.

I had my chance to enter the game when another girl in our classroom showed me some interest and wanted her and me to join into the popularity of this inviting school yard game. But I could not get myself to focus or even attempt to escape from my introversion. I had relied on its comforts for too long. I politely turned her down, feeling like a fool moments later. Did I want to join in? Of course, but where was your hand? I clung on to the belief that there was more to the definition of puppy love than I was told to believe. Even at that age, you couldn't convince me that someone else could tell me how I felt when it was the epitome of my heart that ruled my thoughts. I did not need a Donny Osmond song to concur.

We graduated that year with not so much as a good-bye to each other. I do remember during the ceremonies where we looked at each other. And for a moment, I thought I saw a gleam in your eye that represented that you did understand what I still felt. Whether in sympathy or in actual recognition, you did give me a smile. It is that smile I replaced from the one when you were nine years old, and I carried it with me like a photograph in a wallet. The outcast, withdrawn country boy had something to take with him aside from a report card full of As.

You were entering a different high school than I. So was everyone else in the class. Because of the district in which I lived, I was the only one on a different bus route that would take me to another high school. Something to do with property taxes sent me in a different direction than the kids I had spent the last eight years with. It was a mixed blessing. Although I wouldn't know a soul at my new school, I now had a chance at a fresh start. I could leave all the judgments and upheavals behind me with no record of my past. But with bashfulness as my base, I did not know if I would ever succeed in proving myself as anyone else but what I showed. Or rather what I couldn't show.

During my voyage through life, I soon learned that I was extremely sentimental, mostly to a fault where it could be labeled as a flaw rather than a good characteristic, another weight to be carried along with a heavy heart. Up until the time I was kicked out of my house at the ripe old age of fourteen, I still had the little Valentine cutout you gave me that year. Just above the kitten and above your faded signature that you had written in pencil was the request for me to come out and play in the press-printed type of a thousand cards just like it. I can only wish for that opportunity now.

Later on in life, as my memories of you relaxed their hold through the effects of time, my feelings for you came suddenly rushing back like a tidal wave. Since I was an avid reader of current events, nothing escaped me that happened in the area, or at least nothing that was in print. All the local newspapers were read from front to back in a strange sense of enjoyment of the written word no matter what it was. From the events section of the newspaper, I knew when you had graduated from high school. A few years later, I saw your wedding picture, and below it were the details of your marriage and your new last name. It wasn't as painful as I thought it would be to discover you married. I had gone on to other experiences. Was I expecting you to wait for me? But what was heartbreaking was two years later when I read about the death of your husband in a motorcycle accident. I felt your pain as if it was my own loss. There is no stronger sense of empathy you will find than that which flows from the depth of my soul. Whether it is because of so much time spent inside myself, I do not know. Sometimes it has been a curse to me, but I have always considered it a blessing. I did not go to the funeral because I felt I had no place. But I can now share the absurd idea I had that after a few months of allowing you to grieve, I would try to find you. My life was a fast-paced blur then, a long-discovered knowledge that I could find courage in a bottle. The idea never reached obsessive proportions, and I was able to put you back in my memory banks where you belonged. That did not stop you from resurfacing from time to time in a few lonely, drunken, introspective nights while I lay alone sleep deprived from an amphetamine-driven binge.

I will always wonder if you would have accepted me, given me time to follow through with the emotions dragged from my youth. I am sure you have moved on by now and would only like to state that to this day, I still think of you when I reflect on my past. I wish you the best in life and mention that in some small way, you have had a part in the growth of my soul. You have influenced the way I think of others, and the first seeds of true love has to be planted somewhere. The universal love that affects us all, that surrounds us all and sets the tone of our journey on this planet. You were my first.

CHAPTER 2

April:

My last year of grade school left me with a bleak view of life. If those first years were any indication of what I had to look forward to, I was doomed to sadness. You were the first girl, except for a discouraging bout with what everyone referred to as puppy love, who sparked my interest. You brought to the surface my initiative to make an attempt at conversation and follow that drive of the heart. It is perhaps why I still consider you my first true love. Breaking the barrier that held inside the haunts of ridicule, the inability for me to express my feelings and the constant search for an outlet to my shyness, led me to constant thoughts of you when I found out that you were interested in me. An incident that happened to me in grade 4 still crushed me—a Valentine's Day card, the brunt of mockery that shoved me back into a shell from where my brief moment of valor was replaced with thicker layers of concrete, protecting me from the outside world.

There were other girls who tried to talk to me, with sprinkles of adoration in the air, but the wall was solid, and sledgehammers would have had the same effect as rubber raindrops. Nothing was going to get through, until I met you. My last days of public school were fast approaching, and most of any concentration was on my schoolwork. I had very few friends and even less that I hung around with. So when I was invited to Andrew's birthday party, I had little trouble accepting his invitation even though I was not comfortable in any social atmosphere. It was at this party where I met you. You were actually friends with his sister, but he had invited her friends as well, probably on the premise of getting more presents.

It was your friend Vicky who had walked up to me in Andrew's yard and told me that you liked me. From behind a couple of shades of red, I managed to say to her that I would talk to you later in the day. No one could have known how difficult it was for me to even say that. I saw you looking from the living room window, but with the sun reflecting off it, I couldn't see if you were smiling or simply watching the outcome of your message. The party seemed to separate into two groups, the girls in the house and the boys outside. I could hear music from inside the house, and when the sun faded once in a while by a passing cloud, I could see far enough through the window to see you dancing. I wondered if I could ever find the nerve to dance one day. In the meantime, a game of baseball was suggested by Andrew. This was not a difficult decision for me. I loved baseball and was disappointed when my parents wouldn't allow me to play on a team because they needed me on the farm. It was the only thing I ever gave a second thought of doing with other kids and might have even helped me with my internal struggles.

Andrew's front yard was way too small for the makings of a baseball diamond. The game was not fun, and I kept thinking about you instead. The only real excitement of the game was that ill-fated foul ball that went through the front-door window and put an abrupt end to that pastime. I went into the house for a moment, wanting to approach you, but knowing I lacked the courage, I found a wall to lean against. I thought maybe you would come to me and I could struggle through a conversation that way. You looked at me from across the room, and I couldn't even muster up enough nerve to smile. I turned my attention away, and that was when Vicky tapped me on the shoulder and asked if I was going to talk to you or not. I told her I would in a few minutes and retreated back outside. I hated myself, but I was trapped in my blanket of abashment. I got lost in the noise of the party, and the time went by quickly. I was sitting in the grass by the driveway, away from everyone else, when you and Vicky came out of the house, and I could hear you saying good-bye to the other girls still in the house. You walked past me, glancing at me once, and then turned away. It was only then I realized how attracted to you I really was. A few feet past me on the long driveway to the road, Vicky turned around and unexpectedly blasted me. I can still feel the point of the spear she threw, glaring back at me and her voice loud enough to make one think she carried a bullhorn. She started to call me names, but the word *jerk* stood out mostly. She called me useless and said that you were crazy to even think about being interested in me. I was also a big loser according to her view that day. I watched you walk away with your spokesperson in rhythmical stride beside you and disappear down the road. I sat in the grass a long time afterward stung by her remarks but soothed by the picture of beauty that I now had stuck in my memory. It was this picture of you that I held on to through my first year of high school, pretending that we were together, coping with the real world by living in my own fantasy one.

My first year of high school was horrid. I was small and skinny for my age and was teased for it. Add this to my acute shyness and I was a mess inside. All my efforts went into schoolwork, and I had top marks in most of my courses. That led to further teasing. It was sheer relief when the school year finally ended. Summer holidays had deeper meaning to me than for most kids.

I had one coping mechanism during that first year in high school, and I am not sure exactly what led up to it. But to fight off one particular comment from a girl in my class, I found comfort by growing my hair long. Not only had she said to me that I had an inferiority complex but also that my whitewalls looked goofy. That was the description given to those barbershop haircuts where the ears are, in actuality, definitely lowered. I have no intentions of going into detail about the arguments that persisted with my parents about my hair. But when I refused to get it cut, never daring to challenge my parents before, they literally held me down and cut it. I fought like a wild animal until I finally gave up from exhaustion and cried incessantly as I watched the source of my Samson-like strength (only psychological instead of physical) float to the floor and vanish into the colors of the kitchen tile. For a week after that, I refused to go to school. My father finally threatened to drag me there and sit behind me in class, and that scared me enough to crawl back onto the bus. The next time when by their discretion it was getting too long again, I was given a choice. Get it cut or leave. I left.

This was how I became a member of Andrew's household. I was too young to appreciate it at the time, but the favor that Andrew's grandmother did for me was beyond altruistic. Andrew's mother had been killed in a car accident when he was very young, and his father lived on top of a hotel somewhere, waiting for his next welfare check. His grandmother, on a very limited income, was raising Andrew and his other five siblings. With a gargantuan heart, she had taken me in as well, and I agreed to pay her ten dollars a week for room and board. Before I had left my house, I knew where my father kept the savings bonds that he put in my name each year as payment for my hours of toil in the fields. Tomatoes were picked by hand then, and I became quite efficient at it, struggling with fifty-pound baskets practically from the day I shed diapers. I was surprised to see that the bonds had added up to five hundred dollars, as I had only a small grasp of how compound interest worked. I was also surprised when he did not come after me as he would eventually notice them missing. They were under my name, and there wasn't much he could do anyway. I already knew how to be frugal as I watched my parents stretch their dollars, so I felt that I could survive a long time. At least I had a place to stay even though my sleeping quarters consisted of a mouse-bitten, upholstered armchair. There was an endless supply of Kraft Dinner and hot dogs, which makes for a great staple for a kid my age.

I referred to my new lodgings as a boardinghouse, never quite accepting it as my home. My need for long hair was indirectly the reason

I was given a second chance to talk to you. It was why I was in that house the day you came to the door. You were still friends with Andrew's sister, Susan. I still remember the thumping of my heart when I answered the knocking upon hearing the small tapping on the screen door of the kitchen. When I saw you standing there, I thought it would explode from my chest. Only my rib cage kept it contained. Your sweet hello accentuated the sparkle in your eyes that showed a pleasant surprise rather than a shock. You had come to visit Susan, but she was at the neighbor's across the backfield. Although it felt very awkward at first, I was able to carry on a conversation with you. You were amazed that I was actually living there now, and you were genuine when you expressed your sorrow when I gave you the reason why. We talked briefly about our first year of high school. During a moment of silence afterward, I found an uncharacteristic act of courage and asked you if you wanted to go for a walk. At first I did not believe the words had come from me and was tempted to look behind me to see who had spoken for me. Imagine my thrill when you said yes.

It had to have been the way you made me feel comfortable, for I found words that normally never formed on my tongue. My normal introversion from acute shyness seemed to have lifted a curtain that day. Most of our conversation was idle talk, but conversation nonetheless. Halfway through our long walk down that country road, I apologized to you profusely about not talking to you the day of Andrew's birthday party. It may have been a long time ago for you, but for me it was yesterday. Your kindness, your acceptance of me that day, was the beginning of a roller-coaster ride of relationships that was based on my new reliance for emotional needs and the start of a spiraling engagement of dependency on the opposite sex. Unknown to you, unknown to me for that matter, was that the rest of my journey through life would never really be fulfilled without a female's shoulder nearby.

I fell in love with you that day. You were now the support beam that would help me survive in this cruel world. I could not know then the depth of my depression. I only knew that I was sad and an outcast by circumstances I felt I had no control over. Before we parted that day with sweet good-byes and a promise to see each other again, you had already taken on the chore as my guide to happiness.

We spent a great deal of time together that summer. We would go for long walks and chat about everything and nothing. I was still nervous around you, but at least I could talk. I couldn't read how strong your feelings were toward me, but your interest and just being with me was enough. I was way too shy to try and kiss you, but the thought was always there. We did graduate to holding hands, and such a great experience it was the first time. Sometimes there would be informal parties in Andrew's yard. I would watch Andrew kissing his girlfriend from town while I cowered somewhere else beside you. I kept wishing for aggression from you. I had to settle for the warmth of our hands and the added act of bravery where I would put my arm around you. I always said good-bye with a yearning for something more. Each time we were together, I was so close to making a move, but the grips of my self-conscience put a stranglehold on me.

You still seemed to enjoy my company despite my lack of fortitude. It was a very memorable summer for me, and I could always rely on you being there for me. Leave it to me to destroy what we had. Late in the summer, on a day you had to do something with your parents, Andrew introduced me to the pool hall in town, and my sheltered existence and our innocent and coalescent relationship began to erode. I don't have to explain the changes that occurred once I became part of the pool hall and made it my second home. With an extreme need to fit into this newfound town life, I redirected my energies for acceptance in the people of the pool hall. To do that, I had to learn how to play pool, and most of my time was dedicated to do just that. By the end of summer and the start of the school year, I had evolved from not knowing which end of the pool cue to hold to surpassing the title of mediocre player. This is where the gambling started. I also had found summer work in a farmer's field picking tomatoes. My experience at that allowed me to make a fair amount of money. I certainly needed this to supplement the cost of losing at the table before I could improve my game.

The pool hall and its clientele became an obsession, and this new group of acquaintances was helping me with my self-esteem. I had no way of explaining this to you. I hadn't recognized it myself, with the abundance of inadequacies I carried with me. I lost track of how important you were to me, and being only fifteen did not help my situation. I still saw you, just not every day, and you did not voice any disappointment. Just before school started, you surprised me with an invitation to supper at your house. I was not prepared for that, but you said your parents wanted to meet me, and I had no choice but to accept. It was very awkward for me to meet your parents, forever thinking that I no longer had a family of my own to go home to. Andrew's family wasn't exactly your typical setting, and I never did feel a part of it. His grandmother provided shelter and necessities. She did not supply guidance. Being in your parents' house made me realize how much I missed my parents. When I watched the food being passed around your kitchen table, I could not help but think of home. Your mother had served pork chops, potatoes, and vegetables that night, quite rewarding after a steady diet of macaroni and cheese.

Even that was mostly fending for yourself, for his grandmother always seemed to be too ill enough to prepare it for us.

I cannot shake the memory of that night and the harshness of your father. My hair had already reached shoulder length by then, and without any sense of style, it hung in my eyes frequently. Your father, although his initial greeting had been respectful, kept eyeing me and then finally made a rude comment to me at the supper table. I sat there helpless, but what he had done was give me future ammunition to hate society. It was already starting with the time I had spent so far on my own, influenced by the atmosphere of a dark and dreary pool hall. The place reeked with rebellion, and it had already penetrated into my bloodstream. It fed me independency, and combined with the cocky attitude of undisciplined adolescence, I was mixing a dangerous brew. I kept quiet, not only from fear of your father, but also as respect to you. It hurt more than fumed me. Later you walked me back to Andrew's, my stomach full but turning. You apologized for your father's actions, explaining that as an only child, he was very protective of you. There was a tone of insincerity in your voice, however, and I recognized it for what was underlining it. What you really meant to say but dared not was that I would never be good enough for you in your father's eyes.

There was a wave of despair running through me that night as I curled up in my mouse-bitten chair, staring at the dark panels of the living room walls. I cried myself to sleep that night, part of me believing that I wasn't good enough for you. It probably hadn't been there, but when you said good-bye to me that night, I thought I saw a glaze of distance in your eyes. I thought I saw you looking at me differently. Your voice had not had the same warm spread and almost tapered to a chilling effect. If only I could have kissed you, you may have been able to truly feel how much I cared for you, how much I loved you. You were my compass, but my tears were my reflections into the future, and the needle of direction was no longer magnetized. And as you know, my introduction to Linda further complicated things between us.

Only I refused to dwell on this. My feelings for you were more important than anything I needed, and these feelings carried me through the start of the school year. Once school started, I did not see you very often, which only made our time together more precious to me. I kept struggling for ways to bring myself to tell you how I felt. I dreamed about you during classes. But instead of acting, I merely soaked in the warmth I felt for you. When you were with me, I gained comfort, escaping the unrest that brewed inside me. I could tell you were tiring of my inability to express myself properly. Granted, circumstances had left me confused and misguided, but surely I had enough intelligence to control some of my own destiny by simply expressing myself. All I was asking of myself was a few sentences from the depths of my soul to let you understand me. You had extraordinary patience with me. We even made a pact to say that we were going out steady. It is difficult for me to admit about how naive I was, but it does not matter now. I was not sure what *going steady* really meant; I had only heard of the term in public school, but it resonated with great sound and led me to believe it bonded us somehow. If I had considered how young we were, I might have been able to figure out that your feelings for me were not as deep as I anticipated. I certainly had not seen that, and it fed my dependency on you. I wanted the world from you, wanted you to be my world. I was so influenced by you that my sense of direction, that compass, did indeed go haywire. Away from you, I became lost in a world I was unprepared for. Kicked out of the nest, with wings that could only flutter at best, and without the option of returning, I was left to fall on my own.

Your patience with me had limitations, however, and eventually ran out altogether. With the weather turning colder, we saw less of each other. If only we had gone to the same school, things may have turned out differently. You were always on my mind, but I always found a multitude of distractions. Unknown to you at first was my friendliness to the girl across the backfield. Andrew's lack of discretion took care of that, as he found it necessary to inform you. Unknown to you was the beginning of my extracurricular pool hall adventures, where I began to spend more and more time. The five-mile walk from where the school bus dropped me off, since I now lived in the wrong district to be picked up directly, was the same distance into town. The long walk back each night on a pair of worn and well-ventilated running shoes was exhausting. I would get a couple of hours of solid sleep before the next trek to catch the school bus. Homework was done on the ride to school with my penmanship unusually creative from the bumps in the road. I was able to keep straight As, but only miraculously, as most of my classroom time was spent staring out the window lost in daydreams, not only about you, but also about the aspects of such an uncertain future ahead of me. I was still too young to recognize my sadness for what it really was. Depression had no registered meaning yet, but its broad scope had found me anyway. Self-diagnosed as simple unhappiness, the symptoms of clinical depression were free to run its course. My view of the world was altered, but I knew of no other. I was surviving, and at that age, mortality had no meaning. I existed for today, my future trapped in the veils of dark dreams, the present sometimes allowed to stretch into the plans of the next day. That is not to say I did not think about the future, but any actions did not abide to its needs. Stuck in survival mode, I crept on hour by hour letting time itself be my guide to what happens. Because of this, I was in complete shock when your friend Vicky delivered your message.

She was standing at the end of the driveway of Andrew's house, straddling the crossbars of her bike, as if she knew that I had broken protocol of my usual trip to the pool hall instead of straight home that day. There was a smile on her face that represented the grin of Lucifer. I never did figure out why she had detested me so much, but she got great satisfaction telling me that you did not want to see me anymore. I was devastated and felt as if I would melt into a puddle of mud right in front of her. She went on again spewing belittling comments to me. She stuck poisoned arrows into me one after the other with a string of name-calling. Once satisfied that she had done sufficient damage to my heart, she rode away spraying me with loose gravel from her back tire, shouting loser over and over again. I imagined a dark gray cloud hanging over her head, following her, and then both she and the cloud faded away in the far distance and disappeared around the curved road. I had stood there speechless as she watched the life drain out of me. I wanted to cry but was so numb that the tears that usually flowed so easily would not come out this time. Whether it was the sudden shock or the sudden pit of emptiness I felt in my gut, the tear ducts sealed shut.

I had nowhere to go. I did not want to go the house where six kids would be running wild, taking away any privacy I needed. Even less desirable was my second home, the pool hall in town. I shoved my schoolbooks in the mailbox and started walking over to the railroad tracks on the next concession. Pretending I was on a tightrope, I tried to stay balanced on the track as long as possible. I fell to my imaginary death several times. I had to yield once to a train that had come rumbling from behind me, but I waited until the last minute to get out of the way. The engineer's horn blast announced his disgust with me. That one was not pretending. There had been a whispering voice inside my head that urged me not to get out of the way. Another more inner voice encouraged me to see tomorrow. That one prevailed.

It was well past midnight when I returned from my long solitary walk, my mind empty from thoughts, replaced by the push of fatigue. I was freezing, shivering, and wet from the light rain that had started. I curled up in my chair, letting my body heat dry my clothes, too tired to even take them off. I slept, but not deep as my subconscious thoughts took over where my waking mind had quit from exhaustion. I went over and over about what I could have done differently for you. I cursed my shyness. I cursed the fact that I had taken you for granted. Even through my sleep, I could feel the excruciating pain in my heart. I pondered over why it hurt so much. I knew the answer, but it did not alleviate the pain. I loved you more than the world. It wasn't your companionship, your friendliness, your uncanny way to make me feel good about myself when I was with you that bothered me when I thought of how much I would miss you. It was the power of that feeling, the one that can only be described as love. I needed to tell you how I felt. I need to make you understand how important you were to me. By the time the first pale light of dawn broke through the window and changed the shade of the dark-paneled walls of the living room, I was determined to find you that day and finally profess how I felt about you. If I was ever to get you back, I knew I had to find the courage no matter what it took.

This is how I received my first hitchhiking lesson. I had seen others do it, but had never quite found the nerve to do it myself. Your high school was way too far away to walk to, and my determination to talk to you that day was the only priority in my life. I could have waited until you got home from school and found the fortitude to knock on your door. The thought of facing your father flung that scenario clear off the map, away from any sense of tangibility.

It took two different rides to get to your school. It was twice the size of mine, and when first standing outside of it, I was very intimidated. I dared not enter the massive line of front doors and went to the side of the building and entered that way. Even then, there was quite a bit of hesitation. Aside from getting caught, I also had no idea how I was going to find you. When I turned the corner into one of the main halls, my footsteps seemed to echo through the empty passage. A loud shrill of a bell startled me, and a few seconds later, the halls were full of students pouring through doors that simultaneously flew open to drain classrooms. I backed up against the wall for fear of being run over by the herd and studied hundreds of faces as they passed me by. Not one of them was yours. After a moment of thunderous roaring and the resonance of a stampede, the halls were completely silent again.

I stood there alone, frightened and wondering how I could ever accomplish my mission. How could I possibly find you in this ocean of students? I was disheartened by thinking I was probably not even on the right floor and that my situation might be hopeless. I found the door to the gymnasium at the far end of the hall and, hearing no noise, entered it. Taking a seat on the empty bleachers, I stared at the frayed basketball nets, feeling lower in stature than I had ever felt. I was tired, beat-up inside, and as empty as a milkweed pod on a windy autumn day. And then the sealed duct work let loose. I could hear my sobs echoing off the cement walls of the gym and watched the teardrops forming puddles on the floor. There was always a quiet feeling of relief when I cried, as if releasing some form of poisonous chemicals through the tears. There was no change this time, and this lack of relief only made me more determined to find you.

I thought of going to the front office, but I couldn't come up with a valid-enough reason to have you paged. I never did master the ability to lie. When I looked at the huge white face of the clock on the far wall, I realized that there was only enough time for one more class of the day. I now understood that if I was to find you, my best chance would be when you were on your way to catch the bus. I lay down on the bench for a while, wiping away the remnants of my tears, knowing by my agitation that I was in no danger of falling asleep. When I felt the time was right, I entered the hallways and found the main entrance to the outside. There was a long and narrow patch of grass between the building and a long curved driveway where some buses had already pulled up. It was where I paced back and forth waiting for that final bell, as restless as a robin on a lawn void of worms. I finally stood still at a vantage point directly in front of the doors, hoping for an open view of the fanning spread of students flocking to their assigned buses.

Sometimes, on my slow path to destruction, I was blessed with small strokes of luck. Like the time I won twenty bucks off the best player in the pool hall. That day, I was blessed with the luck of spotting you out of the unexpected size of the enormous crowd that came flooding out of the doors, shoving and jostling one another for positions. When I yelled at you, I did not recognize my voice for I had not learned to shout that loud yet. You looked around at the sound of your name, and only my convulsive waves allowed you to spot me. Otherwise the crowd would have swallowed me. You worked your way back through the flow of students and stopped a few feet in front of me. A deep frown that I had never seen before appeared on your forehead, and you asked me what I was doing there. All the planning and orchestrated words I had gone over and over again for a perfectly delivered speech vanished. Suddenly losing my ability to form words, I blurted out that I didn't want to break up with you. Before you even answered me, I could tell that your response was not going to be good. Your facial expression changed from one of concern to one of sympathy and pity. My goal was not to have you feel sorry for me. I wanted you to be with me. You bowed your head, avoiding eye contact, and said that you were very sorry, but you had to move on with your life. Those words sounded so strange coming from a fifteen-year-old girl, as if she had wasted so much of her life already. Little did I know that I was on one of those paths to such waste. Before I could respond, before I could search for that planned speech and make a futile attempt at changing your mind, you walked away repeating that you were sorry.

My heart died for a moment, and I am not sure how many beats it missed. And then to add insult to my injury, I saw your bicycle-courier friend walk up beside you. She spotted me and flipped her middle finger at me accompanied with a glare that could have crushed anyone's sense of hope. Raised in the boondocks, I had only recently found out what that middle finger meant, but I had no inclination or energy to reciprocate the gesture. I was defeated and wilted as the dandelions in the grass I stood in, recently sprayed with pesticides. I stood there drooped over long after all the buses had pulled away, standing in the center of a world that had left me to my own demise.

It was almost three years later before I saw you again, although I carried you around inside my chest every day and your sorry still bouncing around inside my head as clear as the day you said it. Whether by sheer coincidence or by the hidden powers of synchronicity, I found you working as a waitress in a restaurant that I hadn't been to in several months, where I would go for my budgeted meal of a plate of french fries doused in free ketchup. I froze solid when you walked up to my table as we both recognized each other at the same time. I had been drinking that night, as I had been every night then; and the quantity levels were reaching the point that suppressed my timid ways, my inhibitions. You said hello to me in such a soft tone that it sent shivers though me and started to melt my heart all over again, flooding me with emotions back toward the surface, back from where they had never really been in any danger of evaporating. I carried the torch out of the wind.

I was taller and perhaps carried a bit more weight, but I hadn't changed that much externally. Inside, I still balked society, but now lost in a sea of drugs and alcohol. My hair was now down to my waist, which probably wasn't a pretty picture for you. You, however, had blossomed into the makings of a beautiful woman, arousing my past yearnings even further. Once I focused on the reality that it was actually you in front of me, I said hello with confidence in my voice, a redeeming quality gathered from my drinking habit. But it did not help me from being stumped on what to say to you next. I finally asked you what you were doing there, and you said you took the waitressing job to start saving for college. The fact that I was a high school dropout remained out of the conversation, but your words did remind me of my own pipe dreams of college. We chatted idly for a while, and then you took my order, giving me a smile that tore another hole in my heart. Although I never got over you, I had enough distractions in my carefree existence that I had been able to suppress some of the obsession. Three years is a long time, especially to a teenager's view of a calendar. All at once, my feelings for you came rushing back like a tidal wave as I watched the more mature version of my first love walk gracefully away.

The night I met you at the restaurant was the official start of the third month that I had ownership of my own transportation. It was next to junkyard material, with a few dented fenders, but it was what I could afford, and it was mine. With this car came new freedom, and although I still only had a beginner's permit to drive it legally, it did not stop me from exploring the liberations of the open road. With that came many options. By the time you had returned with my grilled cheese sandwich (I had skipped the french fries for once), I had already envisioned you sitting beside me in my car. Before I lost my nerve, before the effects of fermented fortitude wore off, I asked if you were going out with anyone. You shook your head and looked away from me. My heart was racing, but I managed to get the words out before I froze and asked if I could talk to you later. My head was spinning in numerous directions and full of conflict when you told me that you didn't think it was a good idea. Uncertain that I would ever get the chance again, I pleaded with you. I begged you for just one date, just a little time to talk, and how important it was to me. After a cornucopia of various ways of saying please, you finally relented. We agreed that I would pick you up the following Friday night at your house. At first I panicked at this suggestion. Meeting your father again was not part of my agenda. But I would just have to bear.

I said good-bye to you before I left, and the smile you gave me carried me through the week. Whenever I grew fearsome of the impending scrutiny of your father, I would remember your smile, and the dread would subside. I could have asked you to meet me somewhere, but that would have indicated that I was a fool and a coward, not exactly great characteristics to show you, if I was to shine with second impressions. So with the help of a bottle of vodka, compliments of my reliable supplier at the pool hall, I knocked on your door that Friday night armed with liquid courage flowing through my veins and little chance of the smell of alcohol on my breath. Your father answered the door, and although he was not tall, he still intimidated me. I simply said hello, refraining from calling him sir for that would go against the grain of my disrespect for society and its mannerisms. I guess I had more deep-rooted problems than I was willing to admit. Raising myself for the past three years had left me little guidance. I needed influence for that, and now, I had all the faith in you to do just that. My week of anticipation for our date was filled with thoughts of how much you could help me find a path to get my life on track. I felt much wiser now since I was fifteen and wanted to prove that to you. You would be my guiding light once you saw how changed I was, a big assumption on my part for one that had to beg for the opportunity to talk to you.

Your father stepped aside, his eyebrows moving up and down as he scanned me from top to bottom. A frown of disgust appeared on his forehead that I tried to ignore. I remembered a similar frown on your forehead once. When you came around the corner of the hall, my memory of your frown quickly vanished, replaced by a vision of angelic beauty. My heart skipped a beat when I saw how beautiful you were. How three years had changed you, your looks enhanced by a low-cut summer dress in lieu of your waitress uniform. I was almost swooning in your presence, my heart filled with gratitude for this second chance to be with you. I told your father that I would have you home early as a gesture of fake respect, and he quickly snapped back that you were to be home by midnight. I nodded and walked you to my car and, in a weird act of chivalry, rushed ahead and opened up the door for you. The hinges squeaked in defiance. I was waiting for your father to shout out to me and ask if my car was safe, but he had already closed the door.

As I pulled out of your driveway, my lack of concentration made me swerve the car. I suddenly realized that in my absorption of the reality that I was actually taking you out, I had made no plans where. We were too young for bars, and I had doubts you drank anyway. In my eyes you were too classy to take into the pool hall. I fought for direction, some quick plan, and came up empty. In desperation, I asked you if there was any particular thing that you wanted to do. You were of no help. Signs of dusk were already appearing in the sky when I finally remembered that there was a drive-in theater in the next town west of us. You had no problem with this idea, so after veering across a few back roads, I found the main highway. At first our conversation was strained, and I turned up the music to help with the uncomfortable silence. I eventually found the sense to ask you questions about your life of the past three years, and we slowly eased into a comfort zone. After all, we weren't complete strangers. By the time I found the drive-in theater, the music was turned down low, and we were talking to each other fluently. My answers to your questions were without detail, though. Even with a week to prepare for our date, my cursed introverted ways rose to the occasion. I was so afraid of not saying what you wanted to hear and what you might not. I thought I did okay even without the elaboration that a good conversationalist should have.

Although my life was not completely unlucky, destiny seemed to deal me more than my share of bad hands, and that night was no exception. The movie theater was closed. A sudden flash of despair ran through me, that familiar addition to a trail of disappointments, and I almost swore. I had no way of knowing that it was closed, but still found it to be no excuse. I began to apologize over and over. You said it was all right, but I kept showering you with apologizes until I finally recognized your annoyance. This was supposed to be the perfect date, my chance to prove to you my worthiness, and it was turning into a nightmare. The only thing left for me to salvage my chances was the night itself.

The sky was full of stars, and a full moon has just begun to rise. It soothed me as it had many summer nights before. The beauty of the night sky had been shared with you three years ago. Now that we were older, we could share a much deeper magic and connect as soul mates. I drove back to Westlake with a new sense of hope. I took the back way into the campground where I had spent many days by myself soaking in the mysteries of the universe. I parked the car directly over the same cliff where I had spent hours letting the magnetism of the lake wash over me. Now, finally I had you to share this with. My mood was melancholy but with small brushes of joy just to be sitting beside you. The moon's rays glistened off the dark water, the small whitecaps dancing colors in rhythm to the gravitational pull. I had not told you where we were going, but I thought I could feel you relax, thought I could feel you sharing the beauty and vibrations pouring through the windshield. Just being at the park had always filled me with tranquility, and any tenseness I had felt earlier drained from me. I looked over at you, your beauty matching the night sky, and I was overwhelmed by the extraordinary image of elegance you portrayed. And then like a flood, I began to spew my theories of the universe out, rambling on with deep philosophies much too detailed for any understanding. I was trying to share my cosmic knowledge with you enunciated with words that did not fit the true meaning. I was trying to impress you and make you realize how deep I really was. I was no longer the shallow country boy whom you gave up on.

I reached over and whispered into your ear, "I always wanted to do this." I planted a long and sensuous kiss, concentrating on sending as much of my heart through the electrodes of sensuality, transferring from the depths of my soul, through the sensors of your lips directly to your heart, all that I felt about you. It was to be the most magical kiss in the history of mankind. It was supposed to represent the most powerful love available in the universe. It was to be the ultimate token to all my past mistakes and a testament to how important you were to me and had never voiced. Your response was sensuous, but I could not feel your heart, no phenomenal signs of adornment sending sparks through your lips. There was a certain sense of detachment coming from you blending in with the softness. I should have expected it, but my world had become fantasy, and you were what made it turn. When the initial spark I felt was gone, I stopped kissing you. The magic of fairy-tale kisses was not going to happen. But the fact that I finally kissed you after all this time, after all this time dreaming about doing so, was an answered prayer in itself.

I cannot judge how coherent I was that night. I only knew that what I had to say to you had to be said if I was to ever win you back. I told you how much I missed you and then laid it on very thick. You had been so important to me three years ago, and I was sorry I had never told you. Being with you was the only important thing in the world to me. All my inhibitions moved aside for me that night as the magnitude of my need to explain to you how much you meant to me preceded anything else. I spilled all my inner feelings out to you that night, laying my heart out on the dashboard for you to do with what you wanted. Whether the full moon was deactivating parts of my brain that night or it was the obsessed need to fulfill my dreams with you, I babbled on and on how much I loved you. I had total disregard for how uncomfortable I might have made you feel. You sat in silence, whether out of astonishment or carefully considering how you should answer. When you finally did speak, you asked me how I could feel this way after all this time. I had no answer. You provided your own theory, and even before you started, I knew I was in for pain. Your words were condescending, and my mind tried hard to change their meaning. I fidgeted back and forth in my seat and lit a cigarette without asking your permission. You were analyzing me. This was not what was supposed to happen.

According to you, I was still stuck in my childhood, unable to move forward, clinging to old memories to cope with my life. It was only an infatuation of you from three years ago that I was acting on. I was depressed and needed to look inside myself, to a path to maturity instead of looking in the skies. Without goals for myself and being happy within myself, I could not be any good for someone else.

I shut out most of your words as they began to cut me up as if I had swallowed razor blades. My wall went back up faster than the speed of sound. I had to protect myself, seal a barrier of this attack from the girl I loved. When you were finished with your thesis, which I assumed came from a crash course in psychology, I went completely numb. The statement that you had made that did the most damage was the one stating that I was only clinging on to you as a sense of delight from my past, as a self-diagnostic way to help with my depression. I would not admit to depression. It reeked of weakness. I was simply lost in life's shuffle. Depression sounded like a disease that needed to be hidden from public view.

Most of what you had said that night did have a ring of truth, but the little self-esteem I had needed to be protected, creating my stubbornness, my refusal to believe any of it. I loved you, and you were the most important thing in my life. That was all there was to it. I knew there was no common sense in this thinking, but how do you get around feelings? One summer together, a young girl paying attention to a naive country boy did not draw a display of eternal cosmic love. Tell my heart that, and since when did raw emotion hold within the boundaries of common sense?

We continued to let the moonlight filtering through the windshield of my car spread over us, but any sense of magic was gone. I tried to talk to you, make you understand that there was much more to me. But to truly explain, I would have to admit to some of the things you said. Confessions may have changed the way you felt about me, but nothing was about to change the way I felt about you. Before I could change my mind and completely open up to you, your impending curfew and the need to get you home prevailed. There was gnawing in my gut eroding the lining as I tried to elude the fact that you didn't love me. You didn't know me. The ride back to your house faded into silence. I played the *Magical Mystery Tour* tape by the Beatles on the way, the tape that always sent me into a trance when I mixed the tunes with marijuana. It helped me not think about the disastrous way our night was ending. I turned it off when I pulled into your driveway. I was struggling on what to say to you. I did not dare ask you if I could see you again for fear of the answer. I said thank you instead. You nodded, not caring for me to elaborate on what I was thanking you for. We said good night, and I watched you disappear into your house with not so much as a wave.

I didn't quite feel like those wilted dandelions I stood among when you left me standing in front of your school that day, but I certainly felt empty. You had just broken up with me again, but there was no sorry to go with it this time. Call it infatuation, desire, devotion, obsession, stalking, I couldn't get you out of my mind. But I wasn't completely delusional. I did not call you at home, nor did I try to track you down. I knew I would eventually have to find a way to get over you. I did make one last attempt to talk to you, however.

Several weeks after our troubled reunion, I was in the middle of a weeklong binge of beer and pot, completely wasted and feeling sorry for myself. You kept filling my head with past pictures of yourself, kept echoing your words in my brain. My angelic view of you in the moonlight over the lake that night kept popping up in front of me as real as the darkness of my heart.

I had spent the last few weeks committed to getting over you, but my intoxication levels overruled any logical thinking. I had to find you, losing the battle to fend off my feelings. Calling you was not an option. I couldn't deal with your father answering the phone while slurring a request to talk to you. Going to the restaurant where you worked made more sense. When I pulled up to the curb out front, scraping my tires along the side of it in a poor attempt at parking, I almost changed my mind. I could not think of what I would say to you. I decided to wing it, and with my back arched to alleviate the staggering process, I walked in asking for you. The manager was quick to tell me that you didn't work there anymore. I went back to my car and headed for home, a small part of me knowing I had reached my limitations. I fell asleep behind the wheel that night, ditching the car only a few feet from my house. There was only minimum damage, and an understanding farmer helped me pull it out in the morning. Thankfully, there was no police involvement. My trouble with them came much later. But it did shake me up enough to know I had to get on with my life. I finally realized I had to let you go. And in my scrambled mind, I ditched not only my car that night but you too.

I never saw you again until several years later at a social club that I frequented. My rebellious days were behind me. I spotted you among the crowd sitting at a table with your husband. I knew that you had married, had read the announcement in the town newspaper next to the classifieds. My heart had fallen briefly from its proper place, but I had done a half-decent job of getting over you and was actually happy for you once the news had filtered through my bloodstream. I had healed and was making great progress in turning myself around. The fact that I had gotten married too was of great value. I waited until your husband went for drinks at the bar and took the opportunity to say hello. I still had remnants of shyness in my actions, but I was at least socially adjusted to functional levels. Alcohol was still the basis of suppressing my inhibitions, however. We talked briefly and commended each other on how good we looked. You gave me that warm smile of yours as I stated that I was glad to see you found happiness. Your husband was returning, and I wished to avoid introductions, so I wished you the best and said good-bye. That was the last time I ever saw you.

Do I still think about you? Of course, I do, but not every day as now my mind is jammed with too many other thoughts and past experiences. I still wonder from time to time if I had tried harder that I might have eventually been able to win you over. I still wonder what it would have been like to share a life with you. Was I lost during my time with you? Most definitely, but I still think you might have held the key that opened up the path to my dreams. Even after all this time, I do not think you were right about me, that it was just an infatuation of my childhood. I think I loved you.

CHAPTER 3

Linda:

My childhood sweetheart? Well, not in the true definition of the word, but you definitely were by my side during some rough periods of adolescence. I was lost and foolish, unprepared for the real world when I was suddenly cast into it from the shelter of my parents' home with a boot print on my butt. I had met you a few weeks before April had added another boot print to my collection, so even at that young age, I was juggling women.

It was Andrew who introduced us. He had a lot of influence on me since I moved into his house. His grandmother had taken me in after my request, and the fact that she was sick all the time and had six other kids to watch did not deter me from imposing. I needed a roof over my head. I always called it a boardinghouse because not only did I pay a minimal sum for keep, it also never felt like a home to me, and therefore I couldn't label it as such. Both your house and Andrew's were farmhouses surrounded by farm land, but on different concessions. By road, we were three miles apart. By field and by the way that the crow flies, we could see each other's house, and visits were made by cutting through cornfields. You had three brothers and two sisters, so when all of us got together at the same time, we had quite a brood. This menagerie of kids was like a scene from a school yard at recess whenever we would gather outside, making up new rules to sporting games.

I had already been out of my parents' house for almost two months when I met you, tossed from the nest before they taught me how to fly. Naive as a mountain goat trapped in the median of a major highway, I was caught in the middle of a slow and cruel learning process. I thank the powers above me that it was not a city that I was looking at as a means of survival. I would never have endured such a jungle. The town of Westlake, and especially the pool hall that I was introduced to and soon called my own, had the atmosphere of friendliness. I was taken by its amiable air, the streets were safe, tempered from the dangers of a large metropolis. Andrew helped me find my way for a while, but his carefree attitude was not exactly the real guidance I needed. I had quite a learning curve ahead of me.

When our two groups emerged, field hockey was our game of choice, and we played for hours on end. Both farmhouses had long driveways that opened up to huge parking areas, so our gravel rinks were of good size. We actually had gone so far as to write up a schedule for visitor and home games to be played alternately. You were somewhat of a tomboy with a competitive need against your two older brothers. When Andrew introduced us, I felt immediately attracted to you, your long blonde hair and well-blossomed development sending the juices of any teenage boy into motion. I was thrilled to find out you were going to play too. I was small for my age, but I did have athletic abilities. I had to prove to the bigger kids in school I could hold my own against them, just as driven as your need to prove your worth to your older brothers. It made us a good match on the field and great competition when we juggled for possession of the ball.

I had no real idea what flirting was at that age, but when I think back now, that was exactly what you were doing. The purposeful body contact during our hockey games, the harmless teasing tossed in my direction, delicate enough so as not to bear on my sensitivities, your smile that represented more than just friendliness. I didn't think about you much at first until you started to enter my dreams at night, and I would sleep with your smile in front of me. Soon after, as the frequency of our visits had me spending more time with you, your smile entered into my daydreams as well. Through Andrew, our mutual messenger, we indirectly found out that we had a deeper interest in each other than just companions with hockey sticks. I was absorbed in the need for attention and was thrilled that you were interested in me.

I was in a constant search for someone to talk to but chose carefully who to share things with. Fourteen is much too young to go without proper guidance. Andrew and his siblings took up any available attention of their ailing grandmother, so the very least thing I anticipated was direction or advice from her. She did talk to me from time to time, but understandably the younger kids were her priority. I wasn't sure what she could tell me anyway, with my adolescent, self-centered ways settling in already. I could barely appreciate her burdens as it was, but I did have enough sense to know that I wanted to be no burden at all. I did not want to give her a reason to take my roof away. And so as much as my shyness would allow, I began to talk to you, looking to you as my guide through my thoughts of this unchartered territory I was discovering on my own. I need not bore you with my eventual demise with April. You found out all about that through the indiscretions of Andrew. I learned soon enough what not to say to him.

Our time together slowly progressed into more than just a friendship, fed by my imagination of my dreams, my search and yours as well to belong, leading us both to thoughts of fantasy about where our connection would take us. The more we talked, the more we trusted each other, and soon we were opening up to each other in ways I was not accustomed to. I began to rely on you very much. That summer I turned fifteen, and you turned sixteen, our birthdays only a week apart. It was during the celebrations of your birthday that we officially stated that we were now girlfriend and boyfriend. Our dates consisted of social sibling gatherings, late-night card games, bicycle rides. We graduated to long walks in the woods, alone and holding hands.

When I wasn't with you, I was busy getting to know my other new domain, the pool hall. It was a four-mile walk to town, but long walks had become easy for me. I walked farther than that just to catch my school bus. By moving to the boardinghouse, I was in a different school area. I didn't want to change schools, fearing a new start and a new environment would affect my grades and any sense of well-being I was still managing to hold on to. I had enough changes to deal with. But it left my school bus route way out of my way. It meant that in order to catch my bus, I had to walk five miles every morning. As some of the farmers in the area became familiar with the strange kid walking down the dirt road at six in the morning, I was able to catch rides most of the time. I was extremely grateful for this when winter came out of nowhere and stayed around for eternity. It was odd for me how little I had to say to these farmers, and they still seemed to understand my needs. Some would go out of their way to get me to the bus on time. Others would give me advice that I would never remember anyway. What you had to say was more important.

You wouldn't have thought that as I was soon spending more and more time at the pool hall, our time together diminished. I did realize how much I relied on you and needed you, but not only did I never say it, it also left no explanation why spending time in town seemed more important. Inside my head was mass confusion, my thoughts spinning in a hundred different directions all the time. I was already suffering from bouts of depression, not quite understanding its process, and it was also unknown that I would be plagued by pieces of it for the rest of my life. After the hardest, cruelest winter since the end of the ice age and my first Christmas away from my family, I was able to pick myself out of the doldrums when the first signs of spring lifted my spirits. With spring came the outdoor life and more time spent with you. I knew you were upset that I didn't see you every day, but it seemed the time we did spend together meant so much to both of us that you were able to overlook it. When school let out for the summer, I felt like I had just gained the freedom of a soaring eagle. I basked in the long days and the sense of no responsibilities during those long summer evenings and in the feelings of romance in the air when we began to know each other considerably better. You had no curfew to speak of, but we weren't about to risk you being out all night. I had no curfew.

Those warm, moonlit summer evenings spent with you were heavenly. There was a sense of peace within myself, but it was caused only by the weather and your pleasurable distractions that could shut my mind down for a while. It was the start of our experiments in petting, my first true experiences in sexuality. In the hay mow on old straw, in the slopes of soft grass behind the barn, and even in the clover fields, oblivious to the small creatures crawling around and underneath us, we fondled and petted ourselves raw. We aroused ourselves into a flustered frenzy many nights, and our need to wrap ourselves around each other was like an addiction. We explored every inch of our bodies, never tiring of the sensations it sent through us. We learned extraordinary places to leave hickeys once we learned how to give those. If there had been competitions in foreplay, we would surely have been king and queen and owned a shelf of trophies. To this day, I am not sure what stopped us from going all the way to the ultimate act of intercourse. We drove each other insane at times but were soon to discover there were alternative ways to reach the point of orgasms. I am sure you had the same drive to go further with our experiments, but my inexperience and your phobic fear of getting pregnant combined a mixture that allowed us to ride the fringes and stay on the edge of desire.

We kissed like fish at first, like carp out of water; but with practice and various approaches to our petting festivals, we were able to discover that the softer attachments of our lips created better sparks than those found in the patterns of slobber. Because we had spent so much time together in this pastime, our inhibitions, our embarrassment was mostly concealed in the passion that drove us. Was it love or simply hormones? I believe it was both, but either way, I was left confused by it. I could not tell if it was genuine, heartfelt emotion or just infatuation of the feelings we gathered from our display to each other. We carried on with our teenage passion in routine fashion, regardless of the reason, both escaping the grips of the real world around us this way.

Your mother had abandoned you at a young age. Your father raised you on his own until the time you were introduced to your future stepmother. You told me you could never really accept her and that had resulted in many clashes between you. Life had not been easy for you, and you struggled with school. Although I was far from the complete development of my future pitfalls of pure empathy, I did feel for you, probably more to compare my own hard life than the understanding I should have had. You certainly had given me a shoulder, and I tried to do the same. Our conversations were never really deep, and we seemed to be careful not to go too far into detail on how we felt about each other. The three famous words with love as the verb were never said, just understood. We left our unspoken words to love through the actions of our display of physical touch. In my undeveloped mind, it was the same.

My trips to the pool hall eventually ran great interference to our paradisiacal playground and our petting zoo of sensation. I was addicted to both pastimes, but I was filled with restlessness that when I wasn't with you, I became more and more curious about the lives of the town people. Their acceptance of me was the key. I was one of the youngest customers of the pool hall, and maybe my lost look had enabled them to take me under their wings. I felt protected, and after each visit, I grew more comfortable with the people there. I slowly fit in with a sense of identity. And with the introduction of alcohol and eventually drugs, a whole new world opened up to me, one from which I would never return, my simple existence no longer enough. With no overbearing parents to shelter me, I was free to try my fortune with substance abuse and no boundaries for sensibilities. If there ever was a teenager with no borders, without restrictions, that would be me. My older peers from the pool hall knew no better that I was without guidance, nor was it their responsibility to give me any. When they introduced me to booze and drugs, they had no way of knowing that I was an early social outcast with possible psychological problems. They were simply introducing me to the doorway of altered states of consciousness, normally meant for a social atmosphere. To feed an introverted thought process was of no consequence to them. You were aware of my adventures with alcohol, but you were not sure how deeply involved I was with the drug scene I had become. It was a good year before I slowed down, before I either suffered from brain damage or shell shock from bright epiphanies. Depending on whose opinion you ask, it could have been both.

I put you through hell as you stood by, watching me slide from being a grade A student, a reliable friend and companion, into a high school dropout, derelict, drunk. Yet you stayed by my side and were always there for me during times of need. I used you, and I apologize from the depths of my soul if I dragged you down with me. I became self-centered, my only interest becoming the feeding of internal combustion to dead brain cells. You watched me progress from beer and acting stupid to guzzling whiskey and cherry brandy straight from the bottle, and you were there in the beginning of my stone age. Marijuana, at first, did not affect me until I graduated to THC in the pill form. That must have induced some chemical reaction because after that I couldn't get enough of smoking it. They claim weed is not physically addictive, but it certainly is psychologically. Without the altered state that it gave me, I felt empty. Mescaline came next, the happy drug. There were many nights in my world where everything in it was hysterical, a wonderful feeling for a kid who didn't care for the world too much. Finding drugs in the pool hall was easier than finding candy. I was in the middle of its culture.

I spent less and less time with you. Many nights I didn't even make it back to the boardinghouse. I cannot emphasize enough how lucky I was to end up in a small-town atmosphere instead of a city. City streets can be very mean with environments so harsh and dangerous that life itself can be endangered. My small-town streets were almost blanketed in comfort, no looming threats down the next alleyway. The lack of crime, the familiarity of the people, and the compassion of communal civility were all attributes to survival on the street. There was a sofa in the waiting room of the doctor's office that was never locked. It was perfect for temporary and free lodging, although I don't think that was its true purpose. There was free food from friends and acquaintances of friends borrowed from the refrigerator shelves of unsuspecting parents. There were local farmers and fisherman on routine chores who would stop and talk to me, noticing me sitting on the bench outside the pool hall early some mornings waiting for it to open. They would drop a line or two of advice, concerned with this poor street urchin. I am sure they didn't think I was homeless, but they must have thought something was wrong as I sat there staring into space. It was precisely one of these encounters that led me to the information that the canning factory just outside of town was looking for help. When I got the job by lying about my age, I put your concerns to rest when I told you about it, claiming I would go back to school after the canning season was over. You believed me. I believed me, but it never came to pass. I needed money, and my savings bonds would not last forever. They were depleting much faster than expected, especially with my newly added expenses of drugs and alcohol.

I had learned the better skills of playing pool quickly, well enough to win my share of gambled money, but that was not steady pay. Losing was also an easy proposition, especially on the nights when I couldn't see straight. My job also gave me the incentive to get a late start on what had already become a daily drinking habit. Marijuana got me through the working hours, smoked behind the warehouse during breaks. You watched me slowly turn into someone you no longer knew, and I did not have the inclination or the words to tell you that deep inside I had not changed. You let me constantly hurt you and sometimes even degrade you. And although I clung on to my job as a lifeline to sanity, it was also the mundane duties of robotic work that fed my need to further my crutches on drugs and alcohol. I had prided on myself on being an honor student and therefore considered myself on the upper levels of intelligence. This small piece of self-worth was supposed to be enough to blanket over the detriments of my low self-esteem and also enough to deny my actual naivety and distorted picture of the real world around me. Topped with a total lack of responsibility and stunted growth of maturity of a runaway adolescent, I was on a path of collision with calamity. Depression was always boiling just below the surface, suppressed by my delusional and fast-paced existence.

I hadn't seen you in three days, and instead of heading straight to the pool hall after work, I was missing you and went to see you instead. It was Friday night, so in my convoluted logic, I was making sacrifices to see you. But further in, where the parts of the brain that controls emotion, I needed you that night, feeling unusually more vulnerable and sad. You confronted me right away, screaming at me that I couldn't just pop in whenever it was convenient and ignore you the rest of the time. I hated confrontations, but it didn't stop me from arguing that night, my compassion already weakened by a quart of brandy on the way to see you. Our small tiffs from before were always resolved, but that night, it turned into a shouting match. My hopes of a romantic evening were floating away, and there was a throbbing in my heart as I watched your anger spill over enough to push me. I went to push you back and was able to stop myself. I can't remember all the contents of our argument, as most people never do after time settles the dust of friction. I do know that the things you said stung worse than hornets. I walked away, leaving you standing in the driveway, trying to ignore your hurtful insults.

I wasn't quite at the point where the tears flowed in an instant, nor can I pinpoint when the seals started to erode around the tear ducts later to cry at something as simple as a touchy commercial. What I do know was that the faucets sprung open that day, and I couldn't shut them off. The more I cried, the more I could feel the depression finally finding a way out of my pores, bursting through in waves of anguish. The anger I had felt during our argument melted instantly into puddles of despair. I lay down on the side of a ditch that separated the fields, unable to watch the sunset. Dark clouds had piled high on the western horizon. I stared up at the gray dismal sky and felt a hollowness inside me that seemed to resonate from the very marrow of my bones. I was suddenly awakened to how meaningless my life had become. The path of my future was entangled in sheer futility. My life flashed in front of me with enough illumination to light a kaleidoscopic screen of memories from childhood until present day. I felt a void, like falling into a bottomless pit. The tall grass I lay in swallowed me, and the sky gave me no comfort. The thick, muddy waters running just below my feet matched the viscosity of my heart, weighing it down as if a huge piece of concrete had taken its place.

I cried and I cried to the point of dehydration and then cried some more. I began to pray. I had no religious background to speak of, a couple of Sunday school Bible stories in the basement of a church at the age of four and later, when I learned how to read, a few passages from the Old Testament that didn't hold any degree of logic to me. Religion, while I was a child, was replaced by a good, solid moral upbringing. But I prayed that day, and not for salvation. I asked for one thing only, over and over again, first in a whisper and then in shouts. Through my sobs, I screamed at the sky for God to take me from this planet. I visualized a white-bearded man hidden above the clouds and begged for him to let me join him. I pleaded, I begged, I implored him to take me and not let me suffer anymore. I asked him to lift me up, that I didn't want to be here anymore. I did not recognize my prayers for what they were. These were the thoughts of suicide. I was asking God to slit my wrists for me. My request went on and on thinking that if I was persistent enough, he would tire of me and lift me into the clouds. My prayers went unanswered.

The sky shaded into the darker colors of night, and I finally cried myself to sleep. I woke up in the middle of the night to the crack of thunder, and the heavens that had abandoned me now answered with a sudden downpour of cold rain, drenching me in seconds. I ran to my boardinghouse, guided by flashes of lightning. Once inside, I waddled to the living room and, like a sodden sponge, left a trail of water behind me. Everyone else was asleep, and I curled up in my armchair into a ball equivalent to a fetal position, shivering myself back to warmth without even the common sense to change my clothes. I had been wet before. You eventually dry.

I did not dream that night, my mind as empty as my heart. While I slept, I pushed the protruding bubbles of depression back through my pores, but only just below the skin where they could fester and remain part of me. My prayers did get answered temporarily a week later, unknown to me that there was another indirect route to the heavens through the inner mind. After finally changing my clothes the next morning, I forced down a box of macaroni and cheese, the usual staple regardless of the time of day. I did not leave the house that weekend, drained of all energy and purpose. I turned the black-and-white television on, but watched the show displayed from the single window of the living room instead. In the front yard, the thick branches of the trees swayed their leaves gently in a calm breeze, and I watched the birds flutter from branch to branch, content in their simple yet meaningful existence. Oblivious to the other kids running around me, I continued to stare out the window in hypnotic trance. Andrew asked me to go to town with him, and I declined him several times before he gave up and left without me. When the rest of the kids finally went outside and left me alone, I turned my attention to the inside of the house. I had never looked at the house in detail before and was slightly appalled at my new awareness about how old the house actually was.

There were layers upon layers of wallpaper, various patterns showing through, where different depths of rips and tears curled over to display different colors. The stucco ceiling was a sickly yellow, and in the grooves were the pepper droppings of ancient houseflies. Rotting wooden slabs could be seen where some of the plaster had fallen away. The dark brown carpet was so worn that the floorboards underneath had raised through. The glue of the carpet and the rusted nails of the wood were all letting go randomly. The linoleum floor tile of the bathroom and kitchen had loosened from its original coating of paste, and the corners peeled back in spots, waiting for the next unsuspecting toe to collide with them. Some of my own skin had been sacrificed in untimely night excursions to the toilet. The bathtub was beyond approach, and there was limited evidence that a porcelain finish might have been attached to the interior at one time. Sponge baths were the extent of my cleanliness. The toilet didn't flush anymore, and with eight people in the house, you can imagine the disgusting chore that their grandmother had with a ladle and a bucket.

I seldom went upstairs because of my lack of fondness of cobwebs and mouse droppings. The few times I did go up, the stairway creaked so loud that it would make you freeze, wondering if your whole leg was going to go through. The list in my head went on, the faults of my domain my entertainment for that day. The paper-thin curtains flapped from the breeze outside, wind whistling through the cracks of that lone window. The sill was still stuffed with crusty towels from last winter in preparation for the next blast of cold winds. All this sudden awareness of my surroundings, and yet my uncomplicated cognition couldn't comprehend the measurement of poverty. I had a roof over my head, and that's all that mattered. The only clarity in my mind was a sense of embarrassment that refused to let me call it home.

I missed you terribly that weekend, but a certain stubbornness stopped my access to find ways to apologize to you, to tell you how important you really were to me. I spent the weekend in my chair instead. Monday came quickly though in spite of my dormancy. I did my routine morning walk (only to work now instead of school) and tried unsuccessfully to put the weekend behind me. I hibernated that entire week, coming straight back from work each day. The pool hall beckoned to me in my mind, but I was punishing myself. It became more difficult for me, but I refused to visit you. Even Andrew had enough sense to tell me to go see you, recognizing how miserable I was, but making sense was not a high priority. Feeling sorry for myself lent a bizarre perception of comfort.

Friday night, I decided I had enough of a hiatus from the world and ventured to the pool hall. I could never have imagined the adventure in front of me, could never have dreamed that I was about to enter into such a mind-altering experience, that my view of the world would be changed forever—an unexpected shock therapy to an already-scattered brain. After a steady week of living in an armchair, listening to wallpaper curl and mice racing each other in between the rafters, broken only by trips to work and back, I was ready for an attempt at fun. One of the regulars at the pool hall was also the main source of drugs. He had introduced me to a variety of pills, from barbiturates to amphetamines to THC to mescaline. That night he had something new in his collection and was anxious to sell them. They were little blue pills that he called LSD. A new combination of letters was all it was to me, and when he described it as the door to a great ride, I jumped at the chance to try something new. I had heard of acid before, but completely oblivious to the extent of the hallucinatory effects, let alone any danger. I bought four pills, swallowed two immediately with no information from my dealer about what to expect. A warning on the bottle that read take only one at a time would have been enormously helpful.

I will try my best to describe what happened to me, my adventure of a lifetime, a trip that would change my view and perspective of the world, drive me to studies in philosophies, and change my life in general permanently. The realities and pressures of everyday life always push other possible dimensions or other visions and outlooks to the sidelines, but once awakened, you are never far away from the underlining truth of cosmic understanding. On Earth, the practical purposes of this knowledge are very limited. It does leave a deeper sense of appreciation to the world around you and an insight to its mysteries and different planes. This, too, is easily dispersed into faded memory with the onset of hardships and disappointments and pain. But that night, as sure as the Earth turns on its axis, my life changed from simplicity to an underlining knowledge of the cosmos, never to think the same way again.

I had taken pills before with mediocre hallucinogenic effects where it was fun and temporary. Twenty minutes after I popped the LSD tablets, I knew that I was in for something I was totally unprepared for.

I was sitting on one of the pool hall benches that lined the one side of the hall. The place was unusually quiet for a Friday night. Two acquaintances that I didn't particularly care for were playing on the far back table, cursing the cue ball as if it might have helped with the inaccuracy of their shots. I was watching the game of two farmers still left over from the usual gathering of locals in the afternoon. This was when the hallucinations first began. I noticed a trail of color left in the felt cloth from the snooker balls as they traveled across the table, and then the trail would slowly fade away. The clash of the balls was too loud, almost like thunderclaps. Then the hallucinations came in a fiery of changes. In the next shot when the balls collided, I watched one shatter, and pieces danced above the table like butterflies. The dark oak-paneled walls on the opposite side of the room began to throb, pulsing in and out toward me, first convexly and then concavely. With each beat of my heart, which I could now feel thumping on my rib cage, I would see the panels move a bit farther out each time and then back in again, bending so far out I thought the wall would explode at any moment. The Styrofoam ceiling tile joined in, compressing the room toward me.

The holes in the ceiling from where pool sticks had been raised too high spread open. Dark earthworms were crawling out of them and dropping onto the pool table. When I looked down, the farmers had vanished; whether they had left on their own or not, I did not know. The whole hall filled with rays of reds and greens and blues, and they bounced everywhere. The straight lines turned into curves, and everything in front of me was pulsing at incredible speeds. I looked to the back table to find the other two players and saw that a forest of tropical plants had grown and sprouted high enough to hide the back table entirely. The ceiling was moving closer toward me, and I thought I could hear the nails of the wallboards popping out. I was suddenly very afraid and wanted to go outside. I did not want to be crushed. I felt heavy and had to lift myself from the bench with my hands and headed for the front door, concentrating on looking at my shoes to guide me there. The hardwood floors were rolling like small ripples of a waking lake on a calm morning. I moved with the waves, finding balance difficult. Each time I would take a step, I would be pushed back by the next roll of the floor. After considerable effort, I was able to outpace the waves and found my way to the sidewalk outside.

There were no windows in the pool hall, and I had lost track of time. I was not prepared to find it dark already. A car swished by me, and its headlights blinded me for a moment. I lost my footing and stepped out into the street to be met with a blaring horn so loud that it echoed inside my skull instead of my ears. The few streetlights that dimly lit the main street bounced beams of light off the night sky and exploded like fireworks, leaving small yellow holes in the black firmament. The holes would then flutter away like tiny canaries. I closed my eyes for a second, only to be flooded with a million colors penetrating my eyelids. I shook my head and watched a school of startled neon fish disperse in all directions. I opened my eyes back up, and for a moment, everything was normal again. But then the sidewalk began to move like the pool hall floor had. Panic was now setting in, for now there seemed to be no escape. I had nothing to tell me what was real and what was not. I needed someone to help me.

I thought of going back into the pool hall, but my only choices of aid in there were the two acquaintances in the back that had already been covered in vines and fronds. I had no idea where the elderly caretaker was or what he could do to help me anyway. My mind raced as I watched the post office window across the road form red lines swirling into intricate patterns of rose petals. I suddenly remembered the two brothers from Newfoundland who had befriended me and only lived around the corner a block away. I had spent quite a few nights playing cards and drinking strange brands of beer imported from their home province. They had recently moved here and found permanent work on the fishing boats. They were much older than me, but I had nothing but good memories when with them. They were also a reliable source of alcohol, and I thought that maybe that was what I needed to flush this poison out of me. Another car streamed by me, and the headlights felt as if they pierced. Without any further delay, I headed for their house.

The sidewalk began to move again, the separate slabs of cement lifting out of the ground in precarious angles, and I walked up them as if balancing a seesaw. My concentrated effort to get to the Newfoundlander's house allowed me to keep my balance on this delusional moving path. They lived on a side street, and as I turned the corner, the last of the streetlights were behind me. The sidewalk leveled out as if it couldn't raise itself in the dark. Memory guided me to the right house, and just as I thought that the hallucinations might be over already, something burst in the night sky above me. An extraordinary mass of flowing colors that could easily be mistaken for the northern lights if it hadn't been for the strange mix of colors covering the entire sky sent me scurrying to the front door. The door sounded hollow, and my rap was weak. I looked up again to see tiny yellow faces where stars had been. I knocked louder.

It swung open to the girlfriend of one of the brothers. I had met her once before, and she had been friendly. She invited me in, explaining that my friends would be right back. They had stepped out for beer. My legs had increasingly started to turn rubbery, and I grabbed a seat on the couch. She sat across from me on a sofa chair, a glass coffee table between us. She asked me if I was okay, saying I looked very white. Hesitant at first, I explained to her that I had taken something and it was beginning to frighten me. She repeated that my friends would be home shortly and they could probably help me, and if it was acid that I took, they could talk me down. I thought deeply about the word *acid*. My attention quickly drew away from her.

The room was lit with a pole lamp in the corner of the room, casting shadows that now twirled into moving shapes. I saw them form into colorless geometrical shapes, mostly diamonds, and paste themselves on the glass top of the table to fade slowly away like the trail of the pool balls had done. There was an old wooden stereo system on the left wall playing a soft rock tune, only this stereo had real notes floating out of its side speakers, rising into the air and floating across the room in a steady stream and disappearing through the opposite wall, notes from a scale I could only possibly recognize from a music lesson from public school. In an array of rainbow clefs, they danced across the room in beat to the song. For a moment I relaxed, amused by this less-frightening visual. I took a deep breath and could feel every square inch of my lungs in motion. There was a huge wooden picture frame hanging across the room from me containing a picture of a forest with extraordinary detail and colors. The leaves had many different tints depicting the start of an autumn day. Thousands and thousands of streams of colors began to emit from the picture, and all the rays went directly into the center of my eyes. It reminded me of driving though fine snow and watching it come at you in fine lines through the windshield, a tranquil, steady stream of hypnotic proportions, countless hues of pliant textures drawn into my pupils, transfixing onto my retina and back out again and drawing me with it. I felt my body transform into the stream as my whole body was engulfed in the rays. I was pushed along the path, and then in a flash, I was transported into the picture.

If this was only a hallucination, then hallucinations are real. As sure as I was breathing, I was standing in that forest looking up at the majestic qualities above me. The beauty of it all suppressed the fear for a moment. I was lost in a wave of euphoria and then was quickly jolted back to the couch. My friend's girlfriend was shaking me vigorously, her hands grabbing my shoulders and squeezing. I could feel fright raise the hair on the back of my neck, and I quickly pushed her away. She asked me what was wrong, and for a moment, I regained composure. I told her someone needed to help me as I felt the fright reaching panic levels. She repeated that I just needed talking down and she would try to help until her boyfriend came back. She asked me if I had any other pills on me and suggested that I should get rid of them. I had no intentions of ever swallowing another one and gladly handed them to her. I watched her walk to the kitchen and flush them down the drain. When she returned, her face began to melt, dripping like hot wax to obscurity and deformity. Her eyes remained, but they had turned into red-hot embers, like round rubies the color of blood. Just before her lips dissolved, I could hear her voice change to gravel, and it graded like stone on steel. I screamed in terror and shouted out that she was evil.

In deafening screeches, I called her the devil, and then I heard a door slam from behind me. I vaguely remember my two friends entering the room, for they were not my friends for long. Before I could ask them to help me, I watched their faces dissolve as well, turning into monstrosities of anyone's worst nightmare. Horns sprouted out of their foreheads, and the same red fiery eyes were pulsing, appearing to push toward me. Panic was in full mode by then, and my only thought was to escape. The rest of my memory of my time at their house is obscured by a massive onslaught of hallucinations and by my total lack of sense of time. There was an overload of adrenaline, and my physical strength grew beyond human capabilities as I tried to run. Someone grabbed me, and I turned around and swung. My fist went through the wall, but I felt no pain. I do remember picking up the coffee table and throwing it, hearing but not seeing it shatter. I remember being pinned down on the ground but able to get up to be tossed around in a whirlwind of arms and legs. Sometime during the fray, the police had to have been called, for I remember three uniforms added to the mix. Two had held me down, and a third leaned over me with his hand around my neck, crushing my windpipe. This resulted later in a flashback that would not go away for a long time. I could see the devil sucking the breath from my lungs and feel my Adam's apple squeezed to dust. I was fighting against the epitome of evil that night.

There is another big gap in my memory after that. The next thing that I can focus on was being carried away on a stretcher and shoved into the back of an ambulance. I was shrouded in red. Whether it was a blanket or the flashing light of the ambulance, everything had turned to shades of crimson. I cannot say why because any remnants of the real world were gone after that. I remember looking at my toes turning to blood, certainly unconcerned that my shoes were gone. First the skin disappeared, and then the bones. It was as real to me as the earth had been a short while before. My legs soon followed as they dissolved into red liquid and followed a path upward to my pelvis. I could feel a slow warm drain of my organs, but I was surprisingly not afraid. It was a tepid anomalous sensation. The rest of my body liquefied into a red pool, succulently and peacefully. The last and weirdest sensation was the realization that my head was gone as well.

Yet I was completely aware and alive. I was floating upward but had no binding body. I was soaring though time and space as part of the universe. I rose above the Earth through the stratosphere at infinite speed, looking back long enough to see the Earth, its bright blue oceans, and the vibrancy of its lands warming me somewhere where my physical heart used to be. It was so real and natural, so blissful. I shot briskly through the solar system and out through other galaxies never imagined. I saw Jesus pass by me briefly, or at least what my mind conceived him to look like. It was only later in retrospect that I wondered why my whole trip had such contemporary religious overtones to it. From the Devil to the supposed Son of God. I did not see God, but I certainly felt him all around me, guiding me through my flight through the cosmos. There was an understanding of the realities and the meaning of other dimensions, but now they are buried somewhere inside me, hopefully to be rediscovered later someday. There was a brilliant light shining to the purpose of afterlife, far beyond the debates of the literary. I floated among the ethereal and esoteric secrets for an eternity, and then I slowly faded into darkness.

I woke up the next morning strapped to a hospital gurney, unable to move. I had no memory of getting there. I could feel a recent needle pick in my arm and was told later by the nurse that they had given me something that they thought would counter-effect whatever I had taken. They had no way of knowing what it was. I had just taken a journey into the heavens to return and feel no differently than when I had left. It did change me, and I was never able to look at the world the same way. But the weight of the world quickly returned, and unless you want to be labeled insane, you follow its normal perspective.

Shortly after the nurse unstrapped me and brought me a glass of juice, a social worker entered my room. He was rambling, and I paid little attention to what he had to say. I did hear him tell me that there would be no further police involvement and that he was there to help me. Who sent him? I did not know. He offered me advice and where to go for counseling. He asked me about my parents, and I simply explained to him that I didn't live with them anymore. When he could see that I wasn't cooperating with him, he asked if there was anything he could do for me. From that offer, I was able to get released and even swindle a ride from him back to Westlake. I had him drop me off at the pool hall still dressed in my hospital slippers. I had no intentions of going in, but hadn't wanted the social worker to see where I actually lived. I smelled trouble.

I walked back to the boardinghouse, the bright sun hurting my eyes. My eyes had changed somehow. I sat in my armchair for hours and hibernated for the rest of the weekend, thinking that for once I was glad to be alive. I never did speak to the Newfoundland brothers again. They did not frequent the pool hall, and when I would pass them in the street, we would just nod at each other in some strange form of recognition about what happened. I owed them a coffee table, but I thought it best not to volunteer to replace it. They owed me a pair of shoes, so I called it a wash.

Missing work was something I tried to never do. Ingrained work ethics from my time in my father's fields and my acquired taste for a full paycheck wouldn't allow it. But that following Monday, I took the day off. I went for a long walk in the woods with a new appreciation of the vegetation around me. I later walked down my favorite set of railroad tracks. I made room for the freight train meeting me with no second thoughts not to. I stopped at the general store in that little hamlet with the three houses and the grain mill that fulfilled the entire community. I bought Cokes and chocolate bars and enjoyed my first overdose of a sugar buzz. I bought my first pack of cigarettes and, after choking on the first few, had another habit to add to my collection. There were worse things to put in your body than nicotine. Aside from a brief conversation with the owner of the general store, I spent the day in complete solitude. It was a window of opportunity to work on extinguishing my self-pity trips that I had focused on. The fresh country air cleared my mind, and I was ready for a fresh start, to face the responsibilities of my own actions. It would be an uphill battle, though, still stuck with the undeveloped brain of an adolescent. I felt more mature, but I had some way to go before I stopped blaming my problems on the world and on my parents.

After that day of seclusion from the outside world, I came back to the boardinghouse long after dark. I was exhausted, and I slept very soundly. When dawn arrived, I was already bringing reflections of reality to the forefront. My acid trip, my brief vacation to the cosmos already filtering into dark corners of my memory banks, listed as past experiences for retrospect purposes only. I had a clearer understanding, a better insight to what I needed for happiness. That, too, soon faded as the basic needs for life destroyed the verity of it all.

I waited until the weekend to see you, gathering up courage through the week on what to say to you. I crossed through the cornfields, my brief, obscure sabbatical over. An apology for everything was to be my opening statement. You happened to be outside by yourself when I cleared the field and walked into your backyard. You were sitting on the homemade swing that hung from the huge oak tree, motionless, staring at the ground lost in your own deep reflections. When you looked up at me, the solemn expression on your face, I felt the pangs of remorse. I finally recognized how selfish and inconsiderate I had been to you, a disregard for your feelings that approached lewdness. I had taken you for granted, expecting you to just accept me whenever I showed up. I stood in silence in front of you, and as I looked into your eyes, a wave of discomfort hit me. I finally bent over and kissed you and whispered to you that I was sorry.

Your lips were warm and sensuous. Instead of acknowledging that I had just apologized, you told me I tasted like cigarettes. If that's all you had to offer for an icebreaker, then I was ready to accept it. It only occurred to me later how you would know what cigarettes tasted like. Instead, I offered you one and helped you in finding your own addiction to nicotine.

And so life with you went back on course for a while. I spent more time with you, and we regained most of our feelings back for each other. But it was only a matter of time before the pool hall's beckoning call would interfere with my priorities. It was only a matter of time that the pleasures of my destructive lifestyle would allow the return of my selfish ways and begin to disregard your needs.

The night before I was drawn back to the pool hall atmosphere, I was in your backyard again. We were lying in the grass out of sight of your house, admiring the starlit sky and soaking in the warm night air. You said something in such a low voice that I couldn't be sure what you had said. I would swear that you had said to me that you were ready to go all the way. This caught me so off guard that I couldn't get myself to ask what you had said for sure. Before I finally convinced myself that I had to ask you to repeat it, your brothers came storming out of the house, the screen door slamming behind them and as if they had radar, found us right away to torment and tease us. If there was to be an ultimate magic moment between us happening that night, the chances were now gone. We were stuck with the company of your brothers now, and I left you late that night with a kiss and a warm hug, never to know if I had heard you right. I live with that to this day, wondering how much my path might have changed if the circumstance of that evening were different.

We slowly drifted apart after that night. When I would visit you, there was distance between us that hadn't been there before. You were upset that I was spending more time in town again, cutting into our time together. Our conversations became more trivial, like acquaintances rather than the closest of friends. Our physical contact had dwindled to almost nothing, but we held on to the belief that things would get better. I needed you, just didn't have the common sense to tell you. I fell back into the pool hall routine, relying more on alcohol every day. Change is never a welcome venue, and the farther away from my journey to the cosmos and the idle promises I had made to myself to change, were soon buried behind the comforts of routine. All my bad habits returned, and I wallowed in the spaced-out view of a substance abuser. Marijuana was infrequent for a while, for what was explained to me as flashbacks would occur, and my mind would fight against panic when I experienced the shadowy visuals of the bad parts of my acid trip. Paranoia would set in, and thankfully I did have friends that helped me through it, caught in the memories of their own trips. Eventually the residue of the acid left the cells of my brain, and I became a daily pot smoker again, not willing to go without the enhanced feeling of that existence.

Stuck in my routine as inescapable as quicksand, I accepted it as a cozy, safe, and amusing way of life. I was not prepared for any disruptions, so when I got hit with a double play of bad news, I struggled to keep depression from totally ruling me. That unwanted change was inevitable but still crushing. Andrew's grandmother had taken a turn for the worse, and at the hospital, she was diagnosed with advanced lung cancer. She was not coming home. All her grandchildren were being moved to an aunt that lived a hundred miles away. Andrew was staying behind to live with an older cousin that lived in the next town from Westlake. When Andrew delivered this news to me, nonchalantly as if he was talking about the weather, I suggested to him that we could rent the house together and stay right where we were. He was quick to tell me that social services had been there the day before and condemned the house. It would more than likely be torn down.

I was trying to digest all this, suddenly aware that I would be homeless, when Andrew handed me the envelope that you gave him to give to me. I held on to it for a long time, afraid of what it might say. Later when I was alone, I sat outside on the back porch and opened it and read it in the light of the sunset. I did not know what a Dear John was at the time, but not knowing its definition did not lessen the impact of receiving one. As I read your carefully chosen words to tell me that you didn't want to see me anymore, my heart did stop for a moment, and I felt something let loose inside me. I did not want to give you up, but you had enough. Close to the bottom of the page, just before the line that wished me good luck with my life, was the news that you had found about my philanderings with the minister's daughter. Andrew might have been a good friend, but he had the indiscretions of a neon billboard. He had told you about it; to what purpose, I had no idea. He had no trouble sharing details with you, and this was your final straw. The camel's back was broken.

I am not sure if I ever loved you in the truest sense of the word, but I certainly needed you and relied on you. I did feel. When I read your letter for the second time, searching for any choices, I knew we were through. It wasn't quite heartbreak I felt, but it was pain nonetheless. The piercing effect of being dumped hurts at any level of emotion, whether it even is as shallow as a bruised ego. I did not pursue you, did not try to make things right between us. I had too many other distractions to get me by, the least of which was my impending homelessness.

I went begging to my paternal grandmother, whom I had abandoned with the rest of my family. Against the wishes of her son (my father), she took me in. She had been a widow since I was two, and I am sure her own lack of companionship influenced her decision. She had no way of knowing that I would rarely be home and, although with no conscious intentions, would only be taking advantage of her for a roof and food.

The walk to Westlake and the pool hall would increase significantly as she lived out in the country even farther. I had discovered hitchhiking, however, and its relative safety back then. It was convenient and faster.

I thought of you often, especially in my long walks home at night when I discovered drivers were less likely to stop and pick you up in the dark. There were more than a few frigid walks home that winter. But it left me time to concentrate on the past. I missed you. We had spent a lot of time together, sharing adolescent struggles, losing some of our innocence in teenage play and emotion. I doubt if I was a great deal of help to you, but I was your friend, and I did relate to your own troubles.

I never saw you again, but I did bump into one of your brothers a couple of years later. He told me that you had become pregnant and you had insisted that you would be a single mother and raise your child on your own. You had the backing of your family and even your stepmother. Your brother had gone on to say that you were with the father for only two weeks and then he disappeared off the planet. I thought I had been a jerk to you!

I still think of you from time to time, especially after I finish destroying another relationship with someone. I always wished I had found some way of making up to you all the hurt I caused, some way of finally showing you that inside I had heart and cared for you more than I had shown. I have changed since you have met me, but I am still lost. I have internal struggles that follow me through life, but now I have an overwhelming amount of empathy to help me keep my morals in check. I have had a bumpy road to travel. I hope you have not. It would have been so nice if I could have had another chance to talk to you later in life when we had matured a bit, to reminisce and to see if there still is a spark or two left between us. But my guilt weighs me down, and I doubt you would have wanted to see me anyway.

I hope your life is full of bliss now, full of happiness and dreams that you rightfully deserve. I am still searching.

CHAPTER 4

Margaret:

    Sexual experiences are usually attached to memory by the meaning and quality of their value. And although my heart warms for many other reasons, when I reminisce about my time with you, it is your sexual prowess that stands out the most. You were one of the few girls that were pool hall regulars, and a reputation preceded you. You were given unusual freedom for a minister's daughter. You lived on the corner lot off the main street in that huge three-story brick house that towered over the others. So with the pool hall a pebble's throw away and some very lenient parents, you made good competition for me in the contest for the most-frequent-client award.

    I had been drawn to you from the start, and aside from the stigma of your reputation, you were extremely attractive to me. I was also intrigued by your freedom. None of your supposed escapades ever took place in the pool hall, leaving me with the threads of doubt I needed to overcome the comments made behind your back. The pool hall was simply a place for you to hang out and to find attention. My own mix of curiosity and attraction eventually set aside the hearsay and the rumors that the locals had filled my head with about you. I began to believe that the stories of how loose you were could only be mean gibberish. It had been many weeks before my attraction to you became powerful enough to break the barrier of my shyness. You had never really paid any attention to me except for the odd hello, preferring the conversations of the more outgoing. You looked surprised the night I followed you out of the pool hall as you were walking home.

    The streetlight added even more glamour to your looks, and my heart was pounding. I was almost shaking as I asked if I could spend some time with you. I envisioned you laughing at me while I shrank in front of you. But instead you were very friendly, seemingly aware of my bashfulness, and had a concealed understanding of my need for companionship. The instant comfort levels you made me feel allowed idle conversation to flow freely in a way I did not think was possible. That brief encounter on the street that night was the beginning of our shared summer as fellow playmates.

In retrospect, we were just two lost teenagers, biding time in an incessant course through adolescence. I could not imagine you feeling as lonely as I did. You had family to support you, but there are different levels of loneliness. The liberal rules you were blessed with and your outgoing ways and the stories of your sexuality left me confused, and I was somewhat leery at first of your intentions. But after my first encounter with you and your bold sexual advances to me, the gravitational pull toward you was the only thing that mattered. We began seeing each other frequently, with an unspoken agreement that we would keep our connection, our unusual friendship, in the most discreet fashion. How you knew to do this was beyond me, but it was important as I foolishly found importance to avoid the ridicule and teasing of my friends, acquaintances, and peers. My ability to keep my heart in check and keep you from totally capturing it was based on the possible truth of the expanded tales and boasts of their claims. By keeping us quiet, though, I could allow some feeling. Whether it was desire or the slow development of my emotions, our relationship did grow, but always on the foundation of our physical contact.

You became my teacher, an elevator to lift me from the depths of my own ignorance and experience. In the alley, in the park, on the beach, long intervals of extreme petting. A couple of weeks later, after my first approach, you invited me to your house and introduced me to your parents. There was an odd respect I felt for your father, probably from the fact that he was a minister. I had no religious background to speak of, except for some self-administered studies from biblical texts read for my own curiosity. I was welcomed into your house with warm greetings and no questions. The assumption was that I was your boyfriend.

Your house was laid out into many enclosed rooms, making each separate room its own den of privacy. The windowless parlor room with the grand piano and the huge leather couch became ours. The soft material of the cushions seemed to embrace our bodies in a blanket of solace, and this couch became our playground, seemingly unaware that your parents were only strides away in some other room. It was here where you gave me lessons of marathon groping sessions and attentive detail in the art of kissing. It soon became a habit for us to disappear together from the pool hall for the short trek to the parlor room. As we became more and more of an item, our discretion to the pool hall clientele slowly dissipated, and the secrets of our rendezvous waived. I was waiting for the teasing to start, but surprisingly, any comments were quite tame. I wanted to question you about your reputation and remove all doubt, but I remained silent for fear of upsetting you, for fear of jeopardizing the rewards of my new pastime. I had gained your trust, and you showed such genuine interest in me as a person as well as a new playmate to frolic with.

The verity between us created a bond that wasn't quite love, but certainly some form of endearment.

This bond and your sexual experience, which I never questioned, led me to nothing but gratitude when you first introduced me to oral sex. When you asked me if I wanted to try something different, I was already committed to any experimentation with you. Still a virgin, I was at your mercy. Within the comforts of the dark shroud of the parlor room atmosphere and the ease between us, your advanced steps were much more than anticipated. I am not about to brag or describe in vivid detail, but you were quite aware of the satisfactory levels from the muffled groans that came from me involuntarily. You sent me on a new road of experience and expectations, and the results of your talents were the foundation of all future encounters and comparisons of intimacy for quite some time. The trash talk of other guys now made sense to me with their descriptions, the basis of which to describe their own pleasures. I had more respect, though. My difference was I had already combined the gratification with emotion. Born a romantic? More likely a need to think it instead. You sparked something in me that I couldn't quite understand, and I couldn't quite grasp how I felt. You confused me with this intermediate affection.

We continued our fabled existence through many long summer evenings, fully content with the entertainment of our sexual excursions and the privacy of your parlor. You knew nothing of the country girl that lived across the field from my boardinghouse, nor did I see any reason for you to. I did have a sense of loyalty to her, but that dissolved every time I was with you. Were we just playmates? Our entire relationship seemed to be based on our ability to keep our emotions hidden, to stop when conversation got personal. We both accepted this as if to pass that barrier would mean to break us. But I do know how important to me you actually were and how you lifted my spirits. Suffice to say that you were therapeutic in many ways. But just as most of life's experiences go, our simple existence had no chance of lasting forever. We were happy at first in our little fairy-tale journey of two carefree teenagers, only happy to simplify everything, no expiry date in our minds. Time moves differently in the realm of youthful delinquency, before the responsibilities of adulthood creep in. Did my own immaturity have partial blame for interfering with our romp in paradise? Was it my poor excuse for honesty? Or was I finally becoming susceptible to my peers comments and jabs? Now that I can think back more objectively, I can accept all the blame.

On a quiet rainy Saturday night, one that was even more special than usual, with your parents gone for the weekend and the parlor truly our domain, you were extremely mushy. We were enveloped in the euphorically plush sofa, wrapped around each other, when you suddenly whispered in my ear the ultimate gift. You offered me the chance to go all the way with you, to the ever-elusive intercourse. We had skipped our mandatory visit to the pool hall entirely that weekend, and it had just been the two of us for two days straight. I had spent the night before, all night with you, and I felt so blissful falling asleep in your arms. The intense transcendence of sleeping beside you still enveloped me with such peace. My mind was still soaking in this magnitude of comfort. I was totally caught off guard that when your soft and sweet voice had whispered those words, I reacted to it physically, like instant anticipation to the thrill. Your voice formed a gauge of measurement for a comparison chart to all others later. I wonder sometimes if all life experiences are relative to the next.

Any guy with common sense would not have had thought twice of what it would take to follow through with your offer. When you told me that I could have you, that you were ready to take our physical encounters to the summit, my heart had raced in expectation to finally reach such an opportunity. You had only one request. You wanted a commitment from me and my guarantee that I loved you, for to offer yourself to me meant genuine attachment and assurances to a pledge of devotion. It was a very reasonable request, but one that will always torment me as I forever ponder why I told you that I couldn't do it. Was it the voices of my peers echoing in my head, your reputation eating at my conscience? Was it an adolescent brain whose mental capacities had been slightly altered from an extraordinary acid trip? Was it that I didn't know how to mutter those three meaningful words that would have solved everything? It didn't matter, for the wrong words had already slipped out; and although you showed no signs of disappointment, I could feel some kind of change. What little light that filtered through the shadows of the room were only enough to see the outline of your face. But I could sense a strain, an interruption of the steady stream of vibrations that were always between us. We spent the next few hours still embraced and holding hands as if the serious conversation had never happened. You still felt so right to me, made me feel so at peace, but now I was pressured by the thoughts of what a fool I had just become. I had given you the wrong answer.

Your kisses and caresses meant more that afternoon than ever, but I could feel a crack in my heart from what I had just done. I left that night before your parents were expected to arrive. You kissed me at the door, and you acted as if everything was still the same between us. I walked back to my dreary boardinghouse and my ugly domain in the dark and in a light cold rain. Tears began to sting my lips, mixed in with the rainwater running down my cheeks, but not enough to dilute salt from my tear ducts. I wasn't sure why I was crying, but I cried hard. Were they tears of self-pity, sorrow, sympathy? I had stood at your door, not letting your embrace go. My glazed blue eyes with the new ability from recently altered chemistry, enabled me to see through others. Your eyes were full of the world, everything I needed, and yet I hadn't said the words you needed to hear. When I finally pulled away from you, your beautiful smile ate a hole in my heart. You had some kind of inner peace that I am still looking for. Through the flow of tears that night, I searched for a way to tell you as soon as possible what you wanted to hear.

I saw you three days later for the last time, not before the full effects of pool hall peers spread their mean tentacles through my already-tangled gray matter. I had just won twenty dollars from a run of luck on one of the better players in the room. He lashed out in anger when I beat him and looked for ways of revenge. It was no secret by that time that we spent time together, as our discretion had fallen to the wayside with the pace of our feelings for each other. With the blunt force of a solid weapon, he hit me in the gut and asked if I was getting anything from you.

There were certain aspects of peer pressure that I found able to sideline, and one of those was bragging rights. I told him no. And without a second of hesitation, he laughed and said that was funny because he had taken you twice right on top of the piano in your home. I stewed knowing there must be some truth to it if he knew you had a piano. I boiled, feeling the red blush on my face, but made no reply. His buddy, who had been keeping score of the pool game for us, kneeled on the wooden bench across from the table. He must have caught my agitation and decided to join in on the fun. It was his words that dug in the deepest, the one that twisted my guts into knots. He told me that he had taken you in the backseat of his car. Even with the visualization alive in my head, a part of me was still able to believe that they were just stories. But to hear the collusion between these two clowns inside the sanctuary of *my* pool hall was enough to begin the fragmenting of my faith. I managed to finish the game, gave him his twenty bucks back after my severe beating in the second game, and walked out of the hall. I took the long walk to the park and the beach, where I did my best thinking. I felt the hypnotic effects of the lake and was lost in them well past sunset. The permeation of a late summer night's ambience into the pores of my skin calmed the pace of my thoughts but did nothing to alleviate the dull pain. I had to see you. I knew that would make things right. I cared about you too much to let your past interfere with the way I truly felt.

An hour later, under the cover of darkness, I was knocking on your door, hoping you hadn't decided to go to the pool hall. Your father opened up the door. He did not invite me in but summoned you instead. My insides turned to mush at the sight of you, and my pain melted. I wanted to be beside you again in that paradisiacal parlor room and say the right things this time. All my problems could go away in there. We sat on your concrete porch instead, staring up at what stars we could see. At first we sat in silence, and then I gripped your hand, probably too tight for your comfort. Between the skipped beats of my heart, I told you I had changed my mind about your request for me to give you a commitment, but first I had to know the truth. I asked you about what the pool hall clowns had said. Had I expected you to admit it? If it was true, then what? Yes, we had honesty and trust on the surface levels of our connection, but was there still not an unspoken agreement to have our pasts remain buried? Of course, you denied it. Why would I have expected you to shower me in a decree of honesty that would do nothing but tarnish you? I struggled to accept your denial, the words of the pool hall rhetoric now stinging my brain like sharp objects on a chalkboard. But I had a good feeling that I could overcome my doubts, this stigma of promiscuity suppressed by the way I felt about you.

You gave me no time to reflect on this as you quickly blindsided me with unsettling news. You were leaving Westlake. It was decided by your father that it would be best for you to go to a private boarding school for girls to improve your grades. This school was over three hours away. Worse, you were leaving in two days. I was dumbfounded. Still too young to distinguish selfishness where understanding should be, a sudden heartache common to loss flooded me. I let go of your hand and rocked back and forth in disbelief, wondering how this could possibly be true. I asked you if you had any choice, and you were quick to reply that your father's decision had been final. You claimed you also thought it was for the best. You had already yielded and accepted this, for why else would it be for the best? Was this your way of escaping your own surroundings?

I wanted you to run away with me that moment. As ridiculous as some of my thoughts were, I didn't voice them all, and this certainly wasn't one of them. But it didn't stop me from thinking along the fantasy lines of you and me against the world. I remained silent, searching for something reasonable to say. I took your hand again and transferred the physical touch back into the stream of emotion that I had gathered through the summer with you. For the longest time, I sat in silence and then made you promise that I could spend the next two days with you. We talked for a while, but it was strained. I thought it would be best if we waited until tomorrow to talk, letting some time to allow this sudden news to soak in. I left that night kissing you on the cheeks instead of on the lips. I do not know why. It was the last time I ever saw you.

When I knocked on your door the following afternoon, your mother answered the door. She had always seemed to be in the background somewhere, and I really didn't know her. But I will forever remember her that day. She explained to me that your father had taken you ahead of time to the boarding school to settle in before classes. You had packed up after I had left you and had left early that morning, far away from the influences of the pool hall and our obscure little farm and fishing community. I stood there lost, probably with my mouth dropping toward the ground. At first, your mother was polite and compassionate about it, as if she could read how I was feeling inside. It helped lessen the shock, lessen the pain I would now hold on to. Deep inside, I knew it was for the best. The abrasive but somehow elusive truth about your reputation was not going to go away. I knew but could not admit that peer pressure would eventually erode any chances we had of a long-term relationship. It is true, though, that I did want to run away with you, where all that would have been left behind—all our troubles, including mine, blessed with a brand-new start. The dreams of adolescence.

Your mother handed me the letter you wrote to me that night, still sealed with colored tape and lipstick marks in the form of a kiss. She wished me good luck in my life and said she would pray for my guidance. The sincerity of her remarks and her original face of compassion vanished as she shut the door on me with a final look that really said good riddance.

I stood on the porch for the longest time, twirling the envelope in my hand, as if kinetic energy would send vibrations through my fingers and open it for me to tell me what it said. I walked to the park and the beach, where the only true vibrations could be felt. I soaked in the surroundings that I had grown accustomed to feeling when I went there. I could feel the earth move beneath my feet, a sensation that could no longer leave me, and took deep breaths of the clean air flowing off the lake. A lone seagull flew over my head, crying out for me to open the letter. I read each line slowly as if to prolong the inevitable. Your words were clear and precise and sad. My tear ducts opened up as they did more and more frequently that year. I still well up when I think of your letter from time to time. The honesty and the passion of your written word, which you never shared in your spoken words, penetrated into the chambers of my heart, and I felt lonelier than ever. Overwhelming grief mixed with the first signs of sincere empathy, which would flow permanently in the future, ran to the core of my soul.

You explained your acute feeling of loneliness, your constant strive for companionship, your regrets of your past promiscuities. You accounted for your actions as a search through your lost world, and I could feel the similarities of my own impoverished journey through the streets of solitude. Now that the truth of your past was in front of me, it no longer mattered. I fell in love with you that afternoon on the shore of the lake, turning the pages of your farewell letter. All the emotions that I had held in all summer gushed out like a broken levy, and I lay back on the warm sand with a strange sense of déjà vu as I prayed for some kind of guidance from the heavens to help me. I watched the marshmallow clouds drift by forming faces and then dispersing in the distance, your letter sandwiched between the palms of my hands as if to offer sacrifice in some ancient ritual. The tears kept flowing until there was nothing left but dust. I closed my eyes and felt the sway of the magnetic pull of the Earth, felt its pulse. In my mind I was part of the cosmos, not caring if it was real or not. I lay there for hours, undisturbed by anything or anyone.

I kept your letter for a long time until it was eventually lost in the shuffle of many relocations. Two months after you left, I finally found the nerve to knock on your parents' door, encouraged by a quart of cherry brandy and an evening of feeling sorry for myself. Someone else answered the door to inform me that your parents no longer lived there and had moved out of town. I slithered away, not knowing where you or your parents had gone. You had not mentioned it in your letter, nor did anyone in town know either. As part of my life, as part of Westlake, you were now only history. I would still ask around as time passed, and over a year later, through the vines of the small-town gossip mill, a question of your whereabouts brought on by me with a constant obsession with my past brought me the fruits of an answer. A friend of a friend's acquaintance knew you and told him that you had gotten pregnant, had married, and moved out west all in the same year.

This news was helpful for me to put to rest the need to know if you were doing okay. I will always wonder, though, if I had simply committed to you that night, even with only the words you wanted to hear, how different our lives would have been. You would probably have still gone to private school, but you might have stayed in contact with me. I can say, with overtones of jocularity, that I remained a virgin until the day I met my wife. Maybe I was honoring you until I found the right person. In actuality, the opportunity never arose again, with the bulk of my teenage years used for a concentrated effort of burning away as many brain cells as possible.

When I think back about my time with you, I cannot help but wonder how happy you are now. I hope you have found the contentment and everything you were looking for and maybe even think about me once in a while. To be truly content and fulfilled has always clouded me, but I certainly do have a small sense of tranquility whenever I remember you.

CHAPTER 5

Melissa:

My only one—my only wife, that is. And now I guess I can only label you as ex. But you will always be the celestial star that finally picked me out of the gutter and pointed me in a direction of maturity and responsibility, at least while I was with you. It was quite a challenging chore to turn an eighteen-year-old alcoholic, psychologically addicted stoner, wannabe hippie, social outcast into a productive member of society, especially for a seventeen-year-old girl with a background of her own childhood problems.

You met me at a very lonely time in my life and at a time where my self-esteem was at an all-time low on any scale. I didn't think about the future, preferring to live in a fog and hoping to make it to the next day without too many repercussions. I can't say I was in a total downward spiral when you met me, but I lacked care and responsibility. But you did lift me out of what could have been the start to the bottom of an abyss and to an eventual landing of total destruction. Partying and getting wasted wasn't exactly a complicated agenda with glorious results and accomplishments.

I first saw you below a crystal clear blue sky in the middle of an early, warm June summer morning. I was already on my third bottle of apple wine, my second joint, perched on top of a picnic table. The air had no movement, as if the Earth had stopped for me to get a better look. I was in tune with nature, engulfed in the beauty around me; the lush green trees, an endless variety of birds frolicking fearlessly among the branches, squirrels claiming ownership to the forest floor, vivid colors everywhere. My campsite was directly in front of the boardwalk, nestled slightly under hug oak trees, acorns sporadically plunking off the wooden boards of the table, temporarily startling me from my trance. I chose that site because the boardwalk was the only route over the creek to get to the beach and the lake. Everyone in this campground would eventually venture to the sandy beach and to view the lake, and this setting gave me the optimum chance to people-watch.

It was at this vantage point that I first saw you. I thought you were an illusion at first as you blended into the beauty of the rest of the surroundings, the effects of my altered state by some very potent weed. Smoking it alone was my method of choice recently since rather than as a social use, I found it enhanced my introversion. I was in the middle of a space-distorted stone when you glided rather than walked toward me and then turned down the boardwalk. Your beautiful blonde hair floated behind you, trailing like a golden halo that had burst into a thousand rays of light. You made no sound as you seemed to float over the thick planks of the boardwalk and disappear down the hill on the other side. I waited patiently, and half hour later, you came back as the same angelic vision. You looked at me for a moment but did not smile, and I watched you disappear down the same path you had come from. An hour later, as my attention withdrew from nature into the confines of my inner darkness, wallowing in self-pity and indulging myself with that weird sense of comfort that I felt from depression, you appeared again. As if in a dream, I watched you glide down the boardwalk a second time, down the hill, and a while later, return again. There was a brief exchange of eye contact this time, possible but not determined makings of a smile on your face, and then you were gone once more. Was it remotely possible that you were interested in me?

I opened up a fourth bottle of wine, a case of it still in my tent, to work on shattering my shyness to the wind. But there was no wind that day, and inhibitions were not going to be easily blown away. I spent the next hour hoping for your return. Whether it was the wine, the weed, the weather, the concentration of my polluted mind had switched to you and only you. The total time for you to walk across the boardwalk and disappear from the direction you came would have been three, four minutes at best. But already I was obsessed with you, a driving force fueled by my perpetual loneliness. I mulled over all the ways I could confront you if you came back. The attraction I felt had become overwhelming. But just as overwhelming were all the negative reasons I was coming up with not to approach you. You had a boyfriend, you could care less about the burnout with nothing to do but sit by himself on top of a picnic table staring into oblivion, you were looking for your friends, you were . . .

I was having another internal war with myself when you did return for a third time. My heart started to race thinking this might be my last chance to talk to you. As a fan of baseball, I kept thinking about the three-strike rule. My hands started to tremble, my nerves sitting on a ledge waiting to leap off, all directly related to my lack of ability that day to cut through the bashfulness. My tolerance levels for alcohol had reached high scale after three years of solid pickling of the brain. The volume needed to suppress my inhibitions to courage levels kept increasing. I watched you disappear over the boardwalk once again. I slipped into obsessive overdrive and finally gave way to compulsive affinity. This was my campground. I should have home-field advantage. What did I really have to lose by approaching you? When you finally came back from the beach that third time, I still watched you turn to walk away down the gravel path. I jumped up and, nothing short of running, went after you, whispering, "Miss, miss," and then gradually raising the decibels to a shout when you didn't hear me. And the rest is our history.

You teased me for a long time about calling you *miss*, but if it wasn't for that word, no matter how lame it sounded at the time, our five years together would never have happened; my brief period of salvation, nothing but a fantasy. You had made me feel so comfortable so quickly. It was as if we had already known each other. Under the shade of the oak trees and the sounds of chirping robins, we had made arrangements for you to meet me later that night and go to a bar in the next town away from Westlake. We said a quick good-bye, and I spent the afternoon with some doubt that I would really see you later. It had all happened so fast.

My drunken buddies had shown up that afternoon, their booze-filled coolers and pup tents in tow, prepared for a weekend of stupor and rowdiness. You had told me you would be back just before sunset, and I had not shared any of this with my buddies. I was still perched on top of the picnic table, being entertained with the antics around the campfire that one of them had lit earlier. You came from around the corner of the gravel path appearing like a vision out of a dream, the crimson colors of dusk painted behind you, around you. My buddies spotted you at the same time and were already whistling and shouting comments, construction workers' display of sexism. You will never know how proud I was that day when you ignored their comments and, without hesitation, climbed up on top of the picnic table and sat down beside me with only the width of my cigarette package between us. The catcalling stopped immediately, and I watched with pride and a not-well-hidden grin as their mouths dropped in awe, their jaws unhinged reaching for the ground. I tried not to show the vanity of a peacock, but it was hard to restrain. In the time of a lightning bolt flash, my self-esteem shot to the top of the charts. All those lonely nights of praying for a change in my life, some sign of guidance, some form of miracle to pull me out of the doldrums, had just been answered. I was already convinced that you were mine, assured that the attraction I felt toward you was mutual. Years of pain and agony were washed away, the beginning of a new journey steaming with enthusiasm and positive thinking. It felt so right. You never knew how much you did for me that day. Know it now.

Conversation flowed freely on the way to the bar that night. And I could tell it was much more than booze affiliated. You made no comments about my beat-up Barracuda, which by that time was held together with duct tape in some places. From the frequent trips in and out of ditches, it had more dents in it than some of the tireless ones lined up in front of the junkyard just outside of town. I was completely enveloped in comfort although I should have been a bundle of nerves. The console and the gearshift separated us, interfering with my desire to sit closer to you. You made it feel so natural for me to be with you. I walked into the bar with you looking like I had known you all along. At first I was afraid they wouldn't let you in. We were both underage, and we both looked it. But with business being business, they didn't ask you for identification, and we walked in as if we owned the place. I should have because they certainly knew me there. I had handed over more than a few paychecks to bartenders and waitresses.

Dancing was something I never did, but you and I danced the night way. There was absolutely no hesitation when you asked me to dance. The music blended into my bloodstream, and I was surprised at my own rhythm and blushed at your comments about my dancing skills. Through intermissions our hands were glued together, save for the raising of glasses filled with double shots of rum and Coke. I had a new drinking partner, much better looking than the clowns back at the campsite. Whatever you saw in me, you were not shy to show it to me in your eyes. On the way back to your parents' campsite that night, we had shared most of the outlines of our background. And somehow I knew what I told you would stay with you. That was important. There was a huge hole developing in the hard shell that protected my inner self, and it was already pouring out in a direct path to your heart. I wasn't alone anymore.

How such a thing could have happened so fast was beyond my perception, nor did I need to understand it. I only knew the reality of what I was feeling. I kissed you good night in front of your darkened campsite, thankful your parents were asleep. You had left out the detail that they wanted you home by midnight until well past any chance of doing so. Our kiss had great spark, and I was glad my days of kissing like a fish were far behind me. I watched you disappear to the other side of the dying embers of the fire pit and into the side door of your parents' trailer. I drove back to my campsite, taking deep, satisfying breaths of night air, and I could feel an involuntary smile on my face for the first time in recent memory.

You were to meet me the following morning at my campsite again, and I was swimming in that thought. I was alone again when I had returned to the camp, my buddies having fanned out to various parties unknown. I returned to my perch on top of the picnic table, only horizontally this time, and watched the stars fade away as the morning sky, as the start of dawn slowly wiped away the darkness. I fell asleep just as the sun rose above the tree line and, under the cover of my own darkness, basked in the hot morning sun, waking up just moments before your scheduled arrival with a midrange hangover. Nothing that a cold shower in the public, bug-infested, and sand-laden facilities and a fresh bottle of apple wine wouldn't take care of.

My hair was still wet when you walked that same path toward me. It wasn't long after you had joined me that you gave me the unnerving news that your parents wanted to meet me and I was invited for supper. As you had known from our sharing of details the night before, I lived with my grandmother, so aside from her constant diet of boiled potatoes and boiled chicken and boiled everything, any other food intake consisted entirely of meatless, condiment sandwiches and chocolate bars. It was self-explanatory why I was so scrawny. Not so easily explained was why I didn't have scurvy.

So I agreed, to confirm our relationship not only on a social level but also on the basis of hunger, for there was nothing in my cooler but a loaf of bread, a bottle of ketchup, ice, beer, and wine. With your help, by late afternoon, only the bread and the ketchup remained, while I worked on augmenting courage to meet your parents with the advantages of fermented liquid. I soon found out that you could hold your own, which was another godsend for someone whose life revolved around alcohol. I had a fellow drinker as a partner, and a beautiful one at that. By late afternoon we were glowing in more ways than one. Between the apple wine and our growing attraction to each other, we were alight. Late that afternoon, hand in hand, you led me to your parents' campsite, only slightly apprehensive.

Your father was not a big man, but quite intimidating just the same with his sinewy arms and his initial growling features. It didn't help that he continued to swing the ax into the chunks of wood stood upright on the ground, continuing to split the wood in great accuracy down the middle even through your introductions. He nodded at me instead of the expected handshake and took another swing. Your mother was sitting in her hand-knitted lawn chair snapping string beans into a pot with one hand and a beer in the other. She looked up and smiled along with a cheerful hello. I had taken an instant liking to her, and I knew right away where you got your good looks from. Your father eventually warmed up to me, and the fact that he had a great fondness of his own to beer was something for me to revere. When he asked my last name and said that he knew my grandfather (who had passed way when I was barely two), I seemed to fall into his good graces. He did make a couple of comments about my hair that day (which by that time was reaching down toward my belt loops), but somehow the memories of my ancestor reflected something worthy he saw in me. I was accepted into your family with miraculous ease, and whether I was looking for some kind of parental figures, I grew very fond of them very quickly. Of course, the fact that both of your parents were alcoholics made my transition into your family smooth.

When I left your campsite that night, it was without pain and with an immediate sense of belonging. An impression was left on both sides. After accepting a second beer from them, I excused myself for a moment and rushed back to my campsite to get my other cooler of beer hidden in my tent, full of backup supply. It was a mixed agenda, wanting them to know that I wasn't a moocher and not liking the warm beer that your parents preferred to cold. I had a cast-iron stomach trained to drink liters of hard liquor straight out of the bottle from my brain-dead years in the pool hall, but warm beer just didn't cut it. After a great supper and an enjoyable evening of lawn darts and card games, you walked me back to my campsite. We kissed passionately several times along the path, the moonlight spreading over us. I could feel the tingles between us and was engulfed with your embrace. When we finally got back to my campsite, you asked me if I had a blanket. And so for a fourth time, I watched you glide over the boardwalk, only this time you had my grandmother's quilt and myself behind you.

Of all the memories I have of you, that night is the most recurring, as I suppose it would be for anyone's first time. I never shared with you that it had been my first time, but you probably knew. I knew it wasn't yours as your display of what you were doing and then later your mother's need to tell me about your past boyfriends erased any doubt of that. In one of my paranoid states a few years later, I thought I heard you telling someone about my virginity and making fun of me. Nonetheless, the magic of that night remains.

I did have professional foreplay on my list of skills from previous rounds of exploration with others, so the moment was not completely awkward. Under a thousand stars, on a secluded stretch of sand, with the lake lapping the shore cresting in small ripples, I entered the realm of sexual intercourse, never to return to a life without it. Under that night sky, I found another escape route from the turmoil inside my psyche. However short-lived or sometimes lacking true meaning, it carried me from each time to the next as an act of pure repose. And each time we progressed with the comforts of familiarity and a growing bond, the need and the desire grew stronger.

We spent that whole summer in a routine where each night was not fulfilled until we ended it with sex. Sometimes in the back of my derelict Barracuda, crunched in the backseat in awkward positions, sometimes on the beach, and then bravely later, in my bedroom adjacent to my grandmother's shared wall to her bedroom. We soon discovered, and thankfully, that she was a very sound sleeper. We lived most nights in the Vista Inn, the bar where I had taken you the first night. It became our bar, our dance floor where many times we didn't care what spectacle we were as the only couple dancing. It was our world. Each night we would take the long drive back to my bedroom and afterward fall briefly asleep in each other's arms. And then I would jolt awake just in time to get you home before your parents stirred and in time for me to get to work. We became inseparable. Whether it was love or simply the symbiosis of each other's needs, I am not sure. Regardless, we were emotionally involved and relied on each other to get us through the day.

As summer quickly turned into fall and the memories of cold weather rose to the surface of thought, I figured it was time to introduce you to my grandmother rather than sneak you in after she was asleep. I should have done this much earlier so that we had other alternatives besides living in the bar each night. It was wreaking havoc on any attempts for me to save money. With our desire to be with each other all the time and our secured comfort levels, we soon found curling up on my grandmother's couch watching her black-and-white television wrapped in a quilt (not the sand-covered and beach-smelling one from the campground); we were just as content doing nothing. We no longer needed the constant social atmosphere that most teenagers feel the need for. It was also a quicker trip to my bedroom when the first sounds of snoring came from my grandmother's room.

We still partied on weekends, but our new pace through the week allowed me the new discovery that I could drink through the week at non-abusive levels. When we weren't at my grandmother's, we were at your parents' house. Many nights they would not be home, busy with their own social schedule. They had their dart nights at the Legion; they had their card nights at friends' homes.

Sex became our main source of entertainment. I developed an insatiable appetite, and you had no lack of hunger of your own. Either we both had raging hormones or, as I later learned to call it, we were anxiety screwing. We came close to getting caught once at your place when your parents came home unexpectedly early one night. I was glad that the outside walls of your house were thin, so the noise of their car tires could be heard on the gravel driveway. *Guinness* holds a spot for me in their record books for the amount of time it took me to fly down the stairs naked with my clothes bundled in my arms and rush into the downstairs bathroom to get dressed. Still out of breath and flushed, I had come out of the bathroom just as they entered the house. I managed a stammered hello and sat down on the couch as if nothing was the matter.

Life was great! Simple but great. That cloud of depression that had followed me around for so long had lifted, a sense of tranquility not felt before. I was content. I was happy. And then with little warning, my grandmother died.

I should have known that something was wrong. She wasn't getting out of bed anymore. I was too busy rushing off to work on a couple of hours of sleep to pay attention. Even on the last couple of days before she turned very ill, I would honor her request to bring her Jell-O in bed, leave her a glass of water on her nightstand, and rush out the door. Trapped in the selfish outlook of a teenager, I didn't recognize how sick she had become.

That last morning, that last day I ever talked to her, she asked me to call her an ambulance. My grandmother was either old-fashioned or afraid of the new world, but she never owned a phone. As you know, my parents lived the distance of a few farms down the road. So for the first time in three years, I stood on the porch of what used to be my home. I knocked on my parents' door, a bundle of nerves and quite apprehensive about what to say. My mother answered the door, but I could sense my father lurking somewhere behind her. There was an uncontrolled tone of animosity in my voice, yet there was a sense of loss as I stood on that porch of my childhood home. I explained to my mother how ill my grandmother was and that she had asked for an ambulance. My father's bellowing voice was quick to respond. He had been standing behind the door. He quickly blasted me, asking if she was that sick, why I had waited so long. I sarcastically told him that she was his mother and left quickly, wanting to avoid all confrontation with him. I had delivered the message, and I felt it was no longer my responsibility.

I drove to work at unsafe speeds and won the race against the final tick of the punch clock. I suffered through an excruciating long day at work, numbing my worries with a joint I borrowed off the co-worker that I knew always carried. When I entered my grandmother's house after work, there was a note left on the kitchen table stating which hospital my grandmother had been taken to. By the time I got there, she was already in a coma. She died the following morning.

My father was quick to blame me, and maybe some of it was my fault. I could have been more aware of her needs. But I knew he checked in on her when I wasn't there, so if anyone should have known how serious the situation was, it should have been him. That was how I coped with it anyway. The diagnosis was stomach cancer that had spread. She must have been suffering and yet said nothing. It was probably due to the French-and-Irish mix of her blood that the stubbornness to endure the pain had helped her through. I hoped that I had inherited some of it to help me through some of my own.

You came to the funeral with me. I kept my composure right until the time the music started, just before the eulogy. Music always affected my emotions to the point of chills sometimes, and the right note or meaningful lyric could make the hair on my arms stand up. I lost it, crying hysterically. Whether out of guilt or out of belated gratitude to what she had done for me without so much as an iota of spoken appreciation while she was alive. I thanked her that day, over and over again, hoping to channel it to her through any higher power that might be interested in listening to me. A few relatives offered me comfort that day, but I cannot remember a single word they said to me. Neither one of my parents spoke to me.

Two days later, on the weekend that your parents had gone away, I kneeled on the floor beside you as you sat on your couch and asked you to marry me—no ring, still drunk from an after-funeral marathon drinking binge, tears in my eyes. You said nothing but quietly nodded your head in the right direction with a smile of joy and then joined me with your own tears. It was only then that I finally realized that you were just as lonely as I had been the day we met. Sure, you had family, but there are different kinds of loneliness. We christened our engagement that afternoon with the passion and the escape that we grew accustomed to.

We decided to wait a few days before we broke the news to your parents of our intentions to wed. I had seen your father's temper by that time, watching him start a brawl in the Legion one night. I needed some time to prepare for any negative reaction. We also needed your parents' permission, and I had my doubts they would give it to us with you being so young. But when I finally faced that awkward moment the following week, stuttering through a planned speech gone awry, and sputtered out a few words instead, they had consented with reserved blessings. Not with overwhelming titillations, but far from scorn. I respected their advice; my foundation of my belief in their wisdom reached from their age and expected experience that goes with it. They convinced us to wait and not marry as soon as possible and gave us a sensible list of reasons why we should wait. We set the date for the following summer so proper arrangements could be made.

We spent a long and cold winter in anticipation for our big day. You saved me from a boring and depressing season as we saw each other almost every day. Our bar trips were very infrequent as we not only were more comfortable on my grandmother's couch, but we were also trying to save money for our future. The word *future* had a funny ring to me, not a word I had commonly used before. The black-and-white television did not bother us, and we did not mind the lack of color, for that television was only a prelude for our mandatory trip to the bedroom anyway. Then every night, I would rush you home at precisely midnight, not wishing to meet your father's wrath for breaking your curfew. You were his child for one more year, and that was not to be rocked. In theory, I wasn't much more than a child myself. But our relationship, no matter how young or simplified at the time, was slowly developing into the fringes of maturity as we began to mentally prepare for our life together.

Although my grandmother had taken me in long after any serious child-rearing had been done, she did influence me enough to muddle through adolescence with a blossoming insight to right and wrong and the path to adulthood. In all fairness to my parents, they did give me a great moral upbringing. My grandmother's death allowed me some respect for her attempt at guidance and a limited gratitude to my parents' raising of me. And so with this background, I finally began to save money, letting someone else take a turn at lining the pockets of waitresses and bartenders. My grandmother had left me a small sum of money in her will, and without my concrete plans with you, I could have easily squandered it on booze and drugs. I was given temporary lodgings at my grandmother's house until spring or at least until the estate was settled. My uncle had told me this, for I am not sure if I would have been given the same graces if it was left entirely up to my father.

Winter did end quickly for once or spring came fast; whichever way time took its flight. With it, however, came the end to our cozy little existence. No time was wasted in the settling of the estate, and through my father's lawyer, I received the letter with the thirty days' notice in it to vacate the house. This was supposedly in order to sell it. I took it as continued punishment for my disobedience and disrespect in not agreeing to my marine haircut of the past. I would never understand it, his anger or his reasoning.

By this time, I had gathered great rapport with your parents. So when I discussed the fact that I needed to find an apartment to rent, the idea was quickly squashed. I was to stay at your parents' house in the spare room in the basement until the day of our wedding, with strict instructions that you were off limits until then. Like that was going to stop us.

And the wedding day arrived, jitters and all. I had promised you that I would not drink that day. You knew of my inability to stop at a couple of drinks. I kept that promise, but I might as well have drank because I remember little of that day. I was still far from allowing bashfulness not to affect my actions, so to stand in front of two hundred people without the benefit of liquid courage wasn't exactly an easy chore. I was a bottle of nerves the entire time, curling up inside myself most of the day, simply going through the actions, waiting for the day to end. My sanity was kept by the fact that you were now my wife and we were about to start a whole new life together, that elusive thought of a great future now within the reaches of reality.

My parents even showed up, but I don't think they really wanted to. The pressure of being shunned by friends and neighbors influenced them. They congratulated us, but conversation was very limited. The most I remember of that day was how beautiful you looked. I know this for a fact because there is no dust on our wedding pictures that I still have and look at from time to time. After your queen-for-a-day celebration, we went up north for a three-day honeymoon. Neither one of us had really been anywhere, and although it was not the Caribbean, we had some good memories to keep.

Later that week, we came back to our new beginning and watched the start of our five years together take off at enormous speeds forward. We moved into our one-bedroom upper apartment in town (rough to fathom at first for a country boy) and decorated it in obscure fashion, wallpaper fit for acid trips. But it was ours, and we were happy. I don't know if it is because my mind has become entangled in jumbled memories of a scattered life, but our five years together seemed to scamper by as if a strong wind had taken over the pages of the calendar. For a while, we sailed with our free wings. Then the pressures and the influences of your parents interfered with our little paradise.

I had not expected their interference to the degree they did, and it was especially difficult for me, for if there was one who knew independence, it was me. But it was your parents, and I had to respect that. First came the relentless bombardment of a request for a grandchild. Hell, we were only kids ourselves, let alone raising one. We were able to ignore that request for a while. After that, though, came the "how to do this" and "how to do that." The consistent nagging rendered us helpless. The fact that we spent so much time with them made the situation even worse. We became members of their dart league, joined the same club to play cards with them twice a week. Not only had I found a new set of parents, I had also gained a new set of drinking buddies.

What turned the tables the wrong way was when they began to offer me financial advice. By this time, I knew almost every tidbit of information about your parents' background. They weren't exactly tight-lipped when they drank. The fact that they had gone bankrupt twice before did not give them much sway for me in their accounting abilities. So after listening over and over again to their unwavering opinions and with my introverted personality slowly pulling outward like fixing inside-out socks and after many a heated argument on how our future should go, I took their advice.

But not in the direction they wanted me to go. They wanted me to start some kind of business with them. Instead I committed to a second goal to run parallel to my life with you. I would become financially savvy with the object to save as much money as possible in the shortest amount of time. I read book after book on investments and tax strategies. I set up retirement savings plans and, combined with my math skills, all the available tools needed to make every dollar work to its fullest potential. You found a seasonal job to help contribute, and the cheap country home we found to rent allowed us to escape the claustrophobic effects of the apartment. We had amazingly saved up over twenty thousand dollars in three years. This was quite a proud accomplishment for someone who, only a short time before, thought of nothing but handing his paycheck over to pay the utility bills of his local bar. This financial discipline did not affect our partying habits. It merely switched the locale to friends and family. There was always room in the budget for alcohol. We ate generic food products to compensate. We bargain hunted for all necessities. We bought used furniture. We shopped at discount clothing stores. We were responsible.

And on top of it all, we decided it was time to honor one of your parents' requests—a grandchild. Our third year of marriage brought to us our daughter, a beautiful baby girl that was the image of you. You spent twenty-four hours of hard labor, and although I was beside you, I don't think I gave you the support you really needed. So whether mental or physical, you had a rough go of it.

It was difficult for me to comprehend all this at first. A comfortable bank account, a wonderful wife, and a beautiful child. I was a father, and my whole life had changed. I was someone. Instincts ran with us, and we became proud and good parents. When I think back, as time melds into clumps of memory, my heart warms as I recall how happy we really were. Our country home, our financial stability, our love for each other, and our daughter would have been so unfathomable for me to imagine only a few years earlier. We were still very young, but we had a future mapped out for us that would envy many. Our social life expanded as we met new friends, close friends. We continued our responsibilities through the week and separated it from our desire to entertain friends on the weekend. We had a sense of harmony between us, and the world was ours.

But like a nightmarish pattern that was destined to reoccur, life always seemed to find a way to turn on me, something always lurking around the corner to sabotage the calibration of a balanced scale. The trouble started to brew during our fourth year of marriage. At first I thought maybe it would just be a bump in the road instead of a deep ditch. It was not the case. It was more like slipping down an old ladder, each rung holding momentarily and then splitting in two to land on the next lower level, a prolonged and treacherous trip to the ground below. I try not to, but I still harbor ill feelings toward your parents for what they did to us. They were the forefront cause of our spiral, not only in fact, but also in my need to blame someone else besides myself.

We were relishing in the numbers of our savings account and were considering taking a plunge into the housing market, a house of our very own. We even weighed the idea of a second child. Not necessarily because we were ready to, but to appease your overbearing father with his request for a grandson. The granddaughter wasn't good enough. There was even one drunken evening when he accused me of having bad genes for producing a girl instead of a boy. There were times when his logic vanished in a tub of whiskey. When I think back sometimes, with my own polluted filters cleaned, I realize how unhappy your parents really were with their own lives. And it is not like I can't relate to why they would drown their problems in alcohol.

It was on one of these drunken weekend binges when we had gone camping with your parents that the troublesome conversations began, the start of many years of regret. Your parents were barely scraping by, and as close as you were to them, you had shared with them the news of our success with our investments. Unlike me and my ability to drag myself to work on the most painful of mornings, your father's hangovers were of such intensity that he was in constant danger of losing his job over absenteeism. Your mother didn't work, but she had two businesses before. Both of them had failed. I had a strong feeling that the main reason for these failures was the consistent opening of the till for advanced trips to beer and liquor stores. At that time, still encased in the naivety of youth, it did not dawn on me that they were just poor managers. It was this naivety and their relentless pestering to the advantages of owning a business that allowed me a trip down the wrong road.

Around a late-night campfire that fateful weekend, your parents came up with the idea that we should go in on a joint adventure and open up a fabric store. You were sold on it right away, not only because you were antsy sitting at home, but also because you wanted more of a challenge in your life aside from being a housewife. The fabric store had come up in many conversations before, its premise for success based on a friend of your mother's similar thriving business in a neighboring town. There was an increasing Mennonite population in our area who made their own clothes, so there was a potential client base and a market for the business. After five hours of relentless explanations of why we should do this, I grew tired and said I would consider it. But I insisted that we meet with your mother's friend and look at her sales. You had your hopes up so high already that I had to at least look at the feasibility. When we did meet with her, she only fueled you and your mother's compulsion by saying she would sell you fabric at a much discounted price to get you started and a jump on future suppliers. She did refuse to show me her accounting books, citing privacy reasons.

After that visit, your mother was relentless. There was only one problem with this joint venture. It was to be all our money that was being invested. Your parents had nothing to offer. Aside from you and our daughter, my growing self-esteem and prestige was based on our growing savings. Take away all the reaps of the climb out of my struggling teenage years, and I was left with nothing. I had fallen into society's trap and how one's worth was based on what one has. Day after day, your mother pestered us; and I finally relented, far below my better judgment. A week later, I signed a one-year lease to an empty store, ironically right beside the Legion where we played darts. I bought an air-conditioning unit with my next paycheck, still hesitant about taking from our savings. I decided it would be best to look for a business loan and let the store take care of itself that way. This would have left our savings untouched and an easy way to keep the business separate. Eight financial institutions later, I was given the rude awakening that this venture was much too risky, and none of the wise warlocks of wealth would even consider giving us a loan. They explained to me that the country was in the middle of a recession, and even if it wasn't, they couldn't help me.

With this knowledge, I was ready to accept the loss on the lease and back away from the whole thing and count my blessings. I would at least have an air conditioner out of it and the free roam of an empty store to call my own for a year.

For the next couple of weeks, I started drinking heavily again to drown out your parents' daily pounding of why we should go through with it anyway. My concerns seemed to be unheard, and the banks didn't seem to know what they were talking about. After hearing a hundred times that we had already rented the store and that we were wasting money by waiting, I finally had enough of the harassment and handed over the key to all my savings. Not six months later, not only did I see every penny gone, but also you had added up forty thousand in debt on the credit lines of various suppliers with a cash flow from sales that might have you pay them off in a decade or two. I sat on the sidelines watching my ruin play out in front of me, now lining the pockets of the Legion instead of the waitresses at the Vista Inn.

I soon lost interest in you, my daughter, my own life. They always claim that money isn't everything. That may hold true when you don't have it. But to have it and lose it remains an argument to its purpose. There is also the security it provides. And I had been far from secure when you first met me. We had to claim bankruptcy a few months later and lost everything. That included that Pontiac Firebird we were both so proud of, which we bought in celebration of our daughter and for the benefit of her safety as well. To add to our misery, the landlord came over soon after and gave us thirty days' notice. His son was coming back from out west and needed the house. He was sympathetic, but that did not eliminate the fact that we were still left homeless and broke. We ended up renting a dilapidated, mouse-infested farmhouse in the middle of a cornfield just before the arrival of a very cold and icy winter. I found an old rust bucket for a car, and thankfully my mechanically inclined friend from my pool hall days was able to make it somewhat roadworthy. Our cozy little existence had vanished into thin air.

We still saw your parents, but the visits were now strained. We dropped out of the dart league. We quit playing cards. Friends became our priority as we lost some of our own connection and bond. By being with friends, we could at least give ourselves the illusion that nothing was wrong between us. I became heavily involved with smoking weed again, easily influenced by our friends now. I had given it up for you and especially for my daughter. It didn't seem to matter now. I was grateful that you didn't drink as much as I did and were able to watch out for the welfare of our daughter. Many nights I would black out. It was as if I had lost all my tolerance levels along with my will to care. I was regressing back into the habits of my teenage years.

Who or what was punishing me and bringing the flow of bad luck my way wasn't finished with me yet. That same winter, I lost my job. Not because of any foolish antics caused by my heavy drinking, but because of just a growing parade of declivity. They were closing my factory and merging it with a company across the border. So now, on top of everything else, I was jobless. We had to live on unemployment insurance, which only paid a portion of what I was used to making.

That winter was the start of our eventual demise. We managed to scrape up enough money to give our daughter a Christmas. I had memories of worse, so it was just another day for me anyway. Since she was only two, it was easy to appease her. It was your own appeasement that suffered. I could see the pain in your eyes, but there was nothing I could do. Part of me was blaming you for our situation. Not out loud, but I was harboring inside the decisions I felt you forced me to make. Our great value of communication was gone, and although I knew I still loved you, I resented what had happened to us.

With the slow return of the paranoid feelings I used to get from smoking marijuana, caused by my constant use again, I began to crawl back into the shell from which I came. Back into the safety net of my introversion and the withdrawal of my youth. From there I was protected from the outside world. From there I could dwell in my pain where the dullness and swelling depression gave me an obscure sense of comfort. To fill the void between us, we continued to rely on friends and a party lifestyle. As we met more and more people through our growing network of friends, it was eventually not unusual for us to go to separate parties.

It was at one of these separate parties that I met Nancy. Whether I was searching for any means of escape to my problems, I cannot say. I know I did not go out to hurt you. There was harmless flirtation at first, and then by spring, after several meetings, a full-fledged affair. You weren't suspicious at first, but when I started staying out all night, it was easy for you to start wondering what was going on. My friends covered for me at first, but they were your friends too. So it became more and more difficult to hide it. When you confronted me, I always denied any wrongdoing, telling you I simply passed out and wasn't sure where. Your doubts grew as I struggled for better explanations as my absences continued. Then one night when I crawled home at four in the morning, we got into a very heated argument.

You kept pounding away at my head that was already throbbing, demanding to know where I was. And tired and weak from all the deceit, I slipped up and confessed to you. I could hear your heart break in two. There are teardrops splattered on our wedding picture for when I hold the frame in my hand and look at us, I cannot help but think of the horrifying feeling I got from you that night. I remember the chills that went through me when your sobs ran ice through my veins, and each time I look at our picture, I relive the agony I put you through. My heart snapped in two that night as well, right alongside yours. But the numbness inside me that I used for my own survival could do nothing about it. Your screams of "How could you!" still echoes in my head as if it were yesterday.

I had no answer for you, and I began to think I was the most selfish asshole on the planet. I had hurt people before, and sometimes self-indulgence was what drove me. I had empathy, overflowed with it. I had felt the part of you that died that morning. I died along with you. And yet how do I explain the excuse I gave you when you relentlessly pulverized an answer out of me. I told you that I didn't love you anymore. It was the farthest thing from the truth, but I said it anyway. What I didn't love is what had become of us. I didn't love your parents' influence in our lives. I didn't love that my self-esteem had plummeted back into a murky pit. How did I confuse that with my love for you? I had felt your heart drop into the bottom of your stomach where the acid would erode the veneer of your hurt and anguish and change it into anger, and then hatred.

You left me a few weeks later with most of the furniture, all of our future, and all of our daughter. Shortly before our fifth wedding anniversary, you left me standing in an empty house and said good-bye with nothing but spurn and loathing in your voice. I watched in complete dismay as you walked out the door and ended our life together. I fell to the floor and cried through breathless sobs over and over until there was nothing left but dry heaves. You had been everything I stood for, everything I had become. You were my future; you were my life. I let you go anyway.

I wanted to stop you, but my disarranged mind wouldn't let me. The moment you walked out the door, I knew I had made a mistake. But I was already soaking in the solace of self-pity, unable to make sense of it all. I knew from the center of my soul that I was about to begin another journey that would send me tumbling out of control. No future but a day-to-day existence, struggling to keep my mind afloat. I was still very young in the grand scheme of things, but when you feel like all the life force is drained from you, it leaves your past in the realm of eternity. There was also that nagging feeling that you were responsible for our demise. Was I blaming you for my infidelity too?

Before I came to my senses and realized how much I needed you and how much I would give to get you back, it was too late. Within two months after you left me, you found one of my old pool hall acquaintances (which I had long ago labeled as a moron), rented an apartment together, and were pregnant with his child. You had wasted no time replacing me, replacing your life with me. Your father was very proud later as you produced that grandson I deprived him of. If it was a contest of who could shovel the most pain, deliver the most arrows through the chest, then you won hands down. I certainly deserved it, but that didn't help me deal with the amount of emotional upheavals you put me through. What hurt the worst and was the most unfair was the way you deprived me of my own daughter. She already looked up to her newfound father as your bitterness toward me left no qualms in not letting her know who her real father was. Your insistence that I couldn't see her without paying first became a nasty battle long before any court dates to legally end our marriage.

Maybe you didn't know where the money was coming from when you first moved in with my replacement, but I certainly did. It turned out to be a valuable playing card for me in your constant drive for vengeance. Drug dealing is not exactly a legal profession, nor is it usually written on a résumé or job application. As a user of the merchandise, though, I knew how profitable it was, and tax-free income as well. Whenever you demanded the eventual court-assigned child support payments from me in exchange for my right to see my daughter, an ugly argument ensued. You knew I wasn't working yet. You knew that it was no direct fault of my own that our life savings had become history. You were strictly out for revenge and nothing else. My threat to turn the law against your new mate was the only shield I had, and it worked. But only at a stalemate level. I wasn't allowed to see my daughter, so in essence, you still won.

I could never understand how you could just erase from your memory the somewhat-blissful times of our past, how we grew up together. I could not grasp how you could simply wipe clean any emotional feelings we had shared. I know it was my words that did that to you, but what about what was in my heart? It hadn't changed. There is a part of you that will remain stuck in there forever, intertwined like strands of rope wound around regard and regret. I had hoped that with the passing of time, it was only circumstances that had changed our path, our life together—that we still had a chance. For you to cling on so quickly to another guy with the same symbiosis of what I cherished so much about us was gut-wrenching for me. But it still did not diminish my feelings for you.

I can never take back the words that I said that morning, but I can know that I didn't mean them. You were my wife for many reasons, least of all for the way I felt about you. I only wish that you had known that from the bottom of your heart and had found a ray of light through the hurt and pain. I wonder if there are times that you deplore your actions of using our daughter as a pawn to get back at me. Please know that if there was a way to change what happened to us, it would have been done. I have spent enough time stuck in my own past, however, that I can't dwell on it anymore. I can only hope that you have found true happiness and just maybe think about me once in a while. And remember that there was a time when we were happy together.

CHAPTER 6

Nancy:

My guardian seraph that showed me a path to another world that I had only dreamed about. From out of the country bumpkin class and into a view of the brighter side of life and all its potentials. I had no idea how naive I was about the real world until my time spent with you. Not that I wasn't well-read, but I was, for lack of a better term, unsophisticated. You were from a higher part of society that one is unaware of in the land of corn and wheat. You taught me more about the world than any amount of literature and newspapers ever could. If I hadn't been going through such deep depression, I could have utilized all the things you taught me, could have used this new light around me in a form of determination and devotion toward my life's goals and turned my world around. Instead I continued to merely exist, but thanks to you there were a few glimpses of hope and flashes of rapture to fend off the darkness.

When I first encountered you, I was still married, the tail end of a fusion gone sour over the pettiness of finances. I guess not that petty when those same finances were the foundation of my social status and my self-esteem. The same society that I detested and shunned as a teenager was the same society I later found a purpose in. But with my in-laws in a perpetual state of running interference, I had watched my cherished existence crumble away. Filled with disappointment and dismay as I sat helplessly while everything I worked for vanished, I returned to my destructive patterns of alcohol abuse.

I was drunk the first time I laid eyes on you. You glistened with energy and untarnished innocence. You were only nineteen. I was pushing twenty-four, but the fast-paced events of less than half a decade of marriage, swirled into a small pack of memories, left me feeling much younger. Or at least my mental and emotional capacities had pushed me into such regression that I had no qualms acting it.

You were from across the American border and in the first year of university. How I envied that. If there was an outstanding disappointment over all others, it was my lack of education. I had dreams of college that had long been suppressed by the drowning of those dreams with a steady infusion of drugs and alcohol. But deep inside, the reverie was still there.

I met you at my friend Ben's house, the one by the lake where all those weekend parties were known and expected. My wife was with her parents that night, filling an obligation to her parents at a dart tournament. Our trouble had already started, and it was not unusual for us to hire a sitter and go separate ways on weekends.

Whether I was searching for a way to retrieve that feeling I had when I first met my wife, all those jittery quivers I felt from meeting a girl for the first time, or something to simply fill the void I was enduring again, I fell for you that first night. We only talked briefly, but I felt such an overwhelming attraction. It was casual introductions in a corner of the living room before our words were swept away and dispersed by the noise of the crowd. You left early that night, and I felt a rising disappointment to see you go. You waved to me at the door, over the heads of drunks that marred our view, but I saw your smile, and it burned permanently onto the back of my retina. I crashed at Ben's house that night, wasted by the stupid drinking games that I had so foolishly joined in. I did not need games in order to drink. Hard liquor was my enemy, never quite learning the lesson that the volume should change when switching from beer.

I woke up the next morning beside a few other stragglers, and as they slowly turned to face the sunrise and with moans of congregated hangovers, the party started all over again. Our host enjoyed a good drinking binge as much as the next drunk, supposedly escaping his own demons and insecurities. A good friend indeed! By late that night, I was well into the land of oblivion, barely remembering my depression, and hanging on to my new vision of beauty from the night before. Your smile and your deep blue eyes were not going to fade away. My wife showed up to break up the prolonged party, but I am not sure how she got there. I remember staggering to my new jalopy that I had parked on the road and then nothing afterward as I blacked out until the next morning, curled up in a ball at arm's length to my wife.

It wasn't just her anger alone from my resurrected hobby of binge drinking that sliced and disconnected us. The bankruptcy proceedings had devastated us emotionally. I had no job, and the little money that I received from unemployment insurance barely covered food and booze. We were behind in the rent, and we blamed each other for the predicament we found ourselves in. To further add to the burden, the country was in a recession, and another job was not about to walk up to me and slap me in the face. It probably would have helped if I went out and looked somewhere else besides the bottom of a beer bottle. Winter was coming quickly and would only add to our distress.

And now I had another pain throbbing inside me, one that I wasn't sure what to do about. I couldn't stop thinking about you. I finally decided to play detective and try to find you. I found out from Ben that your parents had a cottage along the lake, a couple of miles away from Ben's place and close to my favorite campground. Our meeting was only chance, as you had limited connections to the people of Westlake and really only knew one of my friend's sister whom you had tagged along with that night. The odds of me seeing you again were as great as getting my money back from my in-laws. But obsession can become resolution. I needed to find you. To me there was much more than flirting going on between us that night.

As I lay beside my wife with resentment wedged between us as solid as a brick wall, on sleepless night after sleepless night, all my metaphysical energies were concentrated on you. With such a vivid centerpiece to focus on, the mountain of all my other problems seemed to hit the sidelines. My heavy drinking had graduated to seven days a week; conversation between my wife and I had dried up and usually ended up in shouting matches when we tried. I spent less and less time with my daughter. I felt alone again. Two straight weeks of this destruction only increased my obsession with you. I now had to find you, no matter what the consequences.

I cornered my friend's sister, Lory, finding enough coherencies dispersed among my drunken words, long enough to link together a conversation with her to make her understand how important it was for me to see you. Whether she did it out of pity for me or weighed the fact that she never liked my wife, she agreed to contact you and deliver my wishes to see you. She went even further and convinced you to take a break from your university studies and come down to your cottage for a secret rendezvous with me. She told you that I was married, but that it was a rocky one. I insisted that she tell you that, not wanting to deceive you. It was against my intentions. Your curiosity had gotten the better of you, and you agreed to meet me. This was not an easy chore for you, as your parents had closed the cottage for the winter. I never asked you what reasoning you used to convince them to let you reopen it, but it was settled, and I would get to see you.

I spent the whole week before your arrival with the flutters of a thousand butterflies and possibly a few moths bouncing off the lining of my stomach, a bundle of nerves and magnified anxiety. Lory was to call me when you were at your cottage, under the guise of inviting me to a party if my wife answered the phone. When the call finally came, I was home alone, and all of Lory's discretions were saved for later. Awhile later, in a whirlwind of thoughts and anticipations, my Camaro clunker pulled into your driveway just after dark. After sitting in your driveway for at least five minutes, gathering up enough nerve to knock on your door, Lory tapped on my window, practically startling me out of my shoes. I had not noticed her coming out of the side door of your cottage. She smile reassuringly and told me to go in and that she had to leave. I watched her disappear down the road with not even the sense to offer her a ride. I grabbed my cooler of liquid courage, which I knew I wouldn't be able to go without, and mumbled several times to myself the question of what I was doing.

I barely focused on my surroundings, the whole world blanketed in a haze. But when I took a deep breath, my vision opened briefly to the wonderment around me. The well-kept cottage, the picturesque landscaping, the grassy hill that sloped to the generous sandy beach to the calm waters below all went unnoticed until the following day. What I did notice was the full orange moon that was breaking the surface of the water in the far horizon and the reflection on the water glistening like a glossy postcard that it should have been pasted on. I still hold that vision with you in the center of it. My timid knock on your door seemed to disturb the motionless air around me as if the depressive forces inside me disturbed the vibrations. This notion quickly went away when your beauty filled the door frame with an aura that matched the moon. My memory of what you looked like had done no justice. The palms of my hands were soaked, and the whole scenario was surreal, the calm air now disturbed by a heart rate that was fast enough to make it explode.

Memories of my first encounter with my wife were so distant that night that irrelevance was next to amnesia. I stood there completely submerged in the resonance that came from you and vibrated through me. I can still feel the goose bumps from your first words as if they were a song that sends chills, and all you did was invite me in. I nodded slowly in a stunned response, as bashful as a scared child. With my cooler trailing behind me like a suitcase in travel, I entered into the center of your world.

I tried to stop shaking, my nerves tied in knots and in desperate need of a drink. You told me to relax and suggested that we sit in the sunroom overlooking the lake. You had made me feel so comfortable so fast. I sunk into the sofa with you beside me and melted like a snowball in hot sun. Your outgoing ways had me opening up to you and shedding my inner thoughts to you before I was even inebriated enough to even consider doing so. I was spilling out sentences like oxygen to a fire. It was like you reached into my core and pulled out my soul to caress it while whispering to stop worrying. The sunroom had been transferred into a moon room, and the soft light wrapped around us and sent me into a trance. The tranquil effects of your sweet vocal tones sent me into such a relaxed state that for a while, I felt no inner pain. It felt so natural. I was swooning in the moonlight and in your presence.

Ten beers later and several hours later, I was telling you things I never dreamed of sharing with anyone. I was sharing feelings I had difficulty sharing with myself. This was coming from the depths of my soul, and you listened as if you were a part of me. I thought that originally I had that feeling with my wife, but it had all been surface levels. It did not diminish the way I had felt about her; it just left the depths of my inner growth in a state of vacancy.

In that moon room that night, I felt the proof that two souls can intertwine on metaphysical levels and in the physical world at the same time. Does this sound like hopeless-romantic gibberish? You know it wasn't. You were there, and you told me you felt it too. The immediate connection we felt that night would put doubts on the critics who find fault in the belief of reincarnation. We both felt that we had known each other before, and it was far more than a sappy love story. Your love for me may have been more gradual, but it doesn't remove the fact that we were attracted by a magnetic pull even though we were from opposite sides of the meadow. You came from a very rich family, your future outlined for you somewhat in silver with a university degree and a chance at a career. You were also one of the most intelligent persons I have ever met. You were content and happy. I had no education to speak of, self-taught knowledge at best. I came from very modest means, naive about many aspects of the real world and in the middle of a downward spiral into the pits of depression. Our connection had to have come from a higher source. Later our successful experiments with telepathy did not even alarm us, but further locked in our feeling of destiny. There was a bond there so rare that even the most ancient of philosophers might struggle for words to explain. It was with this electrifying fervor that in the floating cushions of your couch I held your hand and, just before dawn, fell comfortably asleep with an anomalous sense of calm and without nightmares.

Late the next morning, we woke almost simultaneously and hungry. I suggested we go somewhere out of town for breakfast, but you found frozen waffles in the freezer instead. We took a chance on an expired bottle of maple syrup and washed it down with the bottle of wine that floated solitarily among the beer bottles in my cooler. We went for a long walk on the beach that afternoon, and the breezes were surprisingly warm for that time of year. I held your hand and basked in the tranquility of the lake sounds and the clear skies. But even with the profound sense of peace that enveloped around me, my morals had me glancing at the houses on the hill, wondering if anyone would recognize me. Not a mile to the east was a boardwalk and a campground that I was quite familiar with. My wife entered my thoughts for a moment, but the intensity of my feelings for you faded them. Back in the sanctity of your cottage, they vanished entirely.

The afternoon swept along with a clock that ran too fast. Our words flowed to each other like tributaries running through sands in harmonized strands to the delta. The magnetic pull of our souls yearning for ways to express the attraction led to our first kiss, a kiss so long and tender and pleasant that now every romantic scene on a movie screen reminds me of you. You took my hand and led me to the shower where we disrobed each other. It felt so natural to be with you that I was not nervous or inhibited. We made love that night after you sent me into a frenzy with my first taste of how erotic you could be. You were only the second woman I had really slept with, but there was something so mystical, so esoteric that until the day of my cremation I will never be able to compare. To intertwine the physical body with the augmented pull of the soul can only be described as the highest point of ecstasy. I know by your own words the entire room had filled with electricity; that we were feeding from a higher source than what this planet had to offer. I was more than in love with you. The extraordinary way that we expressed our feelings physically had me enslaved to you. But it was your ambition, your desires and dreams, your total positive outlook toward life that attracted me the most. I was not entirely sure how I made you feel, though.

You knew how depressed I was, and it didn't matter to you. Your own energies had a way of draining it from me. I was far from believing nor was I even aware of the philosophy that you had to be happy within yourself before you could make others happy. And even if I attempted to wrap that around my minuscule idea of hope, my depression would have repelled it to the far corners of the darker parts of my brain for later reflection. I had no other descriptive methods for my thinking processes if they were not first soaked in sadness. It was the same dark lining I had as a teenager that throbbed as a constant thought of suicide. You told me later, as you became more aware of how far I had fallen into the doldrums of debasement, that alcohol was a slow method of suicide. That one registered for a moment, and then I filed that one away in another darker corner where no later reflection could take place.

We spent the Sunday together that weekend too. The conversation flowed between us in unimaginable proportions. Thoughts of how heavenly you were flashed before me several times, and your brightness had cut through some of my darkness. You had quickly become my purpose in life in my distorted view of the whole. I fought the battle with the flight of time and was unable to stop it. The darkness of another night sky won the battle over my own darkness. I held you tight not wanting to face the reality that I had to let you go. I hugged you hoping to show as well as state the deep profession of my love.

I helped you close up the cottage, checking that everything was in place. I made you promise to see me again as soon as possible. You had commitments to your family, but you were sure that you could talk your father into continuing to come to the cottage, telling him you do your best studying there. It was left that I would see you in two weeks. I walked to your Mazda sports car, which flowed in streamlined fashion and which seemed to match your spirit. I had not even noticed it there when I parked behind it two days before. Somehow, I finally let go of you, savoring one last kiss that was to last me two weeks, and pulled out of your driveway. I could barely focus on the road as an unexpected rush of tears flowed from a cornucopia of mixed emotions. Out in front of that mix were the sudden realization and an adrenaline rush of hidden regret that I had just broken my wedding vows. The euphoria of the weekend was instantaneously replaced with a flood of guilt.

That feeling subsided significantly when I arrived home, to have my wife take long strips of hide off me. I fell asleep on the couch that night, still hearing her screams and demands about where I had been. She got no answers except that I had been partying and I wasn't sure where.

Three more weekends with you, well into the season of barren trees and another meaningless Christmas, I finally admitted to her that I was having an affair. You had begun the small subtle hints that you didn't want to be the other woman, and it scared me into thinking that I would lose you. My constant arguments at home tipped the scales to my continued dishonesty, and I finally blurted out the truth. I hadn't been ready to throw my marriage away, but I also couldn't throw out this new touch of paradise I had found with you. The reality of it was I woke up a few weeks later, under dark gray wintry skies, in my rodent-infested farmhouse, void of furniture, lonelier than I could ever have imagined. She had packed up that weekend and left with my daughter when she gave up waiting for me to say that I wouldn't see you anymore. I took her physical punches as well as her stabs to the heart as she hurled her anger, already dipped in hatred, with piercing results. I had watched in pure agony as she and my daughter climbed into the back of her father's van, knowing that she would probably never return.

"*What have I done?*," screeched loudly inside me over and over again as I watched my original savior walk out the door. My love for you was the only thing that kept me from going completely insane. It was the only logic I could hold on to that could explain how I had just ripped apart the only stability I had ever known. Rock bottom would be avoided when I had you to hold me up. But it was not until that fateful gray wintry day when my family disappeared that I fully understood that what I had signed on with you was a long-distance relationship.

A few weeks later, suffering from immeasurable winter blues, the lack of sunshine adding increased weight on my shoulders, I found myself relying heavily on marijuana, a habit I had given up for a while as a sign of a family man and responsibilities. It didn't matter now and when I found the remains of a stale bag of weed in the pocket of an old winter coat from who knows when; I was going to relieve some pain in proper style. I hadn't been able to see you in almost a month as you were in the middle of exams and essays and whatever other reason you were coming up with. So weed was on the menu that day, and I would fight any paranoid effects somehow, Eventually, as I sat in my empty house with the wind whistling tunes through the cracks of the window sills, my stone carried me to the idea to tackle the Westlake bar.

With the *Magical Mystery Tour* playing in the tape deck, never sounding so good before, I pulled up my rust bucket in front of a parking space in front of the bar, a million or so thoughts bouncing around in my head in total disarray. I found a table in the far corner of the saloon and began to pour back draft beer, pint after pint, in an effort to counter-effect the effects of the marijuana. Most of the afternoon, I spent in solitude, except for an older waitress with disdain for me written all over her face. The only other customers were a few regular retired farmers and fishermen on the opposite side of the room. The afternoon did pass even with the time and space distortion caused by the weed, with many shuffles of thoughts and trips to the bathroom. By early evening, I had lost track of the amount of my consumption, nor did it matter except I should have been keeping track of how much of my most recent unemployment check was going into the urinal.

The place began to fill with the night crowd, which were mostly locals that I knew one way or another. Business was abundant when you were the only drinking establishment of a small town, and that was the favorite pastime. I would nod in acknowledgment to acquaintances, but was careful to show disinterest in their company. I was far from feeling social, yet still wanted to soak in a crowd from a distance. Small-town gossip, whether fact or fiction, travels at very high velocity. I felt the stares of some as if they knew that my wife had dumped me. To confirm that they did, instead of me trying to read their minds, my wife walked in attached by an arm to her newfound mate. She had worked fast. I could tell they were higher than a Benjamin Franklin experiment, and she purposely ignored me. They sat on the opposite side of the room at a table with a bunch of mutual acquaintances that I would normally have sat with. Only then, she would have been at my side instead of that straggly redheaded goon, drug dealing, loud-mouthed piece of garbage.

I ordered a pitcher of beer instead of another pint and guzzled it like water, trying to muffle the taunting laughs coming from their table that always seemed to accompany a group of contemptuous glares at me. It was intimidating enough that I left, staggering and cowering toward the door, unable to hold on to any cohesive or coherent thought. I wanted to flatten him and everyone else at that table. But I wasn't about to win any boxing matches in my condition. I made it to my car, still tormented at what I thought was direct mockery toward me. I looked at my windshield and, to my dismay, found both windshield wipers bent into the shapes of pretzels. There was no mystery on who did that.

I have driven drunk many times and had found a knack to keep the wheels between the lines. But it had been awhile that I had tried it with as much intake in such a short period. I had not eaten all day and also lacked direction of solid rumination. I wasn't ready to go back to my cold, empty house, and so I drove around town waiting for some miracle to happen, which should have been a sufficient-enough one when I hadn't hit any parked cars. And then like a flash, all my thoughts lined up toward you. I missed you so much. I began to think how badly I needed to see you. In a drunken stupor, I came up with the bright idea that I would drive to your cottage, and maybe, just maybe, you somehow would be there. I also thought of driving to your university but hadn't a clue how to get there, and it would have been a bit rough crossing the border drunk. A few minutes later, I found myself parked in your cottage driveway with no valid purpose. I had recently been plagued with crying sprees, the tear ducts opening without warning. In your driveway, I was hit again. It took a long time to stop, and my eyes were still blurry, and with the combined beer goggles that I wore as well, I should not have been driving at all. But I now had gathered enough common sense that I should go home. I didn't make it for not five minutes later, I pulled over when the flashing red lights appeared in my rearview mirror. You know the details of the rest.

My luck had finally run out, and a polite policeman told me that I was about to receive my first impaired-driving charge. He gave me a free ride to the police station and put me through all the procedures. He knew me, as any small-town cop knows the civilians he was there to protect and serve. It was this protection that remained his excuse for not letting me go. I do think he was sincere when he told me that he really didn't want to charge me but had no choice. He knew my background. He had once questioned me as a teenager when I was found loitering in front of the pool hall at four in the morning waiting for the doors to open. He had driven me home that night. And now he drove me home again. He kept my keys and told me to get them the next day. I often wonder how different the night would have ended if I hadn't been chasing your ghost. I am thankful that the penalties for drunk driving were not as severe then, with drinking and driving not as much of a social evil as it is today. But when I finally did go to court and lost my driving privileges, the results were a whirlwind of events and experiences that not only can I not remember properly, but also should not have taken place at all. You only know of a few, but when I work through the blur, I mostly think about the pure angelic way that you had put up with me.

I hibernated the week after my arrest, refusing to allow myself to leave the house. There were enough remnants in the cupboard representing food to sustain me. I was used to eating crumbs and used to being hungry. I also had twenty-three different recipes for the case of Kraft Dinner I had in the closet. I had the phone disconnected, pinching as many pennies as I could to survive. I regretted doing that later as it put you even farther away from me.

At the beginning of the following week, I walked to Westlake to call your dormitory from a phone booth, and after several attempts, the number you had given me finally went through. Your voice was sweet and lifted my spirits enough to even out my shoulders that were in danger of a permanent slouch. They rose even higher when you told me you could meet me at the cottage that weekend even though it was unplanned, but it would have to be the last time until spring. I only cared about right now, and just knowing I was going to see you again left me with enough anticipation to carry me through another week of solitude. When I was through talking to you and telling you that I was officially split up and feeling a sense of relief at your end of the phone, I walked over to the police station, thinking it was about time I retrieved my car. The cop finally showed up an hour later, back from a routine patrol, while I stood there shivering in the winter wind. He handed me the keys with a friendly warning attached. My car was still parked where I had been forced to leave it, and he did not volunteer to give me a ride this time. Just as well because a short lecture was sufficient for me.

The day I was to meet you at the cottage, I watched the sky turn black from inside my car, already parked in your driveway. I still had two hours to go before you were supposed to arrive. Four hours later, my patience was thin, and I began to worry that you weren't going to show. I fidgeted in the car, turning the heater on at intervals, as the cold temperatures took no time turning it into a freezer. I was so relieved when your headlights finally appeared behind me. I grabbed and hugged you until you said your ribs were cracking, not once questioning why you were so late. Like two fanatical lovebirds, we were soon in front of the fireplace that you had me light and were snuggled among shag carpeting and thick woolen blankets. The passion between us flowed like an electric current and sparked just the same. You had no reason to fake it. I had every reason to show it. We fell asleep in the predawn hours to the crackling of apple wood, wrapped around each other. We woke up to daylight in the same position. I could not let go of you. The weight of the world rolled off me that night, still far from understanding that it was only a temporary means of escape. We made love several times that day. When I said I couldn't get enough of you, with extraordinary eloquence, you explained that I was probably *anxiety screwing*. The term stuck with me but didn't lessen my desire. You left me in the shower later that afternoon and drove up town. Armed with the ingredients for a terrific salad and the makings of a feast of pasta, I later ate ravenously as if I was in danger of wilting away. I probably was. How I loved you. It was immeasurable. I was content.

But then my mood changed to disappointment as you softly announced that you had to leave early, because not only did you have more exams, you also were to meet your parents. I opened up the magnum of wine I had purposely not drank yet and tried not to appear that I was sulking. It didn't work, but you soon snapped me out of it with glorious news. With perfect time delivery, you explained to me that your roommate was moving out of the dorm and that it would be yours alone for a while. I could come and visit you. I was so excited that I had almost forgotten to tell you about my antics of the previous weekend. With the embarrassment of a child caught in a prank, I spilled to you the witless events that led up to my impaired-driving charge. You were disconcerted at first, but then you told me things would work out and gave me directions to the university. We made plans that I would see you every other weekend and you would alternate the work schedule of your part-time job. I wanted to ask why you needed to work, but I thought against it.

So this was how I was transformed from the country hick to the eye-opening world of your own. My childhood dreams flashed in front of me. It was still only the fringes of a fantasy, but for every other weekend, I was now part of a university campus with twenty-five thousand students—a chance to search over all the knowledge of the world and feel like I had found a significant place on the planet. I was part of something, and although I wasn't enrolled, just being there was mind-boggling for me. The two-and-a-half-hour ride to see you, the hassle of crossing the international border, the 40 percent exchange rate on my already-limited cash flow, all worthwhile. For every other weekend, I was metamorphosed into a life that I had given up on entirely, lost adolescent whimsy. The five years difference in our age didn't matter to me. The age of the younger students around me didn't really register either, not only because the difference wasn't that great, but also because I looked much younger than I was. Maybe it was all that pickling.

I was in a natural state of euphoria when I was with you on campus. There was a library on the grounds, practically the size of the entire town of Westlake. The times when you had to work for a few hours, I lived in it, totally lost in such a wealth of information. There were mountains of cheap food in the university cafeteria. I wasn't sure how you got me the annual pass to there, and I didn't ask. I had never eaten so well.

Our long walks on the campus grounds, weaving in and around all the buildings, holding hands until they cramped, was like a fairy tale to me. Long sensuous kisses, bundled in parkas while we sat on park benches overlooking the frozen river that meandered through the grounds. I felt as if I had been transported into the center of a movie scene, my heart pumping with warmth and ready to combust. What you saw in me, I could never really grasp, especially when I saw the thousands of guys around for you to pick from. I kept thinking of the George Bernard Shaw story *Pygmalion*, only with the gender roles reversed. I was being groomed. Once I asked you if you thought there was hope for me after I had wasted so much of my youth. Your answer stuck to me through time, and I used your words as a life jacket whenever I lost my way. You told me that many people pick up their lives later, career changes, poor choices to be mended, people leaving the military. Everyone could start fresh, no matter what their ages were. Never too old to fulfill one's dreams was the perfect saying for me, especially later on when I continued to go through life's struggles.

This amazing inspirational journey with my time with you should have balanced my difficulties back home. It did not. Every other weekend without you became another fantasy trip, only with a much darker side. You were aware of some of my drunken escapades, but I dared not share all of them. My weekends without you were filled with despair, with an unbearable feeling of loneliness; and on those weekends, I would end up spiraling into paths of self-destruction. How I was able to hold on to you for so long, how you were able to put up with me for so long, was beyond my understanding. When our situation became shaky at the end, I did finally ask you what you saw in me. You said that I had shown you what love truly was. You got no argument from me. You went on to say that before you had met me, the odd roll in the hay with a jocular jock was sufficient-enough relationship for you. That was comforting for me in an odd sort of way. There is so much gratitude in me for what you did for me over those three years we had together that to this day, I would still melt at the very sight of you. And yes, that was genuine and deep love I had shown you.

All the memories are as clear as if they had happened yesterday. Our mini-vacations throughout your state, our fornicating festivals at your cottage showered with emotion and bliss, our trip to Florida, every day and night of my reflections where it was just the two of us in the entire universe. But all this was not enough to reverse the dark patterns of my existence that always seemed to find a way to erode my sense of paradise with you. It finally forced you to give up on me, to doubt your belief in me and move on.

But the first weekend that I came back from your dormitory, the enchantment and excitement of the weekend filled me with your sense of goals and aspirations and sent my own inspirations soaring high. You had fueled my ambitions so well that I actually looked and then found a job at a wholesale distribution place. It didn't pay much, but it was a start, and at least I was working instead of drinking. I went bargain shopping and refurnished some of the house, even bought mousetraps realizing my small furry friends were not an answer to my loneliness. I had a budget planned, and I would regroup my efforts and begin saving again. I stayed away from bars and even bought groceries for the house. I knew it would be a long trip back to get to where I had once been.

My efforts lasted all of three weeks when the bottom fell out of everything and, on my way down, grabbed the safety line of alcohol to ferment my thoughts and numb them, to freeze them. The endless bombardment of thoughts was causing damage as they bounced off the sides of my skull like loose pebbles. I had to find a way to slow them down. I don't think it was the delivery of my divorce papers. I don't think it was the reminder of an impending court date with a judge that wanted my license. Nor was it the cold winter weather that usually automatically lowered my spirits. It was the sudden realization of my solitude, eleven to twelve days out of every fourteen without you. I had no doubt that I had been one of the most introverted teenagers in history when not influenced by some foreign substance playing tricks with my mind. Eventually, the dead force of my own loneliness again reminded me of my own ineptness. The dark and dreary rooms of my farmhouse, the loud rumbles of emptiness between the barren walls (an illusion created by the heartbeat of my own ears), the echoes of complete silence that now replaced the pleasant noises of my family. Not until later did I realize that it was my self-esteem that was the root of my dismal existence. I had not grasped the fact that it had such deep roots, that it strangled my ambitions, and that it fed my depression. I had sincerely come back from you pumped full of energy and drive. But I had only sponged it off you, and without your presence, its effects wore off quickly. Any attachments to my own core were thin threads that dissolved when I wasn't with you.

I really started slipping around Easter when I realized I would be spending it alone. It had little meaning to me, but it was a family holiday nonetheless. My daughter's newfound daddy absolutely refused to let me see her until I coughed up child support. We hadn't even been to court yet. He had no right, but that privilege had been handed to him by my wife looking for all sources of revenge, and he ran with it. His influence over her was astounding. Drowning in a cistern of self-pity, I left no room for empathy to understand that it was her life too that had been shattered and how it had affected her.

You were going to your parents for Easter, and neither one of us were ready for introductions, especially me with intimidation running at its peak when I had found out how rich they really were. You took me to your house one Sunday when they were out of town for the weekend. I walked into nothing short of a mansion. There was a backyard bigger than some of the farms around Westlake. Your dad had his own library, his own study room, his own office. I knew that house was too big when I got lost in it. I had friends I could have spent Easter with, caring friends. But I wasn't ready to be a burden on someone else.

It was back to the bar scene for that week and almost every day afterward. My budget plans were on hold. I went away from my own town to escape any further ridicule. That was my wife's bar now. Ten more miles out of my way with a whole new set of people to watch. There was no lesson learned yet about drinking and driving, and the risk factor never entered my mind, no lessons on self-control.

On the third night out, I had my first one-night stand. I had brought her back to my house and dropped her off later during a long and high-speed route to work. I did not know who she was, and I was still foggy enough that morning not to remember where I dropped her off. The whole thing was so meaningless that all I got out of it later was a chunk of guilt. I had been in so much emotional pain that the sex would have had more meaning in the privacy of my shower, alone. I was too drunk at the time to even think about it, but I had just betrayed you.

The nights that I didn't go to the bar were only an attempt to dry out. Alcohol had taken over me again and only added to my downcast outlook and brushed on extra layers of depression. But it also left me with that comfortable numbness that slowed down the thinking processes. I talked to you once in a while, shivering inside a phone booth. We had agreed that I wouldn't see you for a while as you needed to concentrate on your exams. This only added to my burden, for I needed a steady dose of optimism from you in order to truly cope. But I understood. You had sounded distant on the phone, but you whispered the three magic words in the receiver, and I was temporarily eased.

So a pattern began. I had two different lifestyles going on. My time with you, and then my detrimental side life without you. Each weekend that I was with you became more difficult to leave. You were a lifeline to keep me afloat, to balance the destructive ways I now lived when not with you.

I had become completely dependent on you to keep my mind from imploding. Each visit, I would feel a trickle of optimism; and then back home, it would be completely obliterated by the vacuum inside me.

One night after another weekend without you, I sat in the Vista Inn. I had finally gotten over the fact that I couldn't enter that bar because that was where I courted my wife. I had fallen into the bad habit of now going to that bar right after work instead of home first. It made sense to me since my work was in this very town. Lexington was past Westlake, so to drive by the very bar I was returning to made little sense. For that matter, neither did a lot of things I did that summer. I was out of control. I had picked up another stray the week before, a barrage of one-night stands turning into nightmarish proportions. The dangers of promiscuity wouldn't even register, let alone my unfaithfulness to you.

That night in the Vista Inn, I sat at a far corner table wanting only to be alone. Everything was already in a fog as I tried to focus on my thoughts and my future. My vision was so blurred from alcohol that at first I didn't see the woman sitting across the table from me. I recognized her as the woman I worked with, or at least who worked at the same place. I can't remember any of the conversation I had with her that night, but I remember driving back to my farm cave and having sex with her. And in some ungodly way, her softness and her tenderness had made it meaningful, and I had let my emotions run with it. This was how I met Veronica, and this was how I began my dual existence, with guilt just low enough below the surface that I was able to convince myself that it wasn't wrong, my own selfish purposes finding reasons. I mentioned her to you, but assured you that we were only friends. So on top of everything else, now I had to lie to you.

My survival instincts were wrapped around sex and companionship. I needed a way to fill the gap between our visits. With loneliness and depression kept at bay, suppressed by two women and a constant state of inebriation, I floated though time. Subsisting from day to day, burying my past with it, and snuffing out future consequences by simply not thinking about them. To keep you separate was an act of controlled schizophrenia. The kid that had once thrived on being honest was now a juggler of falsehoods and fabricated stories to fit his needs. So intertwined was my fact and fiction that they were sometimes hard to distinguish in my own mind. I either loved both of you or I loved the lack of void.

Time passes rapidly when traveling with no brakes, full speed ahead on a foggy road and devoid of planning. I watched two years vanish into misty memory and not a thing to show for it. My visits with you became more infrequent as you carefully planned your own future. Each visit was still glorious uplifting, though. You still were my true world, and I believe that if I had come from a different walk of life, was able to see you daily, and had found a meaningful way to apply myself to the goals it took to crawl out of the dark recesses of subversion, we would still be together today.

I cherish every shining memory that protrudes out of the fog of those chaotic years. I hold on tightly to every moment of our trip to Florida on spring break. I had already lost my job, but I managed to scrape enough money from an income tax refund. We shared the magic of Disney World together, walked along the white sands of the Atlantic Ocean, made passionate love in warm tropical breezes without any distractions of our life back home. We were one. We lived as a couple for ten days with the overtones of fairy-tale existence. I hold on to the bond we had close to my heart and soul as a padlocked memory about how things should have turned out between us by never losing focus on our time together in that Sunshine State. My tears now flow involuntarily whenever I see a happy couple together, their love displayed to the world. I cry at romantic scenes portrayed in movies as I see us instead of the characters. You were so right when you said I showed you what love is. I loved you from the core. That feeling of love, the powerful prevalence of emotion, ruled my deeper thoughts to the point of impediment. I considered you bliss. Our summer weekends at the cottage can never be forgotten either as you pulled me from all my problems, whether it be for only moments at a time. You were my sanity.

I was jobless again though, and I could not go without work forever. So with the job prospects very low in the area, I had to make a decision when I had a chance to go out west where all the jobs were and look for work. You urged me on saying I had to do what was best for me. I was only going for a few weeks, and it was disguised as a vacation as well. When I looked for your advice, when I told you that it was Veronica that asked me to go, you only said that you would have to trust me. That hurt as I always hid the true nature of my friendship with her.

We discussed the trip in great detail. I did not want to leave the paradise of your cottage and my time with you. The summer would be almost over when I got back to you. When we were done weighing the pros and cons, you sent me on my way. I returned later without a job and more messed up than I had been before I left.

Ironically, in spite of my fast path to destructive ways, there were always a few strokes of luck to stop me from turning into road-kill. Before I had left on my western journey, I had put an application into a factory in the same town that I had gone to high school, the same town where my first apartment was. I had almost forgotten. The week after I returned, I checked my mail and found a request for an interview. I got the job and almost fell over when they told me the starting wage. I hated that town, but if I was to jeopardize a high-paying job for the sake of a few bad memories in the middle of a recession, I was more of a fool than most people already thought I was. I had now officially lost my license after many delayed court dates, and with fall and cold weather coming, I had to ensure that I could make it to work on time every day. Hitchhiking in the middle of winter was not going to cut it. So I ended up moving to a dinky apartment in the town I despised, but I now had a telephone again.

My work consisted of weekend work as well, and that meant even less time with you. You graciously came to see me on some weekends and waited for me in the apartment during the day. We made the best of it. Winter came fast that year, and I dreaded every day that brought Christmas closer. I wanted to erase that holiday from the calendar. It was complete surprise when you invited me to your parents' house for Christmas. I had so many reservations that I was a rack of nerves the days preceding the holidays. I still suffered from low self-esteem. To meet your rich parents and have them judge my modest means, be screened for character flaws and have them give me all the indications that I wasn't good enough for you, was not my idea of a good time.

I did go, however, and I survived. But my hatred for Christmas, the no-alcohol clause that I signed at your parents' door, and the strained conversation from all their questions, pokes, and prods left me confined and claustrophobic even in the presence of your majestic home. Watching a philharmonic orchestra Christmas special on a television so big that I had to strain my neck to see, sunk between cushions on an uncomfortable couch, after forcing down a dinner of unusual food items that were far from my normal diet under the scrutinizing eye of your parents was excruciating at best.

It was sheer joy, like you had just caused huge boulders to roll off my shoulders, when you saved me from the rest of the evening by announcing that we were leaving early for the trip back to your place because you were tired. In the quiet comfort of your bedroom later, I knew then that I would never be good enough for you, never live up to expectations. I wasn't in the same league as you, and I didn't know if I could ever even attempt to qualify to give you everything you needed. But that did not stop me from clinging on to some hope that we could find a future together. My early wasted efforts of a failed marriage weighed heavily on my thinking and had eroded any confidence in myself. But I had a good job now, and not all was lost. I held on to my faith that we were meant to be and there was a way for us to live happily ever after.

But still unknown to you was the time I had spent with Veronica with the excuse I had to fill the void when I wasn't with you. I had erased the initial bouts of guilt and was actually convinced that I really wasn't being unfaithful to you. I was instead finding a way from drowning in my own depression by utilizing and sharing my emotional levels with another to stay on level ground. I would be no good to you as a vegetable, my despair making a sieve of my aspirations when I wasn't with you. I had twisted it around so badly that I actually thought I was doing it for you.

When the next summer rolled around, as I filled my head with anticipation of another set of glorious weekends with you at your cottage, you hit me with a brick. Because of your studies in the arts, your parents thought it would be a golden opportunity for you to go to Paris for the summer as an exchange student. I did my best to understand that you had to do what was best for you, to continue your studies, to obtain your degree. It hurt just the same. The time for your departure came quickly, but we had arranged a final weekend at the cottage, a sort of farewell rendezvous. You were leaving for eight weeks, an eternity in my version of time.

So when you cancelled our visit at the last minute, explaining that your parents found you an earlier flight and declaring you had too many preparations and just couldn't make it, I was devastated. I tried to hide my disappointment from you. I didn't want to dampen your excitement. But I am sure you heard it in my voice. My good-bye kiss to you was on the mouthpiece of the phone, and after I heard the click at your end, I broke into a blubbering idiot, my tears forming puddles at my feet, dropping incessantly as if you had just deceased. Going the whole summer without you had suddenly become too much to handle, and I broke down, like a dam that just exploded.

I had not told you, nor could I even have thought of a way to, but I had found a stupid way to lose my license again soon after I had just gotten it back. So I was stuck in this horror town of my high school years, now of my workplace, and visions of a meaningless summer thumping in my head.

My whole balancing act was put on hold, and I began to rely on friends again to get me through. That whole summer was spent mostly in blurred vision and thought, caught in a whirlwind of long benders and monstrous hangovers. I blocked out the hole you left by filling it with alcohol. All was not lost, though. I had enough sense not to jeopardize my job over it. Even allowing for the constant flow of alcohol, I was able to watch my bank account finally grow a little. I found a big home to rent, although the landlord was hesitant at first renting it to a single guy. I gave him the plant manager's name at work for references. He knew him, and he agreed to let me rent it. I was so glad to rid myself of that claustrophobic box someone had labeled as an apartment. I worked hard, one of the attributes acquired from a good moral upbringing and working on a farm as child labor.

I furnished my new abode sparingly but eloquently, and my organizational skills were reflected in my housekeeping. Well, kept, but not the most satisfactory job in dusting, window cleaning, and definitely not a sparkling toilet bowl. But my inability to tolerate clutter left me with a decent-looking bachelor pad. I had a yard again, and many hours were spent around the new picnic table out back. Minus the tent, my backyard was my campground for the summer.

I will spare you the details of that summer since it would only be detrimental to the good memories we do share. But please know that my main purpose was to help the clock turn faster to the direction of autumn and your eventual return. I received a letter from you late in the summer that told me the exact date that you would be back, and I read it over a dozen times, trying to read between the lines of your limited details of your French summer. Although the actual words were not there, I had a sickening feeling that you were not exactly alone over there. You were a beautiful woman, and there would be many French male prowlers who would recognize the same. I spent the last of the summer obsessed with those thoughts, almost raging in jealousy from the fabrication of events that I imagined, a great performance for such a conscientious mind that thought nothing of lying with other women in your absence. I couldn't and wouldn't take the time to recognize my own hypocrisy.

And finally the phone call I waited all summer for. You were back, and you were coming to see me. I gave you directions to my new dwelling, and a couple of hours later, you pulled into my driveway. My French amie, looking as beautiful as you ever had. I held you in my arms forever, my bare feet oblivious to the crushed stone beneath them. All my feelings were with you. I felt the angelic forces that you electrified me with during the very first time at your cottage. There was no conversation as we moved from the driveway to under the bedroom sheets. It was so magical, so sublime that the whole weekend with you was like a dream. The whole summer had become lost and absurd, even more so than it had already been. I cannot describe to anyone how I felt about you that weekend. My heart starts beating faster when I think about that weekend and the strength that you gave me. There was something about that weekend that was so special to me that I sometimes use the memory of it as an antidote to my depression. But it is also marred as I remember how that year ended and how we reached our final good-byes.

You were quick to go back to your job and your studies, leaving you little time to see me. I finally had to admit to you that I lost my license again, but I still found a way to see you, my troubles at the border each time all worth the while. They would center me out, attracted to my carrying tote hanging from my shoulder, the word *suspicious* written on my forehead.

The way you were able to temporarily wash away the demons inside me was worth every hassle. First I would catch a Greyhound bus to the city. A city bus would run across the border underneath the tunnel and drop me off in front of the American customs building for a round of the third degree. Where was I going, how long I was staying, why was I traveling so light? Each time the same interrogation; each time an identification check. Once, I took a chance on sarcasm and asked if they could put my picture on the wall so they could remember me prior to my next visit. He did not see the humor. Each time, my whole history had to be repeated with the same series of questions. I knew the script by heart. Each time, I was shown the door with an approval stamp to enter the country. I took the long walk to the bus station on the American side, which was conveniently placed in the worst area of the city. Zigzagging my way through backstreets and alleys, weaving in and out of drug dealers, panhandlers and street bums, and—I am sure—the odd homicidal maniac waiting for the right reason to satisfy an urge. I could feel the chills of apprehension running down my spine. There were only a few scary encounters though, and I was able to walk away each time unscathed.

I would arrive at your place late Friday night and have to leave early Sunday morning to catch the only bus back that day. I could not miss work, for it was a lifeline as important for my sanity as was my weekend fixes with you. My time with you was very short, as you now had an eight-hour job on Saturdays. My loneliness was exponential with each visit as the hours with you seemed to shorten at the same velocity. But I clung on to every moment, the love in my heart aching as much as it did when I wasn't with you. The pains of depression were losing the war of balance that had been teetering against the scraps of bliss that I had with you. The foggy memory between visits and my increasing fear of how remote the chances were of me being able to spend the rest of my life with you was becoming a lethal combination against any optimism. I was probably clinically depressed by that point, but to seek help would mean weakness. To whom this weakness mattered to didn't register.

And then one Saturday morning, I pushed myself over the edge, tried to push you over with me, but you pushed back and let me go over on my own. I had another six hours to go to wait for you to finish work, and I was already half drunk. Without thinking, I decided to go through your dressers and personal items. What I was looking for, I had no idea. What I found certainly wasn't it. There among Christmas cards and photographs was letter after letter from a guy from Arizona. My heart plummeted toward the ground, and my stomach felt as if it was being squeezed in a vice. You had met him in France where he had been on the same mission as you and had furthered your education together. As I read more, unable now to put the letters back before it was too late, I discovered that you were educating each other in lessons that had nothing to do with the classroom, lessons of the private kind that I thought were only for me. When I got to the point of his professed feelings for you, I started to hyperventilate and had nothing short of a panic attack as the words on the pages spilled out the details of your affair in Paris. I was swooning and had to sit down for I almost fainted.

After the initial shock, I now had to face the dilemma of how to confront you. I did not want to lose you, but I couldn't live in silence to what I now knew. How was I to tell you that I breached your trust and had gone through your stuff? I couldn't change it now. How was I to find a way to deal with this new pain without talking to you about it?

When you returned from work that day, my cheeks were still red from the tears that burned on my skin like acid. When you asked me what was wrong, I didn't take the time to analyze how I should face you. Instead I blew up in a rage and told you what I had found. I watched your respect for me evaporate right in front of me, and after I had spewed out my anger, there was a long excruciating silence between us. And then you tossed a grenade back at me that blew up our entire relationship in a single second. In a voice too calm for the situation, you told me you knew about Veronica, that you knew that we were much more than friends. I felt my world crumble. I wanted to curl up and die.

Lory had known that Veronica had been more than a friend. In a small community, news traveled fast. It didn't help that she had caught us once in a compromising position in the corner of the Vista Inn. But she promised me that she would not tell you. She knew how much you meant to me, but eventually her obligations to your friendship wouldn't allow her to keep it secret. I never blamed her and shouldn't have expected her to stay neutral. You had known for some time but had never said anything to me. I had convinced myself somehow, getting around disgusting, twisted morals, that Veronica had only been a way to fill the gap, a way for me to survive in between our visits. I had convinced myself that I was doing nothing wrong, that it was you I loved. So instead of begging for forgiveness to wipe our slates clean, I became defensive, and we argued incessantly for hours.

When we would get close to logic and understanding, one of us would grow defensive again in the heat of it all with the slightest word setting us off. It had been the first time we had ever argued, the first time we even thought of being uncivil to each other. I had never dreamed a breach of trust between us. I followed the normal escape route and drank beer after beer. The more I drank, the more unresolved it became, the more heated it became between us. In my stubborn and stupid defense mechanisms that night, I couldn't admit that I was wrong. I will now.

I remember the torment inside me that night. I wanted to reach inside myself and rip open my chest and remove the pain. I watched the magic between us dissolve, with only the residue left for me to hold on to. Like a coward unable to face trouble, unable to swim when the waves got rough, I left your dormitory, defeated. I wandered the campus until daylight finding no miracles to mend things. I caught the morning bus home, unable to face you. My guiding light, your heart, my beacon to success and a path away from destruction, no longer in my reach. My mind was still enveloped in my love for you, but so was my pain and anguish. It clashed inside my head like an endless surf pounding on cliffs eroding my sanity.

Back home after a long and suffering week at work, I couldn't take the internal battle anymore, and my love for you won out. After several futile attempts of not getting an answer, I still camped out by the phone and called hour after hour. You finally answered the phone at three in the morning. Your voice was as sweet as ever, and it turned me into a puddle before I even spoke. But there was also a sorrowed and tired tone to it that scared me. And it was soon apparent that my alarm was justified.

I rambled on and on with a thousand apologies. Nothing was more important than winning you back, resolving our differences to retrieve the magic. I felt my love for you pouring through the telephone lines. I could feel yours too, but it was only through your tears as you struggled to tell me that you had to break up with me. I felt that familiar loosening of the heart as gravity pushed it down at too fast a speed not to endanger it from breaking in half. I went to scream *NO* at the top of my lungs, but something stopped me, and I said nothing instead.

You were the best thing that had ever happened to me, and I didn't want to lose that; but I knew from the core of my soul that we couldn't hurt each other anymore, couldn't pretend that our differences and the distance between us could be overcome. I kept apologizing for hurting you as we talked over each other's sobs. We said no hurtful things. We blamed no one, but we did spend some time talking about what went wrong. The long distance between us, the importance of the drive of your career, the sinfulness that you felt but had never mentioned before about having a part in the breakup of my marriage. We were from opposite sides of the fence, but wasn't love supposed to conquer all? An hour went by, and it felt that we had resolved everything—that we were at peace with each other. That didn't stop me from thinking I was making the biggest mistake of my life. I wasn't going to fight for you.

I started to apologize to you again, but you didn't want to hear anymore. You started to cry again and then said that this was the hardest thing you ever had to do in your life. You said good-bye and wished me good luck. I heard the click and then the dreadful silence at the other end of the phone before the dial tone broke it. My knees had already started to buckle, and I sat down on the floor. My heart and stomach tied each other into knots and churned like a cement mixer. I couldn't stop sobbing, and my first impulse was to call you back. I never did.

Once the sobbing stopped from sheer exhaustion and my whole system was drained leaving an almost serene vacuity, I was overcome by a weird sense of relief. I stared into space as if suddenly hypnotized. No more dishonesty, no more eternal long weeks without you, waiting for the next opportunity to see you. Now I could hold you in my heart forever, and every day would feel the same. My love for you had become agonizing, and in confused reflection, I thought that maybe the pain of loving you had actually added to my depression. I snapped out of my trance and drank myself to sleep. I stuck you safely away in my heart where you could always remain and be brought out for memories of past periods of joy. You were mine after all, and if it was only your spirit I could carry, it would have to suffice.

I always hoped that I could have seen you one more time, and there were a couple of times when I was really drunk and thought of attempting it. But I was not always as selfish as one of my buddies' wife had accused me of once. I knew I had to let you go and let you move on with your life. It still didn't allow my mind to completely let go of you. There was one time, a couple of years later, when I drove to your cottage and parked in the driveway, drunkenly thinking that there was a slim chance that you would be there. There was very slim chance.

You had kept in contact with Lory, and I found out later that you had received your marketing degree and had moved to Minneapolis, Minnesota, where you found work for a huge and well-established company. You married a doctor. No surprise there because you could have had anyone you wanted. I was sincerely happy for you when she told me, but deep inside my heart where I still keep you, there was some wincing. Your parents had sold their cottage and their mansion and moved to Florida. Lory also told me you were very happy, and I had said deservedly so. I can assume, since Lory had shared your life with me, that she also told you that I am still the same lost soul you knew. I am hoping that is some consolation to you for any heartache I may have caused.

I do not know if it would have been different between us if I had met you later in life. I kept regressing after you left me, letting alcohol run my life; and for a while, I was a runaway train looking for a place to derail. But you were a miracle for me and gave me more insight than you will ever know. You permeated me with your wisdom and your depth and gave me some light in my dark, miserable existence. You not only live in my heart, but you also rest in the center of my soul. It is there you will remain forever. As the true meaning of love and as my guardian angel. I hope to find you some day in another lifetime on equal ground.

CHAPTER 7

Veronica:

In a word, *voluptuous*. I can describe you no other way. The whispers of acquaintances and even your own self-degrading comments about your weight failed to register and bypassed any other form of description. *Voluptuous.* The word had reverberation, even alliteration, when used with your name. It rid me of any stigma that was associated with being overweight. There I said it, overweight, but never perceived it. Loneliness can be just as blind as love.

I first saw you in passing at work, and we shared the obligatory hellos, but it was done with a smile slightly above politeness. It was like a hidden recognition between us that I couldn't read, but somehow it said that you would make a good friend. But work was work to me, and so I made no other connection but that of a fellow co-worker. It was not until our meeting a few weeks later at the Vista Inn that I saw our similarities and then saw the true reading of your smile.

I was sitting alone, reminiscing the days in that very bar where I used to court my ex-wife. I was well on my way to intoxication, the fog of beer-saturated pupils causing everything to be out of focus, when you suddenly appeared in front of me like a wave of a wand from a magician. You sat across from me at the table, like some heavenly vision. The music from the live band was pounding so loud that it vibrated the butt-filled ashtray in the center of the table. Conversation would have been screaming into each other's ears at best, so until the band's intermission, I simply stared at you with a stunned look on my face and a smile that probably looked like that of a stroke victim.

When the drumming had finally stopped, only the drone of a light Wednesday-night crowd could be heard. My face must have still been brushed with astonishment, for the first thing you asked me was if I recognized you. In certain ways, I did not. As I attempted to shake away the blurriness, your face shone with luminosity, standing out from the dimmer lights of the bar. There was a bright shimmering aura around your head; whether real or imagined, it didn't matter. It was there. Those huge brown eyes seemed to look through me, and when I looked back into them, I could feel the same sadness coming from you that I felt within myself. Our eyes may have been of different colors, and yours lacked the glaze of mine, but they were still windows to our souls that screamed out loud to each other's loneliness.

I do not remember our conversation of that night. I only remember feelings. I must have been coherent enough and likeable enough to pass as appropriate company because after we closed the bar, you sat in the passenger seat of my car as a quiet navigator, watching me weave a path back to my house and bed. The sensuality between us that night was beyond extraordinary. It was more than the excitement of being with someone new. I had proven this as inane with vague memories of one-night stands that left me with nothing but guilt and vacuity. You were different. Stimulated by your talents and washed in a shared outward cry for notice, you raised me to high points of exhilaration, and we collapsed in unison. Such escapism from the bonds of depression, however remote and temporary, was more gratifying than the smothering of drugs and alcohol. Drugs and alcohol was an addiction, a change of view. Sex was release. I still always considered it a display of love, and that is why I was thrown out of whack with the one-night stands. These sidetracked, meaningless acts did not normally cloak the gloom.

I felt the throes from you, somewhat misplaced with your sexual prowess but meaningful just the same, something more unique. It was this display that became the basis of two needy people and the premise of our relationship to follow. We fell asleep in each other's arms only to bolt awaken two hours later in a mad rush to get to work and beat the click of the punctual punch clock. With not so much of a change of clothes, without breakfast or coffee, and with the throbbing temples of a hangover, I rushed us to work with little time to even think of what had happened between us.

We passed each other a few times that day at work, focused on our duties, the normal cordial hello and a smile of recognition, which was now not quite the same, but still only a minute taint of guilt. The workday stretched forever, and I couldn't help but think of you. Close to the end of the day, my heart rate was faster as my thoughts shoved forward, and I knew I had to talk to you somehow. My thoughts of wanting to be with you again marched to the forefront, and I almost didn't catch a shipping error. I needed to make sure that the night before was not just some drunken fantasy I had experienced. I had blackouts before, but they had never manifested into hallucinations or runaway imagination.

I caught you just as you were walking out the door. All remnants of liquid courage had long dissipated, and my shyness came flooding back with a vengeance. I was gasping for words and for air while I struggled to talk to you. I finally squeezed out enough words that hopefully sounded like I was asking to see you again that night. You must have understood me, and without any signs of hesitation, you gave me directions to your house. I was surprised to learn that you only lived two blocks away. I told you I was going home first to clean up. You nodded and looked through me again with those round brown eyes. I watched you cut across the open field adjacent to our building as a shortcut to your home. I had asked where your car was, and you had told me it was at home; unlike me, you had enough sense to walk to the bar the night before.

And so began my journey of juggling my time between two women and yet somehow lacking the fact that it was wrong. Maybe I was as completely selfish as some made me out to be. It didn't matter because I had already confused what I was doing with issues for ways of survival. And survival usually represents priorities. I had to keep the effects of depression as dormant as possible, and if it meant stretching moral values, meant brief interludes of comfort to evade its jaws, then what I was doing was necessity, not selfishness. There was no time to look at it internally and certainly no time to face the responsibilities and implications of my own actions.

I arrived at your doorstep with fresh clothes and revived by a long stand in the shower and three quick beers. You lived in a huge farmhouse on the outskirts of town, but still within its boundaries. It stood out like a weed, with a subdivision of newer homes built around it, as if it had refused to move out of the way of progress. It was extremely spacious, with two stories and a basement, six bedrooms, and two and a half bathrooms. It was well kept, with the original woodwork still appearing as new, and freshly polished.

You were not alone in this big house. Your sister and her boyfriend lived with you, helping divide the rent and other costs. And to my surprise but not shock, you had a six-year-old son and a five-year-old daughter. They took an instant liking to me, but not for lack of a father figure. You shared liberal custody with your ex-husband, sometimes alternating entire weeks, leaving each other time to care for your own lives without the constant pressure of the children. How I envied that. I would have been ecstatic if I could have had such an arrangement with my ex-wife, to share the responsibility of raising my daughter. There was too much ill will between us for that to ever happen, and I had a nagging doubt of my own capabilities of doing a good job anyway. As self-directed sarcasm, I teased myself when I thought of it. My drug-dealing replacement would do such a better job of rearing her.

Tormenting myself with distressing thoughts to add to the burdens I carried inside me was a sick pastime but an involuntary one. The fleeting idea of getting back with my ex-wife combined with a stronger desire to turn the law on them because of their chosen vocation left me with an array of jumbled feelings. With their absolute refusal to let me see my daughter without child support payments, I retaliated by threatening to actually turn them in if she ever enforced the court ruling. It was partially hypocritical, like I had never used drugs. But wasn't selling them a totally different scenario? So about once a month, I would call them; and we would play our stalemate game, as they refused to budge, and I went without watching my daughter grow up. These thoughts often flashed before me later when I got to know your children very well.

On our second night together, later in the confines of your bedroom, the kids tucked in; and with the social prerequisites with your sister and brother over with, we shared our history and a third bottle of potent wine. Both of us were fluent and anxious to share. You had split up just over a year ago after eleven years of marriage. You were not really sure why. You were seeing, but only platonically, someone I had remembered seeing in the Vista Inn on numerous occasions. I would never have taken him for a heroin addict until you told me. My employer was your brother-in-law, and you had some real perks that he was unaware of. I did not judge at all when you told me that you had frequently borrowed from the cash register from time to time and had a tendency to take free merchandise. What did amaze me was your age. You were thirty-five, but certainly didn't look it. I was twenty-five, but I didn't waste much time thinking about our age difference. And in retrospect, thirty-five is not that old.

Your honesty was almost appalling to me, although I cherished the quality. For what it meant to me was I was expected to reciprocate. There was to be no secrets. So just before we made love that night, I told you about Nancy. It didn't seem to matter to you. Instead we continued with the same passion as the night before and later fell asleep in each other's arms in almost the same position as the night before. We had found a cure for our loneliness, and it soon became habit forming, especially through the week. Our relationship was somewhat unusual and unique in that we had an unspoken agreement that there were no strings attached. In our joint effort to fill each other's void, a silent pact that in spite of our symbiotic attachment, our feelings could turn inside our hearts, but never to be spoken out loud. Late at night, though, proclamations would sometimes slip out.

Work became more enjoyable as I waited in anticipation to spend the night with you instead of being in a dark corner of a bar, wondering what the night would bring. To me this was a sign of responsibility, no matter how bizarre in comparison to its real meaning. Since you lived so close to work and so close to the Vista Inn that we still frequently visited together, I spent many nights at your house. On the weekends without your children and the weekends I was not traveling across the border, we spent it at mine. How you tolerated me suddenly disappearing whenever it was my time scheduled with Nancy, I could not fathom. I could only assume that you would fill in your own gap with your platonic friend. You had introduced him to me one night, and the vibrations I got from him told me that your relationship was a step above platonic. But not only did your unblemished honesty say it wasn't true, I also had no right for jealousy. So to keep our relationship intact and special, you had found some rationale to deal with my commitment to Nancy and yet still be with you. We both knew the unfairness of it all, but it had become an accepted prerequisite to continuing our relationship.

Nancy was my true love, but she was also becoming a completely unattainable goal for any reasonable answers to my life's path. But my dreams with her had to be hung on to. The answer to my immediate needs was with you, but the suppression of the deeper source of my depression lay with her. Can you love two women at the same time? I believe so. This opens the door to all kinds of theories and philosophies about the various degrees and levels of love. We never spoke out loud about our feelings except when the infusion of alcohol interfered, and we would give quick bursts of those three lovely words that everyone usually likes to hear. In my mind, it didn't mean the same thing as whatever brain cells I had still left operating knew that my heart was with Nancy. But somehow we continued on day to day never really sure where we stood with each other. Somewhat happy together in spite of our strange circumstances.

To alleviate the pressure of my juggling act, my drinking had become heavier than it already was. My memory of exact dates or even chronological events and sometimes even in the year that they took place were intertwined in confusion. Scary but true. We spent an enormous amount of time together, but I also have many memories of Nancy in that same period. So as I try to decipher how I really felt about you and explain how I do cherish my memories with you, I will eliminate her name.

Time marched on, as it always does, with summer melding into fall and the fast approach of Christmas. And how I hated Christmas. Most people find a way to the joy of the holidays and are able to even separate the commercialization of it and be happy with the time spent with friends and family. A time of reflection on what is truly important in their lives and a time to show appreciation. I learned to reflect on the negativity instead and the things I didn't have. I am sure I am not alone. I am also sure that sensitivity levels are peaked at this time of year. In the supposed season of festivities, I had become prone to crying spells. Even as shallow as some stupid commercial that might remind me of something or hit an open nerve, I would be left blubbering. It was no surprise to me that you were part of the unfortunate group that had the same negative reflections as I did when it came to Christmas. That year, it did not help that it was your ex-husband's turn with the kids. It did not help that your mother passed away two years ago just before Christmas Eve.

Misery enjoys its company, and we were quite content together spending Christmas Day by ourselves. Your sister and her boyfriend had their own plans with his family, and without the frolic of your kids, we went even further to ensure privacy. It was rare, but you did have surprise visits from extended family. I had narrowed down my circle of friends to almost reclusive levels. I knew those who still remained in contact had their own families to attend to. My house would be safe from any outside interruptions, and so my rodent-infested house was where we spent that Christmas. As old as my house was, winter winds easily found their way through the thin walls and through the gaps of ancient windowpanes. With only an old oil stove and a small fan that squeaked with noises that represented death, discomfort wasn't even close to describing our environment.

You made us a traditional ham-and-turkey dinner, minus the turkey, and heaping plates of mashed potatoes and sweet corn. A better meal than my steady diet of meatless sandwiches, I assure you. With only one burner working on my electric stove, usually left on for additional warmth, I was surprised you were even able to conjure up our meal. My television had been struck by lightning that summer, so that source of entertainment was out. I am still fascinated when I remember the day of that thunderstorm while I lay on the couch half asleep in front of a *Green Acres* rerun. The bolt of lightning entered into the center of the tube, exited, and went back out the window it came from. Even you didn't believe that story, but it didn't lessen the fact that I had no working television. I found out later that Arnold, the pig, was all right and had only a few singed hairs.

I had two warm quilts, one still dripping with the memories of my grandmother, another with memories I would rather not share. Under these, we spent Christmas night on my mattress with full stomachs and very close body heat. My telephone was disconnected long ago, so even that had no chance of disturbing us. Merry Christmas, and to each of us, a good night.

We went back to your house the next day and repeated the process of osmosis, relying on each other to get through the holidays. Only this time, without the shivering and with a working television set. It was that night that I lay awake after making love to you. Instead of falling asleep like I normally did, I began to fill my head with millions of thoughts. My reflections were coming faster than I could comprehend them, but they all had the theme of *love*. Did I even know the meaning of the word? Was it always synonymous with *need*? Attraction aside, had my heart confused companionship with strong emotion? My head overflowed with past experiences and how I had allowed drunken stupor and one-night stands fill me with regret and remorse. More thoughts bounced around until it felt like my head was going to burst. I reached over for you, put my arms around you, and then made love to you again. My thoughts dispersed, and I finally fell asleep dreaming about being rich.

We continued our routine, a weird sense of contentment between us, but to concur that any source of happiness for me was eventually to be condemned, my world came crashing in with another round of bad luck.

We still went to the Vista Inn frequently. It was like it reenergized our feelings for each other. The vibrations of its dark-paneled walls bounced the sounds of the bar and band through our ears. It fed our brains with nourishment that awoke the past memories of our time together, our first encounter; a refresher course of our feelings. It was on a Wednesday night again, where we should have been nesting on a couch in your living room instead, but you didn't have your kids that week. The music was as loud as ever, and we poured back drinks as if the liquid would serve as earplugs. I never did find the nerve to dance with you. I blame most of it on not wanting to blemish the memories of dancing with my ex-wife on that very dance floor of the Vista Inn. I had danced since then, but never in the sanctuary that I had shared with her. That dance floor was a shrine in her honor, and I was not to shatter that.

Instead, I held your hand particularly tight that night as our eyes matched the same reflections, the same memories of our first time together. We had never argued yet, never disagreed, and held the respect of very close friends. As we basked in our silent tranquility, I was drenched in amorous waves of desire. I never gave much thought to raging hormones when my mind would only relate it to need and possibly lust. But if I had taken the time to think about it, I might not have found the trouble that found me that night. When we left after last call, the air was still warm outside. My car was parked across the street, and in a sudden impulse, I grabbed you in the middle of the street and, in a warm embrace, gave you a long and passionate kiss. I was oblivious to everything around me, feeling only the reciprocation of your soft, full lips. The streetlights had disappeared behind closed eyelids. I was floating in our world of sensuality.

Two long blasts of a car horn broke our trance, and they were in very close proximity. I looked over to see a cop car with two officers in it, not three feet from us, blocked by our stance. You waved to them and led me the rest of the way across the street. We climbed into my car, and I watched both officers as they passed by at a snail's pace with unwavering frowns on their faces. As stupid as the brain thinks when inebriated, there are still threads of common sense ready to prevail if not officially stupid to begin with. I knew and told you that I could not drive because they would surely pull me over. You told me not to worry about it because you knew one of the cops. I listened to you, but it was against all my better judgment. I didn't even get around the corner of the block when those familiar red lights appeared in my rearview mirror. A horrible feeling sat in my gut. I trusted you, but common sense should have told me that it wouldn't make any difference whether you knew the cop or not. I was in the center of town with witnesses all around.

The one driving the cop car asked me to get out of the car, and the other one shoved me into the backseat of the cruiser. I could hear you being asked why you would let me drive. You followed behind in my own car and waited for me in the police station lobby even though you were well above the legal limit too. Five minutes later, I emerged with my second impaired-driving charge; and for good measure, they threw in a failing to take a Breathalyzer with it. I had refused to take the test on principle, upset about the unfairness of the charges. Day after day, I had driven over the limit and had only been caught once. And now I was being charged for kissing a woman on the street. It wasn't right.

They put you in charge of me and my vehicle, but not before I shared a few choice words with my captors. You drove us back to your house in a very uncomfortable silence. We lay down for a couple of hours of restless sleep and were at work before remorse even had a chance to settle in. We were late and drove your car to work that day. Any discretion we kept from our co-workers was now history as we walked in together, both disheveled and tardy. I worked in fog and illness that day. By late afternoon, the thought that I would lose my license again was deadweight, and I could barely function. Not once did I blame you. I should have since if I had listened to my gut instead of you, I would not have seen the inside of that police station. But I couldn't get myself to blame you when I had such a great part in it. I also had no intentions of jeopardizing the comfort I could continue to plunder from you.

We buried the event in our minds for a while, and it was a long time before I did have to face the consequences. I went to a lawyer that you knew and was prepared not to go down without a fight. I never questioned your circle of acquaintances, so I had to trust the lawyer. Whether it was our age difference or my lack of own experience, I respected you. Even though we shared confusion, were both lost in our ways, I allowed you to be a source of guidance. That might have been a big part of what eventually steered us off track when I eventually developed a bit of disdain in your lack of guidance and your own wrong decisions.

The lawyer did say he could help. He was young and eager to take any case. But all he really did accomplish was prolong the inevitable by many delays and various motions I never understood. We were even able to take our trip out west before the actual loss of my license took place almost immediately after we returned. I ended up pleading guilty after all the effort. After a few private discussions with the prosecutor, they agreed to drop the impaired-driving charge if I pleaded guilty to failing to blow into the machine. I agreed. But the lawyer conveniently forgot to tell me, whether on purpose or he thought I knew, that the penalty was the same. My license ended up being suspended for six months this time since it was my second charge. It was a blessing that it happened back then. Today the punishment is more severe, and if it had been a jail term, I might as well have kissed what little sanity I had left good-bye. A friend of mine, who years later faced the same charge, spent fourteen days in jail and was never the same. But just as conveniently as the lawyer's omission of all the facts, except for the original retainer I gave him, he was never paid. We were even.

After that incident and with the court case forever impending, I didn't want to drink and drive in your town anymore. You suggested I move in with you. It was very tempting at first, especially when I remembered the periods of happiness and stability I felt when I had been married. But even through my confused and disoriented state of mind, I knew it wouldn't be fair to either one of us. There was this problem that revolved around an American girl that my heart held on to. I did find myself staying overnight more often. Part of my wardrobe was transplanted into the bottom drawer of one of your dressers. Also transplanted to your house, however, were my consistent need to be inebriated and an increasing amount of bundled nerves. I had heard of nervous breakdowns before, but I didn't know how to recognize it nor the ability to admit it if I did. To this day, I am not sure if I actually had one or I was just looking for a direct line for pity. I do have you to thank for holding me together, as you seemed to understand what I was going through when I told you I needed to be alone for a while. The mention of a shrink was completely out of the question, and thankfully you did not bring up that option.

I couldn't concentrate on work anymore. I couldn't concentrate on anything. I went to your brother-in-law in complete honesty, telling him that my nerves were shattered and needed some time off. This took effort for me because I needed the money and couldn't afford time off. But I was afraid I was losing grip on sanity and needed to get away from the world. He gave me a week off, but my honesty to him proved to be a mistake.

I spent five full days cut off from the outside world, locking myself away in my dilapidated farmhouse. I spent the days lying in my uncut grass, staring up at the blue skies, turning cumulus clouds into objects, both animate and inanimate. My acid days were long over, but I still had ways to travel above the clouds. I could duplicate the feeling by deep meditation and could almost feel what astral projection must really be like. When I would jolt back, I could feel the earth move underneath me. I could hear the cornfields around my house grow.

At night I would read until I fell asleep. Not for the first two nights when my mind would race at blinding speed on the screen of my closed eyelids in a kaleidoscopic dance of jumbled visions and a theater of confusing dreams. They finally subsided after the third day. For the first time in memory, I dried out. Five days without alcohol or drugs of any kind seemed like an eternity, but when it was over, I felt almost human again. There were no prayers this time, only constant reflections about what went wrong with my life. After my week of sabbatical, I was ready to start fresh, a brand-new outlook. But in reality, it was only needed rest that I received. No hidden epiphanies. My brain was still scattered inside, but at least now I wasn't ready to implode.

Sobriety was short-lived, and the day I decided to go back and face your brother-in-law to tell him I was ready to go back to work, courage failed me. Several beers later, with a coating of false fortitude, I went to face him. I was barely done talking to him when he looked up at me from his huge oak desk and told me he was sorry, but he would have to let me go because the situation was too dangerous. He did tell me he would write *laid off* on my record of employment so as not to jeopardize my chances of collecting unemployment insurance. I left his office in shock.

I waited for you on the porch of your house that day, waiting for you to return from work, too dumbfounded to look for you there. You did not seem to be upset with the news, and instead of really talking about what I should do next, we got drunk together and then made love as if nothing had ever happened. I left you later for a weekend across the border with my college-student romancer and continued to lose myself in booze and sex. I could feel your disappointment this time, but it did not stop me from alleviating more pain with someone else.

With employment insurance only paying a low ratio to what had already been low wages, finances were going to be a major problem. I rolled my pennies. I cashed in my empty beer bottles. And worse, I began to mooch off you. It began with cigarettes. You ran the front of the wholesale store, a division of the warehouse I had worked in; and it was nothing for you to lift cartons of cigarettes, bypassing the till altogether, only now it included my brand. When you had the right opportunity, you would load your car with groceries and stock my kitchen cupboards. I was full of gratitude, but felt little guilt. Desperation can extinguish moral values and allow survival instincts quite an amount of leniency in its tactics and direction. Besides, it wasn't really me doing the stealing Indirectly, yes, but somehow that made it okay. I accepted your charity with open arms out of necessity, out of poverty.

We continued our osmotic arrangement, soaking in a bath of mixed emotion, falling asleep like curled up hamsters, small bites of time allowing temporary unawareness of the pressures of the world around us. But because of the distance between our homes, your job, and my lack of one, there was a slow pulling apart from each other. At the same time, when we were together, our time in bed was inexplicably intensified. It was right after one of these poignant nights that you brought up your potential plans to go out west for a vacation. You had worked for your brother-in-law a long time, and he felt you were entitled to three weeks a year instead of the mandatory two. You had a friend that had moved out west that would occasionally ask you to visit her. You thought it was time. It was a few moments before I realized that you were asking me to go with you. I was filled with excitement at the prospect, but it took some time to sink in as I pondered what it meant.

A trip to Florida, a short stay up north, and a few weekend excursions was the extent of my travel. I couldn't fathom such a lengthy trip, both in mileage and in distance. There was a whole list of deterring factors. I was unemployed, had no money, and most of all, had a girlfriend across the border expecting me. Everyone knew that there were jobs galore out west, cities booming and employers begging for help. Our own province sat dormant in a recession. If there was ever an opportunity for me to find work, it was out there. I stopped thinking about it and told you I would go with you. There was a future out there. I still felt young and could make something of myself. I had been actively seeking work, filling out applications everywhere. But I knew full well no one was hiring. I went through the motions to appease the government, who needed to see I was actively seeking work, in order for them to provide me with the unemployment checks rather than an actual hope that I could remove myself from my rut. You had just offered me new hope and also a chance to escape this godforsaken existence for a while and find adventure. Even though I felt I had already taken too much from you, I had no money to go. I asked you to loan me a thousand dollars with a solemn promise to pay you back as soon as possible. You didn't hesitate for a second before you agreed.

I spent the weekend before we left on the other side of the border. The exhilaration I usually felt from being on the university grounds wasn't there that weekend. Neither was the normal exuberance that I pulled from my collegiate angel. There was uneasiness between us when I first asked and then told her that I was making the trip out west with you. I think I was more concerned than her, but she knew you were my friend and, as far as she was concerned, only my friend. She trusted me. I kept asking how sure she was that I should go. What bothered me the most was that if I did find work out there, was I willing to make the sacrifices necessary to move? In her eyes, there was almost pride that I would finally want to improve myself. She knew I wasn't the most ambitious person in the world, and to take an opportunity, even if it was on the other side of the country, could only be positive. She gave me her blessing. She trusted me.

And so the following week, we packed up your car and, with map in hand, headed for the western frontier. Your ex-husband agreed to take your kids without any disagreements or reservations. My car would have never made it, but it did not stop me from chuckling at yours. The two of us on the open highway in a brown Gremlin with the yellow factory stripe on each side. We were driving in style. I had not thought of cutting through the states to save mileage and time. I soon discovered how big our country actually was. Those few inches on the map took a long time to cover. So twenty-four hours later, we finally crossed the Manitoba border, stopping only for bathroom breaks, gas, and confectionery food. You didn't want to drive, so with the help of some powerful amphetamines, I pulled into the outskirts of Calgary in less than forty-four hours. There were a few hallucinations during the last few hours on the road, but they were caused only by sleep deprivation. I had not slept very well the weekend before we left, and now this straight stretch of concentration was playing tricks with my vision. The road through the prairies was one long stretch of road through some very flat land. As long as I favored the right-hand side of the road, even if I had fallen asleep behind the wheel, I would have eventually glided to a stop in the middle of a wheat field.

Your friend had given us great directions, and we soon found her street. When you called her, she insisted that we would be staying with her for free and there would be no discussion about it. So with only two days gone by and free lodgings, we were off to a great start. I had no way of knowing that our western adventure would turn into nothing but a very long party and a very long period of steady intoxication. It soon was apparent that any goals I had in mind would be sidelined, and instead my time would be spent killing off more brain cells. Did I regret it? You can't regret memory that influences your life or adds to your experiences. Although our three weeks was nothing but a ride into complete escapism, without any sense of responsibilities, it was not without meaning. What was the definition of vacation anyway?

When we first pulled into the driveway, we both felt apprehensive. The two-story house stood among a row of cookie-cutter construction, with small yards in front of each one. We got out and stretched our road-weary legs that by now had almost seized up. On our way into the city, the size of it was very intimidating, but this suburban side street made us feel more secure. We were small-town folk in the middle of a concrete jungle. We stood on the small strip of grass in front of the house like ceramic gnomes, deciding whether we should knock. Your friend Beth decided for us as she burst out of the front door to give you an enormous bear hug, and at first I was afraid she was going to crush you. You turned a shade of crimson red as she kissed you on the lips and hugged you again. I got a handshake.

What later followed seemed like an endless whirlpool of activity. We were rushed into the house with our luggage in our hands, pointed to the showers, which I can assure you we both needed with the layers of road dust we had on us, showed to our room where we would be staying once it was established we only needed one, and were pouring back rounds of beer and tequila at the kitchen table before I could even register the fact that we had made it safe and sound to Calgary. Once settled at that kitchen table, which we were practically glued to most of our stay, I was finally able to focus. The house was astonishingly spacious. It even dwarfed yours. There were six bedrooms upstairs, a master one downstairs, as well as a guest bedroom that was so graciously given to us. She owned the house, and when you asked how she could afford it, she explained that she had four boarders to help her cover the costs. We soon discovered that the cost of living in Calgary was astronomical. It explained the type of houses on the street. It was common practice to share accommodations to make ends meet. It was socially acceptable to have multiple families in one home, a common practice from previous generations that we had slowly backed away from. Now we were stuck in a society that had to prove that we could outdo each other.

As the afternoon approached into evening and as Beth gave us some cultural lessons of her city, while the two of you reminisced fondly about your past times together, the other four members of the household rolled in individually, returning from their work and duties. We were introduced as new members of the household, and we were graciously accepted with an abundance of friendship. I was enjoying the idea that I would be sharing a house with six women. It wasn't something that happened every day. I caught you watching me as I studied each one, a habit I picked up from all those lonely evenings sitting in the corners of bars by myself. There was one blonde in particular that my eyes kept roaming to. I wasn't even aware I was doing it until your look told me it was quite obvious what I was doing. I denied it later, but we both knew I was guilty. A pig like the rest of them came to my mind, and I hoped the thought that nestled there for a moment had not come from you. If I was to be stereotyped and stung by such a description of my character, I did not want it to come from you.

It was on our fifth introduction that my actions were soon forgotten about. Another woman walked in, and if I hadn't lost my mathematical skills, this would make five boarders instead of the four mentioned. You watched in bewilderment and discomfort as she walked up to Beth and planted a passionate kiss on her lips and sat down on her lap. The other four women did not react, but you had a stunned look. She was introduced to us as Beth's girlfriend. We both had our mouths slightly open but speechless; mine out of amusement, yours out of mild shock.

You had not one iota of knowledge that your friend was a lesbian. The reason she had moved out west in the first place was to get away from her ex-husband. We obviously knew that there were such alternative lifestyles, but coming from a basic rural area, the inside of a closet would have been the only place we would find it. Here out in the open, in plain view for us to see, was quite unusual for us. Later that evening, when they were caressing and groping right at the table in manners that would have been uncomfortable to watch even if it had been a heterosexual couple, we noticed that it did not bother the other four women in the house. Your discomfort subsided some, but I could feel you slowly edging your chair closer to me. We excused ourselves early that first night, the alcohol affecting us quickly, the marijuana passed around the table as frequently as the cigarettes we lit, and sheer exhaustion had us in danger of decorating the table with our heads.

I fell asleep in seconds that night and woke up the next morning with pieces of memory missing. You were holding me tight and had been awake long before me. I knew something was wrong, and when I pushed you to tell me after you denied it, you began to explain how bothered you were with Beth. I had been unaware that she had thrown you subtle hints that they wanted you to consider joining in with them and Beth had rubbed your leg a couple of times. Had I been that stoned not to even see that? What about the other four women in the house? Had they allowed it? When I asked you for more details, you began to doubt their real intentions, and it may have been that you were overly apprehensive and had read too much into their words and actions. You were still perplexed though, so I gave you a series of soft kisses and told you that they couldn't have you, that you were mine. I was refreshed and alert now and simply wanted to put the night behind me. You agreed to do the same. We had the better part of three weeks here, and we were meant to enjoy it.

We soon accepted things the way they were as each night turned into the same routine. Seven of us around the table, in no other pursuits but heavy-duty partying. It seemed to start earlier each day, and it wasn't long before I understood that this was going to be one long drunk festival. With the help of the other straight members of our group, we relaxed and soon paid no attention to our two female lovebirds, who never found it necessary to use up two chairs when sitting. The normalcy of the other women, the constant jokes, the constant fits of laughter put us into such a relaxed state that we fell into ease. The steady stream of dope and alcohol put our brains into neutral. But after seven straight days of this, I found enough sobriety one morning to realize that if I didn't at least make an attempt to search for work, I would have a bucket of regrets later.

My attempts at finding employment had been limited to browsing the morning newspaper that appeared on the front sidewalk each day. I would go outside each morning with my lone coffee, enjoy the morning sunrise, and go through the classifieds. I would leave you sleeping, for you were not accustomed to such binge drinking and some extra horizontal would certainly do you no harm. The rest of the household was usually gone to work before I woke or they would still be nursing their own hangover in one of the rooms upstairs. It was difficult for me to keep track of everyone's schedule with my foggy and riddled memory, not only from the steady partying, but also from the constant frenzy of activity in a house full of women. Almost all my memories are centered on that kitchen table, and what guys wouldn't with a kitchen full of pretty women to party with?

My low self-esteem was kept at bay with the uniform intake of alcohol, releasing my inhibitions in the same steady stream. My respect for you was probably the only thing that stopped me from acting on the growing attraction I felt toward one of the boarders. I knew you could sense it, and I knew you caught us with the flirtatious eye contact between us and how she would purposely flip her blonde hair suggestively whenever I was looking at her. Yet you said nothing.

So each morning, outside on the porch, between sips of that coffee, I would browse through the classifieds and circle any potential jobs. And during this time, I was also able to brush off any guilt or remorse of any memories of acting like a jackass the night before. The help-wanted ads were plentiful, and on the eighth day and the eighth newspaper, I discovered an ad for a warehouse position with an address that, when I traced on a map, was in the same side of the city as we were staying. I made it my goal to apply there and talked to you about it and everyone else at the table that evening. I must have opened up an opportunity that Beth had been waiting for. She jumped into the conversation right away. Without any regard for your choice in the matter, she said that since I would be busy, it would be a great chance for her and her girlfriend to show you the sights of the city. They both had the day off, and it was time to show you some fun. It was sensible, for why should you not see and discover things the city had to offer? It was your vacation. I was supposed to be here on business, on finding work. Before I had a chance to recognize your apprehension, I was already drowning in tequila shots. So it was settled without discussion.

The next morning, I kissed you good-bye and told you to have fun and disappeared out the door with my newspaper, my cigarettes, and my map. I had explained to you that I had to do this or going back home without even trying to find a job would eat at me forever. You had said you understood and that you would be fine. You weren't. Neither was I. Walking the streets of a strange and gigantic city, three provinces away from home and away from the comforts of my rural setting, alone for the first time since our arrival, I began to feel an overwhelming sense of panic. My head was pounding from the night before, and tequila tremors ran through my limbs. You had offered me your car, and I might have considered it if the exhaust pipe had not let go the day before on our way to the liquor store. It would have made it extremely difficult for an out-of-province driver to remain in stealth mode and not draw attention to himself. Walking always had some form of invigoration for me anyway, and according to my map, the two destinations I had chosen were within a three-mile radius.

I found the first place with no trouble at all, but when I saw how run-down it was and saw the heaps of scattered junk around the entire perimeter of the building, I chose not to go in. My intuition told me not to. I was ready to turn around and go back to the kitchen table, but the shame I would feel later by not continuing would have devoured me. There was only one other place I had in mind anyway. So I walked and walked until I finally found the industrial site the business I was looking for was supposed to be in, but the ad in the paper had given only the street and name of the business and not the street number. The street wound in and around cross streets, meandering in long curves and straight ways the entire length of the subdivision. To complicate it even further, there was a north and south street of the same name. I walked what seemed like hours trying to find a building with the right name on it. The more I walked, the more intimidating everything was becoming. I stopped twice to ask, but no one seemed to have heard of it. I was weak from dehydration, and after a third walk through the same area, I gave up, preferring to listen to the beckoning call of a cold bottle of beer.

I could have applied in all the businesses I passed, but I was only looking for one. I could have tried again the next day. But with anxiety and intimidation boiling in a pot of panic attacks, that was the extent of my efforts to find work out west. My obscure sense of logic told me that at least I had tried.

I walked back to my temporary home, overheated, tired, and with a parched throat. Beth had graciously showed me where she had kept the key underneath the welcome mat. The house was empty and quiet. I guzzled a cold beer faster than it took to open it and started on a second one. I had a more feasible goal now, a simpler, easier, and more pleasurable one. I would eliminate my thirst. On the start of my sixth beer, I had stopped shaking and was comfortable enough to forget about my search for work altogether. Back out on the front porch, I sat staring at the rows of houses across the street, wondering how I could possibly have thought that I could live in this city. The party lifestyle alone would have killed me eventually. How I missed my lake and favorite boardwalk that day, where I could lay down on that sloping hill and feel the earth move. I took you there once but never stayed. I guess I wasn't ready to share it with you. I could never explain the vibrancy and the energy that flowed to the very core of my being from that spot. This concrete jungle had no outlets to alleviate stress, did nothing to keep my nerves from fraying.

Day turned into early dusk, and I still sat alone on the porch, waiting for you to return, waiting for anyone to return. And as coincidences go in my life, the first one to return was the beautiful blonde with the flirtatious eyes. My heart skipped a beat as I finally recognized why I was so attracted to her. She had a remarkable resemblance to my ex-wife. Could I then be blamed for the way I was beginning to feel about her? We kept each other company on the porch that night well past dusk and into the night. She supplied me with tequila and joints, and it wasn't long before I was well on my way to being wasted again. I don't remember what we talked about. I only remember the ease in which we talked to each other. The lone streetlight in front of the house silhouetted us, and I had visions of romance. No one else had returned yet, and in total disregard or concern for your well-being, I was basking in my company.

When Beth finally returned and pulled the car into the driveway, you witnessed us together on the porch. Nothing had occurred, but my blonde friend had just finished passing me another joint, and she sat so close that our hips and thighs were touching. She moved over slightly when you got out of the car, and your anger was clearly visible. But there was something else on your expression that alarmed me more. It was anguish. It was fear. I couldn't quite place it, nor did I until the following morning when I found myself lying next to you with no recollection about how I got there. I had blacked out and was carried to bed by a harem of females sometime through the night. It must have been one hell of a party.

Even with a worse hangover than the day before, even more dehydrated than I had been when walking in circles in the industrial park, I crawled out of bed leaving you sleeping. You found me soon after taking my final sips of my coffee, which this time I had spiked with rum. I was reading a fresh newspaper. I had never seen you so upset, but with a blank memory of the night before, I had no idea of what I had done to make you feel that way. And when I asked you what was wrong, you broke down in tears and endless sobs. I had never seen you cry before, and it broke my heart to watch you. I put arms around you and hoped that you would stop. I took your hand and walked you down the street, making sure we had privacy to talk about what was wrong, to wait for the bombshell of what I had done so wrong.

To my relief, it wasn't me after all. Your adventure with your two lesbian friends had not gone well. When you were finally able to compose yourself, you told me that at first it was fun. They had taken you sightseeing, let you discover the prime areas of the city, and then you went barhopping, finally ending up in the swank restaurant on top of Calgary Tower. They treated you to expensive food and expensive drinks and a spectacular view. But during the marathon of after-dinner drinks, they unexpectedly started to pressure you. You started to cry again as you explained how they had persisted in telling you that you were not allowing yourself to experience your rightful lifestyle. I stood on the street, motionless, in total disbelief as you further explained how they insisted that you were in denial and that you were far from straight. You had been in shock at first and then began to doubt yourself as they went on a relentless mission of brainwashing you into thinking that they were right. After hours of bombardment and totally on your own, their description of the advantages and rewards of gay life had you unsure of yourself. I couldn't begin to imagine how confused you had been as they picked away at your past, your vulnerability, your loneliness.

My presence and connection with you had been erased by them, convincing you that I was only using you. Beth had repeated it to you many times, like a mantra. This thought had never occurred to me before. Could I have been just using you and had no way of admitting it to myself? A quick inventory of all that you had done for me weighed heavily as I struggled with this possibility. I shrugged it off as you continued with the details of your night. They had you petrified when they had started to grope you from underneath the tablecloth, soft touches on your thigh and higher. They comforted you with words of adoration, but you were trembling with fear. You were shaking again as you relived it when describing it to me. I reached over and told you how sorry I was for not being there for you and assured you that I was not using you. I was not sure how to really comfort you, but you told me the way. You made me promise never to leave your side the rest of the trip. That was not going to be a problem because my empathy for you was so high I felt that they had done it to me. The terror, the helplessness, the doubts and confusion that you went through were running through me as well. There was a corrosive reaction in my own mind, and I needed you by my side just as much as you did.

Before we went back into the house, we discussed and then agreed that it would be a glorious idea to go out on our own for a couple of days and see the mountains. They were not that far away, and we would be crazy anyway to have come this far and not experience them. Banff was close, and we had read about its beauty. We both went to Beth and told her of our plans together, and there was not much she could say to disagree.

First, though, I had to pretend to be a mechanic and crawl underneath your Gremlin to see how bad the exhaust leak was. I was proud of my ingenuity. I walked a few blocks to the hardware store and bought two hose clamps, a screwdriver, and a can of soda from the vending machine in front of the store. I sliced the can in half after removing the ends and wrapped it around the hole in the exhaust pipe and tightened the clamps to it and the aluminum can. I had an instant repair job. It didn't eliminate all the noise, but it dropped the decibels low enough from the thunderous roar and was enough to detract attention.

The rest of the boarders were excited for us, understanding our need to play tourist, and wished us a good time. Beth said nothing. You threw a few of our things in a bag and left the rest of our luggage behind. I let you drive while I did the navigating for a change. My head hurt so badly that I didn't think I could have concentrated on the road anyway. I remember Beth standing in the driveway as we pulled away waving good-bye and mouthing for us to be careful. And when she thought it was only me left looking, she formed a scorn on her brow, and I thought I could actually hear her disdain.

For two days, we lived in peace, tranquility, and bliss with not a care in the world. We walked the streets of Banff and were astonished by its beauty. The pictures we saw before had not done it enough justice. The mountains left us in nothing short of awe. We spent over an hour just standing overlooking Lake Louise as if its beauty had paralyzed us. We found a small and affordable motel off the beaten path and drenched ourselves in the mountain air. We retired early the first night, and after only a few drinks and a great restaurant meal, we curled up together naked under fresh, crisp sheets. Exhaustion did not begin to describe the measure of our fatigue. We made love that night, and the feelings for your softness and your passion seeped through me once more. I fell asleep in your arms in solace and feeling very safe. It was my first real rejuvenated sleep since we arrived.

The next morning, we both agreed that everything between us was good, more than good. We could rely on each other with never any more doubts. After a great breakfast, which did not include alcohol and a new positive outlook at our situation, feeling almost human again, we spent the day carefree and sober. Whether it was the mountain air, the recognition of what the world felt like in a normal state, or the freedom of a true vacation day, we felt a natural form of exhilaration. We both had forgotten what that felt like. We were alive. We didn't want to leave, but the next morning, we agreed that we should head back as we watched our cash dwindle. We didn't have the luxury of unlimited exploration.

Just before we left to find the main highway, I grabbed you and kissed you. You asked what it was for, and I replied that it was for being you. I am not sure if you knew what I meant at the time, but know it now. You were good for me, and I never really took the time to show or even feel the appreciation that was inside me. Maybe I was truly selfish. I remember you blushing that day, and I saw a smile that hadn't been there for a while. So maybe, just maybe, I left you with the notion that I did value you, did love you; but in my confusion of the times, I didn't really know how to say it or appropriately show it. I can only hope that our physical connection was able to transmit to you some of the emotion that I did hold for you.

It had already turned dark before we found our way back to Beth's. The regular kitchen-table party had started without us, but we soon assumed our positions. We were asked about our trip, and there seemed to be genuine interest in our replies instead of merely social politeness. If Beth or her girlfriend harbored any ill feelings toward me, there were no signs. I felt no friction at all, and we dug right back into the thick of partying and soon erased any refreshed outlook that we gathered from being only high on elevation on the pureness of mountain air. We both crawled into bed that night, neither one interested in the joints being passed around, but neither one of us wishing to be antisocial either. They were still our hosts. Any rejuvenation efforts of our getaway were wiped out in a single night. We passed out in each other's arms, but now knowing that we now had each other to rely on the remainder of our stay.

If our trip out west was to escape our problems back home, we certainly did that. There were times when we could have forgotten where we came from. It wasn't that we liked our new surroundings so much. It was more the freedom to do nothing. But our trip to the land of oblivion was only a mask. The remainder of our stay returned us into a state of constant waste. It seemed the longer we stayed, the more potent the weed they fed us. There were a few nights when the paranoid effects that had plagued me many times in the past came rolling back like monsters in fog. If I didn't have you to rely on, I might have panicked. We definitely leaned on each other when we came back from the mountains. When the time came to end our trip and accept that we had to take the long ride back to reality and to home, we were a mess, but in a mess together. A long stay in a rehabilitation center was in order, but we would have to dry out on the Trans-Canada Highway instead. It was almost a blessing when the day came to leave. We knew our new friends very well by the time we left, but we were not going to miss them. There were many laughs, many shared stories, and many bizarre ideas. We owned part of that kitchen table, but we were ready to relinquish it to memory.

The morning we packed up to leave, there was only Beth there to say good-bye. We said informal good-byes the night before, or at least I think we did. That morning, everyone else was either scattered throughout the city at their jobs or still passed out upstairs. Beth hugged you and said that she loved you. It was the love of a friend and could not be mistaken for anything else. Her attempts to recruit you to the gay community were over. I got a hug from her as well and a stern warning to take care of you. I promised her that I would, a promise I never kept.

We pulled out of Beth's driveway and never looked back, never discussed our time out west again. When I think back in the solitude of my own recollections, I have difficulty sorting it all out. Most of my memories of those three weeks are foggy and so scattered that I use it as a foundation to never want to have such a stretch of steady inebriation and blackouts ever again. When I sometimes dream of those three weeks, I wake up to the frightening sensation of free-falling into a dark abyss and there is no bottom. I can feel pressure inside my head that pushes it into excruciating pain as I try to grab for a way to stop falling. I wake from this recurring dream each time drenched in sweat and feeling like my lungs had just collapsed. The addiction levels, the lack of any sense of control, had alarmed me and entered my subconscious as a nightmare. Awake, I had visions of ending up in desolation, like the old man that was always in the Vista Inn and lived in one of the rooms upstairs, waiting for his next welfare check—the one that sat alone talking to himself out loud and feeding change into the jukebox, listening to the same Tom Connors song over and over again. That rare flash-forward into my future to display such a bleak and condemned picture sent tremors of terror through me. I did not want to waste my life away.

If this small epiphany was all I got out of our trip together, then it was all worth it—an incentive to finally make something out of myself, to pick up the pieces and build. It might have been my subconscious that caused me to slowly drift away from you when we returned. You might somehow have signified the fear I felt of what I might become if I did not try to make changes. How extremely unfair this was to you, but at that point in my life, I was no good to you anyway.

It took us three days to get back home. I was out of amphetamines, and no amount of caffeine was going to keep me awake forty-plus hours. We were both wiped out. We took turns driving back, but even then, the louder noise of your exhaust wouldn't allow me to sleep. We would stop at rest areas and sleep in the cargo area of your Gremlin. It was extremely uncomfortable, twisted around each other in contortionist positions, but we still managed to catch some sleep. But as I lay beside you, I was already guilt ridden as I had already begun to scrutinize our relationship and already thought of the changes I needed to make. Beth's words kept ringing in my ear, "He's using you."

We got back a day late, causing you to miss a day's work. You weren't concerned, and you needed another day of recuperation, anyway. The next day, I went to court and handed over my license. I had almost forgotten the date, and with the results, I might as well have. I went back to my rodent-infested house and slept for two days straight. And then without even telling you, I crossed the border to see my university angel. I had called her once from out west, but it did not go well. I was drunk, staggering off the walls of the phone booth, barely audible over the street noise. The call was short and curt. And then to show up much later than expected, unannounced with a duffel bag and a sob story, I was not in good graces. It was a weekend of lecturing instead of the comfort I was seeking. I was not cooperative in providing details of the trip, not only because of my own sketchy memory, but also because I had to be careful not be caught in lies about my true relationship with you.

It was my first weekend where there was no intimacy involved. Instead I was pounded with warnings about where my future was headed, the same warnings I was already ripping myself apart with. I came home defeated. I still continued to avoid you and barricaded myself in my house, wanting to disassociate myself with the rest of the world. You showed up at my door two days later, legitimately concerned. I apologized profusely, explaining I just needed some time by myself. You said you understood, but your expression didn't say it. In your hand were all the mail that had been stuffed in my mailbox while we were gone. I had left it there, with no interest in looking at bills. But as you handed the bundle to me, I noticed on top of the pile a letter from a company I had applied to for work.

In an unusual godsend of luck, they were interested in hiring me. My heart beat with excitement, and I had to read it several times to make sure it wasn't a prank. I hugged you and thanked you. You stayed for a while, but even with such good news, our conversation was strained. There was a distance between us that thickened the air. We made no attempt to cut through it. You said you had to leave as your kids were going to be dropped off soon, and I made no effort to keep you. I kissed you as you leaned against your car door. We both had tears in our eyes. You knew. You knew that I was struggling to find a way to tell you that I had to move on. I said nothing. I didn't have to. The solemn look in my eyes had said it all. I watched you back out of the driveway, and it haunted me. It wasn't the first time I stood there watching someone I loved drive away.

I didn't see you again until several weeks later. I had gone for the interview, pulled it off successfully after two days of heavy contemplating of how I could sell myself. It was the vodka trick (you can't smell it) that suppressed my inhibitions and allowed me to express myself properly. The manager took a shining to me and hired me on the spot. I was light-headed when he told me the rate of pay, twice what I had expected and an additional increase in ninety days. I had found a pot of gold, and I knew I wasn't afraid to work for it. The downside was that this factory was in my dreaded high school town of Hilbury. It was also the town where my ex-wife and I had rented an apartment. I wanted to forget that town, but with this sudden path to a real future—first accepted in astonishment and then recognized as the most important thing to never jeopardize in any way—I would get over it. To screw this up, I might as well find a job testing the quality of guillotines, with me as the subject.

When I first started the job, I would get up two hours in advance since the loss of my license had left me with only my feet as a source of transportation. Hitchhiking was easy then, before the days of perversion and weirdos wrecked it. Then, there was very limited danger. But I was always risking a dry spell and not catching a ride in time, leaving me running for miles with severe pains in my chest. I could not be late. Winter would soon start its fast march to freezing temperatures and only add to the hardships of getting to work.

I began to look for a place in Hilbury to stay and found a small claustrophobic apartment to move into. By putting all my efforts into the job, it helped keep my mind off you. But sometimes when the work became mundane and my mind began to wander, I could not help but think of you and all that you had done for me. So one Sunday, after I was all settled in to what I referred to as my hillbilly town, I hitchhiked to your house. Thankfully you were home, because the cold rain of that day had left me drenched and shivering. I had to walk the last three miles to get to you. You were very surprised to see me, and as I dried in the warmth of your living room, you brought me a glass of double rum and Coke. You sat beside me, and we talked freely, but I could feel the lines of distance that now separated us. I ignored it.

And so did you. After my fifth strong drink, I reached over and kissed you and felt the original sparks. It was all I could do to not make love to you. In your eyes was that same look of no strings attached that we had agreed on a long time ago. But now I knew it wasn't right. I couldn't continue to show you such lack of regard. Before I could say anything, before I could tell you that I didn't want to hurt you anymore and it was best that I leave you alone, we were interrupted. Your ex was knocking on the door, returning your kids from the weekend. I felt the agony twisting inside me as I watched your beautiful kids burst in, excited to see me. I gave them both a hug and, for the first time, saw the same innocence in their eyes that had always been in yours.

I spent the rest of the day as a family man. We played board games with your kids, making each other laugh; and although it felt so good, it was also breaking my heart. You made us the last supper we ever had together, and we sat around the dining room table as representation of a family unit. You gave me that smile that was sometimes hard to find, and it was all I could do to hold my tears back. Embedded in my memory is that smile, and it is always mixed with joy and sorrow, a weird sensation of melancholy that cannot be clearly defined. Our quiet family moments were soon dispersed into chaos as your sister and her boyfriend returned home. They were surprised to see me, but celebrated my appearance with more shared drinks. You tucked your kids into bed later, but not before they hugged me. The new responsibilities of work were on the top of my mind, and as I caught myself falling to the traps of alcohol, I told you I had to get home. You refused to let me hitchhike and gave me a ride home. I invited you in, but we both knew it wasn't a good idea, and you were the first to say it. You knew. I gave you what turned out to be my very last kiss with you. I watched you pull away and disappear out of my life.

I did get to see you one last time over a year later. You bumped into my friend Chad one night in a bar, and my name came up in conversation. After too many drinks, you both decided to pay me a surprise visit. I had moved from my dinky apartment by then, and it was a total surprise when you appeared at my door with Chad. I was glad I was alone and not entertaining, but that was not unusual. I had spent a lot of time alone since we parted. My trips across the border were over by then, and I had slipped back to my wandering ways with a depressing but fresh town to pick strays from.

Our conversation was cordial and simple, especially until Chad did one of his narcolepsy acts hanging half out of a chair with rhythmical snores. Only then did we open up to each other. I knew I still owed you a thousand dollars, but I had no idea how badly you might have needed it. Your antics with your brother-in-law and his business had finally caught up with you. He became aware of the missing inventory and the discrepancies in the books. There was no one else to point fingers at. He allowed you to quit in exchange for not pressing charges. I felt partly responsible, for some of that merchandise was for me. But when I told you that, you admitted you were doing it for many people.

I opened a bottle of wine for us and continued to listen to how your whole life had gone sour. You had to give up your house because you couldn't afford the rent anymore. You still lived with your sister but in a much smaller house. Your ex-husband went to court and got full custody of the kids. You still saw them but infrequently. I did not know what to say. I knew your heart. You did not deserve any of this, and I went completely numb when I thought of all the hardships you had gone through in such a short period. I felt your pain, but I also knew that I could no longer add to it, could not be the cause of more. I repressed my urge to kiss you, but it was difficult. I felt the original physical attraction welling up inside me, and instead of even considering acting on it, I lit a cigarette and went to look for my checkbook. I sensed that you would probably never have asked for it, so I wrote out a check for the thousand dollars I owed you and apologized for taking so long to give you your money back. Before you had a chance to reply, Chad woke up from his nap.

I really wasn't able to afford to give you the whole amount then as I was still clearing a back log of unpaid bills from before my new job. I hated myself for even thinking that, especially in the predicament you were now in. Before I could ask you of your future plans, Chad decided it was time to go. I could have asked you to stay, but it would have only led to regrets in the morning. I managed to delay your leaving by insisting that Chad have one more drink with me, but any personal conversation between us was finished. It was of no concern of his, and we were not about to make it so. I walked you to Chad's van after where you hugged me and whispered thank you in my ear. I looked into your eyes and saw the same beautiful, innocent eyes of a lost soul, the same look I first saw across a foggy table at the Vista Inn many moons ago. I started to kiss you and somehow was able to stop. I was suddenly flooded by all the feelings that you and I had shared. But regardless of the pain I felt by letting you go, I was not going to cause you any more. I knew what I was doing was right for you, and it helped me stop the tears after you pulled away.

Whenever I think of you now, I also pray. I pray that you have found success in your life. I pray that you have found someone that can really appreciate you. I pray that you have found the happiness that I am still searching for.

CHAPTER 8

Christine:

My petite French girl. I still hear your raspy voice caused from your cigarette habit, accentuated with the accent that was a dead giveaway to your nationality. You were born and raised in Hilbury, the town I despised but was now stuck in. It was several years down the road before I found the sense to get out of it and as it turned out, only temporarily. The longest years of my life and the eventual awakening to my entrapment were in that town. I met you in the town bar where, in my half-witted state of the times, I didn't have the brains to stay out of.

I soon learned from this hillbilly town that under the disguise of emotional value, one could have quick affairs and use women easily. But my ventures weren't under the pretense of satisfying my own needs, not entirely. I genuinely felt something, and I was far from cold. I had concluded, however, that I would stay away from the traps of my past and not fall in love with the idea of being in love. The strangeness of the mind's ability to suppress loneliness with any form of companionship and justify it regardless of the consequences was something I was only beginning to discover. And although I delved into the practice, it was totally against my grain. It was a perplexing state of mind for me. There were feelings, just not quite to the depths of solid authenticity. Perhaps a good psychologist could have helped me sort it out, but I was in the fast lane again, carrying with me burdens that were best left buried. I had fear of my skull cracking open and coils of steam shoving despair and distress out of the top of my head and nothing to replace it with. It was better to remain anaesthetized and skim along on the surface of existence. Deeper thinking hurt too much.

I was sitting with my new drinking pals on a Friday night after work. The warehouse crew from work, which I was now a significant part of, always went to the bar after work to wash down some dust. They had sense to go home after a few. I did not. That particular night, I was pouring them back faster than normal, and that meant fast. I was watching you at the next table beside us where you sat among a group of your girlfriends. We were playing the same game together, showing interest in the conversation of our respective tables, but truly interested in what was going on at each other's. We both seemed to be trapped in our own thoughts, and we had exchanged a hundred glances over the night. Bill, the closest of my working acquaintances, not only because he worked side by side with me but also because he had fish drinking capabilities that matched my own, saw what was distracting me.

He was married, and yet I had never met a better womanizer. My hero? He could seduce a woman for later rendezvous while his wife sat in the same bar with him. Usually, though, she was sitting at home waiting for him. So I was surprised when he told me to stay away from you, that you were married and your brother-in-law actually worked in the factory part of our company. I nodded in acknowledgment, poured back two more beers, and decided not to take his warning into consideration. By midnight, everyone else had left my table and gone home. Bill was still around, but he was up at the bar preparing his next target, a long-haired brunette with wraparound legs. His warning was totally obliterated when you continued to exchange looks with me. I could never approach anyone until I was inebriated, and then I had to hope that I was not too far gone. A drunk certainly doesn't know when he has had too much. There was also my fear of rejection regardless of the amount of alcohol. I had no assessed measurement for that fear to be eliminated.

Out of my reach at that time of my life was the lack of cognitive ability to understand that I had pressed a self-destruct button, caring less about the poisonous potion of alcohol, amphetamines, weed, and a nasty cigarette habit for good measure. I had my job to keep me on a responsible path, but my emotional levels had regressed back into the teenage years. I was so lost to common sense that I had come to the conclusion that proper sleep was even a waste of time. Maybe I was aware that my lifestyle was shortening my life and wanted to use every hour available.

Some of these thoughts churned around while I looked for reasons to approach you. I ordered another two beers and, trying not to stagger, held one in each hand and walked to your table and sat beside you. Comically, I asked if I could talk to you after I had already sat down. We exchanged a few friendly words, and you introduced me to your friends, but you might as well have given me Latin names for South American vegetation. I was lucky to remember your name.

By last call, there was only you and I left at the table. We had talked a lot, but I cannot remember the slightest detail. I know we didn't discuss that you were married, nor did you mention it when I asked you to come back to my place with me. I was ashamed of my little apartment, but then I wasn't bringing you home to impress you. When I think back on all my escapades in that town, it still amazes me how easy it was to sleep with women. I realized we were in the middle of an era of sexual freedom, but with my pestering inhibitions and my recent deterioration to the tolerance levels of alcohol and my fight against low self-esteem on top of it all, I didn't think I was part of it. But even with a stack of inferiority problems, I was still able to find my share of the pot. Sexually transmitted diseases were not peaking yet, but they were certainly out there. That certainly wasn't on top of my mind. It obviously wasn't on yours either.

Neither was your husband, for we made love that same night; and although I started off as the aggressor, you ended the night as one. There was usually not a thought or emotion to be found when I picked up someone I did not know. My goal was to simply fill a void of loneliness. I had to assume it was mutual. You can easily be married or be with someone and feel just as lonely, as if you lived in complete solitude. But that night was different, and I could feel the tinges of an emotional attachment from you. It was more than casual.

I am not sure when I fell asleep, but I woke up just in time to rush off to work. You were gone. Saturdays were mandatory at that time of year, and I certainly didn't mind the overtime. Work was only a mile from my apartment. When I had lost my license, I needed somewhere to live that was within walking distance. I refused to be late for work. No matter how polluted I allowed my mind to become, no matter how sick or hung over I was, I was always able to drag myself to work. My attendance was almost perfect. After suffering through periods of poverty, I could not jeopardize a good-paying job for anything. Work was my lifeline, and any hope of making something out of my miserable existence depended on it. Not a pot to piss in was a saying that did not resonate well with me, especially when I looked around and saw how well-off some other people of my age were doing. My balking of society days no longer applied, except maybe in my drinking habits.

I don't know if you fell asleep with me for a while or not. It wasn't until I came home from work that day that I found your note underneath my magnetic apple, which was stuck on the door of my refrigerator. On it was your phone number. I had come back with various parts of a greasy bird carried in a cardboard bucket from the Colonels', and later, with a pile of bones and several empty beers in front of me, I began to feel human enough to call you. You answered the phone, and I told you who I was. I recognized your voice, but you said I had the wrong number and hung up. My heart did a round of erratic beats and then dropped a little lower than it normally set. I remembered Bill telling me you were married, and I could only surmise that I had just been the victim of a hit-and-run, the one left empty from a one-night stand. I felt like a fool as I remembered that touch of emotion I felt when you were on top of me. Now I knew what some women must feel when they were taken advantage of.

My anguish was short-lived. An hour after I had called you, you were knocking on my door. After my first initial reaction of total surprise, I let you in with only small reservations. I was still stinging from the phone call, but I thought your presence must mean something. You just didn't decide you were in the neighborhood. This wasn't rejection after all. I opened up a beer for each of us, and we sat down on my couch in the cramped living room. You opened up to me in the fashion of a tsunami. You poured out everything, from your childhood to your unhappy marriage, in an endless stream of vocalized thoughts. I had always been commended as a good listener. This was an ingrained characteristic as of late, folded around an overdeveloped sense of empathy. This was quite a contrast to those who saw me as selfish and self-centered. You finished with an exasperated exhalation of air, as if telling me all this hadn't helped. You had ended by telling me that your husband was not only mentally abusive, but there was also physical abuse from time to time. The only reason you stayed was for your two young kids. There were always kids.

As you further went on to explain in that cute French accent, you told me you really cared about me and was sorry for hanging up. Your husband had been home, and you were sorry for not telling me that you were married. Before you could say anything else, I hugged you and kissed you lightly and explained that I had already known that you were married. I said I wasn't looking for a commitment, but that I liked you and I was very lonely. We both wanted good companionship, so I couldn't see the harm for us to see each other. And so began my first affair with a married woman.

We did not have that much in common, but that did not stop us from nurturing each other in some sense of need. You were not deep, but I wasn't looking for depth then. I wasn't looking for some miracle woman yet. That path had led me to disappointment more than once. With you still being attached to your husband, I was also safe from commitment. It was the right arrangement for me at that time. We could both enjoy a trivial amount of happiness between us and not have the pressures of a full-blown relationship. In some ways, I did miss more meaningful conversations. I had an insatiable appetite for the understanding of the whole. But I accepted you as you were.

For over three months, we saw each other at least three times a week. Weekends were off-limits for you because of family obligations. For me, weekends were off-limits so as not to disrupt my exploratory excursions into oblivion. I considered myself now as only a weekend alcoholic, if there was such a thing. Each visit, I would listen to you talk, listen to you vent about what bothered you at home and with your life. You stated that you usually kept your feelings bottled up and were so glad to find someone to talk to. I understood that, for inside was where I had kept everything recently. I was your sounding board, and although you urged for me to reciprocate, I could not. My concrete wall had been built back up with thicker mortar this time, and nothing was getting through for a while. That miracle woman that I denied looking for would have to break it sometime in the future when she found me. I can only hope that you understand this whenever you reflect back on our time together. It wasn't that I didn't want to share with you; I just couldn't.

We never went out in public. The town was small and also full of your relatives. You didn't want to jeopardize what was left of your marriage, and I didn't want to give you the wrong impression there was more to us than there really was. Our entire time together was spent in my tiny apartment. I regretted later that I hadn't been with you when I found the big house on the other side of town later that spring where we would have more room to roam and more room between the walls in our sexual frolic.

We had a routine. You would share with me what had happened in your life since your last visit. We would smoke a joint and then head to the bedroom with a bottle of wine. There wasn't even a window or a ceiling light in that microscopic bedroom, barely enough room for the bed. On my nightstand wedged between the wall and the headboard was the only source of light, the red glow of the alarm clock screen.

We had sex on every visit. We shared it as a means of appreciation to each other, an answer to our loneliness, and a brief escape from our real worlds. You were old-fashioned, and variety was not a big option for you, and I sensed not to push it. You had never been with anyone else but with your husband, and I should have felt honored. What I did feel was lucky. Lucky that I had walked over to your table at the right time, for you had never even thought of an affair before. And now I was your retreat. I did feel some guilt, but did you not have a choice in what you were doing? I began to reflect on the advantages of having someone to count on and the advantages of being with someone on a more permanent basis, but I was comfortable with the arrangement we had. It didn't matter if you ran home at midnight as if your car would turn into vegetation after the witching hour. It didn't matter I didn't see you every day. It was relief for me to find some form of self-discipline in my mixed-up world and be content with only seeing you some of the time.

But I did rely on your visits. A few hours of companionship, some instant sexual gratification as a prescription for stress release without any commitment, gave me a key to remain on level ground, giving my brain a rest from the constant dwelling of everything else I was missing from my life. I gave no second thought about how I was interfering in your marriage. I thought that was your responsibility. I was not forcing you to come, but indirectly, I was telling you not to stop. I couldn't place how I felt about you. I hoped that you were more than a pastime. I did not want to become that shallow.

The night that you told me that your husband was getting very suspicious when you disappeared three evenings a week was the turning point of our cozy and convenient relationship. This news made me think of the repercussions that would happen, not so much that I might have to face the ire of a jealous husband, but what else you might have expected from me. We did not have enough in common to take any further steps ahead together. It would have been unfair to both of us and would never have worked. To scare me even further the same night you told me about his interrogations about where you were going, you said your lame answers would increase his doubts and he would start following you. You expressed fear that he might eventually find out if you were actually going to ceramic classes. I didn't say it, but I thought you could have been more original than that. But the worst scare you gave me was after our routine carnal performance; that night you told me that you loved me. I knew in the way you said it that I was in too deep. I did not feel the same way about you.

And so for the first time in my jumbled existence, I caught a glimpse of myself as those haunting words from my past came rushing in. Maybe I was a user. It left me scrambling for answers, searching about where my moral values had gone. I was lying with a married woman and felt no guilt. Had I always looked for excuses to escape my faults? Had I always twisted situations around that I could find valid and just reasons for immoral and selfish ways? Inductive reasoning can be turned many ways when diluted in alcohol. Could simple desire override my own guilt?

You lay beside me in all sincerity and told me you wanted more in such simplicity and innocence that I began to hate myself. I did not want to hurt you. But it did not stop me from breaking it off with you almost immediately. At the same time, I was not ready to give up the convenience of having you show up at my door at various intervals for our heated affair, to share our teddy bear holds afterward, and then having you leave at midnight, temporarily satisfied and with no accountability. "I had no one to replace you with" was a sickening but constant thought, and instead of doing the right thing, I simply waited for your next visit, then your next visit, and then your next visit.

I felt an abomination growing inside me though, and the more you visited, the more I was eroding inside to the point that I no longer felt right about us at all. My last shreds of decency prevailed.

I finally realized this wasn't about survival and need at all. I was only patching over some enormous craters of loneliness with some casual sex. And although it felt good, you were trying to take it another step. I couldn't. So with a few rays of intelligence shining through the shrouds of pain that covered my soul, enough light from the core permeated through to let me do the right thing.

I will never know how much hurt I caused you the night we skipped our routine and did not find our way to the bedroom. Count on me still wanting to, still thinking about it, but instead I played the wise philosopher. I tried to be as kind as I could after I started by telling you that I didn't think we should see each other anymore. I asked you to think about what was best for your kids. I degraded myself, explaining that I was no good for you. I told you there was no future with me and you had to think of your own well-being. I pleaded with you to talk things through with your husband. I was wrong for you, and I had nothing to offer. I had found it easy to list my faults, probably because most of them were true. However, I was genuine about my concern on what was best for you. At the same time as I rambled on to you, I was mentally undressing you. What a mess I had become. Some counselor, I would have made.

You didn't cry as I spewed carefully chosen words to ease any pain of breaking up with you. Maybe I was a fool for not at least giving us a chance, for not understanding that sometimes love has to grow, and not flashing neon lights at first sight. But instead I felt a burden lift from me when I knew that now I didn't have to compare you to my past. I had enough baggage with me without adding you. I would have needed a bigger suitcase.

I walked you to the door that night well before midnight. There was a sadness emitting from both of us. I knew that in spite of all the righteous crap I had just spilled to you, I was going to miss you. I still wanted to take you into the bedroom. We embraced for a long time, and that only increased my desire to have you again. And when I kissed you good-bye, my tears were already flowing. I watched you walk away, and the dark murk of loneliness flooded back through me like thick cold mud.

I did not sleep that night. My whole past life was flashing fragments of disorienting pictures on the screen inside my forehead. I lay in pitch-dark, with a dark-colored towel thrown over my alarm clock. I prayed that night, something I had not done in a while. Although probably grounds for a label of clinically crazy, I knew someone, something was listening. It was a sensation, like a tiny revolving sphere just above the heart, and I knew there was a guiding force in there. But I didn't pray for me that night. I prayed for you.

I still think of you from time to time. Through the winds of the downtown gossip mill, I found out that you did separate from your husband for a couple of months. But you returned to him after he agreed to joint counseling, and you have been with him ever since. I was so glad to hear that. Some of us actually can find long and true relationships with a little hard work. Some of us can work out our problems and make the effort needed. I am sincerely grateful that you were one of them.

CHAPTER 9

Bernadette:

I am at a loss about how to describe the relationship we had. Whatever it was, I still am left confused and can't decipher the meaning of it all. Our short time together reflects only sexual encounters. Can we label it as the convenience of sexual pleasure? My own personal masseuse of the erotic kind, a liberated woman of the fullest kind, a wannabe hooker, or simply someone temporarily filling in the gaps of loneliness in her own life. Were you as lonely as I was and only looking for bits and pieces of amorous fancy? In any attempt at describing it, the results are the same. We had a strange arrangement.

I first saw you at work on the factory side of my company, where the operation was seasonal and mostly women. Part of my job was to support the factory with production supplies with my forklift and to take finished goods back with me to the warehouse. Coming from a farm originally, I was a natural at driving equipment. I could operate a forklift with my eyes closed. With my eyes free, I used them to scan the female workers around me, waiting for any signs of mutual awareness and the potential for meaningful eye exchange. I wasn't quite sure why I had picked up this habit, except for amusement and to kill the monotony of the day. I had vowed never to show interest to any woman at work. I would have been too shy to approach anyone at work, anyway. There was no consumption of liquid courage on the job, and I had a reason from my past that I wanted to ensure no involvement with a co-worker. I made a pastime of studying the women around me anyway, and if for nothing else, I liked women.

This was how you and I first made eye contact. At first it was quick glances in my direction, which soon graduated to you looking for me when I drove in. Within a few days, we added a smile to our acknowledgment to each other, but I was never so brave as to say hello. It was not until later, when Allan, my co-worker in the warehouse as well as a new friend, approached me with the news of your interest in me. Allan was going out with someone he had met in the factory, rather successful with his endeavor in the same exchange of glances with a girl named Debbie. The two of them had become quite an item, and as it turned out, she had also befriended you.

It was disbelief at first when Allan explained what Debbie had requested him to ask of me. He began by saying that you had just moved here from the Maritimes, that you were married but your husband was in the service and couldn't join you for another six months. Debbie didn't feel that it was right for you to spend so much time alone and that you should get out. Where she got the idea that I would be the perfect candidate, the perfect gentleman to escort you on a date with only the purest intentions of only providing you with company, was beyond me. For many reasons, I told Allan I didn't think it was good idea, but thanks anyway. That wasn't the right answer for Debbie, and she confronted me in the factory herself the next day.

It was easy to see what Allan saw in her. She was pretty, pleasurable, and persuasive. Somehow she could see through my loneliness. When she told me that she could see that I was honorable and trustworthy, she had already won me over, as she explained to me that all she was really asking me to do was to keep you company and show you a good time as a kind of an escort. She repeated what Allan had already told me. You were happily married but were alone in this town and would be for a while. I was to be your friend, and that would be the extent of it all. I finally agreed thinking I had nothing to lose and it would be harmless, especially the way Debbie had explained everything. We were going on a double date.

I rushed off to the warehouse after she was done talking to me. I had fallen behind since it did take her awhile to convince me. I drove away thinking what a great girl Debbie was and felt an attraction to her. I was one mixed-up character. Nothing a high-pressure firehouse to the brain wouldn't have taken care of. It certainly needed a good cleansing.

And so the next Friday night, after a long day at work and your smiles now displaying a different meaning, I found myself on my very first double date. We chose a bar outside of town, not wishing to bring attention to ourselves. You turned out to be very outgoing, totally different than in the workplace, and how you cleaned up! You bubbled with fun. I could not help but feel some of the dark depression drawn from me when I was with you. You could actually make me laugh, and I had forgotten the last time I had done that. You made me feel so comfortable right away. When I noticed how close Allan and Debbie were and how good they seemed to be for each other, my attraction to her was put in proper perspective, and she became a good friend, right alongside Al. We had a great time that night, and even though you didn't drink that much, I still found myself pouring back double shots of rum and Coke. I didn't get drunk, but it took enough of the edge off me to actually dance with you. You were a great dancer, and I followed you with great precision, and we practically danced the night away. It had been a long time since I had danced with anyone. I was well-behaved that night, no staggering, no slurring, no missing memory. I remember every detail and every piece of conversation we shared. Maybe Debbie was right. I could be a gentleman with a little bit of polishing.

We closed the bar, and then Allan dropped you off first at your apartment. When they picked us up, the order had been reversed. There had been many instances of synchronicity from my past that could not be explained by coincidence alone. But I was still in total amazement and almost shocked when they pulled up to the very same duplex apartment my ex-wife and I had rented when we first married. It stunned me for a moment, and I almost kissed you on the lips instead of the expected gentlemanly peck on the cheek. You thanked me for a great night and vanished through the side door that led to the upstairs apartment. I wondered if it was still decorated in the same funky wallpaper that I had originally put up.

I lay awake that night thinking about you, how you had lifted my spirits, how you had made me smile the whole night. I knew I wasn't supposed to think of you as anything else but a friend, but you had aroused more. I was now obsessed by the way you had made me feel, how you had taken away the weight of my loneliness. That Saturday morning and well into the afternoon, I drank beer after beer as I fought over the idea to go and see you. After a private boxing match with myself to figure out what to do, I lost. I first convinced myself upon knowing that you were married that I should stay away. I also had a recent memory of almost destroying someone else's marriage over my own selfishness and petty needs. But I kept remembering both Allan and Debbie say that you were not just married, but happily married, so you would stop me if I got stupid. You would remind me that we were only friends.

Late that afternoon, I walked to your duplex and climbed the stairs to your apartment; and after standing outside your door for several minutes, still debating with myself, I knocked. You opened the door and were clearly surprised, but cheerfully invited me in when I said that I couldn't stop myself from wanting to see you again. We talked for a few moments, and I told you how much fun I had the night before; and in the middle of a sentence, I invited you back to my house. You did not hesitate and said you would be glad to. I was thrilled because I was very uncomfortable in your apartment. The wallpaper had not been changed. It was much later into our relationship that I explained to you the strange coincidence of which apartment you had chosen over all the other ones in town. It was also the reason that all our time was spent at my house.

We walked back to my house together, and I was proud to let you in. I had recently moved out of my claustrophobic apartment into this older but spacious home. So recent in fact that except for Allan, who had helped me move my furniture with his truck, you were my only guest so far. I had been ecstatic when I found out how cheap the rent was and even more amazed when the landlord agreed to rent it to me. With three bedrooms upstairs and one down, he thought the house was too big for me. He was worried about parties and renting it out to a single guy. Sometimes my pathetic look served purpose and called for pity. He rented it to me against his better judgment. A little honesty worked as well, as I explained that a house like his could get my life back on track and I shared with him a little of my unfortunate past. So sympathy and pity allowed him to take a chance on me.

I fed you strong drinks that night, not that you needed them for any purpose that I needed them for. I found myself opening wide open to you. As the night progressed into the morning hours, when I thought it was the right moment, I reached over and kissed you. Our conversation had been personal, but not deep and philosophical as I sometimes ran with. I was comfortable with your simple outlook, your optimistic view of life. I had absorbed it and let filter out the release of a thousand thoughts in my head that weren't anchored down with the prospects of some profound meaning. To be awake and not have to think that I had to figure out the exact physics of the universe was a pleasant change. I enjoyed our night of unsophisticated exchanges, and I soaked in it with unusual worry-free notions.

We made love that night before we were even aware of what we were doing. It felt like the right thing to do. We did not think about it. We only felt. We made love over and over again, well into Sunday night in an extraordinary volume of various positions as if we were experimenting with each other. You were wild, fantasy above imagination. I had not expected it from you, from someone that on the surface showed such non-complexity. There were sparks between us, but they were only physical. It felt uncomplicated and joyful, yet with a connection I had not quite felt before when the heart wasn't totally involved. Casual sex, one-night stands had always left me with some sort of guilt or remorse, as if the lack of meaning tainted me, and I would only look for a rapid exit to anonymity.

You felt so different. I wasn't trying to run out the door before dawn (dawn had already passed), wasn't trying to hide, nor was it entirely physical. You were my companion, just not at some deep emotional level ready for upheaval. We became lovers without the exact meaning of love to be determined. At times when I was alone, after one of our marathon evenings in bed, I would go back to reflecting and wonder what we were really doing. And later one night, I couldn't help myself and asked you.

Your answer was a bit disturbing to me at first, but then I found it funny. You told me you were using me and said it as a matter of fact. There was such casualness in your voice when you said you loved your husband and we were just having fun, acting out fantasies. And as bizarre as it sounded to me, I continued to have fun. We would exchange glances at work and playful smiles that no one else on the planet knew the reason why. It was our secret, and I would keep my promise to never tell a soul. I had delightful reasons not to.

Sometimes when we took the time to talk before we hit the mattress, you would share your plans. Your husband was going to join you in six months after his first stint in the army. You both wanted to live in Ontario, and you had moved here ahead of him to at least get established. You went on to say that you loved him very much. I had no choice but to ask you what you were doing with me. You always repeated the same answer. You were just having fun, just acting out some fantasies. Before I could even fathom what you were telling me, you would act one out and carry me away from my frame of thought. Fun it was.

We were companions, and if this physical connection was part of our companionship, I wasn't about to put up any arguments. If sex with me was your way of filling the void until you were rejoined with your husband, I was happy to oblige. There were things from my past that could see the logic in your thinking. I was far from chauvinistic, and if this is what it took for you to cope while you waited, I could understand that in essence you weren't really being unfaithful. On the contrary, you were simply biding time with a friend. So was I letting you take advantage of me? I did not have the deep emotional value invested, which would normally leave me in devastation, so it didn't matter. Our situation was not harming anyone.

We understood the rules ahead of time. They weren't quite spoken, but there was a silent pact between us that knew the boundaries of our relationship, of our arrangement. We were never seen together, not only to preserve your future, but your reputation as well. I understood it all. The house continued to be the epicenter of our interludes. You would not come to my house on your own, insisting I call first whenever I wanted to see you. It was a gesture to not interfere with my life, an unnecessary one, however. We shared many nights together, long steamy marathons of sexuality, as we both escaped our own realities basking in each other's pleasures. We were addicted to each other and the sensibilities we shared.

Whenever I was feeling down, sensing that oncoming rise of depression to the surface, I would call you, and you would come prancing to the door.

Sometimes we wouldn't even get to share a weather report between us before we were tangled in the sheets. I was only vaguely aware of the disassociation of love, the adoration of past relationships, the emotional barometer that usually measured the intensity. There was an obvious affection between us, but it was the quick gratification that really nourished us, somehow both physically and emotionally. It scared me sometimes, especially the day that you were acting out a fantasy and telling me that you felt like a prostitute. In a normal relationship, those words would have thrown me into a frenzy, wondering how shallow I had become. A brief visual of you with someone else had flashed in front of me when you had said it, but I couldn't think it possible when you were with me almost every day. I could not see you wanting to jeopardize your friendship with Debbie that way even if you had the time. Your secret was safe with me, but not necessarily with someone else. It wasn't difficult to see that Debbie was very morally bound, and if she found out about our true relationship, this friend-with-benefits act, she would be in an uproar. She would have eaten you alive at the very notion of promiscuity, of infidelity. She did accept us as being friends together. But that was because she trusted us both.

We nurtured each other for another six months. Sex between us had become as important of a staple as food. You were so at ease. But there was one night when you almost went into a panic when my buddies from Westlake had dropped in unannounced and caught us in the bedroom. They didn't believe in knocking first. After the initial compromising position they found us in, I took you aside and explained to you that it was fine. They were from out of town, that they had no connections to Hilbury, and there would be no repercussions to them finding us together. You relaxed, and we partied with them as boyfriend and girlfriend. But there were repercussions, only they were mine. After my friends had left that night, I was suddenly flushed with the awareness that I did have feelings for you. You had become more than a playmate to me. Whether I had too much to drink or it was the joint I shared with our company, I was overcome with emotion. I rambled on about how much I cared about you, how much you meant to me, how good we could be for each other. You put your finger to my lips and stopped me cold. We made love on the living room floor that night, and it was more intense than ever.

I woke up the next morning in remorse. Not from drinking, but from my inexcusable burst of sudden emotion. It had to be suppressed, and quickly. My success was limited, but I did manage to put my feelings back into perspective before you ran away from me. I didn't call you for a few days, never going more than two before. To work out the mixed feelings, I worked on some more liver damage, and unfortunately, through the week again. I had almost curbed that habit. Heavy drinking was to be only on weekends. The more I numbed myself in alcohol, the more I was able to numb the memory of that burst of emotion. It was an unusual performance, when most of the time alcohol did the opposite. But my fear of losing my playmate was enough enticement to actually go against my own personality, and I put my feelings toward you in a back drawer of my mind and sealed it. Don't ask me how.

When I next called you, it finally registered that aside from our physical relationship, you actually did help me learn to function alone. Ever since my teenage years and especially after getting married so very young, I had lost my way in coping when not with someone. I thought I could manage on my own now. I was only addicted to your talents and the way you would relieve me of any problems I was thinking about. My desire to have sex with you had become as addictive as the beer that consistently beckoned to me from behind the refrigerator door. So we moved back on track and carried on with our physical relationship, our stress relief of the sexual kind.

I fell back into the original purpose of it all. I could stifle my past—leave it neatly tucked away in memory banks out of reach for now—and not feel subversive sentience, shut out rumination, and most of all, drown out self-pity instead of drowning in it. You bought me time to breath, time to appreciate the small things in life that I had totally lost focus on. I had finally stopped dwelling on the past and allowed myself to heal some of the scars of my heart that still sometimes oozed. I was in dormancy and yet not in a destructive manner. I can't give you all the credit for that brief period of peace, but I have no doubt that your influence had the most to do with it. But like everything else that came along in my checkered past, it always found a way to end.

It was very close to Christmas, and you were careful not to tell me until after we had made love. Lying next to me, you announced that you were leaving Hilbury. Your husband had called and had decided that Ontario was too far away and that instead he wanted you to go back to New Brunswick. With his decision came the fact that Ontario was also not for you. You were already laid off from your job, the season over. You were joining him for Christmas and had already started to pack. You were going home, your real home. It was not real heartache I felt. It was more an emptiness. Like the echo in the bottom of an empty beer bottle. But I knew there was also a deeper void that wouldn't surface until later in the distant future when I dialed the phone to get no answer.

On our last night together, I told you how much I was going to miss you, and you only said that I would be fine. You crawled on top of me and made love to me one last time.

From the pale burn of the street lamp, yellow light filtered though the shades of my bedroom window. It spread back the darkness enough for me to see the outline of your body. I was shocked to see such noticeable detachment over your face. Had it always been that way? Had you been somewhere else the entire time we shared this room? I fell asleep soon after, caring not to think about it. When I woke up a few minutes later, you were already gone.

I called you two days later, and your phone was already disconnected. You were permanently gone. I spent Christmas alone that year. Only this time I wasn't self-loathing, wasn't drenched in self-pity. Sure, I was depressed, but that was now part of my makeup. But now I had some degree of hope, a desire to improve myself, and a confidence in myself that I would find a path to a promising future. I would find independence, and in your own subtle way, you had helped me with that. I knew this wasn't going to be an easy task, with a brain full of memories that all pointed to my brief interludes of happiness dependent on others. Love thyself was never a concept that I could grasp with any firm hold.

But it was starting to register that if I was to be any good to anyone else, I had to be good to myself first. I had been too busy in my past stuck in the philosophies of the meaning of the cosmos instead of concentrating on what everyday life had to offer. I needed a fresh start that did not include my past. I knew that was never going to happen, but even as a perplexed task, I had to try.

You had at least given me enough insight to find enough confidence to do so and see past the bottom of my next drink. There are many things that I am thankful for when it comes to you. I cannot list them nor am I sure I completely understand them. You did light up in me the strong hope of a new beginning and a new outlook. You placed in me some positive feelings that I could get through life on my own. Perhaps you were sent by way of an answered prayer to drop in and give me a wake-up call. Or maybe you were just another coincidence. Either way, I thank you. May your life be filled with joy and your marriage last forever.

CHAPTER 10

Mary Beth:

My enigmatic Mary Beth. You contributed more to my distrust and apprehension of the intentions of women than many combined. You accomplished this without any perception that you were doing it. Whether in massive confusion in which direction you were going or in your own unmentioned distrust of me, it doesn't matter now. The damage was done. All the signs of a disturbing relationship, as we went through various intervals, were there when my obsession with you began to rule the way I thought, the way I functioned. Our paths crossed several times, and I was far away from stable most of those times. Maybe you recognized it and only felt sorry for me. The question has always remained unanswered for me.

Each time we met by coincidence, you fed my belief that we were eventually destined to be with each other. It didn't start that way. I first met you in the pool hall, the pregnant girlfriend to Keith—motherhood at the ripe old age of sixteen. He had just turned eighteen and was floating through life alongside me in the same rubber raft, oaring through a sea of drugs and alcohol. Only he wasn't wearing a heavy coat of inferiority complex and a suit of bashfulness.

Keith and I became good friends by default. He was one of the few that could hang out with me on the street all night. Most of the others had responsibilities or parents to answer to. So did Keith, but he had very lax rules to follow, which meant no curfew and no need to explain his whereabouts. I am not sure where he met you, but I first laid eyes on you when he brought you into the pool hall to display you, to show off his trophy. And a trophy you were. I was instantly attracted to you, as would every other breathing male. As well as I knew Keith, I could assume that although trapped in a life of partying, he was searching for a life of responsibility and stability. It would be another year before my chance at that.

How I envied him. Your girl-next-door portrayal and your appearance of innocence left you with a glow that sent me into wishful and covetous thinking. You were together less than two months when he got you pregnant. The two of you decided to rush into marriage in a supposed effort on his part to do the right thing. To honor my friendship and our many shared sunrises on the street, he asked me to be the best man. I found an outdated suit at a thrift store, finding a frugal way out of this unexpected expense. A few weeks later, we were standing in the city municipal office in the middle of a civil ceremony. I flanked Keith, and his sister was to your right. I stood there, my eyes wandering around the stuffy room, pretending to listen to your vows, still envious.

We drove back to your parents' house for a late-afternoon lunch, and I followed behind Keith's van in my Barracuda clunker, which I had only recently obtained, but long enough to rearrange the shape of some of the fenders. Your parents served us wine with the meal, and I tried not to guzzle it. I avoided looking at you. I now had to work on stamping out any attraction I felt for you, and it wasn't going to be easy. There was no reception planned, and it had been decided that a few drinks at the Vista Inn would be the extent of your celebration, the same windowless rock-and-roll bar that I would court my own potential bride a year later.

Only a handful of friends and family were invited to this bizarre wedding reception. You chose this particular saloon because they never checked for identification. Underage drinking was the norm there, and Keith and I were already regulars, our hangout whenever we ventured out of Westlake.

I do not remember much of that night. I had guzzled a bottle of brandy that I had hidden in my glove compartment on the way from your parents' place. I was nervous and had to take the edge off. None of our group danced, and the main courses of your reception were a variety of liquor shots and a bowl of unshelled peanuts. My first introduction to tequila that night was of no value to my memory banks, and I faded in and out of blackouts to the events of the night. I woke up in the backseat of my car the next morning, still in the hotel parking lot with no recollection of how I got there.

Except for a couple of visits to your apartment, I saw very little of you after your exchange of wedding vows. I went back to my partying and left Keith to attend to his new life. It was well after your son was born that my visits became more frequent. I had met Melissa by this time, and the four of us started to spend time together. My attraction to you now was well-balanced, and my feelings for my fiancée relieved any remnants of the gravitational pull I felt toward you. We had a group of mutual friends, and together, we had many memorable parties. The memories of those parties are now overshadowed in both of our minds when both of our marriages eventually failed. Long before my marriage ended, yours had already disintegrated. Keith had returned to his old ways of drug use and it took over any rational behavior that he had accumulated with you. He became physically abusive to you. Not only did he lose you, but he also lost my friendship. I could find a way to condone many things, but hitting a woman was not one of them. Nor could I watch as he hit a road that led to self-destruction. I had my own road to self-destruction to try and stay clear of and couldn't help him with the right directions.

After you broke up, I would run into you from time to time because you never left the Westlake area. Not six months after your split, you were living with another guy from our small town. I vaguely knew him, but I remembered him as a scrapper and having a hair-trigger temper. There were holes in the pool hall wall with his name on it. I said nothing.

Then there was a long period where I never saw you at all after a sporadic series of quick hellos and quick how-are-you-doing conversations. After that dry spell, I bumped into you coming out of a grocery store, and you had startled me. I had been walking down the street, going nowhere in particular. Melissa had just left me, and I wasn't doing well. We talked in length that day, and we stood in the middle of the sidewalk, almost oblivious to the pedestrians that had to walk around us. As I watched the sunlight hit your auburn hair and as I looked into those piercing hazel eyes, a rush of my original attraction flooded in, but I was able to suppress it. I had stronger feelings elsewhere to distract me, new profound dreams and experiences enveloped around a certain cottage.

I shoved my feelings about you into a crevasse once again. You told me that day that you were happy now and realized that Keith had been a mistake from the start, but there was something in your expression that didn't make your declaration of happiness ring true. Regardless, I had to believe you. I gave you a hug and wished you all the best. That was the last I saw of you for three years while I went off to fulfill my destiny that turned out to be one of slow self-destruction.

The next time I saw you was at the same bar that you had your obscure wedding reception in, the same bar where I courted my now ex-wife. I was coming off the tail end of two losing relationships almost simultaneously. I was drained of ambition, of dreams, and my previous goals dangled in the winds of internal turmoil. Even common sense levels had been marred by a blend of emptiness and disappointment. Only the forces of addiction controlled me then, and aside from keeping a job, I had too much idle time and no guidance away from my demons.

I came back to the Vista Inn on a regular basis. It had many memories for me, and it was the best place for me to wallow in self-pity and to try and count how many more steps I had left on the stairway to reach rock bottom. That night, I had put back on my thick beer glasses; and because of the blur of my vision, I almost didn't spot you sitting in a corner at the far end of the room, barely noticeable through the dismal lighting and crowd.

You were with a girlfriend that I did not know, and at first, I watched carefully to make sure no one else was with you. My normal shyness was already submerged in a drenching of alcohol, and with inhibitions drowned in it, I did not hesitate to approach your table once I established there were only the two of you. My heart warmed as you expressed not a surprise but a look of earnest expectation when seeing an old friend. You jumped up and gave me a big hug. But this time I was unable to suppress the attraction I had stuck in that crevasse dedicated to you. That simple hug released all the buried feelings I kept away from the first time I saw you. You introduced me to your friend, and she said hello, but she eyed me cautiously with an extended look that was warning me that she was there to protect you.

It took little prodding to have you tell me that you were not getting along at all with your boyfriend and you were planning to end it. Whether it was the atmosphere of the Vista Inn or your trust in me as a friend, you settled into an open conversation with me and flooded me with information of your problems. We were almost ignoring your friend. I shared a quick outline of my own screwed-up life, but I focused on what had been happening to you. You talked so freely, so openly to me that I felt part of you, and any suppressed feelings I had about you were now bubbling over, already finding cracks into the barriers to where I kept my vulnerabilities. Alone and desolate and now sitting by you in the right light, I had no reason not to let down my wall. You were next to single, or at least planning it, and you were unhappy.

We talked past last call and were in danger of being carried out by the staff if we didn't leave. I did not want to wait, could not wait another three years to see you. I asked you to go for coffee with me. Your friend did not want to go, and although a bit perturbed, she left on her own with that same stern warning in her eyes that told me that I better be good to you.

In the coffee shop later, the zeal toward my desire to express my attraction to you, my released feelings now on the surface for the right moment to exude them into speech, left me anxious. If I had met you sober that night, I would never have acted, certainly would never have said anything. Instead I bubbled over in romantic gibberish, and it flowed out of me in such a rush that it seemed I was afraid my inhibitions would put a blanket back up any second. I held your hand and flooded you with sentimental comments and a complete admission to how I felt about you since I first saw you. In normal circumstances, the words would have sounded too smooth, like the strategy of a wolf in sheep's clothing. I was not hustling you but simply telling you how I felt. Those sensuous eyes looked back at me, those piercing eyes that could penetrate any guy's heart, and told me that you might feel the same way. But the only real thing you did say to confirm that was when you agreed to come home with me.

My new hometown was Hilbury and no short ride. But I drove home without weaving and with absolutely nothing on my mind but you. I did not get you past my front door when I grabbed you and kissed you, sweet sensuous kisses. I led you down the hall to my bedroom, and if you were uncomfortable, the heat of the moment had hidden it from me. There was a touch of awkwardness. We were rushing this, but when I thought of how long I had to hide how I really felt about you, it did not seem that way. I undressed you in the darkness of my room, and we cuddled beneath the sheets. Once in my bed, it was a signing of commitment to go all the way. I did blame myself later for pushing you into it and ate guilt for a while. There must have been some way for me, some source of willpower inside me, to have just been able to lie beside you that night, to slow things down, and to prolong the sensuality and anticipation for a future encounter. To caress and know each other first before the ultimate step. My extreme desire to be with you overruled willpower, and instead of keeping my longing for you inside, I went inside you instead.

It was awkward between us; neither one of us were really prepared for each other. There was no magic, no heavenly bliss in an explosion of emotion and sentience. We lay there afterward in silence, and I was already regretting that we hadn't waited. You wanted to smoke a cigarette, and although I never smoked in bed, I made an exception that night, and we both lived and did not become another burning-mattress story. You didn't want to stay and asked me for a ride home. Only then did I remember that you had a boyfriend and a child waiting for you at home. We got dressed, and what should have been a glorious night left us both embarrassed and slightly ashamed. The ride back to your country home was extremely quiet, neither one of us really knowing what to say. I concentrated on getting you home safely because by then I was extremely tired. When I pulled up to your house, you insisted that I do not turn into the driveway. I let you out on the shoulder of the road with only a quick good-bye, and I barely had time to ask you if I could see you again. You replied with a *maybe,* but added *not* for a while.

I drove home cursing myself, and as if to augment my own discord, the sky opened, and a torrential downpour of rain pelted against my windshield. I screamed out loud and asked the interior of my car why I couldn't have waited. I swore at myself for my inexcusable actions and kept talking to myself all the way home, preparing for my days as an aged and seasoned drunk. I spent the next day wrapped in remorse and regret, feeling like I had taken advantage of you.

Your *maybe* turned into three months. Not that I didn't look for you. I spent many nights back at the Vista Inn, hoping I would find you there. I drove the streets of Westlake in a futile attempt to spot you somewhere. Several times I drove by your house but dared not stop. It was you who found me.

I had pulled into the corner variety store just outside the main street of Westlake to feed my disgusting cigarette habit. I was on my way to Lexington to spend another night in the Vista Inn, looking for you, looking for something. When I came back out the store, you were leaning against my car. My heart skipped a beat at the sight of you. Even after three months I could still feel tingles running through me at the prospect of talking to you. You gave me a hug and asked how I had been. I could have told you the truth, but you probably sensed it anyway. I was a mess in my desperate search in finding a way to crawl out of the depths of my depression. Your hug alone even lifted me a notch although it had only represented friendship.

We talked in the parking lot for a long time. Again our conversation was open, and it represented the trust of good friends, but I could sense that you were holding something back. You seemed to be protecting yourself, and I thought later that I wished I had learned to do that. You explained to me that you were leaving your boyfriend and were just waiting for the right opportunity to do so. He had become more abusive, and when you said that, I thought I could see a faded bruise under your eye. Again I said nothing.

The factory where you worked had slowed down, and temporary layoffs were frequent, and you couldn't afford to be on your own yet. You didn't want to ask your parents for help, and you had your child to consider. Your pride seeped through when you went on to describe your child's athletic abilities. In spite of your languished relationship with your boyfriend, you said he was a good father figure. I didn't want to hear that part, for what was wrong with me? As you continued to talk, I interrupted you to ask you to go with me for a couple of drinks. I thought it was a harmless request, but then you broke out in tears and started to cry.

I stood there flabbergasted and helpless at first until I was finally able to pry from you what was wrong. You started to sob and then, through broken words, told me that you were pregnant again. I could only hold you and tell you that it would be all right. And without thinking and without any inhibitions, I shocked both of us when I said that I would take care of you. This was not some sadistic form of hustling, beyond any acceptable moral value. There was something innocent about you although your path had so far shown the opposite. I was most sincere.

My words had caught you so off guard that you were speechless. But they were delivered with such unorthodox timing and inappropriate atmosphere that you only had to politely reject my offer without the appropriate amount of fear that I would be hurt. Had I expected you to simply fall into my arms, a knight with a dull armor? You went on to say that you just needed time alone to sort things out. I ignored you and, in those selfish ways of mine, asked you to at least spend some time with me that night. After some coaxing and a couple of pleas that fell just short of getting down on my knees, you agreed.

You left your car in the parking lot of the store, and we headed for none other than the Vista Inn, unsure if I still had a moral compass to guide me. We both decided that discretion was still needed, although we never really spoke of it. We sat in the lounge area, where it was even darker than the dim light of the main floor, away from the main crowd. There was bound to be someone that would know us, and you weren't ready to announce anything, not ready to feed the rumor mill. In your condition, you drank no alcohol. I made up for it and was pouring them back as if afraid the bar had a limited supply.

You were so easy to talk to, but there was much I couldn't tell you. I couldn't discuss how recently I had turned to meaningless relationships to fill a void but then only stretching it wider as a result. I could not tell you how I hurt inside when you disappeared after we had made love. But I had to show you something, had to make you at least aware that my feelings for you were genuine.

When I reached across the table to hold your hand, you didn't pull away. I felt the electricity run through your fingers and up my arms, like tendrils reaching for my heart. I was enveloped with the same warmth that filled me when I felt deep love. Except for that night when I spilled all over you in drunken speech and had convinced you to come back to my place, I had always hidden my feelings from you. You couldn't possibly really know how much I felt for you. You didn't know it was more than my loneliness that drove me to you. I had always seen something in you but had always kept it inside, way inside where it could not be acted on. In spite of my addictions and selfish ways, all moral inclinations arose to the occasion when it came to you. But now I did not see the purpose when the strength of those relinquished feelings was not going to go away. I had already broken the moral barrier with you three months before.

Across from my table was now the sudden answer to my prayers. Not just the answer but also the path to everything I could do right this time. There were years of hidden fantasies with you, buried in such proper perspective that they weren't even at dream level. But now they were bright and vivid and fueled by double shots of rum at unrestrained pace. My jumbled brain was telling me that alcohol was the key in capturing your heart that night once and for all. It may have been the key to vocabulary to convince you, but it was also the key to the door of vulnerability. Instead of blurting out a line of bleeding confessions, how deep my feelings were, I asked you to dance with me instead. This was just as difficult, and I was both nervous and apprehensive. I had sworn to never dance on that particular dance floor again. It was a shrine to my ex-wife. But I found myself on that sacred dance floor when you said yes. It was a very slow dance, and we swayed back and forth rather than any rhythmical steps. For a moment, I was completely liberated, as if chunks of cement had just rolled off my shoulders. You looked at me with those piercing eyes, and I turned into mush. All the work of the previous months brushing layers of veneer over my heart, a shield to any more pain and poison arrows, shattered and dispersed from one dance. Without an ounce of reservation, I kissed you in front of our audience, not caring who else was there, and was lost in a swirling tunnel of intensity and feverish emotion behind the complacency of my closed eyelids. Discretion was gone.

It was a kiss wrapped in all my past relationships into one meaning, my whole journey compressed into this one spotlighted dance. I was on the very top of the world that night, a field of energy extracted from you, evaporating every dark corner of my existence. I can only keep repeating if you had only known how much you meant to me that night, how much I really felt. It translated into the future, our future. Too caught up in the moment, not once did I consider that the power of that kiss was not mutual. You had done nothing to show me otherwise.

A couple of drinks had turned into a couple more and so on. More double shots of rum and Coke, yours minus the rum. I could not let go of your hand, as if letting go of it would take away my energy source and I would wilt away. Your eyes alone sent some telekinetic force throughout my entire bloodstream, forcing my heart to pump faster.

I drove back to your car that night, weaving only once in a display of spitting stones from their proper place on the shoulder of the road, the only interruption of the vibrations still flowing through me from the effects of double rums and double-piercing hazel eyes. I was in a comfortable vacuum, that neutral part of the brain that was usually very hard for me to find. My whole body felt like it was enveloped in sensuous clouds, and that euphoric feeling one gets when first falling in love had filled the cavity of my chest.

When we arrived back in the store parking lot, I shut the engine off. Without thinking, I reached over and kissed you, trying to deliver to you some more of the tenderness swirling inside me. I did not ask you to come home with me. There would be no rushing this time, allowing time for the magic to broil. I had to do this right this time. I wanted to bathe in this new sense of energy pulsating in me and not jeopardize my chances with you on the cheapness of rushing to the sheets. This time it would be glamorous in the pressured way of anticipation. The power of our torrid kisses would carry us to future desires.

You waited for what you thought was the right moment and told me that you should go home. I understood. You had a son that would be sleeping but still waiting to sense your presence. I asked when I could see you again, and you said that you would call. That brought my brain out of neutral, and I was already concerned that you wouldn't. I made you promise, and you did, but you followed by saying to just give you a couple of days. I gave you my phone number, and I agreed with you that I shouldn't call your house. We said good night after you found a polite way to pry your hand from mine, which I had clamped on to in a desperate attempt to prolong the night. You waved to me as you pulled out of the parking lot, and I sat there long after the red glow of your taillights were swallowed by the darkness and the settling of the morning fog. I fell asleep on my couch later, missing the sunrise by a few minutes, and dreamed of you. And in that dream, I told you how much I loved you.

That week, I rushed home from work every day to sit by the phone and wait for it to ring. Each day, my alcohol consumption increased to help cure the boredom of staring at the phone and listening to its silence. By Thursday, I was going to work with a hangover, compounding the pain of disappointment. The clock had lost its momentum as I continued to sit next to the phone, debating but knowing I had agreed not to call you. I did not have your number anyway, and it wasn't my right to disturb your household. When I combined all this with the depression that lurked in every corner of my thinking processes, only the pacing back and forth throughout my house kept me from going insane. I had fallen for you, and there was absolutely nothing I could do about it.

How I had allowed myself to fall into this trap so easily was beyond my reach of understanding. I was obsessed with a woman who I thought had given me indication that we had the start of something special. But had she truly, or was I reading what I wanted it to be? My insides were corroding, my sense of dreams and direction fading into oblivion, overpowered by sadness and substance abuse. All my hopes now relied on you, and you weren't even there.

Friday night I wore trails though my house, back and forth through each room, my head ready to burst from anxiety. I would sit by the phone for moments at a time and then walk the rooms of the house, popping the caps off beer bottles and pouring them back like water. Each minute was eternity. I could hear each second of the clock ticking and the long spaces in between the moving cogs. Each minute increased the intervals between ticks, and I kept waiting for time to stop altogether. By midnight, I was drunk. Thankfully I held on to enough threads of common sense not to leave the house.

The effects of alcohol were already interfering with any rational thought, and my obsession with you would only create chances of very poor judgment. There was a mental fistfight going on inside my head, one opponent wanting to go look for you, the other wanting to stop thinking about you. Two previous impaired-driving charges mean nothing to someone who is already impaired and can't reason with consequences. I knew that if I ever got caught again, I would be looking at jail time. I knew I would come out a vegetable. Imprisonment would cause more brain damage than twenty acid trips combined. I could only assume that I escaped my teenage acid trip relatively unscathed. Iron bars, on the other hand, would prepare me for a role in a zombie movie.

By three in the morning, when I finally accepted that the phone was not going to ring, a knockout punch from the rational opponent of my fistfight won; and I passed out on the couch, dreaming of turning into a carrot and caught on top of barbed wire fences. It was almost noon before I woke up with a heavy head and a heavy heart. All the alcohol from the night before had done nothing to alleviate the compulsion that drove me to want to see you. Several drinks later, poured into an empty stomach, the only thing that mattered in my meager existence was to find you.

In the bottom drawer of my dresser, I found the bag of amphetamines I had stashed in a rolled-up sock. This was an emergency supply, but with my chest about to burst from anxiety and no energy to do anything about it, I popped two and hopped into the shower. By the time I had a few more drinks, the sun was already reaching the western portion of the sky, and I pointed my car toward Westlake.

I had no game plan and instead drove by your house three times, taking a longer scenic route each time, hoping the warm air would arouse some common sense. The dirt roads filled my nostrils with dust rolling in from my open windows, but I was unable to filter any logic from that. I was beyond obsessed. This was insane. Each time I drove by, I would slow to a crawl meaning to pull into your driveway and then, at the last second, drive away instead. Each time I would try to come up with a different explanation for the second vehicle parked by your house, one other than it was your boyfriend's car. My heart was now racing from the effects of the amphetamines as well as anxiety. I pondered over a hundred reasons for an excuse to walk up to your door and knock on it, and every one of them did not fit logic or legitimacy. I couldn't jeopardize what stability of your own you might hold behind your walls. What would you have thought of me?

So finally, with no set direction or plan, I was off to the Westlake watering hole to give my car a rest, to give myself a rest. I usually avoided that place like the plague, for what used to be my bar was now claimed by my ex-wife and her new idea of love in the form of a red-haired idiot. I prayed they wouldn't be there. My prayers were answered. There were only a few acquaintances that I knew there, and the rest were probably tourists from the surrounding campgrounds. It was crowded and noisy, but I pushed through the crowd and found a small table in the far corner with a single chair. A country band was playing, and the lyrics of the song that was currently playing reminded me of a suicide march, music so depressing it added to my own sadness. I ordered a pitcher of draft beer and drank like a camel at an oasis. I was soon on a second one when I was now more than ever determined that I needed to talk to you. If your boyfriend answered, I could hang up.

Scrounging up a quarter from the bottom of my pocket, I headed for the pay phone in the lobby. I dialed information and asked for a listing of your married name to no avail. Racking my brain for your boyfriend's last name was futile, as I had only heard it shouted out in the pool hall once and had no reason to file it into memory. I had more success remembering your maiden name, flashing back to your parent's mailbox from the day you were married. It was comforting to know that not all my brain cells were fried. But after successfully finding your phone number, which indeed was listed under your maiden name, I wasn't sure I had any left that night or I wouldn't have called you.

There was no answer the first time, and that should have been my clue. Instead, I called again moments after and let it continue to ring again. The lobby door swung open as a few patrons went to leave, flooding the lobby with the bar noise inside. I plugged my free ear with a finger and then heard your sweet hello, only it wasn't really that sweet; and when you realized it was me, your tone was one of perturbation. My thoughts were instantly transformed to how stupid it was for me to have called you. I apologized profusely, but explained that I really needed to see you. You said you couldn't and you couldn't talk. You wanted to hang up, and I begged you to talk to me just for a few minutes. You repeated that you couldn't, and I was aware enough to understand that your boyfriend might be standing nearby. I asked if you could at least meet me tomorrow, and I breathed a huge sigh of relief when you said okay. I quickly gave you directions to the exact spot in the campground where I would be. What better place to be with you than the best place for me to fathom the ability to relax. That piece of land was dedicated to me. You agreed to meet at noon and hung up without even saying good-bye.

I stepped outside to breathe some air. The small lobby had started to cave in on me. I should have left then. But I still had a half a pitcher of beer at my table, and if nothing else, my frugality wouldn't allow me to waste that. A group of people stood in a circle on the sidewalk, passing around a joint. Marijuana was always normally known as a social drug, and it was soon passed to me without warning. I hesitated at first, but accepted it with the memories of its soothing effects beckoning to me. The recollection of the paranoid effects that I almost always felt when using it escaped me, and I foolishly stuck around as they lit up a second one.

Later, back in the corner of the bar, the music now enhanced, I could feel the beat of the drums echoing though my veins. At first I was relaxed, and after all the anxiety I had just put myself through, it was almost relief. But then my mind started racing in a thousand different directions as it normally did with the onset of paranoia. I began to feel that everyone was watching me, and I was suddenly self-conscious of sitting there all alone. I heard laughter around me and wondered how many people were actually laughing at me. I was on the verge of panic attacks as the crowd seemed to push toward me, and I felt the serpentine squeezes of claustrophobia.

I guzzled down the remains of my pitcher and ordered another one, thinking that the alcohol would counter-effect my stone. I concentrated on the stage, watching every string of the guitar vibrate, separating every chord, every note. The lyrics of the present song were uplifting, and it was not some sorrowful ballad, and I was able to continue to focus on the stage rather than the crowd. The crowd faded around me and then dispersed into the equivalent importance of furniture and decor. I had beaten the paranoia.

I staggered out of the bar before last call, a feat in itself when I usually took pride to be one of the last to leave. Whether it was sheer exhaustion or a shred of leftover common sense, I went to sleep in the back of my car instead of trying to drive home. It was still dark when I woke up, and although still drunk, I decided to navigate my chunk of metal home and hope for the best. At eight o'clock in the morning, I woke up on my kitchen floor with a few aches, no memory of how I got there, but still in one piece. My car was parked at an angle to the driveway with the front tires resting in the lawn. I wondered what in the hell that weed had been spiked with.

It was times like this that I was sure there was some guardian angel looking after me and at least be guiding me to physical safety. But I still had no inclination that I should be thanking such an entity. It seemed too trivial a matter to be thankful to arrive home safely. Too enveloped in self-pity, any insight to celestial help would interfere with the picture of futility in my life. It was quite feasible that the glimpses of hope and the dreams I held on to were derived from the connection of a higher power. But by not acknowledging the guidance of the cosmics, I could rely on sheer luck and not have to think about the long term. The only thing of importance that day was preparing for my meeting with you anyway.

    I layered the bottom of my cooler with cold beer and a bottle of wine and threw a towel on top of it, a trick I had learned in order to conceal it. More than one park warden had fallen for it when he would randomly check coolers on the beach. Although it was legal to drink on a registered campsite, it was not legal on the beachside of the park. I made several sandwiches and placed them on top of the towel and threw in some wilted fruit I had in the crisper of the fridge. I tossed in a bag of chocolate chip cookies and two plastic cups, and my picnic lunch was complete. As I was placing it in the trunk of my car, I remembered the rosebush in the backyard. So to add the romantic touches to my packed gourmet meal, I cut what I thought was the prettiest of the flowers and placed it in the cooler.

    The ride to the park that morning was accompanied by you. Your vision was displayed in the windshield, in the passing scenery, in the sky. I mulled over the forthcoming afternoon with you, preparing speeches, configuring different ways to woo you. I was now completely convinced that you were my only salvation. You would come with a shovel to bury all my past and to also dig the foundation of my future, our future. In return, I would give you anything you wanted, do anything you wanted, and make you the happiest woman on the planet. In spite of all the dangers of planning complete dependency on you, before thinking of any repercussions to give every ounce of my being to you, it was already too late. I had already begun to worship you.

    That day was extremely warm for that late in the summer, but my hatred for winter never allowed me to mention discomfort when it came to heat and humidity. My favorite spot on the grassy slope that stopped abruptly to the clay cliff, which was slowly eroding over time, was unoccupied. Below were the sandy beach and the low roll of the lake toward shore. Behind me out of sight was a boardwalk that I tried not to think about. I had spread out the frayed quilt, which had become a permanent resident of the backseat of my car, soaked in personal memories; and beside it was my cooler, which held its own set of memories. I was an hour early, but wanted to claim my ground, so much reminiscence in this very spot that I had squatter's rights. This twenty-five-square-foot plot was mine. It was at least mine metaphysically, regardless of how many other footprints were on it.

While I waited for you, I emptied out a beer into one of the plastic cups and hid the empty underneath the quilt. I lay down and watched the cumulus clouds form into various shapes of animals and faces, a pastime from my childhood that I had spent hours at. I had almost forgotten how peaceful I could become here, reaching brief periods of tranquility in such natural states by tuning into the magnetic pull of the Earth. I could feel its gravitational path around the sun as I had so many times before, lost as a teenager, oblivious to any other living soul around me. This was the real thing. There were no hallucinations or chemicals to explain this phenomenon.

The hangover I woke up with that morning was gone, a flush of genuine euphoria flowing though my veins. I was sorry I did not come here as often as I used to. I had lost focus on the esoteric value of my trances and the hypnotic effect of the lake. I pitied city dwellers that never leave the city, stuck between their brick walls and concrete existence, never given a chance to experience this feeling. And as I lay there, I began to think about how I was going to share this experience that afternoon with someone I was now convinced I would spend the rest of my life with.

I never wore a watch, having had no use for regimented time, except for the responsibility to get to work on time. But because of my many summers in this very campground, I could come close to the exact time by the position of the sun. When I started to snap out of my mesmerized and meditative look at my surroundings, I realized it was long past noon. It did not concern me at first as I amused myself with the profound sensations I felt, surpassing and suppressing any emotional upheavals I might have felt earlier. I poured another beer into my cup and, soon after, another and switched my attention to the people gathering around me. This was essentially a family park, a natural reserve of sorts, and catered to the tranquil needs of a family bond. My peers and I certainly didn't treat it as such as teenagers, but we had the park wardens to keep us in line when our rowdiness got out of hand.

I watched the families around me, the giggles and the ease with which they simplified their lives in various forms of disentangled fun, sometimes as simple as the toss of a Frisbee or the splash of a water pistol. There was a gnawing envy in me. I had this once, and I had thrown it away. This very existence had saved me from self-destruction. It had provided me with the ladder to climb up society's plateaus and carve out a life of happiness. When I lost my wife and daughter, I had lost myself as well. I had grown so tired of these repeated paths of regression, tired of following paths that led to instability, that I craved with fixation a family lifestyle to return to.

On this peaceful Sunday afternoon, with now only a small sense of concord between the vibratory pulls of the water below me, I waited patiently for you. I waited for you as my beacon to my return to family life, my security and stability to a normal life again. I waited and I waited and I waited some more, tracking the path of the sun as it found its way by repetition to the western part of the sky. Pangs of anxiety were beginning to pick at the lining of my stomach like open ulcers. My sense of peace was gone. The laughter of children running in and out of the water, splashing in the waves and then running gleefully back to the protection of their parents' arms, wasn't cheerful to me anymore. How I missed my daughter, how I missed my wife. No! It was you that I missed. My hopes and inspirations, my guide to a mended soul, my consequential love of life.

A lone seagull shrieked just above me, momentarily diverting my attention from the family below me. I looked back at the couple with the two young kids and kept taking the husband out of the equation and substituting myself in his place. I visualized myself sitting by the beautiful long-haired blonde, her hair flipped back by the soft breezes as her young toddlers ran around her in circles, joyful innocent laughter and frolic. I turned away. My mood had changed and swamped me with sadness. I felt the sting of salt on my chapped lips and knew it was my tears. After all this time, I still cried at the drop of a dime whenever a raw nerve from my past came along. That should have been me down there enjoying the benefits of family life, not up on this hill wallowing in self-pity and loneliness.

I convinced myself that you were busy with something and you were only running late. My whole afternoon had turned into a mixed bag of emotional melancholy. A roller coaster between the paradisiacal atmosphere to the suffusion of my surface levels of depression, creating a potion of ardor that I could not quite fathom. But the result was a deeper loneliness than I had already felt and a rush of despair.

Where were you? My patience was down to very thin layers. I was now in the most desperate need to share the experiences around me. I had the depths of my heart to give you and to share this harmonious knowledge that came from this piece of ground I lay on.

The sun was setting, and I still foolishly held out hope that you were coming. Only a few families remained as a night feeding of mosquitoes were already sending their scouts out. My beer was gone, so I opened up the bottle of wine, shaking it first to send the plastic cork into the sky aiming it at Venus, the first light of the night sky. The park warden had already passed by twice, and I did not expect him back, so I made no attempt to hide the bottle. Instead of using a cup, I drank long swigs right out of the bottle. The sky had lost all its blue luster, and the black velvet was slowly penetrated with pinholes of sparkling light as the stars took their proper place. I was soon alone.

The campground far behind me cast out a few noises from the campers that were staying past the weekend. The beach had become desolate, the wind dying to still air, and a full moon began to break on the horizon, its reflection on the water the only thing to distinguish the eastern horizon. I sat there, miniaturized by the splendor of it all. Dazed by senses of cosmic connection, I stared up into the skies. And as if needing an answer from above first, I finally realized that you weren't coming. I guzzled the rest of the wine and lay down on the blanket. In a continuous effort, I swatted mosquitoes as they stopped in droves for a drink, and it wasn't my wine they were interested in.

Tears started to roll down my cheeks again involuntarily, but I wasn't sure why. Disappointment maybe, but why heartache again? You hadn't truly led me to believe that you wanted me to be your knight in shining armor. Besides, I wasn't exactly a knight, and I was not shining. Had I fabricated any connection I thought we had? I didn't think so, but maybe I didn't articulate how important you had become to me. I fell asleep under the stars and whispered to the heavens that you weren't coming.

There were no dreams to interrupt my sleep that night. I woke up around what I thought was midnight. I did not have the same aptitude of telling time with the night sky. Parched and covered in welts caused from an unlimited drilling process by thousands of tiny bloodsuckers, I arose in pain. I packed up the remnants of my picnic, replacing the shriveled sandwiches and rotten fruit and the wilted rose with empty beer bottles. The sandwiches and fruit went into the trash can, and the rose went over the cliff. I ate the bag of cookies during my ride home to settle my stomach and replace some depleted sugar.

Monday morning came fast, as they normally do. I was tired, but with a heavy workload, the day whisked by, and it wasn't that long when I was back on my couch letting the well-worn cushions swallow me. I began to think of you again, busy enough at work to keep you temporarily in the shadows. Now back at home, you were in the forefront of my thoughts once more. I wanted to call you so badly to see what happened, but the phone remained cradled. My heart still wanted to chase you, but I finally convinced myself that if we were meant to be together, it would happen.

That next weekend, Paul dropped by unannounced and insisted it was time for us to go barhopping. You knew Paul in passing from the pool hall. I agreed without any debate, not only to deter my thoughts of you, but also to wash a week's worth of warehouse dust from my throat. I had not drank that week in some strange effort of reprimanding myself for my foolishness of waiting for you that Sunday. We drove to a town where no one would know us and, without need for recall on how to do it, got wasted. I met up with a stray (as I callously call loose women) and used her to try and forget about you and, as unlikely as it sounds, to forget about me.

You never did call. But I still clung on to the idea that you eventually would. I still drove by your house once in a while to see both vehicles still parked there. I refrained from calling you again, even when I was wasted enough to do so. I still held on to ribbons of hope that someday we could be together, but I was able to suppress most of the obsession. Life went on.

I replaced you with a gypsy from Lindros and put my heart and soul into her instead, only to be pounced and trampled on later. I was destined for a life of pain, but kept swearing I would remain strong and eventually find true independence. But you weren't done interfering with me in any sense of accomplishment with that. My feelings for you might have been buried, but they never vanished.

It was over two years though before I let you play with my heart some more. Not once during that time did I run into you, and it was an eventual "out of sight out of mind" that helped me cloak you. The next time I ran into you, I was much better off financially, but emotionally and mentally, I was still a mess.

It was only a chance encounter that found us together again. I tried to avoid the bars scene at that point in my life, but sometimes when the loneliness became unbearable, I would fall into old habits and head for the bar for a night of studying people. Bars were the only real social atmosphere I knew. I wasn't ready to join any church groups. I tried to avoid the Westlake bar, still wondering about the chances of a plague in there, but the Vista Inn I could still cope with. But it also caused me to be flooded with memories of my past. They would rush in like kaleidoscopic flashbacks in no particular order, mixing past anguish with flickers of pleasantries, and stop in the center of my mind's eye and would do nothing to aid me in my agony of the present. It was like wallowing in a huge pot of lost love and dreams, yet drowning in decaying swamp compost at the same time.

If I was finally going to bury the past, it would not be done by sitting at center stage, running old movies past a retrospect screen, and living inside it. After many torturous weekends soaked in the pathos of the Vista Inn, I switched venues. Two blocks from the Vista Inn was a dark and dreary country-and-western bar that reeked with stale beer and stale urinals. Most of the people in that bar were depressed, and it was easier for me to feed off them. There were too many merry people in the Vista Inn, and my filtering system would deny any vibrations I felt from them. Depressed people were an easier blend for me.

This place had such a depressing atmosphere it almost made me feel good about myself. There is truth behind misery likes company. Even the bartender had a permanent scowl that made one think his mother had just died. The waitresses had failed to learn what a smile was, and their tip jar corroborated this fact. The smoke was usually so thick that you didn't have to light your own, simply breathe in the air, and the whole place was enveloped in another haze that wasn't quite visible but probably just as dangerous as the carcinogens of the manifested one. It was coming back from a session of this therapeutic air that I spotted you.

In order to get home, the quickest and safest route was through Westlake, and a left turn at the only stoplight in town was a direct route to Hilbury. At this intersection, on the left side of the street, was still the bench that I had spent many nights on as a kid. As I approached the intersection, I looked over at that weathered bench and had to do a double take. You were sitting on it, the pale light from the street lamp enveloping you like a celestial vision. I could see that you were crying and paying no attention to your surroundings. My heart skipped a beat as it always had when I saw you.

I parked my car around the corner and walked over to you. I wasn't drunk, but I wasn't sober either. The fact that it had been over two years since I had seen you wasn't quite registering. It was your tears that mattered, and I was coming armed with comfort. It was very late, and there wasn't another soul around. You were so distraught that you didn't even notice me until you felt the bench shift when I sat down beside you. A look of disbelief and shock grew on your face as if you were looking at a ghost. You muttered my name at the same time you wiped your tears away with the sleeve of your jacket. When I asked if you were okay, you burst into tears, and I instinctively put my arms around you. After a few moments, you were calm enough to talk to me. You had gotten into an argument with some new male friend, and he had left you behind in the bar. Your details were sketchy, but when I gently pressured you, the problems of your night were shared.

You had left your boyfriend the year before, finally having to put a restraining order against him as the physical abuse had worsened. You were dating someone new and, as creatures of habit with small-town limitations for entertainment, had gone to the Westlake bar for a typical Friday night outing. You were talking to another guy, and your date became extremely jealous and flew into a fit of rage. It surmounted into a shoving match between the two of you, continuing into the lobby and out onto the street. I had bit my tongue before I said that you sure knew how to pick them. I had to think of my own background. I told you I was going to get you boxing lessons for Christmas, and that was enough levity for you to giggle, and any tension between us that might have been there evaporated.

You continued to tell me that you left him standing in the street as he shouted obscenities and derogatory remarks not fit for anyone. In a low voice, I said that you didn't have to tell me anymore and asked where your car was, only to find out that he had driven and you were now stranded. I asked where your child was, and you corrected me. It was now children. How could I have forgotten that? You now had a little girl, and I saw you light up with pride as you told me. I could feel it from you, and I thought of my long lost daughter. You went on to tell me that your kids were with your mother for the weekend.

The proper thing for me to have done then was to offer you a ride home. Instead, I asked if you would come to my place. When you didn't respond, I tried to clear any ill intentions you might have felt and told you that I just wanted to talk, catch up on an old friendship. So two confused souls headed down the highway.

We ignored the fact that we hadn't seen each other in a long time. You opened up to me like a broken dam and flooded me with details of your recent life—an abundance of details about your kids and your parents, your job and your eventual breakup with your boyfriend. I couldn't tell you that I was really only interested in the breakup; that he was finally out of the picture. Where I was going with that thought so quickly, I couldn't say either. You said that you had only just recently started dating again, looking for some kind of life outside of your children, but they would always remain top priority.

When the subject turned to me, I had fewer details for you. I did tell you about Leslie and how she had taken me for a ride and taken my ride too. You chuckled on the way I described it, but did mean it when you said you were sorry to hear it. I did explain how I had focused on my work and my goal to buy a house. The rest of my shenanigans, I left out. There was no need for you to know that I was probably still messed up as ever, still an emotional wreck, and still no sense of a balanced life.

When we arrived at my house that night, I poured us huge glasses of wine. You asked for coffee instead. We sank almost past the springs of my couch, now completely worn from my countless nights there in lieu of my bed. I hated my bed when I was alone. When our conversation began to trail off, I turned the television on, preparing for the eventual exciting program of off-the-air test patterns. I was careful not to sit too close to you for fear of scaring you off. I wanted so desperately to hold your hand again, to feel that magnetism rushing up my arm that I so vividly remembered. Instead, I whispered to you how much I had missed your company. I wanted to say that I missed you, not your company, but

I wanted to make sure I was not overbearing in the slightest. Your eyes were already closed when I said that, and I wasn't sure if your uh-huh was in agreement or a new way of saying good night. You were snoring softly, and I loosened the grip on your coffee cup and had to stop myself from kissing you on the forehead. I covered you up with a blanket and awhile later dozed off on the other end of the couch with one less frown line than normal.

I arose to daylight and made fresh coffee before you woke up. It was very apparent that you were uncomfortable, and you turned down my offer of breakfast and asked for a ride home instead. I did not hesitate for I did not want to jeopardize any potential chances I had with you. We said very little on the way to your place, and it wasn't until I pulled into your driveway that I found enough courage to confront you. You had given me no indication that you were going to invite me in, so I asked if I could call you, and you said yes. When I asked if we were good friends, you said of course we were and kissed me on the cheek and left me with a trailing thank-you behind you. I watched you walk into the house, and I stayed parked in your driveway for several minutes, holding on to that vision even if it was only of you walking away.

A week passed, and every waking moment was interfered by my refreshed thoughts of you, a constant presence in my mind. The suppressed obsession was awakened, and I wanted to be with you so badly. Each night after work, I would pick up the phone and put the receiver back down before I dialed your number. I was afraid I was rushing things, afraid that you weren't ready to talk to me yet, that you wouldn't be home and then I would have to wonder where you were.

Friday night came and, with it, the usual compounded anxiety. I paced my house back and forth through all the rooms, fighting an inner voice that was pressuring me into calling you. Another voice was telling me to walk up town and kill time in the bar. Deep in thought, I jumped when the phone rang. My heart skipped, thinking it could possibly be you, but knew it could be anyone. When I picked up the phone, my heart not only skipped some more, but it also started to pound when I heard your voice. I was so nervous that I was shaking, lacking words to form coherent speech. At first I couldn't grasp what you were asking. When I finally focused on the fact that you had just asked me to go to an amusement park a few hours away from us, I had to breathe before I said yes. You said it would just be the two of us, that you were leaving the kids with your mother and just wanted some time to enjoy yourself for one day. It wouldn't have mattered because I sincerely wanted to meet your kids, wanted everything to do with you. I told you that I would love to go. You were picking me up bright and early, and you were driving. I thanked you three times and, only after I had hung up, realized I sounded overzealous.

I do not have to describe the day to you. If you have never shared any of the depths of my feelings, you did share some kind of connection with me that day. We both loved the thrill of roller coasters, and we joined in a mutual escape of the real world. You were so genuine that day, as we strolled though the park so carefree, and I felt the constant warmth when you held my hand. I could feel the sparks, and I held your hand like a lifeline, even on the scariest curves of the multi-twisted roller coaster. There are many memories to sort out in my life, but the good ones are limited. That day at the amusement park stands as one of the most pleasant. It surfaces many times. The slow gondola-style boat ride through the water canals of the horror house stays with me like a photograph that never fades. You had reached over and kissed me ever so delicately and so full of meaning that sometimes when I watch a love scene in a movie, I feel that kiss. It will come with me when I leave this planet.

You seemed so happy and content. The nervous giggle I remembered when I first saw you had returned, and there was a bounce in your step that defied gravity. I soaked up some of the energy flowing from you, and it spread light into my core that was shrouded in darkness most of the time. You overwhelmed me, and you were probably every man's dream that day. The confidence that pulsated off you and was transferred to me fueled me with such optimism that I couldn't remember holding so much at once.

The crowds had been sparse, and it was overcast. But to me the day was as bright as if a tropical sun bore down on us. There was no gray to me. We stayed late, absorbing every moment of our getaway. There were shows and thrill rides and corn dogs and cotton candy. We had the innocence and the joy of children. By the time we were ready to leave, we were exhausted.

I held your hand for the long ride home, fearful that if I let go, it would all end. I watched the countryside go by in the window, and my heart sped along with it in such grand velocity of gratification. The music from your front speakers permeated through me, and I was floating on clouds, a sense of peace I had thought I was destined to never feel again. There would be no letting go of you this time. And it felt so real I had no choice to think that the feeling had to be mutual. This was a natural feeling, not some repertoire of my mind to replace the past. You had won me over so much that day that there was nothing I wouldn't do for you. So much for protectionism; so much for my defense mechanisms to block the sources of past pain.

The long ride home was not long, as I fought back time wanting the day to last forever. It was dark when you pulled into my driveway. I asked you in, and you whispered next time. We kissed again, and I almost needed stitches when I bit off those three powerful words before they flew off the tip of my tongue. I did not want to scare you with such a flippant-sounding profession of my love for you. Something told me you weren't ready to hear it yet. Instead I stood in the driveway and watched your taillights disappear in the dark once again, only thinking about how much I loved you instead of saying it.

I called you the next morning, feeling rested and healthier than I had in quite some time. After many rings, you finally answered it with a cheerful hello. You were so friendly on the phone that my disappointment was not severe when you turned down my invitation to come over and let me cook supper for you. I never cooked for myself, and although I wasn't an award-winning chef, I could cook and was looking forward to laying it on thick in an effort to impress you. You explained that you were going to pick up your kids from your parents and were obligated to a visit to your daughter's paternal grandparents. I had overlooked that different fathers meant different extended families. I should have known this, should have been prepared for all the complications with you. But it didn't matter. I had fallen for you and was relying on you now, that having you let me down again was not a matter for focus. You had me hooked now and, whether you knew it or not, had great power over me.

I could not think of the possibility that you didn't feel as strongly about me. It would only jeopardize the dynamics of the optimism you started to roll in me, a bright look at the future after so many pitfalls could not be imperiled. I thanked you again for the previous day, sounding like a grateful child, and blurted out that I missed you already, not really expecting reciprocation and not getting it. You told me you would call me soon.

And then the days of waiting began again. Each night after work, I would wait for the phone to ring. I was my own worst enemy. In my mind, you had again already become my salvation, my sense of worthiness, my motivation. I did have my goal of financial gain as a sideline, but that was such a slow process, not only promising minimal levels of success, but its original purpose was also merely to escape the confines of poverty. It would not begin to fill my void. It was only a distraction from my misguided soul-searching, my search for love. Now that I had become so quickly dependent on you, anxiety was snowballing. Planning, wishing, dreaming about us, visualizing being with you every day compounded my loneliness and made my empty house unbearable. My need for you was exploding into exponential levels. That relentless pounding of desire had come close to driving me insane more than once and was definitely no deterrent to control my drinking habits.

Short-term relationships were meaningless and had only temporarily masked any pain. They only resulted in hurting me more and hurting any unlucky woman who got caught in my selfish ways of using them. I did not mean to, confusing it with a means to stop my own insanity. It was the long term that I searched for, that I could thrive on. The romance, the caring, the true deep feelings that brings stability, and the prospects of a bright and committed future with someone, that was the true goal.

In essence, I barely knew you; but it did not stop me from thinking you were right for me, that you were the one. Despite of my track record, I was willing to walk another tightrope, with you as my safety net. Maybe I should have asked you if you were ready to take on that responsibility instead of assuming you had already volunteered. Before I fell in love with you.

The phone continued not to ring, and if it was a waiting game to see who would call first, you had already won long ago. I did wait until the weekly revolution to another Friday night. Weekends had always brought out the worst of my loneliness. I caved in to my internal pressure halfway through the night and dialed the phone. I listened to the long and aggravating rings and almost hung up before you answered. Your voice was tired. You were cordial, but I had to drag conversation from you. I was expecting more. Hearing you drool on the phone and exclaiming your profound love for me, loud enough for the neighbors to hear, would have sufficed. Instead you turned me down again when I asked if I could see you. Your kids were sick. I told you it didn't matter, that I just wanted to see you and I would help you with your kids. You laid out a line of other excuses, and my disappointment was so high that they didn't even register as what they were. I accepted them. I had no choice.

The temptation to go out and drown myself in alcohol was abated by my determination to find the patience needed to wait for you. I would give you space for now if that was what you needed. You were too important for me to screw it up by pressuring you. It would have helped if I knew what you really needed. It would have helped if you had shown me some degree of honesty.

My friends from Westlake called me the next morning, my lifetime drinking buddies, my partners in crime, my fellow social deviants wanting for me to come out and play. They had learned to call first instead of just popping in, when they risked the drinking-and-driving laws not to find me home anyway. Some time with some old friends sounded appealing at first, but then I turned them down with an excuse that I had a date and told them some other weekend in the future would be great. By Saturday afternoon, I regretted it. By Saturday night, I was a mess. Not because I was soaked in alcohol, but because my anxiety attacks had started again. I was pacing from wall to wall wondering what to do. I wrestled with myself and decided calling you was not pressuring you. You were, after all, my friend before anything else.

A male voice answered the phone, and music was blaring in the background. He was barely audible. At first, I went to apologize for dialing the wrong number, but then I asked for you instead. My stomach had a huge knot in it, like someone had hit it with a brick when he told me to wait a second.

I could tell you had been drinking because you were laughing when you answered the phone. Your voice was slightly slurred, but it was also charming as you talked to me in such friendly manners. I waited for you to volunteer to tell me who was with you, and when you didn't, I gulped nervously and asked. You were quick to say that it was just a cousin to your old boyfriend and that you had remained good friends with him. I felt steam developing inside, but it turned to harmless vapor, any boiling process extinguished with buckets of pain, the throbbing twinges of emotional torture.

You sounded so sincere, so assured that there was nothing wrong with you entertaining another guy while I sat home alone. I heard him suddenly laugh, and you chuckled alongside him. We talked on the phone for a long time, and you convinced me nothing was going on. I asked you about the kids, and you said they were feeling better. Twice during our conversation, I asked if I could come over, and twice you told me it wasn't a good idea. There was no mention of getting together later, no mention of how I might be feeling. I should have been bursting with anger, but I was so convinced that you were the cure to all my problems that I was able to numb both the anger and the hurt. We said good-bye, contentment in your voice, turmoil in mine. I went to bed trying not to dwell on what just happened. I tried to quit asking myself how much emotional pain one man was supposed to endure. I tossed and turned until daylight and rose without sleep.

I was now layered in mistrust and wanted to know how I could continue to be so stupid. Did I totally misread our day at the amusement park? Had I wanted you so badly that I fabricated signs from you that you felt the same? Could I ever stop the ripples inside my gut? I withdrew even further back into myself. Another week went by, and I suffered. I wanted the pain to go away. I talked to no one at work unless absolutely necessary. I lay down on the couch each night after work and literally moaned out loud. I did not hover near the phone this time. I did not expect you to call. And with incessant turbulence bouncing thoughts around inside my head at such a velocity that none of them made sense, another Friday night finally rolled around.

I had spent a lot of time that week pondering over what to do. I could try forgetting about you somehow, could let pride stand up for me. There were a few ounces of that left in me, almost an involuntary trait that can never entirely be stomped out of a person. But to give up on you with such a trivial aspect of self-worth, pride listed as one of the seven deadly sins, would be something I dreaded later. It was better to finally confront you, finally find the courage, and tell you where I stood with you. If you backed away, it could not hurt anymore than it already did.

So I stood by the phone, taking deep breaths as if the air itself could fill me full of fortitude. I dialed it, and when you answered it right away, I almost froze. A part of me didn't expect you to answer. You were very friendly and talked to me so naturally. I thought that you really must have no idea on how I felt about you. Had you forgotten? But before I had a chance to fix that, you invited me over. Like a bumbling fool, I asked if you were sure that was what you wanted, and you confirmed my stupid question with an appropriate answer to match. You said you wouldn't be inviting me if you didn't want me there.

An hour later, I was sitting in your living room, nervous and as shy as I would be if it had been our first date. Your children were up, and they were full of energy. They were both beautiful kids and full of fun. I played with them for hours, more because I wanted to than as a means of distraction. I had always been commended about the way kids took a liking to me. Yours were no exception, and they warmed to me almost immediately. I could not help but think that indeed I would make a great father. I looked at you and thought I would make a great husband as well, but I pushed that thought further back. When I considered my past, the truth of that belief saddened me. I brushed the start of tears away before you could see me. I needed to remain strong that night, to show you I wasn't as messed up as you might think. I would show you that I was grounded, solid, reliable, and a potential mate.

As I swirled your daughter in the air, she giggled, and it was almost a mockery of your own. She had the same piercing eyes, and her aura shone with life. I looked back at you, and you displayed the same warmth and care that I had shared with you at the amusement park. You were melting me all over again, and as if suffering from short-term memory, all the pain I had felt through the week was gone. When it came time to put your kids to bed, I asked if I could do it, and the kids loved the idea. I had formed a bond with them so quickly that it was almost surreal. You smiled, and with that smile was my confirmation that it was once again time to tell you exactly how I felt about you, but I still had to find carefully chosen words. In spite of my determination to face you head-on, I did not want to frighten you away.

Later as we sat on your couch a safe distance away from each other, I mulled over what exactly I should say, what precise words would finally work. All my previous thoughts were useless now that I faced the moment of truth. I could not mention the hurt that you caused me the weekend before, for that would erode the pureness of what I really wanted to say. I had not drank much that day, and although my words were coming from deep within my heart without any blanket of liquid courage, they were not quite coherent. You listened intently though as I showered you with sentiment and my oath of complete devotion, the words flowing out, released from storage in a direct path to you. The conversation was one-sided at first as I sprayed out all my caged-up feelings and showered you with every available compliment I could muster. If this was only a string of pickup lines, it was applied so thick you could have laughed. But I had never been so sincere, and whether you believed me or not didn't matter at that point. I had to release it, had to open up the vent of an imprisoned heart. When I was through, you played the devil's advocate, but this was strange because we were the only two parties involved.

You first told me you had little to offer me. As you sat there and degraded yourself, it was the first time that I recognized that you might be struggling with your own past. Your charm and charisma masked it well. You pointed at the back bedroom where the kids were sleeping and asked me why I would want a ready-made family. I explained to you that you and your kids were everything I needed for the stability and responsibilities to succeed in life. You weren't buying it.

I couldn't get you to understand how introverted I really was, and for me to spill my guts to you, to stand before you and admit my troubled past and failures, was the most righteous and genuine signs of my commitment to you. As you carefully listened to my words that suddenly poured out of me in a desperate attempt to reach you, to make you believe how much I had fallen for you, a few of my words got through, for you stopped coming up with reasons why I shouldn't feel that way. Your switch to neutrality gave me hope. When I ran out of things to say, I felt completely drained but strangely relaxed. I reached over for your hand, and we sat in silence and stared at the television. The late-night news had come on, and although we couldn't be described as sharing a comfortable silence, it was far from tense. I had not found many sleeping hours that week, and as I soaked in that familiar electric current I always got when I held your hand, I fell asleep. I did not wake up until morning. I was horizontal on your couch. You had gone to your own bed and were already up making coffee. I apologized for being so tired, and you said it was all right, that you were just as tired.

Your kids woke up soon after and were busy trying to make me laugh before they even had their cereal. Regardless of any doubts you still had, it felt right to me. The only discomfort I felt that morning was my lack of usual reliance on alcohol and the uneasy feeling that this was your house and not ours. The liveliness of your kids and their incessant energy took my mind away from it, and I reveled in their play and innocence. I was afraid to ask you what your plans were for that day. Out of earshot from the kids, I finally did ask and was relieved to hear you say you had none. I asked for you and your kids to come to the park with me, the back of my mind still trying to erase my wait for you there. You made me an extremely happy man when you agreed to spend the day with me.

I watched your kids while you went to town to pick up supplies at the grocery store. I was sure you could pack a better picnic lunch than I could. I was smiling when you returned, and the corners of my mouth hurt. I was not used to smiling. I was going on a real family picnic. I could stick my tongue out at the other families around us, possibly the same ones that glared at me in scorn when I sat among them alone.

I can never describe to you how meaningful that day was to me. To truly taste the life I dreamed of, the stable family life with you at the center. I could have easily married you that day. To suppress all the sophistication of my troubled mind and compact it all into a far corner, even for one day, was nothing short of fantasy, only now it was tangibly real. This was beyond any help to my sanity than anything else on earth could do. The unusual warm weather of another late summer was picture perfect, no breeze, no bugs, no booze. Sure, the craving was there, but here was proof that I could live without it. Well, at least function without it. You and your kids were what I truly needed.

I frolicked at the edge of the water with your kids, the windless day leaving the surface like mirrored glass. Their shrieks of laughter were contagious, and I found myself laughing with them. I had forgotten how to laugh long ago. The beach was crowded with families taking advantage of the last remnants of summer. The crowd did not bother me. In fact, I had a strange sense of vanity. I thought there must be something to this pride after all. I was certainly proud to be with you.

We laughed, we ate, we played, we lived. Those penetrating eyes of yours were even more enhanced by the reflection of the lake. They bore through me like lasers, and combined with your radiant smile, I was glowing inside. I did not want the day to end. But as the laws of subjective time took its course, so did the sun's path across the sky. After a full day of fresh air, the kids grew tired, and we left before sunset. Back at your house, I helped you unpack everything and helped you put the kids to bed. We plunged onto the couch, exhausted ourselves.

The safety gap we left between us the night before had closed, and we sat side by side. I felt our bodies meld together, and as we pretended to watch the movie on the television screen, all my attention was concentrated on the vibrations I felt from you. I reached over and kissed you. I had no intentions of pressuring you into anything. It was a kiss of gratitude. I also had my shyness to deal with. There was no alcohol in my system to conceal the effects of my inhibitions. We slept on opposite ends of the couch that night, time undetermined about when we fell asleep. Knowing that you were beside me was as exhilarating as if I had slept in your arms all night. That Sunday morning, we shared coffee long before your kids were up. And then you casually launched a grenade at me.

You broke the news to me that you were to be at your parents' house at noon for a planned visit. I told you that I would gladly go with you, but you said you weren't quite prepared for that yet. You thanked me and told me how grateful you were for our time at the beach. I wasn't listening. Disappointment had flushed thought and hearing from me. I had looked so forward to spending another day with you. You poured me another coffee, and I accepted it although I normally only drank one. I had enough addictions.

Later, standing at your door after giving both your kids a huge hug, I had difficulty pulling myself away from the door frame. I was delaying every minute before I said good-bye. I fought back my tears, not wanting this new sense of worthiness to end. I looked to you for support, and you gave me a kiss that represented to me your proclamation of our chances at a future together. We agreed that I would see you next Sunday.

I wanted to see you before that. My work enabled me to get through the week, though, without dwelling on you too much. It was busy season at work, and I worked long hours of overtime including Saturday. So although I was constantly thinking of you, I was preoccupied enough to cope with the waiting process to see you again. You had filled my heart to the brink, and there was light inside me. We did talk over the phone a couple of times though the week, and I carried those calls with me. There were no fancy words of romance, quoted stanzas of smitten poets, but you left me content and confident.

Sunday morning did finally come, but also unexpectedly came anxiety. My confidence had started to erode, by a foreboding fear that I might possibly lack all the qualities you were looking for in a man. My insecurities rolled back in from nowhere, as I started to fret over how to prepare for my visit with you. I could not afford to be paranoid, wondering about my own faith in my abilities. The signs were there for success, a slow, steady pace to a long and fulfilling relationship. Why now was I succumbing to the haunts of my past?

I knew of only one way to rid myself of this sudden burst of anxieties—alcohol. At first I was only going to drink a couple of beers to relax me, to calm the nerves. My heart rate was rising and with the onset of a panic attack that was so unexpected, it was more confusion than fright. And then I remembered the dreams I had through the week. Each night, I had fallen asleep full of anticipation of the upcoming Sunday with you. My impulse to make love to you filtered into my dreams and fed my imagination of such high expectations of what Sunday night would bring. I knew my drive; my libido would eventually pressure me into pressuring you to repeat the act of closeness we once attempted, only this time it must reach magical proportions. In my dreams, I was planning the perfect night together, as if preparing for an appointment. Recurring dreams do not leave room for spontaneity.

There were times in my past where my thoughts took on a life of their own, scraping against the grain of the very person I wanted to become. Primitive thoughts would wrap around virtuous reflections, like a stranglehold of creeping vines, and squeeze out the morals. It was ludicrous to think that I could retract these vines by atomizing them with alcohol and make them vanish. I could only benumb them, and so I did. Already in the beginning stages of intoxication, I packed my cooler full of beer and headed for you.

We had agreed on one o'clock. You had told me that you had to go to church in the morning for the benefit of your kids. So when I pulled into your driveway at one thirty, I was expecting to see your car. I knocked on your door just in case, and when there was no answer, I sat down on your concrete porch and began to wait for you. By four o'clock, empty beer bottles were lining up on your step, agitation winning over patience by way of a hundred variations of malignant scenarios about where you were. Blinded by my infatuation with you, guided by my perpetual need to be with you, I squashed each thought individually. By five o'clock, what threads of common sense I had left that could bypass my inebriated brain cells told me it was time to leave. It took until six o'clock to remember that I was leaving at five. Just as I was finally ready to give up and leave, you pulled in beside my car. Your kids rushed out from the backseat and tackled me together in playful hugs almost sending me to the ground. That one act rid me of the entire afternoon's buildup of agitation, frustration, and heartache. Your kids had equivalent power over me, your power running contagiously in their blood and infecting my own. Was I in such dire need for companionship that whatever spell you held over me could not be broken? It certainly rang true when all you had to do was say you were sorry that you were late and I accepted it without question. I needed no explanation about where you were, and my incessant afternoon was answered by being able to spend the night with you.

Later, back in the comfortable hold of your couch, I watched the light from the single living room window fade away from dark blue to black. You lit candles instead of turning the lights on. You put the kids to bed early, and I had wore them out enough in another round of play that they put up no fuss. But they had worn me out too, and I secretly grabbed two amphetamine pills from the bottom of my pocket that I had brought with me. While you were in the kitchen, I brushed the lint off them and washed them down my throat in another gush of beer. Drowsiness was not an option. I had no intentions of falling asleep on you.

When you lit the candles, the dreams I had through the week flashed back, and I was already undressing you with my eyes. I slapped away the thought that this was all that my complicated idea of goals and inspirations amounted to. I couldn't help it if I wanted you. Only later reflections in the light of remorse and an analysis period following a hangover could cut through such simplicity. For now, it was simply that I needed to make love to you. It was of ultimate importance, the highest of priorities under the guise of having to show you how much I loved you.

You came back from the kitchen with snacks, but I was far from hungry. You looked like an angel when you glided into the living room. The scented candles flickered in their crystal holders and spread quivering patterns of shadow and light on your face. Your eyes glistened as if tiny fireflies were blinking from behind your irises. Your body was accentuated by your tight clothes, and your aura appeared bright white and shot off in every direction like small solar flashes. You were beautiful in every sense of the word.

We talked that night. We talked forever and about everything. And when we didn't, the silences between us were now comforting. But unfortunately at my very core, unable to be buried by the effects of the alcohol, was that growing recognition that you did not recognize the disappointment of the nonchalant way that you had stood me up in the past. Tonight of all nights for this to bother me; but my confidence depended on you understanding this. With my increasing desire to make love to you, knowing it was in danger of changing into forceful determination, I had to make absolutely sure you knew how important you were to me. So with my alcohol-amphetamine concoction at full brewing stages, I began to ramble.

I told you how much I suffered when I wasn't with you, how I spent all my waking hours wanting to be with you. I told you how much I loved your kids and how we could become the perfect family. I cannot remember how many different ways I came up with that night to profess my love for you, but I am sure that I must have eventually started to sound like a blubbering idiot. I do remember my tear ducts opening up several times, unable to find the macho faucet to shut them off. You talked to me that night more than you ever had. But you kept the same theme as before when I tried to reach inside you. Everything from you weren't good enough for me; you still had to find your own direction, that you couldn't understand how I would want a ready-made family, especially from two different fathers. You kept saying no one would want the extended family that came with you, with different sets of relatives always in the picture. I knocked down each of your excuses individually, and each pessimistic statement I replaced with explanations of how we could overcome anything, that it was our world to tackle together. I was tireless in my efforts to make you understand, ready to battle any of your defenses to keep me out. There would be no fatigue to stop me from convincing you that we were right for each other.

Subconsciously, I was fighting for my own future. Relentlessly, I picked away at you; and as the night progressed, you grew weaker. By midnight, our ping-pong game of words and various emotional scenarios had slowed to a crawl. My mind was very numb from the day, and the chemical potion sloshing around in my head still did not prepare me for your shocking statement. It was conflicting but not upsetting, and when you surrendered such a secret to me, I accepted it as your surrender to me.

You told me that when you were pregnant with your daughter, you thought it might have been mine. For one of the few times that night, I was silenced. I had never thought of the time frame before. You went on to explain about all the anxiety you had gone through during your pregnancy wondering if it was mine. You had blood tests done later, and the results showed that it wasn't mine but in fact your boyfriend's. While you were telling me this, I had found myself hoping it was mine. I do not regret what I said afterward. I do not regret thinking out loud when I said that DNA test or not, your daughter was still mine. We shared the blood and connection of the heart.

You were very emotional when you told me about your anguish during your pregnancy, never knowing for sure. I cannot be sure if I consciously took advantage of this, but our emotional evening turned physical at that point. It was my own aggression that led the rest of the night, and with such sexually repressed urges and energies amalgamated with my admiration and affection toward you, my mind was bursting at the seams. We kissed softly at first and then, with an overflow of passion, more deeply and firmly. This led us to petting and groping, and you were a willing participant. But you would stop and light a cigarette as if to tell me that was as far as you wanted to go. I was too overworked to let it go. I was very persistent and continued to search for tools to seduce you. In the early morning hours, you gave in and let me dominate. I blew out the candles, grabbed the comforter from the back of the couch, and laid it on the living room floor.

You let me lay you down, and we embraced each other, any unease blanketed by the darkness of the room. My desire for you had reached unbearable levels, all the waiting and the disappointing moments of your evanescent showings now gathered into the momentum of the present. I slowly took your clothes off and, soon after, removed mine. Whether I was expecting some overwhelming act of passion from you or some mystical shroud wrapped around us, I did not feel the magic I had anticipated. But with the buildup of penchant to be with you, it didn't matter. I blamed what I thought was your first lack of enthusiasm as nervousness. In my mind, the most important thing in the world was to physically show you how much you meant to me, how much I loved you. You did participate, and our foreplay was setting me on fire, but I delayed and delayed.

It might have been that delay that flipped the resolve to the ultimate moment of passion into a steep slope tumbling me into a bad dream. As I lay there with you, there was a sudden rush of rumination, flooding my brain with flashbacks, not from leftover residue from a bad acid trip from my teenage years but from a blast of scintillated memories of past sexual experiences. A total mixture of passionate nights, meaningless one-night stands, tear-jerking emotions, insignificant climaxes for cheap thrills. It all swirled into a concoction of dismay and despair, confusing the meaningful with the paltry. All the pain and joy in my life flashed in front of me in kaleidoscopic visions and feelings that swallowed my concentration into an abyss of mass confusion. I tried hard to fight it, to focus on you. The physically driven part of my brain fought back and tried to enter you, but the whole process was shattered.

Instead, I entered into every man's nightmare and couldn't perform. In absolute dismay, I had become temporarily impotent. As I struggled, you tried to help me but to no avail. After several minutes, I gave up in frustration and rolled over beside you in consummate embarrassment and shame.

I wanted to cry, but my own disgust prevented it, and self-abhorrence took over. I must have told you a thousand times how sorry I was. You kept telling me it was all right and that it happens. It had never happened to me! What else were you going to say? You could have laughed at me; you could have humiliated me enough for me to want to crawl into a cave and die. You weren't like that, and I was doing a good-enough job of tormenting myself. I wanted to swear out loud, but the acoustics of my own thoughts were probably fulminating enough for you to hear.

The first signs of daylight were sprouting, the living room windowpanes changing from black to a dark shade of blue, just the opposite of only hours ago. The songs of birds were sending different choruses from the line of evergreens in your front yard. I had to go to work, and time was not stopping for me. Anguish had turned my insides into knots. I turned away from you in modesty and dressed, cursive words still reverberating inside my skull. You slipped on a housecoat that had been draped over the arm of the corner chair and followed me to the front door.

I felt like I was running for shelter, avoiding capture by the horrifying animal of humility. I probably was, but my main purpose was to get to work on time. I had difficulty making eye contact with you, needle points of shame pricking at my skin, the sweat of mortification oozing from my pores. I gave you a hug and then, holding you by the arms, asked you for a chance to make it up to you.

What else could I have said? How else was I going to slither away from what happened? It could have been the mixture of booze and pills, the stress, the anxiety. I could come up with a list of excuses, and it wouldn't really help me grasp it. It had never happened before, so why now?

You kept telling me it was all right and to stop worrying about it. You hugged me, but I couldn't be sure what it really meant. There was also no way of me knowing that it would be the last physical contact I would ever have with you.

I drove straight to work that day, beating the final toll of the punch clock by two minutes. I had finally cursed out loud, my shouts echoing through the interior of the car. The sun hurt my eyes, and there was no palliation from the morning air. Fatigue was my escape as the amphetamines wore off, and waves of depression were of such force that I could barely function. My whole past flickered in and out in a relentless pattern of jumbled memories. I fought to understand how my life had taken so many wrong turns, where all my optimism had gone, why the only thing left was survival instinct to promote my existence.

I knew I had to find the source of inner strength to defeat my own demise. I knew that my external search for something had to come from within, not some futile search for peace and serenity by way of female flesh. I had to start focusing on any blessings I did have. I got as far as "I was alive" and quit counting. My whole day was infected with a muddled mass of conflicted contemplation. If there was ever a guardian angel that helped me before, it wasn't around that day.

A week went by, and I spent each night waiting for you to call. And like so many other nights, you did not. By Saturday night, the turmoil seemed to want to find a way out of my chest by way of explosion. I called you. You answered after a series of long rings, each ring adding to my torment. In the background, I could hear your music blaring again, but worse I could hear the laughter of a male voice. I recognized the voice of the cousin, and you confirmed when I asked if it was him. I asked if I could come over, and you said it wasn't a good idea right now.

Those words were very familiar to me. You were polite, and the charm in your voice always carried the weight of validity, but not that night. And as if hit by an asteroid, I finally realized this was more than a friendly cousin that was with you. Even as my stomach made its journey to the ground, part of me did not want to believe it, that I could still trust your word. When I asked about Sunday, you pulled your son's paternal grandparents visit, from a long list of various relatives, as an excuse to avoid me. And as I felt the ripples of pain rip me apart, I had one defense from being cut to shreds. I had finally woke up.

As much as I cared for you, it was now obvious to me that there was no future with you and probably never was. It was effort for me not to think and then say demeaning things to you over the phone that night. I was able to decide that you were simply as messed up as I was and searching for answers in your own regressive style. I would go no further in blaming you for any of the hurt that I felt. I had a column of other names for that, and you would have to wait your turn for the proper place on my scale of sufferance. I was only fooling myself, however, and I knew that you had done further damage to me. I said good night and hung up before I could say anything that would be regretted later. I did fall asleep that night, for my week had not been restful and I had been working on several insomnia records.

I never called you again. You never called me. It was as if you had never been with me, and if it wasn't for recurring memories that would manifest themselves as nightmares in my sleep, you might not have. There were times after a while that I could repress my memory of you. But it took the start of another relationship to truly forget about you. But it was more like cloaking my memory rather than forgetting you. I dropped you into my cauldron, where my past experiences simmered in, and let you swim in the steam of that vat of failed relationships.

I saw you one last time, but it was several years later. By coincidence, I had walked into a sports bar where you were. I spotted you right away, and I stopped in front of your table. I introduced you to Kathy, who was with me, and I mean truly with me. You introduced the guy that you were with as your husband. I congratulated you, but I did have a lump in my throat when you told me. Other than that quick rush of memory of how I had felt about you, our meeting was not that awkward. Neither your husband nor Kathy knew about our past connections, and neither one of us had any reason to volunteer that information.

You had the same astonishing, piercing eyes, and there was a moment when I had to be careful not to be taken aback by them, to have my memories turn into present feelings. There was extra depth in your eyes now that had not been there before. I recognized it as maturity. You had found yourself. I could only hope that you saw the same in mine.

We chatted for a moment, as old friends do, and then exchanged pleasant good-byes, but not before you told me that you had three children now, and not before I took a good look at your husband, wondering if this was the cousin. I had waited for him to laugh, to hear that tormenting gleeful laugh that I had heard in the background of your phone, but it never came.

Later, from my table at the back of the room, I watched you leave out the front door and disappear from my life for the last time. I never saw you again. Over time, I was able to convince myself that you really hadn't been that important to me. But whenever I think of you, I always wonder if we could have had a life together. I wonder if I had pushed you more, tried harder, explained more in depth what I could have done for you instead of what you could do for me. Maybe if I had rambled on about my sincerity when I was sober, you would have listened more. There is only room for retrospect now, and I will never know.

I have stopped focusing on regrets. But please know, you still hold a piece of my heart, and perhaps it might not ever grow whole again. I am trying to piece it back together, trying to piece my life together with it. If you had only known how I really felt.

CHAPTER 11

Leslie:

Our meeting was by chance, yet with the vibrations we felt that first night, we had labeled it as destiny. When I think back to that weekend, the odds were staggering when confronting all the variations that might have occurred for us to have never met at all. It was the start of another summer, my hatred for winter a distant memory as the thriving months ahead projected me straight into the center of the year, the center of optimism. Depression was still bubbling just below the surface, but kept from festering by a prescription of positive thinking and the ambience of the summer season.

Since last Christmas, I had been able to curb my drinking habits. I had received a layoff notice just before the winter holidays, and my goals for any significant savings in my bank accounts were put on hold, the viability of it as alive as road kill. Unemployment insurance checks were beyond late, and for almost three months, I went without any cash flow at all. I watched in dismay as my rent payments depleted my savings to nil. Paying the rent was a priority, for living on the street in the middle of the winter was not much of an option. The comforts of my house were my sanctuary. The claustrophobic nights of that small apartment of the year before were still in the forefront of my nightmares. Before the first unemployment check finally arrived, it meant searching the back of my kitchen cupboards for crumbs. It also meant the longest dry spell without alcohol since my teenage years. I had lost fifteen pounds off what was a bony frame to begin with. No worries though; I had my vitamin pills.

I became a recluse and very seldom left the house. There was the odd trip to the mailbox where I would throw my gas and electric bill into the garbage pail and then call the utility companies and, begging for mercy, ask them to give me more time to pay. My dream of buying a decent car was also deflated by my layoff. I did have my beater still, but it was so road unworthy that I had parked it for the winter. I had nowhere to go anyway. My friends from Westlake would drop in from time to time, hauling a case or two of beer with them, a token of appreciation for what friendship I had to offer them. I would get drunk with them and then send them on their way and thank them privately the next morning for the reminder of what a hangover felt like.

This was the extent of my connection to the outside world for the bulk of the winter. Ironically, with the arrival of my first unemployment check came the call to go back to work again. So with a new sense of worth that winter had stolen from me, I began to focus on my goals again. I continued my newfound ability to stay at home, to cope with being alone. I strayed from this pattern a few times, influenced by co-workers to go for drinks after work. With my tolerance levels down, I would get drunk easily. I would scan the bar for potential women, an ingrained habit of my past, a ritual of no deterrence. But before I could gather enough nerve to approach anyone, I was already staggering and slurring and, I have no doubt now, quite unpresentable and unappealing to them.

What I am trying to say is that when I met you, it had been a long time since I had been with someone. I was slowly adjusting to a coping mechanism that left me able to function on my own. I would win no awards for my abilities in this, but I was getting by; I was surviving.

It was my Westlake friends that deserve most of the credit for our meeting. You know their names—Chad, Ben, and Paul—a small-town version of the Three Stooges. I am not sure what that made me. They showed up unannounced on a warm summer Friday evening in Chad's conversion van, telling me that I was going with them to Winston for the weekend. This was the farthest thing from what I had wanted to do. I had gained enormous comfort in my hermetic existence. Except for those occasional after-work excursions to the town bar, I had shrunk away from social atmosphere. I adamantly stated that I was not going, but I was outnumbered, three to one. After two hours of steady debate and several beers later, I found myself in the back of Chad's van, heading down the highway for a weekend adventure—against my will, against my better judgment, yet not totally disappointed with myself that there would be much dwelling on it.

There was enough booze in the van to carry the inventory of a small bar, and we were well into a horn's turndown, ground-kicking, stampeding start into the path of a marathon drinking binge before we even arrived at Winston. The game plan was to visit a friend of Ben's who had moved there and then go barhopping the following night. As typical for my friends, our visit was not expected, and his Winston friend was a bit apprehensive when we all showed up at his doorstep. He knew Ben very well, so three strangers were not quite enough to deter him from partying with an old buddy.

I turned down the weed that was passed around quite soon after our arrival. The last time I had smoked dope, the paranoia had set in with a vengeance, a feeling that I could certainly do without. I had my beer, and I had my amphetamines that Ben had handed to me in the van as if they were candy. They would be sufficient to help me counter-effect the alcohol.

Dawn had arrived quicker than expected, and I watched a beautiful sunrise through the living room window, the morning's rays embracing me. Ben's friend had long passed out, and I watched the rest of them nod off one by one, leaving me alone with only the chirping birds outside to talk to. I went outside to join them, to feel the warmth of the summer morning and to breathe in the air of a brand-new day. My replenished source of oxygen that had been depleted from the stale air of the house gave me second wind. I popped another amphetamine pill and spent most of the morning by myself on the patio.

Chad was the first one to wake up, and since he was in charge of the van wheels, he gathered up the troops, and onward we traveled, leaving Ben's friend fast asleep, hanging over the edge of an armchair. After a healthy breakfast of immeasurable amounts of grease at some bar and grill, we found off the main highway, washed down with the beginnings of another alcohol-drenched day, the barhopping plans had changed direction. We were going to Lindros instead, influenced by Paul's suggestion that there were more bars to choose from.

By three in the afternoon, we had rented a motel room with double beds that we found on one of the side streets of the main drag. By six in the afternoon, we were sitting in our first bar, picked from a bar directory we had ripped out of the phone book from the desk of our motel room. Our destinations were chosen by taking turns pointing a pen at the torn page with our eyes closed. The fifth bar was chosen at around nine o'clock, and we drove into the parking lot shortly after, well on our way to three sheets blowing in the wind, or in our case, four.

When we entered the lobby, a wave of comfortable ambience first enveloped and then filtered through us. The rustic decor, the vibrant colors of the patterned carpeting, the live music instantly sending shared chills through our veins—all these brought an unspoken understanding between us that this would be our last stop of the night.

This was how we came to be at the same bar as you were, and you know the odds of us picking the right one out of that long list in the yellow pages blindfolded. Chad had already started to weave the van, and the rest of us were not about to drive anytime soon, but it was the place itself that sealed our stay—four country boys arriving at their final destination in their wondrous discovery of big city life.

We had pooled some money and placed it in the center of the table, and the pitchers of beer began to flow at an alarming rate. My past tolerance levels found their way back to me that night, obstructing any potential embarrassing intoxicated acts. But also did the amounts needed to escape the binds of my introverted ways.

The speakers on each side of the stage were the size of portable outhouses. Until the band went for a break, conversation meant shouting into earlobes. My buddies were content bellowing out jokes at excruciating decibels without my participation, anyway. I slouched back in my chair, studying the room and inhaling cigarette smoke as deep as my lungs would accept it. This was one habit that I could do without, but another addiction just the same.

I had begun to reflect on the past where I had spent many hours alone in bars, back to the wall, separate from everyone else, separate from the world. In hypnotic trance, but strangely still very alert to my surroundings, looking for answers to my loneliness. To hover just above the normal way of thinking, in a different sense of reality, escaping the normal process of logic. That night detached from my buddies' antics, I was soon back into that familiar trance, however diluted from the pressures of everyday life and society's disbelief and unacceptability of the powers of the subconscious mind.

I studied the crowd one by one, separating them from their physical surroundings. I sent the telepathic waves that I had learned to use long ago throughout the room, searching for any hints of receivers, of authentic reaction. Spending so much of my time alone, I had spent a great deal of time practicing this art. I knew telepathy as real. No one could convince me otherwise. Seldom have I had chances to share my results, my proof, that no matter how stoned or how removed from sound rationality, this was not imagination. I would probably only get a passing grade at clinical tests, but to those whom I have connected with through the mind only, that speech without the speech, that internal vibratory touch do share and know the fact of its existence. I could never discuss this with the clan of friends I sat with that night. They found me strange enough.

The bar was overcrowded, not standing room only but sufficiently packed for me to practice. There were many beautiful women in that bar, many single women, mostly on the dance floor. I lost concentration briefly as I felt a pang of loneliness and suddenly realized that my new coping skills to find satisfaction of being home by myself was only a mask to hide the real pain I felt inside. I still craved companionship, still wanted to find love, to be in love. I felt the odd chill, heard the occasional thought as I continued my experiments, interrupted only by the repeated action of filling a beer glass. And then like a lightning bolt, I could hear a sound inside my head, as clear as the voice of my own thoughts.

You had your back to me, but your friend was in open view. You were several tables away, tucked away in a corner to the left of the stage, and I couldn't directly place the vibrations, but they were definitely coming from your direction. After carefully observing your blonde friend, I could tell that she was not the one back-boarding my thoughts. I knew it had to be you.

It wasn't actual words I was picking up but more like pulsing vibrations, well separated from the music and synchronized with my own vibrations. With so many past experiences with the sixth sense, hallucinatory or not, I could not write this off as my imagination. I waited forever for you to finally go to the washroom, to get a good look at you. I had been careful not to make eye contact with your friend, wanting absolute proof that any connection you might feel was guided only by a metaphysical connection between us and no other influence. As indiscreetly as I could, I watched you cross the room in total astonishment of your beauty. I wiped my chin with the palm of my hand, thinking that salivation might be part of my reaction.

Your long auburn hair hung past your shoulders, glistening in the stage floodlights and swinging to the rhythm of your graceful walk. You were tall, at least an inch taller than I was. Your body was so beautifully proportioned that anyone could have mistaken you for a model. Your face was so smooth that it could have been the result of sculpturing. My heart skipped several beats and then came to sudden rest when I realized that you were way out of my league. It is that first vision of you that stays in my mind, like a photograph in a wallet to be pulled out for quick reminiscence. You hadn't seemed to notice me at all, but I could still feel the vibrations I first felt from you. Your total physical beauty, which I already recognized as well beyond my reach, snapped me back into focus, and I came crashing back to the surroundings of my table. I guzzled the contents of my glass and lit up another cigarette.

I watched you return to your table, still fantasizing that you would look at me. My heart rate increased for a moment and then throbbed with disappointment. You were beyond approach, but the feeling that I got from you wouldn't let me rest the case. But even if I could have bolstered enough self-esteem to think that you might have some interest in me, I could never have gathered enough courage to walk over to your table. I had a collection of rejection slips I didn't want to add to.

My buddies got up during intermission to go outside to smoke another joint. I refused to go with them. Paranoia was the farthest thing away from my needs at that point. I drank another glass of beer instead. By the time they returned, the band had started another session with the skill and the noise to take away the crowd from any other attention. Time took its course in the fast fashion it always does when having a good time. The announcement of last call came fast, rudely interrupting my evening of flowing memories and thrashing over my past. I had retreated back into the comforts of my shell, quiet solitude, and sulk. There had been no more experiments that night, but it did not stop me from concentrating on the flow of your auburn hair still sparkling from the stage lights. Your friend had caught my eye once, and I quickly looked away.

After the last encore, the bar remained full, only a few people trailing to the door after realizing that this band was not going to play all night. Ben had been wandering through the bar from time to time and got up again. There were no inhibitions holding him back. He had already confronted several women and had actually scored a couple of dances, but that was the extent of his attempt to bed one. Nothing held this guy back. Rejection meant nothing, and his total disregard for society's rules was probably what amused me about him the most. We had been kicked out of more than one establishment in the past and laughed all the way out the door. He had a collection of bouncer's shoes stuck up his butt. Of course, when it came to being turned down by women, he merely had to go home to his wife.

I watched in combined horror and wonderment as I watched him head straight for your table and sit right beside you in the empty chair with not so much as an inquisition to see if he was welcome. Ten minutes later, he came back just before the bar staff began their difficult chore of shoveling the clientele out the door. The curiosity got the better of me, and I had to ask him how he made out with you. Imagine the fluttering going on inside my stomach when he told me that you had said that you were interested in me. My head started spinning, not from dizziness but from panic. When he told me that you had said that you were receiving vibrations from me, it almost took my breath away. Hyperventilation was not new to me, but this was an unexpected attack.

I knew then that no matter what it took, I had to find a way to approach you to find the truth in Ben's words. You had just given me a direct hint, but I was still unsure. It was obvious you were not going to come to me. I sat there kicking myself for a while, ripping myself apart for allowing myself to grow into such low self-esteem. My feelings had regressed back into the danger zones of my teenage hood. I had to stop this.

The bar was slowly emptying, and although it was always a prerequisite for my clan to be the last ones to leave, that didn't mean you played the same nonsensical game. I took several deep breaths, gathered my cigarettes and lighter, and found hidden fortitude to drag myself to your table just as you got up to leave. A moment later, I would have watched you walk out the door and disappear into eternity. With a timid hello and wasting no time thinking of something wrong to say, I asked you if you wanted to go with us to a party. You and your friend exchanged looks and nodded in agreement. When I explained to you that we were from out of town and staying in a motel room, it didn't seem to matter. Your friend mentioned that she thought Ben was hilarious, and by that, I assumed she meant his witty humor had influenced your decision to go.

Your friend was from the city and quite familiar with where we were staying and said that you would meet us there. I was still partially stunned how quickly things were happening, and when you turned back to me on your way out the door, I did not dwell on the strange question you asked me. You wanted to know if I was older than nineteen. I forced a smile and told you I was way above that and I only looked young. Satisfied, you nodded and then showed me that graceful walk that even the most depressed would enjoy. It wasn't until much later that I discovered the reason for your question.

Chad passed out the second he jumped into the van. It was routine for him. He suffered from some form of narcolepsy, especially when he drank. You could be talking to him one minute, and he would be sleeping the next; you never knew when. Ben found a number for a taxi from the billboard in the lobby and summoned one from the pay phone. I could hear his brain ticking away on his expectations of the evening with your friend.

The taxi took forever to arrive, and I was in a frenzy that you would get there before us and grow tired of waiting. It finally arrived, and in drunken disregard, we left Chad passed out in the van and quickly jumped in. The ride seemed like forever, but judging by the cheap cost of the cab fare, we arrived in good time. But there was no sign of you. I ran across the street to the twenty-four hour variety store to get more cigarettes and found you at the counter doing the same. The coincidences were piling.

I hopped into the backseat of your friend's car and guided you to the visitor's parking area of the motel. From the backseat of her car, I was finally given your names. But to this day, I cannot remember your friend's name. I can remember the capital cities of South American countries from grade 6 geography and correctly spell most of the English vocabulary, but I can't remember names. Selective Alzheimer's in the making.

At the motel room, a party ensued, my friends proud to share their entertainment skills with amusing but absurd conversation. You and I sat in the corner of the room in the two cloth armchairs separated by the small writing table that had one of the leaves broken off. Your friend sat between Ben and Paul, content to be their center of attention. We slowly shared rationed pieces of our background, purposely omitting most of our history. It was an odd environment to share secrets, anyway. With profound coincidence continuing its path, I found out that you were from Dendron and lived only thirty minutes from me.

The word *synchronicity* kept popping into my head as I began to add all the variables it took to meet you. You had taken the bus to Lindros to visit your friend for the weekend and were heading back the following day. You showed no surprise when I told you we were heading back as well. I asked you if you had ever been to that particular bar, and you said never. You had chosen it because you liked the name of the band.

When your hazel eyes met mine, I could see my own, that deep pool of refection that allowed us in but wouldn't let us all the way through. They were like tinted windows letting a certain amount of light in, but behind them a new world of discovery and many secrets. The same eyes I saw in my own mirror. I fell in love the moment I saw the mysteries inside your eyes. All the protectionism, all the years of building internal guarding from a lifetime of disappointments, dispersed in a single flash. A stranger in the night, melting me, turning me into molten lead. I am not sure if you knew that night how much power you held over me, but you certainly knew later. I still shudder when I think back on how quickly I allowed you to tear down my walls, faster than a tsunami against straw huts, and how I left myself without a shield of any kind to protect my vulnerability.

As the late night turned to dawn, you easily agreed to trust the country-boy clan to give you a ride home instead of a long bus ride. You left with your friend, skipping my invitation to breakfast, to get your luggage. Both Ben and Paul passed out moments after you left. I went outside and spent most of the morning on the wooden bench in front of our room. I would rest one eye at a time, afraid I might miss your return. Chad pulled into the parking lot around noon with his party wagon, finding his way back after several wrong turns. If he hadn't remembered the name of the motel, he would probably still be searching for us.

After his long nap in the captain's chair of his van, his steering wheel for a pillow, he was ready to party again. Before I joined him for breakfast drinks of vodka and orange juice, I claimed rights to the shower and scraped off the night with a long spray of warm water. When I went back outside, you were sitting beside him, suitcase trailing behind you. You were wrapped in a visual aura of spirituality that I only caught glimpses of the night before. You were one of the few people I ever admitted to that I could see auras. I had trouble distinguishing the colors, but could see them just the same. It may have been the residual effects of my acid days, but it didn't lessen the fact that auras were real.

My heart filled with an intense passion, a feeling I had buried but had not forgotten. My self-preservation had tried to extinguish the memory of the feeling, but one look at you that morning and I was completely absorbed in it again. It was love at first sight. I felt that I had known you forever and that your eyes were talking to my heart, directing me to heaven. Your smile made my stomach dance. The fact that you were sitting there took away some of my insecurities. The world had lifted off my shoulders that morning. Here miraculously sitting in front of me was the woman of my dreams.

I put aside the seriousness of my thoughts, both of us caught up in the shallow frivolity of Chad. We helped him flip the mattress over, spilling its contents out onto the floor, namely Ben and Paul. An abundance of obscenities flew out of their mouths, causing us to laugh even louder. We were definitely giddy from lack of sleep. By mid-afternoon, after a lunch consisting of junk food items from the shelves of the same variety store across the road and many toasts of vodka to nothing in particular, we were ready to tackle the highway. You climbed into the very back of the van with me, ready to be chauffeured home by my triad of friends, and now, your friends as well.

We talked freely on the ride home. I am not sure who started the conversation about the paranormal, but it was soon apparent we were both fascinated with the subject. The similarities of our beliefs were profound. The supernatural was part of your daily thinking, and to finally share my own experiences with someone further enhanced my feelings for you. When you confirmed that you did feel the vibrations coming from me the night before, my destiny with you was sealed. The music from the back speakers of the van masked our voices, and our conversation went unheard to my buddies, who would have found ways to ridicule. I felt as one with you already.

By the time we pulled into my driveway, with you previously agreeing I could give you a ride home later, the first signs of dusk were already painted on the sky. I invited my friends in for a drink, but they were officially wiped out and were heading home. We both thanked them, and internally, I was also thanking them further for bringing you to me. My emotions were already spinning out of control, all the previous lessons of my past erased by my overwhelming attraction to you. I felt your magnetism, and I was convinced that for it to feel that strong, you must have felt the same. Those hypnotic eyes filled me with joy, an exhilaration of such voltage; I was already at the point of no return.

We made love that night. There had been enough caressing and foreplay to match the intensity of teenage years. Your perfectly formed body, your long legs wrapped around me, brought me to a degree of sensuality higher than anything experienced in the past. There was a spiritual connection that could not compare, and when attached to the physical passion, I was sent spiraling into the ethereal regions of my brain.

It was like taking all the bits and pieces of my fragmented memories of happiness from past relationships and merging them into totality. All the hurt and pain and disappointments shoved back into distant caverns, replaced by a dazzling array of optimism. How quickly I had allowed you to overpower me, my aforementioned hopelessness grasping for your beauty, overwhelmed by your charm and charisma. Regardless of the reasons, I fell asleep in your arms that night forever yours.

I did know that your self-assurance, your confidence, your self-respect, would boost my self-esteem high enough for you to never recognize that I had none when I met you. I would gain great confidence in myself and convince my tattered rationalities that I could do anything, especially defeat depression. This did happen, but erroneously I channeled it all through my love for you, leaving you in complete control of all my certainties. I was left completely vulnerable, but could not see it at the time. The thought that I was in love with being in love still escaped me. Self-analysis did not matter and had no place. I was simply yours.

Three weeks later, I had rented a truck, filled it with the furniture from your apartment, and you moved in with me. Also along for the ride were your six-year-old redheaded son and a black cat of the same age. Both had a mind of their own. You had revealed their existence on the second day I knew you, but with only you on top of my mind, they were not quite personified to me. They were part of the furniture stacked in the rented truck, until I realized all the cargo was not stationary. I was still too dumbfounded to understand the responsibilities I had accepted. I had an instant family. It was a slow awareness that brought me to realize I had entered the category of so-called stepfather. Your son's carrot top left him unfairly judged by me. My ex-wife's newfound husband, my windshield-wiper-twisting friend, had red hair, and I despised him.

My ex-wife was the only relationship that I shared with you in detail. You knew I had a daughter, and I could assume you expected me to accept your son with open arms. I tried, and I did to a certain extent, but sadly I could not find the emotional attachment that should have been there. I left that all up to you. I could only guide him from right and wrong, a good challenge for someone still sorting it out in his own head.

The fact that he was a borderline brat did not help, but I could not discuss that with you and with you alone at the helm in the discipline department (agreed from the start that I would not copilot that adventure) I had no choice but to cope with his attitude. Such a contentious mechanism to ignore and accept child disobedience was significantly eased by your son spending almost every weekend with his father. He lived in Lindros, but did not seem to mind the long Friday afternoon ride to pick him up. I gained complete respect for him to have such dedication, although some of it was compelled by your agreement not to ask for child support in exchange for this visiting arrangement. You had kept a friendship with him, and it was so unusual that when he sat at our kitchen table the first time, drinking the beer I offered him, it did not feel strange at all. Even the tinges of red in his hair didn't bother me!

Weekends were ours alone, so how could coping be any easier? The black cat was more of a challenge. After a couple of airborne attacks, with sharp claws directed straight at my head, only my quick reflexes winning the matches by deflecting it against the hard wall at no-mercy speed, did we gain a mutual respect for each other. The house was big enough for the two of us to go our separate ways. When we were in the same room together, eye contact was still necessary just in case of poor memory about who won the initial battles.

And so began our fantasy existence, resting on a loving couple's impending plans for a long and prosperous future. I went to work every day, my growing seniority lifting me from the danger of another layoff. The job paid well, and this is one blessing that I was not soon to forget. But saving money was still difficult because of my previous setbacks. The five-hundred-dollar winter beater of a car I had picked up before I met you was constantly in for repairs. Only recently had I begun to dig out from the debts, the repercussions of that long winter layoff. You had been living on mothers' allowance as a single parent when I met you, scraping by from week to week. You had wanted no legal backlashes, so when you moved in with me, you told the government, and they immediately cut you off social services. I hadn't given it a second thought, for I had all the intentions of taking care of you.

You did fill my house (our house) with furniture, filling the gaps of sparse decor and turning it into a home instead of a dwelling. It was without sadness that I gave up my milk-crate end tables, which were wrapped in shabby towels, and the thick cardboard box I used for a television stand. Three months later, your contributions to the household grew enormously when you took a job at the town nursing home. Even though it was part-time, our dreams of an enriched future became brighter. It was still only the pecking of society that had made me think that material was important. It was you and our happiness that drove me to fill in the gaps about why materialism was a scale to success.

At first we spent many of our weekends completely alone, preferring to cocoon than spend time with friends. I thought it was creating a bond between us that could never be broken. This was how I found out so much about your odd beliefs, which put the strangeness of my own beliefs well to the bottom range of a strangeness chart. You studied witchcraft and were adamant in your ability of understanding its powers. You worshipped the likes of Edgar Cayce and other names I had never heard of, all messengers of the secrets of the occult. You had done séances in the past and could make the oracle of a Ouija board almost fly off the table. You had your own special tarot cards, whose use and their meaning you were well versed in.

Once when I watched you do a reading for the neighbor, she had left afraid of you with your stunning accuracy about her life. You put my simple beliefs in the paranormal and my insights into the afterlife to shame when I read some of the strange literature you had collected in your home library. You left me stumbling behind when I felt the vibrations pass from you with a single touch, the electricity of your aura sending shivers when you concentrated on shooting pulsars of heat, like invisible solar flashes. My experiences in telepathy and the odd sensation of astral projection could not compare. I had doubts about the witchcraft part of it, but it never left me thinking any less of you. The only thought I had with the smell of sarcasm was that it explained your fondness for that evil cat you called a pet. In spite of the differences in some of our beliefs, my own connections to the paranormal made me feel even closer to you. It certainly gave us a deeper connection physically.

When I reached for further growth in this astonishing connection, I was drawn back into the use of marijuana. You were fond of it enough to warrant calling it an addiction. For a while, I refrained from using it with you, but then realized that if I ever was to beat the feelings of paranoia, it would be with you. My first attempt was not successful, and you had to work to calm me down. Once you gained my complete trust, the feeling was minimized enough to control. I was soon entering comfort zones, your intellect and your guidance, my path. You were five years older than me, and although I considered us equal in intelligence, there was something about those five extra years that gained my full respect. It intensified my love for you.

Your sexual experience was fashioned in extraordinary erotism, leaving me in a constant peak of satisfaction. You had a great appetite for sex, and you seemed to intertwine it into your spirituality. Alongside the occult books were many books about sex. I did not consider myself a novelty in the field, but whenever you weren't around, I found myself reading them. The techniques and your confident style had left me at times feeling a bit inadequate, but my own insatiable need soon eliminated any doubts of my own abilities. It also helped that I felt that the sex between us was strictly love induced, and the memories of my past casual experiences faded and were placed into the banks of back shelves as useless playtime. Our time in bed was truly ecstasy for me, and although I cannot speak for you, you showed me that it had been the same for you. We were together for less than two years, but the blissful connection stands, and you were the barometer of comparison for many years to follow. God, I loved you.

Our social life consisted mostly of visits to Ben's house, never losing the fascination of the lake view from his backyard and the big picture window of his living room. You had taken an instant liking to his wife, and we spent many weekends with them under the influence of weed and alcohol. During our nights alone, we shared more pieces of our past, careful to omit details that might rock the boat of our perfect existence. I was extremely happy, a feeling that had eluded me most of my life. I worked hard each day with my main goal to save for our future and rush home after work and be with you. I paid no attention to your signs of embarrassment when I would sometimes publicly proclaim my love for you. I turned you into my purpose for life. My mind never stopped to register the dangers of that, how in the long term it would be detrimental to my own growth.

My depression was gone or at least set in neutral, and I had not felt so content in my life since those first few years with my ex-wife. There was still no comparison, however, to the warmth you instilled in me; yet I still did not take the time to appreciate how lucky I was, letting the dangerous way of taking things for granted interfere with expressions of gratitude.

We never argued then; our physical attraction never dwindled, and our spiritual connection seemed to grow each day. One particular weekend stands out in my memory that will remain there as firm proof that the connection we shared was not a fabrication of the imaginary part of my mind. You had opened up that bottom drawer of your jewelry box and pulled out a small crunched piece of tinfoil. You unrolled it and held out two tablets of mescaline that you said you were saving for a special occasion. I hesitated and explained to you my bad experience with hallucinogens as a teenager. You assured me the effects would be mild. So with the complete trust I had in you, I popped the pill.

Thirty minutes later, the spiritual connection we had always felt between us materialized, slowly encircling us in tangible substance. To explain the validity of this to anyone else would be grounds for insanity and a request by the listener for me to seek professional help. You know differently. You were there to share the experience. Your own steadfast belief in the occult was ingrained in you to the extent that you had no choice to believe what happened between us was more than hallucination. The sudden enhanced visual of our auras spreading colors previously undetected, joining into one another in a swirl of patterns that kept rhythm to our heartbeats, was authentic. It was not hallucination but an enhanced perception not normally used. The electrical current between us flowed as surely as that to a light bulb in a lamp. This sudden extrasensory perception was not only physical to the touch, but it also enveloped in a sentient exchange of thought.

We had experimented with this before but only touched the surface of the sensation, the effects of alcohol interfering and throwing doubt into the process. I cannot stress enough how real it was, how totally euphoric and blissful the fervency between us was. This was more than emotion. This was a connection of souls correlating to the heavens. In the darkness of our house that evening, we created our own light, rays of cosmic energy that one could only read about. Words were not needed, though. The effects of the mescaline, the opening of a door to the heavens, lasted all night. Our physical interactions bolstered to extreme intensity whirling in unimpeachable macrocosm.

We fell asleep in each other's arms just before dawn. I woke up in the afternoon reaching over you but grabbed air instead. I found you on the couch reading, and for a brief second, I was startled. Whether it was remnants from the drug or a premonition, I watched your face age ten years right in front of me. I shook my head and brought you back to the present. I accepted it as an omen that we would be together forever. We carried on that day as if nothing had changed, as if nothing ever happened. Your indifference to what we had experienced would still not allow me to think that you were not enveloped in the same omniscience that I had been. After all, it was us that the sensations had come from and a higher connection through us. There was no removing our bond now.

For six months straight, we lived our lives in happiness, and the joy of shared dreams, not a disagreement to be found. I was even brave enough one night to bring up the prospect of marriage. Your reaction displayed deep consideration to such an idea, even without an actual affirmation. With this, I ran with the idea that it was part of the planning of our future.

Life followed the path of routine, as mundane responsibilities usually take it. Along with that comes the easy path to taking things for granted, and because it snuck up on me so gradually, I wasn't aware I was doing it. I think back now on how the first signs of my lack of appreciation came with my growing use of alcohol. I didn't need the booze with you, but I needed it to counter the effects of the weed I now frequently smoked with you. The addiction levels of my drinking habits were returning. You were not used to the steady stream of alcohol, preferring the milder effects of weed. Our preferred drug of choice was shared to appease each other. Between our work schedules and daily chores, we were able to balance our partying even as it stretched past the weekends into week days. We did not let it interfere with our peaceful existence. Until that dreadful night.

We were coming back from Ben's house on a cold, wintry Saturday night of drinking and pot smoking. Even in the winter, Ben's view of the lake was much better than our view of the street outside. Our exchange of visiting one another was enormously lopsided, but Ben and his wife preferred it that way anyway. You were driving that night as I had drank too much again. There was a light snow starting to fall, and the roads were covered in a dirty slush. The blades on the windshield wipers were worn out, and in my frugality, I never bothered to replace them. Before we drove out of town, you told me you were going to stop and buy paper towels to clean the windshield because you had a hard time seeing through it. Not entirely aware of my surroundings, foggy cognitive abilities from abundant alcohol and anxious to get home to a horizontal position, I did not think before I spoke. I blurted out that if you couldn't drive, I would.

In the whole time I had been with you, I had never seen you angry. You had shouted at your son a couple of times, but even then, there didn't seem to be enough raise in your voice to pass as anger. Your temperament had never been one of rage nor one without rationale. I was not prepared.

That night was the turning point in our unblemished relationship. You took immediate offense to what I had said. I had meant nothing by it, a senseless statement from a thoughtless drunk who simply meant he could drive. You slid into the store parking lot, bouncing the front tires off the curb, the abrupt stop shoving me toward the dashboard. I heard the driver's door slam shut and then later watched helplessly as you almost ripped in half the roll of paper towels that you bought from the store and wiped the windshield down with way more force than necessary. I saw the anger in your face, the beat red tones and the deep frown of disgust. Your usual soft, hypnotic eyes glared at me. Your contorted face scared me enough to look away. I was so shocked by your reaction that I froze, struggling about what to do to alleviate the problem.

Hostility was not new to me, but the last thing expected was it coming from you. We sat in silence the entire ride home. Once in our house, you sat on the couch, lighting cigarette after cigarette, still fuming hotter than the embers at the end of them. I finally approached you to break the silence and said I was sorry, over and over again. I explained to you that I didn't think I had said anything wrong. You finally spoke to me and accused me of being a chauvinistic pig and of being completely ignorant. I kept denying it while you became more descriptive about what kind of an asshole I really was. The more I tried to explain myself, the more defensive you became. I kept apologizing until I was too tired to say the same repetitive words. Completely exhausted, I went to bed; and after a considerable amount of time waiting for you, I passed out, oblivious to the fact that we were about to spend our first night sleeping alone since the day I met you.

I was so relieved the next morning when I got up to see you in the kitchen with a strained smile and said a quiet good morning. Your angry look had been replaced with one of hurt. I gave you a sober apology stating that nothing like that would ever happen again, and although still somewhat reluctant, you accepted it. We did not talk much that day, diverting our attention to watching television, something we seldom did. The snow outside kept piling up, and although I didn't say it out loud, I was so glad to have you by my side. We went to bed that night, and you allowed me to curl up to you in that perfect set of spoons that we made. I was saddened, but this time aware that not only had we spent the night before apart for the first time, but today also was the first time since we had met that we had not kissed. This haunted me and left a crack in our magical existence.

Things did go back to normal, as our routine took over our lives again. When the car broke down again a few days later, this shared dilemma brought us back in line to poetic partnership. The transmission was shot, and because of the age and condition of the car, common financial sense had put it beyond repair. Money was still tight. We did have some savings, but not enough to afford a reliable car. So for the first time since the days preceding my bankruptcy, I found myself inside a bank looking for money. You came with me for moral support. My credit was still shady, the damage done by my ex in-laws still haunting the prospects of my future. You had no credit history to back me in any way, so although very disappointing, it was not unexpected when that beady-eyed loans officer with the goatee turned us down flat, reeking with arrogance and enjoying his power over us. He did say that if we could find a cosigner, he would consider it.

There was no way in hell that I would impose on friends to do this. Before I could explain that, you volunteered to ask your blonde friend from Lindros to help us, the one that had no name to me. In desperation I finally agreed, trying to allow myself to think that asking for help was not a sign of weakness. You invited her down for the following weekend, and during the midst of your reminiscing party, thrashing over all the history you had with each other, you squeezed in the question at what you thought was the appropriate moment. Your friend was a widow, her husband tragically killed in a car crash, leaving her behind a bag of money from a life insurance policy. I still didn't feel right asking her, but it was your friend, and certainly a good friend. She agreed to help us without any hesitation, without as much as one thought to her own welfare or jeopardy to her own finances. She really had no idea of who I was, only her trust by association to go by.

The following Tuesday, we pulled into the driveway with a shiny new Camaro. Not brand-new, but brand-new to us and a century away from the junk I was used to driving. We shared a sense of pride and intravenously took a dose of what materialism can do to the senses. To leave your ability for credit open and giving us options later, we decided to leave your name off the loan and my name off the ownership to the car. With your income to help with other household expenses, I could pay the car loan off within a year. It all made sense at the time, but now when I think back on how quickly the paperwork was signed, there was a bit of logic missing in the whole situation. I was completely indebted to your friend, however, and it was heartfelt thanks I gave her when her signature appeared under mine. We put the insurance under your name to avoid the higher rates that would not be avoided otherwise because of my past driving record. They didn't need to know I existed behind the wheel as long as I was careful. The restrictions and regulations were more lax back then, and investigations were minimal.

I remember looking out the window that day watching the metallic paint of the car glisten in the sunset. It was not only the pride of ownership but also the symbolism of our bright future behind those wheels, our long life together. Except for that one disagreement over the benefits of a clean windshield, I thought our lives were perfect. My search for a soul mate had become a reality and not some hogwash apparition of my own dreams or a romance novel. I felt your love as strongly as I felt my love for you.

All fairly tales do not end blissfully. When I dwell in the past, I am always pondering over our time together, revising in my head a thousand times where our erosion first started and what I could have done to stop it. Our lives slipped into routine mode, rutted into a path of hard work and hard partying. Was it my addiction to alcohol that was the reason for the end of our ethereal connection? Was it my inept attempt to change the ways of my selfishness? I thought I treated you well, but unknown to me, your mind and aspirations were drifting somewhere else. It was very gradual at first. Our beginnings had started with all the efforts of a promising new start to a binding relationship. We had been prepared to start fresh, leaving all our baggage from the past behind. I was so blinded by you that my focus and view of my surroundings passed through you first before the final decipher. You were another intoxicant to me.

I cannot place when the arguments first started or when they started to increase. The growing list of your disappointments of me stung deep at first, but I wanted everything to remain so perfect that your rude comments were accepted as constructive criticism and I was able to deflect the full brunt of your offenses. I had never fully appreciated the intelligence of women in the past to the degree of equality that I should have. This did not make me the chauvinistic boar that you accused me of. I simply had not met a woman that I considered equal to the intelligence I proclaimed to have; that was until I met you. I never told you directly, but I assumed you were aware of the respect I held for you. Even if you did feel it, I am sure the slow deterioration would have whittled it down to nothing as the intensity of our arguments increased.

You were not a morning person. Innocent jabs of pre-coffee conversation bordering on mortifying insults became more frequent from you. When you first moved in, you would send me to work with fanciful kisses and fond farewells. With the growing comfort levels allowing us to be more demanding, you were able to allow your agitations to rise to the surface and had no qualms to voice them. We were soon spending mornings arguing about nothing, or it seemed to be about nothing when I later tried to remember what we were arguing about in the first place. I would rush off to work sulking, disappointed and hurt. When I returned each late afternoon, it would all seem to be forgotten. But my mind had been tuned to expect bliss between us all the time, so there was no escaping the gathering of tiny thorns piercing the outer layers of my heart when the numerous pricks began to annex to memory. At first we wiped these smears away, our projected perfection allowing forgiveness and forgetting. Our love would smooth the roughness, and we were able to iron out our differences.

Our routine and our ability to make up sailed us into the beginning of our second summer together. Our first anniversary together, with a vault of memories of great times with friends, shared laughter, a shared promise of a great future together, forced our differences down into trivial levels. It wasn't the total bliss we had expected, but we were happy.

This all changed over one tumultuous and revolting weekend by a visit from an old friend of yours. You had a network of friends that you kept in touch with by letter and by phone. One of these friends lived in Prince Edward Island, close to the military base in Summerside. Ironically, that was where Ben was from originally and where his family still lived. Your friend Susie (I can't help but remember her name) had moved out there two years prior, marrying a soldier ten years younger than her. In the grand scheme of things, I guess that isn't that much of a gap. You and I were almost six years apart, and I felt no difference in our maturity levels or in our long-term goals.

Her husband had been given a three-week-long furlough and wanted to travel across Canada, and while passing through, they wanted to visit you. You and Susie wanted to catch up with each other's lives, and you asked me if it was all right. That was only to appease me as you had already made the arrangements. I went through the motions of saying of course it would be okay. I am sure no was not an option, and I sincerely thought I could find insight about your past through your friend anyway. Our house had extra bedrooms upstairs, so there was plenty of room; and inhibitions aside, I did enjoy meeting new people.

They arrived a week later to begin my nightmare, slowly at first as the constant partying and obligatory need to like your friend overshadowed her boisterous personality and obscure beliefs. Your no-name blonde friend knew Susie as well, so she and a new boyfriend of hers were to join us. To round off this reunion, another friend from Lindros, a platonic male friend of yours and Susie's, would also be part of this fanciful occasion. For a moment, I had a bout of jealously wondering how platonic he actually was; but not only did I trust you, when I saw later how meek he was, there was also little doubt that he was only a friend.

Your friends from the island arrived first, and I could feel the warmth from your greetings, the vibrations of a long-cherished friendship filling the air. It had felt very natural to accept Susie and her husband into our home. After all, I was a part of you. Her husband was quiet and reserved, and I could see the discipline in his eyes, something even more than the military would have given him. I could relate to him, that underlining intelligence and his lack of need to portray it. Susie, on the other hand, was loud and opinionated from the second she arrived and scanned me cautiously when I spoke, forming a judgment that I was sure would be shared to your benefit later about my degree of lack of worthiness. She made me feel uncomfortable at first, but with the breaking out of the social tools of alcohol and marijuana, that initial discomfort vanished; and as my own inhibitions evaporated, I no longer felt like I was under Susie's microscope every moment.

The three from Lindros joined us, arriving in one car, and we rolled out the red carpet for the start of a weekend binge to celebrate and enhance the steady reminiscing and exaggerated stories of your pasts that steered the agenda of conversation. I was able to sit on the sidelines most of the time, for until recently I had no part of your past. A few times while I watched the weekend progress, I was reminded of the classic movie *The Big Chill* where old friends got together, although under completely different circumstances than our gathering. The sharing of the kitchen chores, the mixture of different levels of exchange in personal thoughts interweaving between moods and reflections, the music influencing the direction of flow. There was even a group dance between you around the kitchen table. It was festive, cut-loose frolic, and the natural high of close friends and shared musings. I was proud to be a part of such a meaningful connection among all of you.

Your shy and platonic friend, Jim was his name, I think, was especially easy for me to get along with. I could relate to his inhibitions and his reliance on meditation and philosophy. His only problem was the heavy overtones of religion that he found necessary to interject into conversation, whether befitting or not. Susie's husband was a man of few words, so when he did speak, his contributions bore weight. I considered myself the same way, but when the brain is fuelled with a steady diet of alcohol, it sometimes strays from its view and off subject. Her husband had a cemented tolerance for alcohol and hardly ever showed signs of inebriation while holding high volume levels that still didn't quite match my own. How proud I was to be a better candidate for liver damage as a way of undermining his better way of articulation on any subject.

It soon became obvious why he was so quiet. Susie was overbearing. A blatant women's rights activist, women's liberation practically tattooed on her forehead, and to worsen it, a huge superiority complex. When the topic of women's liberation came up on our second day of partying, the debates became loudly one sided and passionate. Her husband and I shrewdly refrained from voicing our opinions, leaving Jim to his own demise. His sudden unwavering need to voice his religious philosophies would serve no purpose in Susie's opinions, which had long been set in stone. He was no match and was about to get eaten by a lioness. He had drank too much, but he still thought he was capable to hold up a different point of view. I watched your reactions as the trouble began to brew, but you were about to sit through it, with layers of neutrality brushed on thick. Perhaps your lack of experience with alcohol couldn't allow you to extinguish the fuse, but it still surprised me that you did nothing while Jim was cut to shreds.

The debate between Jim and Susie turned from a difference of opinion to an outright war of words. None of us were prepared for the decibels or the ferocity. Nor were we prepared for the strength of Susie's dagger used to win the battle. It hadn't sounded that brutal, but her delivery skills and pure insolence secured it. She accused him of spouting dogma and couldn't think himself out of a wet paper bag. I felt his pain as if her words were meant to cut me open instead. There was a long period of awkward silence around the table before Jim finally got up and staggered outside. This had happened well past midnight, and I followed him outside to ensure that he didn't take it on himself to walk off and get lost.

It was exactly what he was determined to do. After another different debate with me about his desire to walk home, he lost another round, only I didn't need any knockout words. I was able to convince him to shrug it off and that tomorrow would bring a brand-new day. I helped him up the stairs as his legs had suddenly turned into rubber, his weakness surmounted by the abandonment of his religious philosophies to protect him.

The rest of us carried on as if nothing had happened. You and I shared a brief look of understanding that it had to be let go, but then as I took another look into your eyes, I felt a growing fear turning in my stomach and saw something in them that I had missed or purposely avoided before. My memory flashed to some of the arguments we had recently. I caught the slivers of comparison to Susie from your past words, saw the domination in your actions; and what I had previously thought of as your inner strength was the facade of women's liberation taken one step further than its original intentions of equality. Even with this unexpected awareness able to be overlooked, later the slow, corrosive effects of our supposed soul mate connection from the increased volume of our arguments dissolved into eventual obliteration. That evening these thoughts flirted dangerously around in my head holding on to my love for you, as some of the weaker moments of our weekend party forced negativity out of the darker corners of cognition.

With the exception of Jim, presumably snoring up a storm upstairs, we all watched the sunrise. We shared the chores of an early breakfast—grease intake equivalent to a gas station service floor—eggs, sausage, and bacon. A very melancholy Jim eventually joined us, turned down breakfast, and insisted that he needed to go home. With your no-name friend and her boyfriend as his ride, his request was not honored until later in the day. The incessant party was moved outside to our newly acquired picnic table. That day now all melds into another binge of fragmented memories, morsels of recollection missing entirely. I remember almost crawling to work the next day, another night without sleep and feeling quite ill; but I always used the theory that if I was going to be sick, it was best to go to work and vomit on the boss's shoes rather than let drinking interfere with my paycheck. As long as I made it to work, my work ethics would still allow me to function, and I could defeat my internal struggle to admit I might have a drinking problem.

I had to entertain your island friends for another week, skipping part of Monday night for sleep and bodily repairs. The partying continued through the week, and I would join right after work. It was an easy process for me to fall back into drinking every day. I had plenty of practice in the past. My younger years had seasoned me in such a way that endurance levels were of Olympic standards. Such simplicity of achievement needed for an alcoholic's mind!

There was another instant in Susie's stay that I did not expect for you to sit idly by. When I took it on myself to step in, I do not know for sure if it added to your discouragement with me. I found your friendship with Susie so unnatural when you let her even command the discipline of your own child. We were sitting at the kitchen table for supper. Your son had just come back from a lengthy summer stay with his father. I had just returned from work, washing warehouse dust down with the help of what was a third beer; so principles, not abundance of alcohol, led to my confrontation. Although I never dared say it to you directly, your son, indeed, was a brat, spoiled beyond repair, and I was not about to analyze why. But this particular night, when he decided that a display of complete juvenile delinquency was in order, I reached my limit.

I won't win any awards for proper etiquette, but I do know that you are not supposed to eat mashed potatoes with your fingers. And so did your son, but regardless of his reasoning, he was determined to do so. You told him not to do it, once and then twice; and with his lack of intention to listen to you, you took his plate away. Whether Susie was too stoned that night or it was her obsessive need to show superiority, she stepped in and handed the plate back to him, stating he had plenty of time to learn how to use utensils. You said nothing, did nothing. What power did she have over you?

I had never once stepped in with the discipline of your son as you are well aware of. But this was a situation where toleration had been pushed above its confines. I yelled out in a volume that frightened even me, let alone the rest of the table, and told Susie to stop it and took the plate away. Susie glared back at me in great contempt, and I glared back at her. She asked me if I was testing her. I calmly said no but that she had overstepped her boundaries. It was not a moment of mutual respect that ended our conflict but a stalemate. Your son was clever enough to know when it was a good moment for proper behavior and picked up his fork, his cue to me to give him back his plate. You stayed silent, and so did everyone else. It made for an awkward dinner.

Afterward, Susie's husband and I moved into the living room, and I brought out the chessboard, a game I knew as having minimal conversation. I apologized to him and simply stated that I had reached my limit. He responded by telling me not to worry about it and that he had long ago but didn't know what to do about it. I knew what he meant, and he did not have to elaborate, and we spent the evening involved in a speechless board game except for the obligatory check or checkmate.

We continued to party the rest of their stay, but I could feel a strain in the conversations after that. There was never any mention of what had happened, however. There was still a steady stream of marijuana through the balance of their stay. I never did agree with smoking dope in front of your son, but it did not stop me from joining in. I still suffered from mild bouts of paranoia, but with the weakened effect when combined with my drinking and what I thought was my ability to still pick up some of your thoughts, it eased me into comfort.

Your friends left that Sunday in preparation for the rest of their voyage across Canada. We shared good-byes in the driveway, sweet exchanges of gratitude and fondness. Susie walked over to me and gave me a hug and said the situation called for one. I couldn't know if she was genuine. Her husband and I shook hands and nodded in recognition, a silent beckoning of good luck to each other. You stood in their driveway long after they were gone as if a part of yourself had left. And it had. I tried to feel that connection of our souls that we had before, but it didn't seem to be there anymore. I wondered how much influence Susie had on you while I was at work. Our conversation after they left did not have its fluent flow anymore. Our openness to each other was now elusive.

Life went on, but now our bickering would start over nonsense. This was wearing at my heart, and I was sure that as deeply confined as you had become, it was wearing at yours as well. Then one afternoon, you unexpectedly showered me with hope and the return of glorious expectations that we could regain all the magic of our first subsistence and connection. We had argued loudly that morning just before I left for work about how I didn't do my share in the kitchen, how I should be helping more with the cleaning and the cooking. You were right to some degree, but I had become spoiled by your original way of taking over the domestic chores, and I also weighed the fact that you were only working part-time. It was not something to argue over. But without even thinking, I had snapped back that your sheep-following procession into the belly of women's rights was interfering with the logic of your everyday life. This brought an immediate return to the infusion of your male-chauvinism accusations, which continued to echo through my head all day long as loudly as the forklift engine did off the warehouse walls. I dreaded coming home that day, thinking of a thousand ways to apologize to you, knowing you would probably not accept a single one.

You beat me to an apology in a style that I could never match, but certainly one quite acceptable to me. When I opened up the door, preparing for another round of torment, you met me at the door completely nude. At first I could not fathom what was happening, but when you led me down the hall to our master bedroom, my heart certainly did. You were of unimaginable beauty, the late-afternoon sun gleaming off your smooth, silk skin. You always were the picture of fantasy to me, and all the pride I held when walking down the street with you or even when we were all alone came rushing back like a tidal wave.

You had sent your son to the neighbor to play, and the last of the afternoon was ours. I couldn't help think later, wondering how much you had smoked that day, if you were satisfying one of my fantasies or catering to one of your own. It didn't matter then. It certainly doesn't matter now. My anticipation grew in leaps and bounds as you led me to the bedroom, my mind racing across the memory banks of our past experiences in that very room. Our sexual relations had always been exalting, your talents to bring me to states of high exuberance, halting, teasing, aspiring me for more. Your physical skills brought climatic endings to complete fulfillment. I was destined to destitute comparisons for the rest of my life.

That afternoon sealed that fate, as well as the fate of my heart. My love for you was flowing in my veins, my soul filled with the ecstasies of a woman's touch, wrapped in the throes of your sexual expertise, your profound proficiencies engulfing my own identity. Of all the great memories I have with my time with you, that afternoon romp stands out the most. You were giving me a message far beyond my selfish comprehension, but I could feel it just the same. Everything that I wanted in a true relationship lay beside me, your inner soul stretched out for the taking as well. Why my supposed well-developed soul and levels of maturity couldn't totally grasp it, I fail to know. I missed the target of my own wants and desires, a slightly distorted mind, from the scars and misgivings of my past. Forever forgive me. Forever forgive myself.

We did spend many days after that with a strange sense of peace and any small quibbles quickly squashed by our new outlook. But a few months later, with Christmas fast approaching and the pressures of winter life, we seemed to slowly drift apart again. I would catch you staring out the window when I came home from work, and the house would reek with marijuana. Our conversations lost their flow again, gradually rationed to the words of necessity, and a growing wedge between us shoved thick shadows of dissent and distance into the gaps. A few weeks before Christmas, my world turned upside down, and all the hopes of a glorious and emotionally filled Christmas fell apart.

I got up to carry out my routine in preparation for work, agitated and slightly moody from the arrival of the short winter days, lack of sunlight, and dealing with your increasing mood swings. You were consistently distant, and it was eroding at my own demeanor. There were a few times when you had suffered from migraines, and when pain killers didn't work, harsh venting seemed to me your medicine of choice. But this morning, you went into a rage, and I was reminded of our very first argument over dated windshield wipers. We had argued the night before over such a trivial matter of my frugality when it came to buying groceries. Had we become that desperate in finding things to argue about? We went to sleep that night when the raising of voices was switched to not talking to each other at all. An unresolved petty argument broke through already-bothersome dreams.

When I came out of the shower the next morning, I could hear you stirring, so I asked if you could do laundry later on that day. You turned rabid, as if I had attacked you, as if I had backed you into a corner. Your temper exploded, anger I should have known was gathering at the surface ready to boil over, ready to roll over any signs of my idiosyncrasies, any imperfections, and any lingering disappointments in your expectations. You had become a walking time bomb, and probably anything would have set it off that morning. Had I been that blind to your needs? That morning it didn't matter because my own frustrations in my inability to please you anymore, entangled with your own disenchanted views, collided, and we clashed in a battle of our own arrogance and pride.

At first, all I wanted to do was try to reason with you, to calm you down, to resolve this new set of disparities. Confrontations were as harmful to my heart as was your recent indifferent attitude. But the more you cursed at me, the more you tossed the insults with rock force, the more my own anger began to brew; and when it hit the surface like a geyser letting off steam, I lost control. I told you I was going to be late for work, and you threw another line of insults accompanied by curses that had no apparent need. I snapped.

I picked up a ceramic angel off the top of your dresser, some memoir from your past, probably a memento of another period of happiness in your life, and fired it at such velocity and enough force to shatter it against the wall into a thousand pieces. It had just missed your head. I had no recollection of ever being that violent before, no memory of ever wanting to hit a woman. My heart dropped down from shock and shame as I watched in horror what I had just done.

I knew the fact, that lurking reality from the depths of my conscience, that I had just shattered the remaining connection between us, shards penetrating your heart just as real as the pieces of tempered clay that lay around you on top of the bedspread. Your shrieking commands to get out drowned out my pleas for forgiveness. Your heart had immediately turned to ice. To turn back time just a few seconds entered my internal prayers as I stood before you completely helpless. I kept apologizing over and over again, but the barrier was up, your shock and instant defense mechanisms bolting forward to raise emotions to hatred levels, an instant drain to any affections. I left you that morning with a trail of apologies, dripping in sorrow and tears, but to your deaf ears. I went to work that day, managing my work responsibilities, but in the state of a zombie. There was numbness inside me, a frigid cold attached to a solidified heartache that throbbed endlessly. I could not think of a way to undo what I had done, no way to mend this except a solemn promise never ever to do it again.

I went home right after work, cowering as I entered the house. It was an empty house. You were not there. Hour after hour, I paced the floor, time crawling to that of a snail's world, waiting for your return. You did not. I left for work the next morning without any sleep, and it was difficult to function. With my good work record, I saw no harm in asking to leave early and was granted an hour off. Cement blocks rolled off my shoulders when I drove home and found you sitting in the living room. The silence between us, though, was beyond awkward. It was tormenting. We were supposed to be soul mates. Where did you go? What had happened to us? Eventually you broke the silence. I listened to your every word intently. I was prepared to do anything to repair the damage I caused between us.

You kept repeating that all the trust was gone, that you had no choice but to move on. I kept begging that I would prove myself, kept ensuring that nothing like that would ever happen again. You let me plea for hours, well into the night, stressing over and over my love for you, accentuating that you were everything to me. My tear ducts opened up several times, and I couldn't stop the flow. The tears ran down my cheeks, and huge salty raindrops puddled on the carpet where I stood. All my emotions were stocked into one, my entire soul held in your hand, my very being at the mercy of your discretion.

Whether out of pity or empathy for the melted fool in front of you or it was a devise of your own temporary needs, you finally gave in to me and said I could have one more chance. You stated that it had to be under your terms and without a second of weighing the consequences of that; I agreed and relented all power to you, anything not to lose you. You had become my world, the foundation on which to base my goals, my dreams, my inspirations. My own self-esteem was melded into my love for you. If I lost you, I would lose myself. The past, present, and future all intertwined into a state of consciousness of compulsion, my very existence dependent on yours.

I knew how dangerous this was, but I had no control over how I felt about you, and I was convinced my stability depended on it. As I handed over all ascension to you, I should have known that I had to cling on to a certain amount of pride, hold on to a certain amount of my own identity. Rooted in my subconscious was the need to be my own person, a normal, independent drive to my own authority. As much as I wanted to change for you, I needed my own decisions, my own directions, or at the very least, to partner as an equal. Such eternal conflict would eventually clash with your demand for dominance and your extreme independence. And it did.

We were very mellow at first, sleeping together again, but with a new game where sex was off-limits. That was the worst punishment you could think of for someone who had routinely used this act for escapism and had also learned to use it to display his love. You were taking away a channel to many outlets. Our conversations were civil, but they were of only practical use.

Christmas Day arrived. We spent it alone. Your son was with his father. You were estranged from your parents, and we had learned to lean on each other with those similarities. The sentimental, the emotional levels of the Christmas season affected us the same. It led us to the same feelings of doldrums, dissension, far away from the merriment and festivities. We had agreed earlier not to exchange gifts that year but to pay down the car instead, and we had both honored that agreement. Your guard came down Christmas Day, and you let me trickle in, and I could feel some of the feelings you used to share with me. You made love to me that day, but some of the spark, the magic, was missing. I did not dwell on it, content that we were heading down the right track. I was wrong.

I began to resent the empowerment I gave you, as your demands, however small, rendered me helpless. Maybe you knew that all along. Although you would probably never admit it, you had not lost any resentments, your begrudging ways more than need. It was never about forgiveness for you. The smallest of things I did were bubbling disgust inside you, even minute, trivial character flaws were ballooning into loathing.

Three weeks into the new year, you announced that you were leaving me, that there was no use carrying on the charade. I felt that familiar drop of my heart and the thundering beat of it off my rib cage, the fear and dread of heartbreak just below the line of panic. I started to talk, and you told me there was no reason to discuss it. Your mind was made up. I tried anyway. Day after day, I begged to hold the frustration of your discordant neglect to my feelings, churning inside the very anger I promised you would never resurface. But my manic compulsion to keep you in my life kept it from boiling over. My persistence, my pleas only furthered your distance and indifference. I had moved to the couch, your callousness and silence too painful to bear while I lay beside you.

We went on like that for several weeks while I still grasped for ways to win you back. When we did talk, you kept pointing out that your decision was final. I even stooped low enough to involve your son, but only briefly, reaching out for his understanding, his influence, no matter how small it might be. It was to no avail as you read right through me. I had never been much of a father figure to him.

We tried our best to hang on to civility. You had given me no time frame about when you were actually leaving. I didn't want to know anyway. It left me shreds of hope that you might still change your mind. You began to spend time away from me on the weekends, but you always came home. I basked in misery waiting for you to return, wondering where you were and what you were doing.

One night when you were gone, out of nowhere, I got the notion to go through your personal belongings. Every moral fiber told me not to, but I was searching for some understanding, something from your past that might help me figure out what made it so easy for your impassivity. I did not really expect to find anything, and now wish I hadn't. In the bottom of your armoire, bound in red ribbon, was a leather journal. There were no entries in it since you had met me, but before that were detailed listings of previous relationships. Inside the pages were the details of your marriage, its breakdown, his philanderings, your own as well, in vivid details that gnawed away at my gut. In between the descriptions of your various affairs were attributes to your ability to feel. It had bothered you that your ex had married a stripper. They had married on Valentine's Day, and that had devastated you for a while. I did not need to be reminded of that day. I had no use for its meaning, either.

You had clung on to good memories, always taking a chunk of him into your next bed, your own hopes of reconciliation still lost in false hopes. The time and efforts of your acclaimed love for him still held a purpose. Why then, I had thought while reading this, had you not understood me? I started to skip paragraphs, the guilt of prying into your private writings starting to eat at me. I read certain excerpts, eventually skipping over entire pages, embarrassed and hurt by the descriptions of your affairs. I always knew how much sex was a part of your life. I had the benefits of your talents to prove it. What I did not know was your obsession with it. Page after page was filled with erotic details. I sped ahead to the last few entries and was served my just reward or rather penalty for invading your privacy.

Only one week before you met me, you were still involved in a long-heated affair with a nineteen-year-old. I felt my body and my mind cringe at the same time, a flush of inadequacies flowing through me. In the most explicit erotic fashion I have ever read or even imagined, you wrote whole compositions on this kid's abilities to satisfy you in bed. With way over a decade between your births, sex was your only commonality. Line after line of vivid description displayed for my despair as you described your addiction to this kid. I closed the journal, carefully replacing the ribbon, dizzy with the compounding effects of my anguish.

The next weekend, Ben and a clan of his friends dropped in unannounced. It was not totally unusual, and even less unusual that his wife was sitting at home. We both put on a face for a while, trying to show that nothing was wrong between us, and played the obligatory host and hostess together. But the weight of the heavy burden of excruciating gloom inside me, waiting for either implosion or explosion, became unbearable for me to play the hoax any longer. When Ben asked us to his birthday party for the following weekend, you said you were sorry but we had other plans. In a fit of rage over your deceit and speaking for me, I blew the facade. I blurted out to everyone that you were leaving me, and it set the faucet to my tear ducts on high.

Ben, in his extroverted ways, took us aside and decided that he could fix things between us. I knew better and, between uncontrollable sobs, said that I was done letting you destroy me and that I would find a way to be strong. I left you standing there alone with Ben and did find the strength to compose myself and grabbed another round of beers from the fridge for everyone. It had been a glorious deception, and I was able to go through the rest of the night, hiding my true pain and fooling my own sensibilities. It was short-lived.

Two days later, as I was getting ready for work, you told me that you were leaving that week. The anger was brewing, but I again deferred to begging, saying that we could work it out, reminding you how I felt about you. I reminded you of how we once talked about marriage, how sincere those conversations had been. You kept repeating it was over and that even counseling wouldn't work, that you had tried that before. We had never discussed counseling, so I am not sure if you were flashing back to someone else or fending me off any chance of proposing such an idea. My whimpering, my persistent pleadings, my repeated professed love for you must have finally set off your tolerance levels. In your coldest fashion yet, you shouted out to me, "Don't you have any integrity?"

This question caught me so off guard that I turned completely numb and let anger rise to the surface. *Integrity* was one of those words in my vocabulary that I knew the meaning of but used with such infrequency that I never did grasp its suggested content when connected to emotion. Your eyes were filled with a dull glaze, a bitterness mixed with more indifference than disgust. My anger subsided before it even found a way out, your unfocused glare causing it to be replaced with grief. I echoed your question over in my head a few times and then, with sudden awareness, realized that we were truly over. I finally had to admit to myself that we were through, finally had to accept that I had lost you.

You took care of that for me when I returned from work that day. Your son had not been brought back from Lindros that weekend and, in my disordered state, had paid no attention to it. Cognition was at a minimum. But it was not difficult to see the suitcases lined up on the kitchen floor, especially with you standing there beside them. I tried talking to you one more time but with futile results. In an almost nonchalant manner, you asked me for the car keys. My heart dropped. I was not expecting that. For all intents and purposes, it was my car. I had made all the payments and had only one more to go in order to wipe the bank's fingerprints off the ownership entirely. Although I had considered us partners, something had allowed me to think that the car was not part of us, that this particular item was mine. I adamantly refused to give you the keys and walked into the living room. Five minutes later, I watched a police car pull into my driveway. You had called them without my knowledge, attention deficit now among my frailties. I felt defeated, but I couldn't just let you take the car.

Your eyes turned away from me, but in the corners, just before you answered the knock on the door, I saw one last small look of empathy, which you had completely diverted away from me long ago. *How could you?* were the only words I could muster, and they reverberated in my head. It was the same words my ex-wife had uttered the night I had announced my infidelity. Was this karma in the offering? Was I being punished for my selfish ways long before the cosmic records should be read?

I argued with the cop that it was my car and that you had no right to it. That argument was quickly squashed when they asked me whose name was on the ownership. When I explained that it was only under your name for cheaper insurance rates, it did not matter to them. The threat of going to jail if I didn't produce the keys left me helpless. I yielded, feeling part of my life force drain from me and my knees buckled in defeat.

The whole thing was wrong, but I had no strength left to fight with. I handed the keys to the cop, who in turn gave them to you and went so far as to help you with the suitcases. You wouldn't look at me as you walked out the door, but you did say that you were sorry for how things turned out. It was genuine, but it served no purpose now. I watched you pull out of the driveway, taking with you not only my only source of transportation but my heart and soul as well. You damaged me, sending me into a familiar spiral, but this time with an underlining sense of self-efficiency.

But I wasn't ready for that just then. That night I got drunk. I had walked up to the bar uptown, not wanting to face the empty house, and sat at a bar stool away from everything and everyone. My only contact was the bartender, and I kept him busy, contributing to my goal of reaching alcohol-poisoning levels. I staggered home, possibly crawling some of the way, and passed out on the kitchen floor. I woke up with my bones creaking and late for work.

The chance for surviving was in my own hands, and I woke up determined not to let you leave me stomped into the ground. I pulled myself together as best as my hangover would allow and found the stamina to not let you destroy me, to not let me destroy me. So through the murkiness of that morning, I picked up the pieces and found a route back to optimism and forced that upward funnel of depression back into deeper recesses. I walked to work and faced my stern boss, who had the reputation of being hard core. Complete and utter honesty was the grounds for my success that day. I told him nothing but the truth, that my nerves were shattered and I needed three days to sort things out. He gave me one day, with the advice that I shouldn't let any woman rule my life.

I spent the rest of the day in a whirlwind with one goal in mind, to have a car parked in my driveway by sunset that day. I walked to the car lot just outside of town and bartered for an hour with a salesman to lower the price of an older model Grand Prix. My fondness for Camaros was not part of the process. I know he gave up part of his commission to accommodate me, but it was a price within what I thought I could afford. I told him I would be back that afternoon and walked to the insurance company office on the main street. I was surprised to find a reasonable rate. I did omit the details of my past foolishness when I was younger from the application. They could find out about that later. I needed to focus on the time restraints. I could face the inability to lie later.

The last thing to accomplish was the most difficult. I had to face the bank and their control over what financing I could get. I went home first for a few bottles of liquid courage, afraid of what the answer was going to be. Armed with a shield over my inhibitions, fear replaced with the fortitude of fermented drinks, I walked into the bank prepared as I ever would be. After waiting nervously, I was soon sitting across from a loans officer. The fact that it was a woman relaxed me a little, but I still wasn't quite sure how to present myself. She had piercing eyes and was not that much older than myself. I struggled at first, but then with the help of that internal guidance that sometimes kicks in, I opened up to her. I told her I didn't know if I should talk to her on a personal level or a business level. With my hands trembling, I spewed out everything in complete detail and complete honesty about what happened between you and me and how I desperately needed the car. I felt a few warm tears on my cheeks as I went on to explain that I needed this to keep some form of dignity.

I sat there in shock as she quickly began the paperwork, discussing only briefly my income and my expenses. My past finances did not enter the picture. I watched the approval for the loan appear before my eyes. I am sure she broke all the rules of the bank's protocol. Had she felt that sorry for me, had I looked that needy, that pitiful? I had difficulty making eye contact with her afterward, her compassion affecting me. But when the final papers were signed, I knew she must have seen the gratitude in my eyes while I thanked her over and over again.

Within a period of eight hours, I had found a car, had insurance for it, and had found an affordable loan to buy it. I drove that car into my driveway that night with a sense of pride and triumph. You might have knocked me over, but I was getting back up. I wanted the words I said to Ben that night when I blurted out you were leaving to ring with truth. I would remain strong. I would prevail.

I entered my house that night and looked at all the belongings you had left behind. I thought that you might have taken my car, but I had your furniture. A twitch of revenge, thinking I had gotten even, ran briefly through my veins. I fell asleep on the couch that night, completely drained, a rewarding sense of vengeance numbing any heartache. The next day, I changed the locks.

For the next few weeks, I concentrated on my work, asking for any available overtime. You were still with me, but I thought time would eventually create the distance I needed to get away from you. I walked to the town bar one night, thinking that would help me forget about you. My reclusive lifestyle was not working that well, especially with your presence still within the walls of my home. It was at the bar that I realized how far back I had withdrawn into myself. The pretty girls on the dance floor could not hold my attention. I could fool myself for brief intervals and feel attraction for a moment, but you were still on top of my mind, regardless of what I wanted to admit to myself. You still filtered through all my thoughts. The satisfaction of replacing the car had been short-lived. It was only a cover for the hurt. The pain still ran deep. You had done some severe damage, crushing my aspirations and my ego. The strength I vowed was not really there. But survival instincts are not as easily crushed. I had been alone before. I could be alone now. I staggered home that night without a stray woman in my arms.

A few days later, I received a very unexpected phone call. Your friend Jim had obviously taken a great liking to me. Like a traitor to your friendship, he called to warn me that you were coming for your furniture, but he wasn't sure when. I thanked him, still not exactly sure why I was honored with this information. I knew the neighbor across the street, and although I found it difficult to impose on her, I asked if she could watch my house while I was at work for anything unusual and call me if anyone was around. She was inquisitive, so I told her what might happen.

The next Friday afternoon, she called me at work to tell me that there was a moving van in my driveway. I rushed home, my good attendance record saving me from reprimand later as I simply yelled out that I had to leave right away and vanished. You were standing on the lawn with a guy I did not know, and your nameless blonde friend and her boyfriend also stood beside you. Two cop cars were pulling up in front of the house. You had called them when you realized your key no longer worked. To my complete dismay, one of the cops was the same one that let you steal my car. And now he was back to help you move the furniture. I argued with the cops for a while, explaining to them that the furniture was ours, not just yours. The other cop called some attorney general and was told that you had all the right to take the furniture. Why I had thought that you were going to be decent enough to leave the furniture for me in exchange for the car was beyond my own logic, but I had thought it all the same. Even with some of your personal items still left in the house, I was convinced up until Jim's phone call that you were not returning. What a fool I had become.

I watched helplessly as, under the watchful guard of the police, you emptied out the house. As I watched the items leave, I was hit with a sudden flash of recognition. You had blinded me with such a witch's brew of love potion that I had previously been unable to see the fact that most of the stuff passing before me was from other relationships. The stereo system was from a past boyfriend that I now remembered you had told me he had left behind. I watched the numerous pieces of artwork that you had hung on my barren walls pass me by in the arms of what was probably your new boyfriend, your new victim. I now remembered you saying that they were all gifts. Now I doubted that. Most of the furniture was your ex-husband's. I had buried all these facts, shoving them in the darker corners of my brain so as to leave a perfectly uncontaminated picture of you.

The spell was gone, and I finally saw what you really were. I wondered how much, if any, of this material was actually yours. Still, I made one last attempt to talk to you as you plundered the remains of the house's contents. I asked if it bothered you at all that you had taken my car. You bluntly told me to consider that you were taking it out in trade for the time we spent in bed. I felt that final blade go through my heart. I went numb, and except for pain, all emotions were frozen. My soul fell briefly into blackness. I had one last flicker of desired retaliation flirting on the edge of my tongue. I wanted to tell you that you weren't that good, but couldn't. It would have been a lie.

I didn't cry as I watched the four of you pile into the cab of the rental van. I was empty, void of any perception except for one last look at you. In a hollow chest, my heart was on intermission. I watched you leave with your head down, saw you for the last time, but not the bewitching eyes, those penetrating eyes meant for the studies of the occult, leaving the shells of lovers behind like dreary debris and collateral damage.

In one last attempt at retribution, I went to a lawyer the next day, to see if there was anything I could do. I think it was more for relief to the financial bite than actual vengeance. He did inform me that there was a way to get the car back from you, but it involved a bond and a sheriff. The more I thought about it, the more I thought it wasn't really the car I wanted back. I was only prolonging the inevitable. You were gone. I told the lawyer to forget about it.

Contrary to my belief that I could remain strong and forget about you, it wasn't that easy. I would hear the songs we shared, see a show we watched together, or simply feel a calm breeze that sometimes reminded me of your own freshness. Every corner of my miserable existence reminded me of you. In a fit of self-pity one night, I ripped off my neck the gold chain you had given me for our first Christmas together and threw it in the trash. It had no further meaning.

My life did carry on without you, but regardless of how you treated me in the end, part of you welded to my very being. The love that I felt for you is hard to compare. Whether the good or the bad that you developed in me, I did eventually develop some defense mechanisms to try not to ever become that vulnerable again. I am still meant to feel and feel intensely, but my journey for perfection has been obscured. I still think of you, but finally not every day, and I can see and appreciate things in this world not associated with you. In the purpose of your own survival, of your own self-interest, I don't think you understood the true agony you left me with.

There are permanent scars, but I am mostly healed now, aside from a lingering fear of commitment, trailing mistrust, and an eternal search for true love gone sour. May you finally find the love you are looking for in such a way as not to continue to leave a trail of destruction behind you in the process. At least find a way to alleviate the volume of pain you inject through your voyage. You are not malevolent, although my own survival instincts may interpret it that way.

The love for my gypsy still remains.

CHAPTER 12

Melanie:

Westlake was a small town, and given enough time, especially with regular attendance at parties and social gatherings, everyone eventually knew someone who knew someone, and everyone had a connection to everyone that knew that person, and so and so on.

I had been to many parties in our small town, and I had seen you several times. We were eventually introduced at one of them. You were still with your husband when that introduction took place. That was many moons ago, and I was still in the puppy stages of any signs of maturity.

I was always attracted to you and would look for you in crowds. You were almost a full decade older than I was, so a little fantasy for me was in play. I was actually still married when our first words of any meaningful conversation ever took place between us. When you split up from your husband and divorced him, you talked to me more often, but you always seemed to be with a new guy all the time—a long line of replacements. But I always held that hidden attraction and always dreamed what it would be like to be with you. Even the reputation you were gathering by being with so many different men did not deter me from that.

When Leslie left me, I was determined not to go into a tailspin, but emotionally I was walking along the edge of a cliff. She had ripped my heart out and part of my will with it. I didn't want to go into another period of regression, but the pain that throbbed at the center of my core needed medication. I bathed it in alcohol, but it left me precariously faltering at the rim of an abyss to self-destruction. You knew Leslie, and although you hadn't said it out loud, your frown and other body language showed your dislike of her. She had met you at Ben's numerous house parties, and she never failed to tell me of her dislike for you. It had been mostly about your flirtatious ways, but as a guy, I didn't have a problem with it. The fact that we talked to each other would set her off, even though all our conversations were of trivial nature. I liked to talk to you and, of course, feed my fantasy. I do have to admit that your multiple partners had given you a reputation that preceded you, but this was only a fleeting thought for me.

When Leslie and I parted ways, or rather abandoned me, I spent a lot of time with Ben and his wife. They were very understanding friends, and it also allowed me the choice away from the bar scenes to occupy my lonely weekends. As much as I had convinced myself that I would be strong this time on my own, determined to stay focused on a prosperous future, that raking emptiness in the middle of my gut kept dragging me down to impending levels of depression. Sitting in dark bars alone, wallowing in self-pity and drowning in my past disappointments had put me back in dangerous territory. Soaking in the dreadful atmosphere of barroom dungeons, scanning for strays that might give me temporary comfort in the sack, should have been grounds for insanity. This was only a recipe for a catalytic downward spiral, a cycle of repetition that I was still trapped in, broken only by a few flashes of hope and false senses of security.

The familiarity of friends was better medicine, and although the need for steady doses represented imposition, my fear of working my way to rock bottom was worth the risk of wearing thin my welcome. It validated my pestilent behavior that Ben and his wife did not seem to mind in the slightest, and their habit of partying every weekend was probably a mask of their own unhappiness and insecurities. With my close and loyal friendship to them, we fed off each other and yet knew our limitations when it came to advice and digging in to the centers of our cores. We were self-professed psychologists to each other. And as each week brought more of my growing pessimistic outlook, I thrived on their friendship and the comforts of their hospitality and understanding more than ever. I had many acquaintances, but very few close friends that I could confide in, so my dependence on them at that time was a safety line.

The weekend that you and I took our friendship a few rungs higher, I was set for another weekend of marathon drinking with Ben and his wife. There were eleven miles of winding road between my new hometown and Westlake, and with the drinking and driving laws getting stricter by the year, Ben's couch was to be my sleeping quarters for the weekend. Their ability to party incessantly, their solid friendship, and their uncanny way to be able to remind me that I could laugh once in a while made them almost another item on my list of addictive behaviors. It also gave me temporary escape from my maddening search and insatiable need for female company. I was still far from understanding that you had to be happy within yourself first before looking for outside sources. Bound in the depths of my forlorn feelings, there was no room for such veritable philosophies. I stole my inner strength from women.

So when I walked into Ben's house that weekend and saw you sitting among all the Friday night revelers, that familiar skip of my heart started involuntarily. It had been the first time in memory I did not see you with someone else. Whether it was my loneliness, my drive to be with someone, or the lighting, you looked more beautiful than I had ever recognized before. I had skipped the routine priming process of pouring back half a dozen beers before I left, so my bashfulness was in full swing. I was almost blushing when I said hello to you, and your return greeting had a softer, sexier tone than I remembered, enhanced by a sweet smile that had more than just friendly overtones.

I tried to remember the name of the last guy you were with, but it became unimportant to me. What was important was the sudden rush of feelings I was wrapped in, this sudden increase of my attraction when realizing you were there alone. I noticed your aura in depth for the first time and the swirling mixture of bright colors that livened up the room. I almost shook my head to disperse them from my vision, totally amazed that after all this time that I had known you, I had ignored that electrical field around you and had only memories of neutral grays. To finally look at you this way without the influence of any drugs was incandescence. With a room full of people and the din of the festivities, my concentration was quickly interrupted, but the sensation from you was now etched inside my brain.

Ben had an array of sofas and chairs in his living room, some backed against walls, others sandwiched between various shapes and sizes of end tables. The kitchen and living room were all open, leaving a spacious area for parties. A long line of floor-to-ceiling windows that overlooked the lake in his backyard gave the illusion of vast expanse. He was the envy of his friends with this lakeside home, and although he only rented it, he was quite proud. That night the lake was ominous as the waves were pushed to shore, and with the windows starting at ground level, it was easy to think that the water would come crashing through the living room. Only a small strip of sand separated the foundation of the house from the water's edge. There was always a hypnotic draw to the shore, where the waves would break into foam and temporarily swallow the sand but return it in equal intervals. But that night I kept going back to you. Your clear blue eyes were focused on me in a way I had not seen before, and although you were involved in conversation with others, you would indiscreetly keep looking back at me.

Everyone in the room was an acquaintance of another, so there were no strangers, no new members to the party. Only a couple of them were obnoxious, so the atmosphere in the room was essentially delightful. I had taken a seat in an empty chair across the room from you and began to pour back beers into my gullet at a fast pace, as if to regain a couple of lost laps in a drinking race. I eased into conversation with a few others, mandatory replies to those who talked to me, but I couldn't keep my eyes off you. I fought for a reason why I had this sudden flush of attraction, and when Ben came by, I asked him if you were with anyone. In his usual blunt way, he told me that he had flown the coop and snidely remarked that you were available. I gave him a frown and then a smile of embarrassment, wondering if he saw right through me.

I dug into the partying, trying to avoid thinking about you. However, the more I drank, the more I wanted to talk to you. But something inside me knew that I would never have the courage to approach you in the manner that I had in mind. I was just someone you knew in passing and would never be interested in someone that was that much younger than you. I again tried to put you out of my mind. The night went on with revelry, and slowly, the more rational ones left. The diehards weren't going anywhere, their awareness and cognition significantly diminished.

When I came back from another trip to the bathroom, Ben had eased into my chair. Friend or not, I wasn't about to tell the host to get out of my spot. I caught your eye while looking for another place to sit, and you patted the cushion next to you with your hand. It had been vacated earlier by someone who had left. I grabbed another beer out of Ben's community fridge and sat down beside you, with my stomach unsettled, in a slow churning of nerves. I was excited to be sitting this close to you, but was still unsure about how personal our conversation should go. Even as harmless an enterprise as talking to you, it had a fear of rejection attached. Had I forgotten that you invited me to sit down?

Your friendliness and pleasant demeanor eased my fears, and in little time, we were exchanging information through casual questions just as we had done in the past. You made me feel comfortable very quickly, and with the alcohol suppressing any surface shyness, I relaxed. Your soft tones released any remnants of tension, and under the radar of the loud partiers left around us, you talked to me as if you had known me forever. I sank further into the couch as you opened up to me with unexpected personal levels. When I asked why you were there alone, you were quick to tell me that your boyfriend had left you. You told me he was a truck driver and you had recently found out that he had been cheating on you, with someone in another town, not two months after you let him move in with you. I listened intently. When you asked about me, I did mention about my gypsy friend and some details of how she had left me and was surprised to feel that it helped for me to talk about it with you. I had clammed shut, refusing to talk about it even to Ben and his wife. But here I was sharing personal issues with you when only moments earlier, I was feeling too bashful to even approach you.

There was a mutual exchange of empathy through the invisible rays passing between us and an understanding that both of us had checkered pasts, best left in the darker corners of our brains. Your blue eyes were reading me, and I saw in them more than just friendliness. Electricity was discharged through me when you moved closer to me, your leg brushing up against mine. The onrush of warmth through my veins knocked down any barrier I might have had set up to impede my attraction to you. I was still not over a relationship that had ripped my heart out, and yet I was doing nothing now to curb my feelings toward you. I was still full of pain, yet the complacency you were already placing in me and the alcohol eating holes into my armor of protected sentience was now allowing that familiar flow of adornment to radiate from my heart.

I did not once stop and think that this was happening way too fast. The brain thinks differently when soaked in alcohol, but the basic principles usually remain the same. With effort and a buildup of tolerance levels, poor judgment can be minimized. Many times I had fooled myself with that theory and disallowed the consequences of my actions. I wanted to be with you, and there was no debate with any internal voices. I was not misreading your actions, and they only further inflamed my desire.

This was not picking up someone at a bar and discarding them before sobriety hits. I knew you, and I had certain attractions to you in the past. And the communication between us that night was fluid and genuine. Despite all my exclamations that I could finally survive on my own, I knew the truth. The vulnerable side of me that thrived on female companionship had already lost any argument to stay protected, and the only thing that mattered was to pursue you. I fueled this drive with more alcohol and replenished your own drinks in the process. Getting you drunk was not my intentions, but I did want to erase any doubts you might have had about my younger age and wipe out any ideas that I might not be a worthy candidate for companionship and beyond. There would be no time or effort set aside for courting. If we were going to do this, it was now. We would either hit it off immediately or carry on separately with the rest of our uncertain futures.

It was almost three in the morning when the thunderstorm hit. Our legs had become intertwined at the ankles, all our inhibitions and discretions gone with the crowd and our guard eliminated. The sudden lightning bolts across the surface of the water added to the mystique of the night. The view out of the window was almost surreal as it lit up the dark to show the tips of the whitecaps rolling toward the house, close enough to spray the windowpanes. This magical exhibition of nature was further enhanced when the lights inside the house flickered and then went out. With a cigarette lighter to guide her, Ben's wife shuffled through a kitchen drawer and found candles. The radio had gone dead in mid song, and there was an eerie silence in the room. The flames from the candles cast mysterious shadows on the walls and fed my senses, fed my feelings for you.

Ben, in his perpetual attempt at humor, asked if anyone wanted him to sing a song in lieu of the radio and was answered by a harmonious chorus of nos. You became edgy a few minutes after the lights went out. I asked you what was wrong, and you explained that your kids were home alone. I knew you had three kids but, with the exuberance of the evening, had given it absolutely no thought or consideration. I had almost forgotten that I had met them when they were very young. I reflected back on the vague memory I held about actually being in your house when you were still married to your husband, when Paul had dragged me there. Paul was your cousin, my buddy. We had only stayed for two beers and had interrupted your breakfast when we barged in looking for something to do after an all-night drinking spree. I remember how uncomfortable I felt, wondering what the hell I was doing in the middle of someone else's family life.

I placed your oldest son now at thirteen, and you confirmed it when I asked. You said he was quite responsible, but you were worried about the younger ones waking up in the storm and being alone in the dark. You decided you should go. Earlier in the night, you had told me that you had taken your share of the house that was sold and divided as part of the divorce decree and used it to buy another house only a few doors down the road. Since it was on the opposite side of the road, it had been reasonably priced as opposed to direct lakefront property. I had felt a sprinkle of envy as I thought of how I had squandered my money throughout the years, and owning a house was still a dream for me.

As you got up to leave and say good-bye to everyone, I whispered to you that I would like to go with you, more as a request than a statement. You nodded to me and, in a very soft and sexy whisper that sent a chill through me, said, "If you want to." Although it was only companionship I was truly seeking that night, the Neanderthal urges were already lurking, filling me with anticipation. I could hear a snicker from one of Ben's leftover company as we got up together to leave, but I focused on Ben and his wife. Ben gave me a comprehending wink that portrayed his chauvinistic ways. His wife gave me an understanding look, sympathetic to my loneliness and past history of loss. When she was sure no one else was watching, she mouthed the words *be careful*, to me. I thought about what a cherished friend she had become, as loyal to me as Ben, but more sophisticated. She had lent me an ear many times in the past while our fellow drinking troops passed out around us, including her husband, leaving only the two of us to conversation. We had watched more than one sunrise together, and she had helped me through some difficult times. I nodded to her in recognition and to her genuine care.

It was only sprinkling when we first started to walk to your house, but halfway there, the clouds opened up like a rain forest waterfall and drenched us in seconds. We ran the rest of the way hand in hand, precariously balancing each other from slipping in the loose gravel and the dirt that was quickly turning into mud. Once inside your house, I stood at the door while you fumbled around for a flashlight and candles. After lighting the candles, you took the flashlight to check on the kids to find them all still fast asleep. You brought me several towels to dry off with and sat down at your kitchen table. From the corner bar in your living room, you pulled out a bottle of wine and two glasses and set them in front of me. I smiled in gratitude and watched you disappear down the hall. You returned a moment later, dressed in nothing but a velvet robe that you left seductively open in the front. I felt the familiar risings and the inner voice that shouted that this was going to happen. But alongside that voice was another that said this was happening too fast.

Had you feelings for me all along? What had happened to my promise to myself that I would not fall for anyone else again, as a tribute to the pain I carried around with me, as a service to past love? I had many questions rolling around inside my head, but had already allowed my feelings for you to spin them in circles to stop any answers from cohering. An awful thought occurred when my defense mechanisms tried to kick in. Maybe I could treat you like a one-night stand. There was only remorse to deal with that way. I took a big gulp of wine just before you sat down beside me and replaced the taste of wine with the taste of your plentiful and plush lips.

I felt the flush of desire, your sensuality flooding me. My inner conflicts quickly subsided, and my mind went blank as you led me down the hallway. I followed you like the lost soul that I was. In the darkness of your bedroom, you took me back to the blissful memories of soft skin next to mine, and all my files of comparison were set on pause, all thoughts hushed and lost in a vacuum of sexuality. The impending gratification of the moment was my only grasp of consciousness. Your intensity and display of your own desire overpowered me, and I was submerged in your hold. With you on top and in complete control, my satisfaction mixed with pleasure and some escape of my internal anguishes. It was quick and feverish, my willpower minimized by your aggression.

I lay beside you afterward, an awkward silence between us while I held your hand. I was sound asleep a moment later, an instant and peaceful slumber as deep as anesthetic inducement. I did not wake until morning and to the sounds of chirping birds outside the window. I did not recognize my surroundings, and I had no idea where I was. The grogginess left me unaware and with no instant memory. I looked over and saw your bare back and your long blonde hair flowing down to one side. The memories of the night rolled back on a slow screen of recognition.

You were still asleep, and I could only think of your kids getting up at any moment, finding me in their house. I had no preparations for any explanations to any questions they might ask. Nothing was preparing me on how to properly face you. So in cowardice fashion, I slipped on my wrinkled clothes, still damp from the rain, found my way to the front door, wincing as the hinges of your screen door squeaked in defiance. I walked back to my car, which I had left parked in front of Ben's house. The morning air refreshed me, the smell of wet ground pleasant to the senses as the early sun was already baking the mud. I had a fresh start to a new day that would definitely be intertwined with liberation and limited remorse.

It was not until after my car was safely back in my own driveway, until after a long cold shower and two breakfast beers, sitting on my backyard picnic table caressed by a warm summer breeze, that I reflected on the night's events. It was already too late to protect my heart. My feelings were with you. I began to wonder what was wrong with me to feel this way again so quickly. Was that gaping hole in my heart only loneliness and could easily be filled back up again by merely being with a woman again? Could I create such adornment on sheer potential?

I really didn't know you, part of me still judging you with your reputation and string of relationships. Some of them were just rumors, but even fabrications sometimes leave no room for doubt. You had three children, almost a decade more of experience and probably a greater understanding of what you wanted out of life than I could ever grasp for myself. But my runaway heart was also telling me that it was you I wanted, even though I had sworn that my shields—to protect me from any more amorous feelings, shields that were shellacked in pain—would remain up as barricades to any emotional entrapments. One night of your company, and it all turned into sawdust.

Clearly I was directionless in my needs. My mind was still clogged with the idea that romance and true love was the path to my internal and external goals. Short-term memory was a curse when my drive for success and my fight to ward off depression depended on women. I mulled over these thoughts over and over again that warm summer morning, fueling my bloodstream with a fresh supply of alcohol. With each additional drink, my night with you would resurface over all other thoughts and memories.

After a quick, uncomfortable afternoon nap on the top of my picnic table, I woke up determined not to spend the night alone. I found your phone number with the aid of a helpful operator, but regardless of my determination, I still hesitated to call you. I wasn't sure if I was ready to tackle my feelings for you verbally yet. If I gave you time before I became completely vulnerable to you, I could let you decide how you really felt about me. Surely you would wait for me a couple of days for me to explain my quick getaway. Maybe my own confusion would be sorted out if I waited. I fought with myself, and a toss of the coin would have been less tedious and less painful in deciding. I did surprise myself when I decided not to call you until later. But I still was determined not to spend the night alone in my house, so I did not see the harm in going up to the town bar for a few drinks and quicken the pace of the night. If I stayed home, I would only pressure myself with all angles of thought and never be able to sleep.

If only I had some grasp of how really screwed up I was. If only I had been able to rid myself of the stigma to get professional help, I might have had some enlightenment about how serious my downward spiral was becoming. Down in the center of my soul, however, was always a faint light that kept me from drowning. My goals, my dreams, the hope and the faith that a good and happy life awaited for me somewhere in the future, still oscillated in there somewhere. Hard work, time, and possibly some small acts of divine intervention, would help me pull through this. I had to believe that. It was the basis of my survival instincts.

I retrieved two amphetamine pills from my hidden stash and washed them down my gullet with another beer. I walked the sidewalks to the town bar. How I hated this town, this bar, but always went back for more. I found my favorite bar stool empty, the one at the far corner of the bar out of the way of everyone, my study vantage point. I claimed squatter's rights for the night and began to order a steady stream of pints of draft. The bathroom was directly behind me, and as all true beer drinkers know, there is usually a steady stream that exits as well. So with all necessary details in order, I began my night of temporary escape from you.

There was a clear view of the dance floor, the entire bar for that matter, from my assigned viewing sight. The bar had only been half full when I arrived, but an hour later, it was packed. I was uncomfortable with that size of crowd, the claustrophobic part of me raising distress. At the same time, I thrived on the vibrant energy of groups, enhanced by the music and the drone of the crowd.

Time took its course, and the alcohol-infused environment was working, and I was able to stop thinking about you, but only in intervals. There were only a few people in the bar I recognized, but my preference to remain a loner in this town wouldn't even label them as acquaintances. Most of my concentration went to the dance floor, where with the summer weather also came some scantily clad women. My rampant appetite for the female body was an involuntary reaction, and that night was no exception. But I was only looking at scenery, not drooling with anticipation or even remotely interested in any encounters that night. There were previous nights where I sat in my corner in solitude, preferring to avoid conversation with anyone except the bartender. And even that I would find strenuous, pointing for a refill and limiting my words to a polite thank-you. He had never cut me off in the past, probably from my knack to not appear drunk. I usually didn't stagger until I hit the outdoors, as if the fresh air triggered a response.

I watched the flings and bounces of the young women on the dance floor, leaving little room for imagination. On a normal night, I would pick one out and focus on her alone, making my best effort to sending psychic vibrations to her. I usually struck out, my abilities contaminated with alcohol. As much as I hated this bar, I had turned it into my drinking hole, and no amount of liquid courage would allow me to approach a woman outright. I remembered one exception, but that was when I first moved to town and was a relative unknown. The fear of rejection now would jeopardize the sanctuary of my little escape, the safety of my bar stool. This was my fuel depot to absorb any kinetic energy I could pull from the human race.

Just as I thought I was absorbed enough to put you out of my mind entirely, you came flashing back. I don't know if there was a particular dancer that suddenly reminded me of you or I had picked up a telepathic thought from someone that was close to my own. The dance floor melted in front of me into a colorful display of mixed auras and propelling arms and shuffled legs, and I suddenly realized that I had no interest in being there. There was no desire, no meaning to my gawking game. My curiosity to what these women were thinking, what their lives were like, vanished. All my thoughts were with you. Even with all the distractions around me, I couldn't shake you. I stowed away the idea that I couldn't possibly be in love with you so quickly. My heart was already amiss. I suppressed the possible fact that I was only looking for someone to replace Leslie, to extinguish that incessant ache inside my chest.

Absolved of all logical reasons not to go after you, I drowned all my defenses in ale that night. The lessons from my past dissolved with them. I allowed myself to plunge back into my cauldron of emotions. There was no room for debate about getting hurt again, and any voice of reason was shoved back into far corners of my subconscious mind, leaving the door wide open for the return of obsession. That was my last coherent thought of the night before I blacked out.

I woke up the next morning on my couch, obviously finding some way to crawl home. It took until noon for my head to stop pounding, subsided by several morning cocktails of vodka and tomato juice. But it was replaced with another kind of pounding, the drumming of an obsessive mind. I had to call you, no choice but to act on my feelings for you. I had to act on this chance for romance in my life again and defer a closer look at my jumbled life. I took several deep breaths and began a series of calls to you, on the hour every hour, before I finally got an answer.

Your voice sent a chill through me, your soft hello representing a hold on my sanity. Our conversation went well, nothing awkward and mostly straightforward. You explained that you had just come back from visiting your mother as you did most Sundays. Your children had a special bond with her, and they did spend a lot of time with her. I apologized for leaving you without any notice and used the excuse that I wasn't sure how your kids would react to me. You told me it would have been all right, and before I even let you finish, I blurted out that I wanted to see you again. There was only a moment of hesitation, and then you surprised me by inviting me over for dinner on Wednesday night. I said yes before any thought processes could mess it up on me. We shared cordial good-byes, and I fell asleep soon after, no longer jittery and restless. It was a peaceful sleep of the floating kind, and you drifted in and out of my dreams.

I dug deep into my work that week, and Wednesday night came more quickly than I had anticipated. If there were any other fragments of optimism holding me together besides my search for romance, it was my job. With steady paychecks, I could save, plan for a future of financial gain, and prove myself in this materialistic world that society demanded I fit into. As many times as I had rejected such a role for myself, mostly because of all the setbacks in finding a way, I knew that if I was ever to crawl out of the pits of depression that periodically swallowed me whole, there had to be a mature path to follow. I couldn't be a rebellious teenager anymore. But curbing my drinking habits was secondary and was not allowed to be linked to any of my problems. And for this reason, I showed up at your door with fresh-cut flowers under one arm, but a case of beer under the other.

You opened the door with a warm smile, and a golden aura wrapped around you. Your blouse was very low cut, and your cleavage had instantly set off arousing thoughts. But no matter how hard I tried to suppress it, there was one abrasive thought, and I could hear the annoying voices of past acquaintances that had sprouted stories about you that tarnished your reputation. My own needs preceded the effects of those stories, and I swatted it into the background. That was then, and it wasn't like I had a great reputation of my own.

Dinner was superb—mixed vegetables, mashed potatoes, and meat loaf that reminded me of something my mother might have fed me long, long ago. A home-cooked meal was a luxury in my world of a steady diet of sandwiches. Not many people like to cook for themselves, and I wasn't the greatest of cooks to begin with. After helping you clean up and sneaking a kiss to thank you, I settled into the living room to get to know your kids. They had not been the least apprehensive of me, and aside from trying to impress you, I had genuine interest in them. I always carried my daughter inside me, wondering what she was doing, and a gnawing useless desire to be part of her life. Except by default of my immature bias toward Leslie's son, I had refined my thoughts of my own daughter with the concern of other children.

My time with your kids that night was split evenly, several games of table hockey with your oldest son, which I gracefully conceded to his better skills, helping your daughter with her math homework and noticing how she shared your good looks, to a card game with a revolving set of rules with your youngest son. There was an odd sense of tranquility in your living room as your kids accepted me with next to open arms. My normal craving for beer had vanished with my time with your kids, and over half the case remained. They stayed up late, as if I was a special occasion, and I was humbled when they all said good night to me like I had invariably become part of their household.

We sat on your couch after the kids went to bed, and I instinctively held your hand. I felt the permeation of magnetism through our intertwined fingers, feeling it rise up through my arm and into the tributaries of my heart. After several minutes of staring blankly at the television screen at a show that captured none of my interest, in my blunt and blurted fashion, sounding like a teenager, I told you that I wanted to go steady with you. It was the only terminology I could get to roll off my tongue. Was I asking you for a date or to marry me? You were far from simple. You knew what I meant.

You stumped me for a moment when you promptly asked me if I was sure that I wasn't just on the rebound. I told you I could go to some sleazy meat-market bar for that and was almost in danger of not avoiding a hastened I love you. Instead I said that you had captured my heart, and I knew this was fast, but I could not help the way I felt. You sat there for a while in careful consideration, and for a second, I felt a pang of rejection flickering in my chest. You extinguished it quickly when you said that if we were going to be together, we would have to take it slow. I agreed immediately and told you that you had the reigns and to slap me if I started to move too fast. I reached over and gave you a quick kiss, which you reciprocated with soft kisses that created sparks. It also contained the unspoken message of "to be continued later."

We talked quite a bit that night, the casual talk of close friends and mutual respect. You also told me that you had just started a steady job recently after trying to survive on part-time work. I took the hint, realizing that it would be no easy chore to get three kids ready in the morning and also get yourself off to work. I left at midnight, but it was not easy.

At the door, you agreed to spend Saturday night at my place, since your kids would be spending the weekend at their grandmother's. I drove home that night content and warmed by the idea that I now had the potential for a long and loving relationship. That was if I didn't screw it up. The fact that you were ten years older than me was only a fleeting thought, and I felt that an older woman was precisely what I needed to keep me on the right track. I fell asleep that night feeling good about myself, a rare commodity for me.

The rest of my week was longer than the first. I would constantly think of a future with you, probing into my subconscious depths looking for all the ways to do everything right this time. The clocks slowed to a crawl, making concentration on other things difficult, and even at work I was daydreaming. At night I was restless, and whenever I did fall asleep, I would dream of you. It was complete repetition of my obsessive ways.

Friday night was the worst, as they usually were when it came to my mind turning around like an over-revved engine. But my drive to do things right this time left my beer collection chilling in the fridge, and I stared at the television screen instead. The shows were consistently interrupted by you though, and there was a constant shadow of your presence, with or without my eyes closed. I had already thrown all precautions to the wind to protect my fragile feelings this time, a broken promise to myself when Leslie left me. I was back in dangerous territory and letting another woman carry my heart. In essence, I barely knew you. I didn't care.

You were three hours late Saturday night, and I was pacing floors again. It took great effort not to call you. There were deep sighs of relief coming from my lungs when you finally pulled into the driveway. You apologized right away for being late, but I wasn't listening to your words. You were dressed so provocatively that I wanted to sweep you off your feet like some cheesy romantic comedy. I managed a quiet hello instead. We had known each other for a long time in passing, but this new plateau of romantic involvement had left me with initial discomfort. That and the persistent fear of messing up. Alcohol was the cure for that as it was my cure for many things. Heavy volumes of quick intake of the cheap champagne I had bought for this occasion soon had me relaxed.

Words were few, and groping sessions started early. We shared the taste of champagne from the tips of our tongues in a fury of long sensuous kisses. I was swept up in the moment after thinking about you all week and led you down the hall into my bedroom, where you allowed me to slowly undress you. We landed on the bed, molded together and wrapped around each other like the world depended on it. For one fleeting moment, Leslie flashed in front of me, an apparition on the surface of my eyelids. You sensed something as I jolted slightly at the vision. You felt me and asked what was wrong. I whispered that nothing was, and I shook her away in a display of broken butterfly wings. For that brief moment, I felt like I was cheating on her. This had been her bedroom too. And then finally the reality of her being gone hit hard and fast, no prolonged wishes and false hopes of her return, no resurrecting the past. I could finally bury her.

We made love that night, over and over again. And then again on Sunday morning while the first rays of daylight filtered through the bedroom window. It reminded me of a description of it from my past. We were both anxiety screwing. *So be it* was my only thought. Just because you were a woman did not ban you from the same access of this escape route in your search for comfort. We made plans to go out for lunch and then showered together. The passion began to flow again, and one shower became two. I felt so at peace. Peace from love was not a new concept, but certainly not a universal one.

We eventually made it to the restaurant, where we finally really talked. I am not sure how the topic was started, but you opened up to me about your past, as if you felt it necessary. You came clean about your reputation when I mentioned that I had heard stories that I didn't believe. Your past reputation was not all fabricated. It was not all galloping gossip. You were searching, exploring, finding independence after an abusive marriage. I thought of my own regression and could easily relate to why you would have taken such a path. Your husband had become very abusive at the end of your marriage, the behind-closed-door verbal and physical assaults, where no one could really know the truth; know the extent of the mistreatment from the hands of your ex-husband. Your later promiscuity after your breakup did not take solid hold on me, and it was easy for me to accept the reasons. I wasn't exactly an angel in my own search for meaning and direction. That still didn't allow me to fully open up to you, and I dodged most of your questions about my past. I wanted to forget about it all. I didn't want to risk filling your head with doubts about me by sharing my checkered past. I wanted you to be my past as well as my future.

After lunch, I wanted to enjoy some of the summer day rather than go back to my house right away. There was a river just outside of town with a sloping bank where a small park had been built. It was far from as serene as my favorite site on the beach outside of Westlake, but it would serve its purpose. We took a long walk along the banks, scaring a pair of Canadian geese from a patch of thick reeds, watched a trout jump out of the water in an attempt to catch a dragonfly; a gray squirrel scampered to the opposite side of an oak tree. I loved nature, and now I had you to share it with.

I retrieved out of my backseat the frayed quilt that was always a permanent residence of my car and stretched it out under a secluded willow tree. Out of the trunk, I pulled out a magnum of wine, a bottle that had been there awhile as a mandatory emergency supply. It was warm but still drinkable. On that blanket, we spent the afternoon, disturbed only by the odd passerby. Two fishermen were on the opposite bank and showed no interest in us. We watched huge cumulus clouds sail by, moving portraits on blue velvet, changing into various forms of animation before our eyes. I lay there beside you, our fingers intertwined once more, and I could feel the pulse of the Earth beneath me. It wasn't even close to the energy of my favorite spot in Westlake, but I could feel the same pull of the Earth's core regardless. And I could feel you.

Your hand melded into mine, and I couldn't distinguish my own from yours. When I closed my eyes, my whole body seemed to float, but you came with me. I have had the hallucinatory effect of drifting many times, but that afternoon, it seemed more real. This was natural, like the orbit of the Earth itself. I had found another soul mate.

Without so much as a single thought, I leaned over and whispered into your ear that I loved you. In your enchanting voice, you whispered back the same words. I was enthralled, wrapped in a tranquil moment of a spiritual connection to the cosmos. I disregarded the thought that you might have repeated such cherished words only out of necessity, out of obligation, out of requirement for appeasement. Instead, I took them to the center of my heart as any hopeless romantic would.

You left late Sunday night, and when I stood in my driveway hugging you and not wanting to let go, I could feel a void approaching. When you drove away, the tears started to flow. I was not sure why I was crying, but I was grateful that I was able to control them until you left. A bag of mixed emotions blended with a cornucopia of past relationships made for a potent potion of melancholy reminiscence. I was watching my past, present, and future drive away. You represented it all. You held my whole deck in your hands in such a short time. So much for my inner strength, so much for my independence, so much for my invulnerability. I was now walking precariously along a cliff in windy gusts of susceptibility once again. It didn't matter, for the power of love overruled any rationale, now the fuel for my existence.

We had agreed that because of our work schedules, it would be best if we only saw each other on weekends. After our shared proclamations on the bank of the river, you repeated that it would still be best for both of us if we took things slowly. I had agreed, but such plans lacked sustenance when my love-craved mind spoke differently. I understood, though, or so I tried to convince myself.

I would call you through the week, but I was never fond of phone calls, lacking the ability to carry on a meaningful conversation through speakers and wires. The calls were short, but hearing your voice was enough encouragement for me to get to the weekend without you. My expectations of my time with you was also enough to curb my bad habits. I was smoking less cigarettes, drinking less beer, and had grown more comfortable at home by myself. But it was all based on the anticipations and sureties of our weekends together, my source of fuel and energy to get through the week.

Time has a tendency to accelerate when measured in routine. As we alternated weekends at each other's house and the long waits in between, autumn was fast approaching. I began to know your children as well as I knew you. They were quick to accept me as a houseguest every other weekend, and there were the odd times when they would let me win at the games we played. My fake sulk helped with that. I was family now. I settled into the comforts of our routine, but as all routines go, there is always something that will eventually interrupt them.

Both of your sons were in hockey, and travel hockey at that. You had warned me about hockey season, and I had pretended that I was prepared that most of our weekend time would be swallowed by their schedules. I had no choice but to tag along if I was to spend all available time with you. At first I had no interest, but then as I watched their games, I was there to support and to cheer your sons to victory. I did not say it, but the cold arena was not pleasant for me, but I hid my shivering with the fidgeting that comes with sitting on hard wooden benches. I applauded at the appropriate times, but I could not progress to the shouts and the screams of other parents who held dancing visions of their sons joining the National Hockey League.

Always distracted by my strange habit of studying people, the crowds around me entertained me enough to fill in the gaps of my actual lack of amusement in the game itself. Sure, I could feel the excitement when one of your sons would score a goal and could feel the symbiotic thrill of your own. The travel games were the most enjoyable with strangers to analyze. The home games left me feeling uncomfortable when I looked around the stands and spotted acquaintances of my teenage years from the now-defunct pool hall. Many were considerably older than I was, and to increase the difference, I still looked much younger; I had always joked about being pickled in alcohol when people would comment on my baby-face look.

These acquaintances had now become adults, matured into productive members of society, kids and wives in tow. Responsible members of their communities with good jobs, mortgage payments, and volunteers in various social groups. They probably even went to church every Sunday. I envied them, their collective dependability, their confidence and success. I felt inferior. I knew it was not too late for me, and I did have goals and aspirations still alive in me. You sat beside me as proof of a potential end to a final search and a path to a proper place for me. But what made it uncomfortable was what these people might actually be thinking about me, with only their memories to judge me by. I was the street urchin, whose pastime was drugs and alcohol, and that dreaded description, a burnout. I was the moron who gave up a beautiful wife and daughter to run off with a college girl and still had his life running off the tracks.

I still prayed for the day when my inferiority complexes would disperse and coincide with my belief that I didn't care what other people thought. But at that moment, I needed an outside source, and that outside source was you. Sitting beside me in those cold arenas was the ultimate package to steer me to a great future. A lovely woman to love and to plan things with, three beautiful children to help raise, and a straight direction away from all my past pitfalls. You represented my security, my safety, and a proud self-image. But I could not shake that the people in the arena were probably wondering what you were doing with me.

You had said to take it slow. That had been difficult for me to grasp, but if I was not to jeopardize my chances with you, I had to let you stay in the driver's seat. Taking it slow was precisely where our relationship was. I missed our first days together already. Then I did not see the great confidence of a single mother, who had the strength to carry on her own. Was I just companionship after all? The inner strength that I grew in small pieces at the end of each relationship was mostly my own deception. It was masked, covering its only real need, survival. I could analyze all this in numerous ways, but I was truly helpless in changing my ways. Why else would have I left myself so vulnerable to a woman again?

Between work and the hockey schedule, our real time (or quality time, as it is known by) was quite limited. Because of the hockey games, weekends became predominately spent at your house. We made love infrequently now, with a variety of excuses, none of them particularly unique. Winter came and stayed, and only your company was left for me to hold on to.

My Christmas work party was two Saturdays before Christmas, and I asked you to go with me. I had not gone the year before and wanted to make an appearance this time. After first confirming that your mother could take the kids to hockey that night, you agreed to go.

The party was in a hall just outside of my town, so I left in plenty of time to pick you up. You were stunning. A short black dress that showed your flawless legs, and your makeup had been done professionally, illuminating your astounding facial features. I was dressed in an old three-piece corduroy suit, oblivious to my outdated fashion statement that would have appropriated a disco ball.

I was gleaming with pride as I walked into the hall with you on my arm. The evening started smoothly as we ended up seated with the guys I worked with in the warehouse. You always had the ability to strike up a conversation with people you didn't know, and you soon had the entire table in captivation. I sat back and had never felt so comfortable in a social situation while you led conversation for me. So there was no excuse for me to have pounded back the drinks as if the oasis was about to run dry. We danced once, an inhibition that wouldn't quite go away, oppressed by some recurring memories of my many nights on the dance floor of the Vista Inn with a teenage wife. There was something sacred about dancing when held to memory.

Halfway through the night, one of the older workers from the factory part of our operation wandered over to our table and sat beside you. He knew you, and there was a long cordial exchange between you, like that of old friends. You briefly explained that he was an old friend of your ex-husband. After you caught up to date with each other, he looked over at me and crudely asked you what you were doing there with me. At first, I took no insult when you answered him by saying that I had asked you to. In retrospect, the words had reverberated to almost shame when I thought of all the other answers that you could have come up with. Your ex-husband's friend knew there was a ten-year difference in our age. I had disregarded it long ago, and when it did filter in once in a while, it gave me nothing more than a further sense of pride in being with you. Any Freudian remarks, even in a fleeting thought that I was looking for a mother figure, would hold no validity. But it did bother me later that you had not described us with further depth than just a casual date.

Pure idiocy alone left me feeling no pain when the company party wore down. I knew long ago not to touch tequila shots, yet my arm did not seem to hurt from whoever had twisted it. I was already starting to slur my words, and the steadiness of my feet needed the aid of my concentration. You were hesitant, but when we were invited to a house party, you agreed to go. It was the house of one of the factory workers that I didn't know that well, but it was a small company I worked for and explained the invitation. You took over the steering wheel of my car, and I gladly let you. You followed a string of cars belonging to the others, and we easily found the house. And in that house was where I lost my self-control with no explanation or prior need.

There was a pool table in the basement of the house and a wall with mirrors the entire length of the room. A full-length bar stretched across the other wall, stocked with every liquor bottle imaginable. There was thick carpeting and brand-new leather furniture in every corner. It was my dream house, the one that I should have owned by now. I was too drunk to recognize my self-pity, too drunk to know envy. Instead, I got plastered and avoided any sense of jealousy. I still managed to play a good game of pool that night, although I was far from showing my true skills. I poured shot after shot down my throat as it was offered to me as if to show my drinking skills instead.

I don't remember leaving the house, but I remember parts of our ride home. I kept putting my hand on your thigh, stammering out how much I loved you. You kept removing my hand to either concentrate on your driving or to protest my loathsome behavior. I remember dropping my cigarette twice, barely finding it in time to avoid burning a hole in the seat. I remember you helping me into your house and flopping me on your couch where I passed out still mumbling how much I loved you.

I woke up the next day not knowing where I was at first. Wiley, the coyote, was chasing some bird with a strange-sounding bicycle horn down its throat, which I soon recognized as coming from the television screen. I was finally able to focus on your daughter sitting on the floor, fully involved in the safe escape of the roadrunner. You were at the kitchen table holding a coffee mug and butting a cigarette into a full ashtray. There was no smile, but you strained out a good morning. I took the coffee you offered me and then had to bum a cigarette off you, having no idea where my package was. I began to think of a string of apologies, but only one I'm sorry rolled off my tongue. You only nodded, and your silence was enough to make my heart drop into my stomach. I felt very sick, and the noise from the television was pounding into my eardrums and sending throbs to my temples. When you finally spoke to me, it was to tell me that you had another hockey game that afternoon. I asked if you would mind if I skipped the game, and you told me that you would prefer it. That one had hurt, but I certainly deserved it. I left after a second coffee, waving good-bye to your daughter on my way out. I kissed you on the cheek when you turned your head away from me.

Back at home, I spent the day on the couch full of remorse and shame, praying I had not damaged our relationship. Two days went by before I called you, thinking somehow that the passing of time would make any problems go away. In a sense, it usually did help, especially with painful issues. Time also had a fleeting way to suppress anger and hurt, and forgiveness is easier to find. You were cordial when I called, and I thought it would be best if I didn't bring up the party at all. I also thought it best if we could meet in neutral territory to talk and not have you feel intrusion that might still linger from my drunken night on your couch. You said that it would have to be late, but you would meet me at that quaint little restaurant down by the fishing harbor at nine o'clock on Friday night. I did not question why so late, and I did not question why there.

When I pulled into the dark parking lot of the restaurant at exactly nine, your car was not there. I walked in to wait for you, and except for the waitress, who doubled as a cook at that time of night, and an elderly couple in the far corner, sitting beside the aquarium, the place was empty. I now understood why you had chosen that place and that time—privacy.

I chose a corner table by the window that overlooked the harbor and the line of fishing boats parked for the winter. I had all the intentions of ordering coffee, to talk to you completely sober. I ordered a beer instead. At ten o'clock and four beers later, you walked in. You sat down across from me with a quiet hello and ordered a coffee. You wore a pink knitted sweater under your winter coat, and my heart sank with a sudden weight attached to it as I saw in you the light of the home life that I so desperately needed. If I could only have convinced you how I truly felt, what I really wanted out of life, instead of my recent scary stammering, incoherent display of my drunken profession of my love in the car that night.

I asked how you were, and with a small smile, you said that you were okay. But the warmth was missing, and your eyes were glazed over. I ordered another beer, and I felt your aversion. We talked mostly nonsensically right up until closing, not in gibberish but like the talk of acquaintances keeping a conversation flowing. You were distant, and you fidgeted like something was wrong and you needed to say it. When I finally asked you what was wrong, I regretted it. I had opened up the door for you.

Your words still ring, like the sounds of discontented wind chimes and sudden impact. You told me that you didn't think things were going to work out between us. I slouched back in my chair as if you had just dropped two cement blocks back on my shoulders. I was not ready for it. I grasped for all the reasons, grasped for straws for you to change your mind. You denied it was because of my actions at the party even though after, in your next breath, you explained to me that your ex-husband was an alcoholic. You denied it was our age difference when I asked about that. I looked for other reasons when you finally said that it wasn't me, that it was you. I couldn't figure out what that was supposed to mean except you were trying to soften the blow.

My whiny, spineless, simpleton act came bubbling to the surface. I pleaded. I begged between sobs, tears big enough to bead and run down my chin, as I asked for another chance, repeating over and over how I could change. But your mind was made up, and to fortify your decision, any eye contact from you ended. You said that you were sorry and walked out the door.

After a desperate attempt of composing myself, under the indiscreet view of the waitress, I rushed out after you just as you were pulling away out of the parking lot. I stopped you by knocking on your window, and you rolled it down. The cold wind pushed your hair awkwardly back. I had not picked out a Christmas present for you yet, trying to decide on the best gift. But I had already bought presents for your kids. They were tucked away in the trunk of my car, already wrapped and waiting for a transfer to your Christmas tree. I asked you to please accept the gifts, and you nodded and stepped out to open your trunk. I placed the gifts carefully around your spare tire, just as the first sleet fell to remind me that winter was here to stay. I closed your trunk, and for a brief moment, we shared a deep look of understanding. You hugged me, and I thought I saw a tear of your own when you repeated that you were sorry. You got back in your car while the sleet cut into me, and I stood there motionless until your taillights faded and then vanished into the dark. God, I hated taillights.

I spent another Christmas alone, almost in a catatonic state. There were no phone calls from anyone, and I wouldn't have answered them anyway. My friends were with families, my family and relatives somewhere on the planet, and my love sprawled all over the countryside in various scenes of past encounters and memories.

I became a hermit that winter. I had enough seniority built up to not get laid off, so aside from work and the odd visit to the grocery store to stave off starvation, I had no use for the outside world. Invitations to the bars from co-workers were turned down flat, and calls from friends were ignored entirely. I even hid in my house pretending not to be home when Ben and his clan dropped in one weekend unannounced as they sometimes had done in the past. I felt like a fool cowering in my bedroom, hoping I had locked all the doors.

I was in self-rehabilitation. Since New Year's Eve, I had not smoked a cigarette or drank any alcohol whatsoever. It was March before I was even aware of my success, so withdrawn within myself to even attribute willpower to my success of abstinence. I did feel healthy and had actually gained a few pounds from my new craving of sugared items. Depression was still lurking everywhere, but I was able to function, and a constant need to check my bank account for growth added merit to my seclusion. The total of my savings was slowly creeping up to significant value where a down payment on a house was within reach. My goal now was to see how much I could save, and it was a sideline that kept my mind occupied when I felt it wander. The bigger the down payment, the bigger the house. Frugality replaced loneliness. A very strange substitute, but a practice that had been there all along. It wasn't long though when my past emotions would let loneliness rule again.

Spring finally arrived, and with it, a losing battle with the onset of cabin fever. Regardless of how secure I had become with my hermetic existence, I missed the interaction of friends. One thing about close friends, especially those who catered to the party lifestyle—it was quite acceptable to drop in without notice. Two weeks after the start of another cycle of blooming tulips and daffodils, my car found its way back to Ben's driveway, ready to be parked for the weekend, while its owner delved into some well-deserved partying. I was welcomed with open arms and the charm of family. Nothing had changed in their lifestyle, and there was already a small gathering of people in his living room, and a night of alcohol abatement was in the offering. One look out his lakefront window, and I was set in a softened mood as the waves rolled toward shore in hypnotic resonance. Settling easily back into the flow of beer after beer but refraining from the joints being passed around, I was in a quiet state of relaxation. The minute effects from the secondhand smoke were quite sufficient, and I had no need to take dosages that would almost certainly relapse me into bouts of paranoia. If there were any signs at all for me to grasp that pointed to signs of my maturity, it was to recognize that my days of marijuana were crossing the finish line.

Two hours into my visit, as I was mesmerized by the hues of red and orange reflecting off the water in a spectacular spring sunset, there was a knock on the door. Ben, his eyes already bloodshot, shouted out to come in. I turned around to watch you walk in.

I had no chance to prepare, no expectations of seeing you. I had been standing at the window when you knocked, my mind in tune with the breaking ripples of the water on the sand and the outstanding exhibition of colors. My heart immediately started palpitating. It took several deep breaths to lower my heart rate, but when your eyes met mine, you sent it soaring again. I had spent an entire winter getting over you and in a certain sense that deserved pride.

We exchanged hellos and smiles that said we missed each other's company. After the initial heartache and instant flush of attraction, I had an unusual feeling of indifference, not quite lacking emotion but a sense of control. For the first time in my life, I was controlling my heart, regulating any possible fluctuation of emotion. Had I finally reached a point where I could not allow pain and despair to command my thoughts?

I knew I was still attracted to you, but with back-to-back spears from you and Leslie still fresh in my mind, my blood had coagulated into the beginning of ice cubes. A very strange feeling, not one I was sure I liked very much, and it was a contradiction of my very core, but I recognized it as a new tool for survival. This was protectionism at its best. I had many nights to reflect on the development of my character during my winter hibernation, but I could not think it possible to find this odd sense of power. Had I found a way to never get hurt again?

Now looking at you and not feeling my guts turning into a mass of mixed emotions, there was a sudden epiphany that startled me. I had finally gathered enough scars on the outer surface of my heart that I could look at you and all the other haunting images of my past and not let the hurt and the pain interfere. It wasn't to say that they were gone, but I could see a different path that allowed for them to no longer rule me. My heart had finally hardened enough to let out some of the air that shared the same compartments of self-pity and empathy. It was a strange mixture anyway.

I didn't get drunk that night as you are well aware of. I monitored my pace in a way I thought I wasn't capable of. For this reason, I was not quite caught off guard when you walked up to me later in the night and asked if we could talk. My calmness and borderline insolent behavior surprised me some, and confidently, I suggested we go outside. It was dark on the back deck, but the clear night was enhanced by a full moon that the sun had long relented the sky to. Even the stars glimmered off the smooth surface of the water as if the wind had been banished by the moon as well. It was still cold at night, and a biting temperature kept the rest of the houseguests inside.

Under normal circumstances, your words would have sent shivers through me, for not only were they so totally unexpected, they should also have sent my heart and mind into a tailspin. You apologized to me profusely and that you had been too quick to give up on me. You wanted us to try again and added that your kids were always asking about me. I stared over the water as you offered me another chance with you. Not even realizing I was doing it, I began my first experiment in this novel strength of indifference. But somewhere further inside, I had a deep gnawing sensation that screamed of the immoral implications that might follow such a path. I agreed that it was worth another attempt, and with sarcastic overtones, I said that we would have to take it slow. We hugged under the cold moonlight, but we did not kiss. Together we walked back into the house like nothing ever happened and carried on with the party still as separate entities, as if to hide our renewed connection from the others.

I drove home that night, dropping you off at your house. I had abandoned the idea of a weekend binge. We both agreed that it was too soon for me to go into your house, and I kissed you good night in your driveway. We agreed that I would see you on Wednesday, as if to concur a day of reminiscence. I accepted your invitation to dinner and a chance to reconnect with your kids and hopefully you as well.

My wait to see you did not bother me as waiting did in the past. This new outlook for me felt very strange and was too recent for me to truly decipher. I did enjoy that my mind wasn't full of nerve-racking thoughts, anticipation, and restlessness, which usually would have preceded such a wait. When I pulled into your driveway that Wednesday night, I was tired; and for the first time in memory, I wasn't dragging a cooler full of beer along with me, as was mandatory for any social visit. I did bring you flowers as a symbol of our new start together. I had no signs of nervousness and no signs of shyness. Granted I knew you, but I still should have had some jitters, should have felt the tickle of butterflies. I had a feeling that they were still in there, just lying dormant.

You had made another spectacular meal and had bought expensive wine to ease any discomfort we might still be feeling. I joked with your kids, helped you with the dishes, and afterward the five of us played Monopoly as one big happy family. We let the kids win although I was always a competitive player. I have never played the game again as if a tribute to that night. It was a great night. There was something missing though, but I couldn't quite place it, and I didn't want to, settling for the comfort of the evening. We held hands on your couch after the kids had gone to bed. A school night meant early bedtime. We watched television and sipped wine, an unusual aspect for me, instead of gulping it. My natural urges were stirring, and I wanted to bed you, wanted to follow through with the drive I felt by being near you again. But something stopped me.

Among all the other mixture of feelings was an underlining protectionist force, compelling enough for me to wait. Instead of following through with the intensity building up, I acted on the fear of sliding back into vulnerability. And with a willpower that I did not think I was capable of, I convinced myself that indeed I would take it slow this time. I whispered that I wanted to make love to you, but told you that I wanted to wait and was going home. You nodded and reached over and kissed me, a reaction that meant to me that you totally agreed, totally understood. I kissed you at the door that night, but my heart was not fluttering, and I paid no attention to the lack of spark. I told you I would call you.

I woke up the next morning refreshed—no hangover, emotional or otherwise. There was no remorse or confusion. I felt in control of my destiny for the first time in memory. It was a strange but welcoming concept for one who has spent most of his life engulfed or manipulated by his surroundings, by events, by experiences. I missed you that week, but I did not call you. I had to stand firm on this feeling of independence or it had no purpose. I kept to myself that weekend, and the urge to call you was strong, but I had to prove that I was not fooling myself with some false sense of determination.

The following Friday, I was invited to a house party scheduled for Saturday night by one of the co-workers that worked in the production area of the factory. He included the warehouse staff in his invitations, and after spending almost ten days at home alone, getting out seemed like a good idea. I called you right after work, and after some idle conversation, I asked you to go to the party with me. You agreed right away, and I should have been thrilled. I certainly would not have gone alone since almost none of my co-workers would be there stag. After I said good-bye and stood there listening to the dial tone for quite some time, my mind seemed to burst into uncontrollable thoughts, sending various emotions in all directions. I could not place what I was feeling, but there was a sudden void in the center of my chest. I wondered where my feelings for you had gone. I started to pace, and I could feel the onset of an anxiety attack, but I could not figure out quite why. The walls of my house started to pull in, and I thought of calling you back. Regardless of how confused I was, I knew most of my anxiety had to do with you. If I could stop thinking about you until tomorrow, I felt that everything would be fine. It was this logic of keeping my mind off you that sent me to the bar that night.

I had sat at my kitchen table after wearing the floor out, already on my fourth beer and a complete wreck. The anxiety attack had come so unexpectedly that I was almost in panic. I had spent the winter with great focus on my desire to function on my own, to survive and provide my own sense of comfort, without the flickering dissemination lurking in all corners of my mind. But now, in an abrupt wave of uncertainty, my concentration and clear outlook had run offtrack. After the sixth beer, the walls were in danger of crushing me. All my recollection of my loneliness compounded each repressed memory, put pressure on me, and bubbled to the surface looking for escape.

There had been many times in my life when I should have stopped analyzing. It would have eliminated some of the bizarre thinking processes that were detrimental by definition alone. I was always able to find an excuse for my predicaments—too young, too drunk, the world was against me, malicious acquaintances purposely stacking the deck, women using me. I had an entire list of misgivings to choose from to point the reasons for my problems away from me. All that was supposed to be behind me, mature enough now to take responsibilities for my own actions. That was why it had been so confusing for me that night when the fringes of self-pity leaked back in and began to pick away at honest contemplations.

Not quite unconsciously but certainly without deliberation, my need to focus on my future vanished that night, and temporary regression into rash behavior was overlooked. There was no reason for me to go to the bar that night except for the pressing urge to escape myself. I was no stranger to that, but I had spent many years reaching for other different ways to do so. Not that night.

I was soon pouring back beer after beer from my favorite bar stool, my mind bouncing around my past radioactively and in no coordinate pattern. In a state of trance, I let the alcohol rule once again. And I probably would have been fine had I been able to have been left alone, letting the music of the disc jockey flow through me to help me regiment my thoughts and march them back into the archives of my memory banks, back into the dark corners of dusty filing cabinets. I wasn't studying the crowds that night but looking through them instead. A steady liquid intake process was my only mission, to drown the mechanism that was operating my thoughts, crawl home, and shut down. And I almost made it to last call, which was an important function to arrive at, without the proper dosage to do so.

One of the more obnoxious regulars, who in the past I had strained conversations with, plopped down on the bar stool beside me. We didn't like each other, and we both knew it. It was difficult to refrain from outright arguments. That night, he wanted to resolve our differences with a fight. There was always one in every bar, but because I had a habit of keeping to myself, I managed to steer clear of trouble most of the time.

I tried to ignore him, but he was having nothing of that. He put his hand on my thigh, which raised my temperature automatically. I am not proud of it, but I am slightly homophobic. I also have a rather large circle of personal space that was easily violated, even when someone got too close when talking to me. I grabbed his hand and tossed it away. And then out of the blue, he asked me if I was queer. I neglected to answer him while I boiled inside. He put his hand back on my leg and repeated the allegation, only with a string of expletive words in the description this time. Steam spewed, and I stood up, knocking my bar stool over in the process and shouting at him to tell me what his problem was. He got up, and although he was almost a foot taller than me, the adrenaline had already expelled any intimidation.

I had been in a few scraps as a teenager but never in a real fistfight, so I surprised myself even more than I surprised him when I cocked my arm back in an overdose of adrenaline. He was caught completely off guard when I let go with a closed fist and hit him on the right side of his face so hard that I knocked him down on the ground, his head just missing the table behind him. He got up shaken and confused, probably discouraged that he wasn't prepared for a southpaw. Before he could compose himself for a counterattack, his girlfriend came rushing out of nowhere and stood between us. His eyes were smoldering with revenge. I could feel my own fire, blood running furiously to my head. There was enough anger and hatred brewing in me to have fueled an army. I was shaking, and it wasn't from fear, and I wondered later how animalistic I could have become.

He let his girlfriend walk him out the door and did not look back. The music had not stopped, and it had happened so quickly that only a few people even witnessed what had taken place. I picked up my bar stool and finished my beer, but now I could feel eyes on me. With the adrenaline rush now dissipated, I was drained of all energy and ironically had also sidelined all the torment that had originally been inside my head. I waited a few moments and left, hoping not to meet up with him in the parking lot. I didn't.

There had been a natural high from my fight, and I finally understood why some people would actually look for one. There was a powerful rush from the adrenaline, and it had its own addictive qualities. I knew it wasn't for me though. I had enough addictions.

I had difficulty sleeping that night, but I did drift in and out. Saturday afternoon finally came, and the fight was long behind me. I now wonder, though, if it had still affected my mood that Saturday night. If I had been left to soak in my own contemplations, I would have simply crawled home, and my anxieties would have been transformed into a melancholy outlook. Instead, in some stupid and imprudent way, I took the experience as fuel and confusedly added it to my new sense of independence.

It was early in the afternoon when I picked you up. Because you lived on the opposite end of the county, there was a long distance between your house and to where the party was. I asked you if you wanted to stop for dinner somewhere, and you told me you were not really that hungry, so I disregarded my own hunger. Starving myself was nothing unusual for me. I had my cooler full of party essentials, not wishing to impose on the host for drinks, and an assured supply of my own needs.

I was distant, and I felt that you could sense that I wasn't acting the same. But I took for granted your sensitivities and was wrapped up in myself. This weird display of egotism did not fit me, and I hadn't planned for it to happen. And why I would take any of my frustrations out on you was very debatable. I do know that on the ride to the party, while we sat in silence, I kept envisioning a dark parking lot with stinging sleet hitting my face and fading taillights. I took this vision into the party with me and framed it with copious amounts of alcohol.

The party was loud, but there was a lack of mixed company. Most of the guys were huddled around the dining room table in a nickel-and-dime poker game. I was no stranger to gambling, and the stakes were quite appropriate to one who mixes frugality with such a pastime. The women had gathered in the living room, either exchanging their favorite recipes or thick in the midst of gossip and comparisons. And while I glanced into the living room from time to time to see how you were doing, in a contentious recognition of reality, I noticed how much older you were than the other women. And I let it bother me instead of the pride I had felt before. You looked stressed, and the youthful beauty that I had preferred to see was hidden. I shook this new look I had of you away with a diamond flush and the winnings of a ninety-five-cent pot.

I was still uncomfortable in social gatherings, and as I watched you fit in easily with your outgoing ways, I grew restless. I started pouring back beers at an alarming rate again, and regrettably so. My tolerance levels were down from my winter lapse of steady partying and my volumes of the night before. Throw in an empty stomach, and I was looking at disaster. I lost sight of you entirely later that night, literally and figuratively. As I concentrated on my cards and threw my brain into simplicity gear, I lost rational reasoning. I lost thoughts of you.

Late in the evening, the host's wife brought bowls of chips and pretzels to our table. On her way past me, she commented to me that she liked my girlfriend. I have said many things in my past that I had not meant, said things off the top of my head in drunken moments, but I was usually able to decipher them later about why. But I felt the horror this time before I even finished the sentence to my reply. Without forethought, not a second of hesitation nor regard for logic, I blurted out that you were not my girlfriend. My concentrated simplicity did not recognize the harshness of my tone.

My hostess had always kept a certain distance from me when she saw me at past occasions, not the purposeful kind but the type that you can sense from psychic vibrations similar to distrust and aversion to unsavory opinions. She turned away from me when she said it, but I could hear her distinctly accuse me of being a gigolo. I felt a sharp pain go through my heart and was not insulted but hurt by the accusation. Not only did I not have the personality for such a portrayal, and probably in many views, not the physical prowess for such professed and heartless exhibitions, my sensitivities would also never have allowed it. Even if I was finally approaching levels that I could thwart some of the crippling effects of my empathy toward women, I could never imagine reaching that kind of hard core and self-centeredness. But none of that explains why I did not stop myself from hurting you that night.

I looked for you right after I had made that horrific comment. You had your back turned to me, talking to someone around the corner of the living room I couldn't see. For a second, I wondered if her words had a ring of truth to it. I had separated myself from you, yet was still there with you. I stopped thinking about it entirely. I was free of the burden of an overworked brain and reached my goal of simplicity. I had shut off the thinking process. May I never reach that ability again.

I drove home that night, although too drunk to do so. You offered to drive, but I insisted I was all right. Except for a few bites into the shoulder of the road with the front passenger tire, I did get you home safely. I had rambled on and on the whole trip back. I had suddenly become an expert about life, about its meaning. There was probably a lot of repetition in my words as I voiced pent-up anguish and accumulated disappointment. It wasn't addressed to anyone in particular, but you were available. You became my target.

I can't remember half of what I said, but I know there were brushes of meanness in my words. I felt the remorse and regret the next morning, but it was somewhat offset by my incessant act of ventilation. All my frustrations from past relationships, all my blighted hopes of life in general, I exhaled in your direction. You were the fault of it all. I turned it away from a display of ranting and ravings about my own life to confrontational patterns of what was wrong with us. I was not malignant, but cruel just the same. You know more of what I said that night than I ever will, but you do not know that none of it was meant to be said.

By the time I found your driveway, irreparable damage had already been done. I had told you that it was never going to work between us, that we were two different people, that we wanted different things from life. None of it was true, but it didn't matter because I had tied all the roots of my drunken frustrations of that night to that haunting vision of standing in the dark, being pelted with sleet, and watching you drive away. There were many women driving away that night I let you go, and you just happened to be there to collect the retributive reward.

We probably didn't stand a chance together, not with me still haunted by my past. If I used you for anything, if I have any explanation to why I let you go that night, it had to have been an obscure way to finally confirm a sense of independence, some form of self-reliance, some way of gaining a defense mechanism against the relentless erosion of my emotions. Why that night and why you, I cannot answer for sure.

The ride home that night must have been an eternity for you while I emptied out my poisons. I cannot recall you saying a single word, not even a good-bye when you were finally able to escape from my vehicle and my torturous rhetoric. I don't remember driving back to my house that night, so I can't honestly reflect on how much of my regrets were immediate. I can only remember a strange sensation caused by an unchartered autonomy growing inside me where it had never existed before. How real it was remained to be seen.

We did remain friends, as you had once stated to me that you had preferred. You probably have regrets that you had not left it there in the first place. Our social paths in our small town could not avoid us from interweaving our journeys with so many mutual friends. We did not avoid each other. Although awkward at first, we were able to talk to each other and keep a friendship. I was so appreciative of that. I would catch myself once in a while feeling the same attraction as before and wondered if we could have made it together or if our combined baggage had always carried doom.

Regardless of how I truly felt, it was difficult for me to see you with another man. It wasn't long after we split that you committed yourself to another relationship. He seemed nice, and for three years, you and your family accepted him into your life. When I saw you together, you both looked happy, but no one really knows what happens behind shut doors. Your relationship with him did fall apart, and by that time, I was spending less and less time in Westlake. But the small-town rumor mill would tell me that you had regressed back into the wild side of life. I had nothing to say about that, having absolutely no difficulty relating to regressive ways. Just because you were a woman didn't mean you weren't susceptible to the same pitfalls. You were allowed the same mistakes and the same feelings of raw emotion that I was. It was society's job to frown on you, not mine.

I have never stopped thinking about you, and even as my days of visiting my hometown diminished to almost nil, my memories of my time with you have never faded. But each time I reflect back, I cannot help but feel extremely sorry for any pain I might have caused you. If it is any consolation, my sense of independence never did cohere. All my frustrations are still inside me, and my ventilated attack on you that night was only a temporary fix. May your life turn out better than mine. You certainly deserve it.

CHAPTER 13

Donna:

At the time when I met you, I was thoroughly convinced that I was done with women. It was time to do some soul-searching internally instead of this futile attempt to find it floating somewhere beside its mate. I had gathered a significant amount of disappointment and heartache in my hunt for the perfect companion that a long hiatus was in order and probably the best therapeutic solution. Recoup the losses, bury the memories, and find an internal way to deal with my depression and feeling of sorrow. My track record was enough proof that I couldn't use women for medicinal purposes, and even my attempts at casual relationships were not adequate enough to even temporarily release the poisons inside me. My mind lacked the filtering system to rid me of residue of the malaise of failed relationships and, by increasing the list of assorted encounters, only added to my burdens.

Sooner or later, I was going to crack and turn into that burnout I had heard whispered about me from across the room from time to time, my acute hearing sometimes a detriment. The word *burnout* scared me. It meant mindless to me, and if I had one iota of self-esteem left, it was based on my belief that I was of high intelligence. This did not stop me from using alcohol as the main source of my escape and to dull that persistent pain inside me. Although there is no tangible screen to keep venom out of the brain, the thought processes did make a valiant effort. The body is a different matter. You could rely on the liver to eventually filter out the alcohol. We won't mention sclerosis to dampen this theory. Drinking was always a reliable source in the process of forgetting, even if it was only a temporary cloaking device. So exchanging broads for booze made sense in my twisted logic.

In order not to completely abuse this transition, as I had done so many times in the past, I began a regimental process of not drinking through the week. This was very difficult at first, but there had been very few dips from the well of willpower in my life so far, so there was plenty to pull from. Miraculously, I was able to stop smoking through the week as well; but this habit was directly linked to my drinking anyway, so maybe it wasn't such a battle of will after all. This turned out to be the most refreshing part of my Monday-to-Thursday sabbatical for breathing was a good thing!

But when Friday afternoon rolled around, it meant my first beer and then a cigarette and a chain event for both habits the entire weekend. So I began a journey of a weekend alcoholic and was treated to the thickness of a solid cement block for a head each Monday morning and eyes the color of molten lava to greet my boss with.

Not that my weekends had changed, but now I felt I had some control over the addictive powers of these substances by refraining from their use through the week. These weekend-only escapes were a balance to alleviate the turmoil inside me, instead of a steady stream of daily need. While I was in the business of this sudden concern for my welfare, I also realized that venturing out on my own was not a recipe for mental health either. Those hours upon hours and night after night sitting in dingy bars by myself in a dark corner somewhere had only added to my misery, paving the way to more self-pity and the return to an external search for female companionship as a crutch to my own survival.

This was where Paul came into the picture and why he was with me the night we met, my drinking buddy and guide. A friend since my early pool hall days and always a reliable drinking partner, he shared the same miserable existence I did. He had his own past problems with women, although not nearly close in number to my menagerie of discord and discard. His drinking problems made my situation look like I was a teetotaler. He had very low tolerance levels, but that didn't affect the volume he drank. Such a great and influential friend to be proud of! I can only really remember him with two girls in his past, both lost to him before he was even twenty-two, directly related to his drinking. He had a Jekyll-and-Hyde situation going on with his personality. Sober, when you could find him that way, he was the most thoughtful and generous person you could meet. Drunk, he was obnoxious and wallowed in such huge vats of self-pity that he put me to shame. I didn't care. He was my friend, and even when he got to the uncontrolled intoxicated levels, we always seemed to find a way to share a few laughs.

Recently, Paul and I were spending every weekend together, subconsciously feeding off each other's misery. My car would lead the way, and it was in charge of which bar we would end up at. We both had grown tired of our neighboring watering holes and had graduated to exploring the saloons of other towns. Sometimes we would rent a motel room minus any potential female catches, him too drunk to fish, me feigning disinterest. At other times, we would drive home drunk and, with him as the navigator, would call the evening a success if we kept the car out of the ditch. His drunk-driving skills were worse than mine. His most recent impaired-driving charge landed him fourteen days in jail and a year without a valid license in his pocket. He was never quite the same after his six-by-nine experience. It hadn't stopped him from driving though, and I was glad to see that although his life was miserable, he was blessed with some luck and never got caught at this.

It was the start of one of these weekend binges that we found ourselves pouring back pitcher after pitcher of beer at your local establishment, a town thirty miles away from our own. It was a depressing old country-and-western-style bar, the scratched walls beat-up from various bar fights, windowless, desolate and dreary, and very poorly lit. It was just the kind of bar that Paul and I had grown to like as we reveled in our moods that matched the decor. This place was even stranger though than the ones we were accustomed to, even more so than the dives we had previously found in our travels. It could have easily passed for a United Nations meeting. There were people of all creeds and colors, shapes and sizes, young and old. From Indians to Asians, to whites and blacks. Not that it led me to any discomfort, for I was the farthest thing from a racist, as you soon found out. But there was a sense of amusement with such a variety of people, most of them seeming to be engulfed in their own self-pity and sorrow flowing from their dark auras. I fit right in.

Paul and I were well on our way to the journey through fermented frontier when the twang-twang beat of the country band had finished their second set. You were still nonexistent, and Paul was already slouching and dropping cigarette ashes on the table, unable to coordinate their direction with the ashtray. Behind him walked a girl in a plain dress carrying a big bunch of long-stemmed roses. I had seen the occasional flower girl in other bars, trying to etch out a living selling flowers. This one looked quite successful at it as I watched her exchange money for two of them at the table beside us. Her timing was her trick. By waiting until past the halfway point between when the entertainment started and the rush for last call, ideally the guys would be unwound enough to buy them as wizardly wands, potentially creating enough magic to earn them favors later on in the evening. I usually never entertained this idea. Not that I didn't buy flowers in the past, but it represented too much of a game to me. Besides, flowers only wilted and died, like my relationships.

So when the flower girl laid down a bright red rose in front of me, I immediately shook my head. It still took me a moment to register what she was actually saying to me, for it threw me for such a loop that I couldn't make sense of it. She pointed at you and said that the rose had come from you. This was a twist of gender roles that I couldn't quite place, wasn't quite accustomed to. I looked over at your table for the first time that night and saw your pretty and alluring smile, the round saucer eyes shining bright even through the gloom of the room. I did not smile back, still a bit confused over receiving the rose.

It was not that you were black that I initially thought of rejecting your gesture entirely. But when I realized your genuine expression of interest, I began to wonder why I had interest instead of shunning you in my mind. I had given you no indication of my interest in you nor my availability. I was still in the thick of avoiding women under the guise of finding myself. The truth was I had too many wounds, hurt too much, still gluing together the cracked lines of a broken heart—too busy falling hard. So my first intentions were to ignore you, possibly even leave the bar to find one with better music. You have Paul to thank for us ever getting together.

He looked over at me in the comical way where his eyes were above the top rim of his glasses, resting precariously on his nose, and looked down at the rose. In his gravelly voice, he said, "I hope you don't turn this offer down, or you're more stupid than I thought!"

He was referring to the weekend before when a beautiful girl walked up to me and had asked me to dance, and I had turned her down. Paul knew about the string of women from my past, and although I never talked about it, he knew I was hurting inside. But that still did not stop him from ridiculing me from what he crassly called turning down a free piece of tail. I am sure you know the phrase.

I still wonder if Paul would have edged me on if he had seen you first. You were behind him, out of his view. Paul was the definition of prejudice and had been quite uncomfortable when we first walked into the bar. But we were in this adventure together, and I convinced him to stay, saying we could always leave anytime. He did mutter something inaudible when he had me point you out. You were with another girl whom you later introduced as your cousin. You were both extremely attractive.

I followed Paul's advice but with some major reservations. I knew in my heart that I was carrying around too much baggage to ever truly clear myself of my past, but this self-imposed attempt at celibacy was nothing but a joke. Instinctively, the drive for female companionship would win out long before any sabbatical-based cure took effect to what ailed me. And so when the waitress came around, I ordered drinks for the both of you. I asked her not to tell you where they came from as if I had become involved in some bizarre parlor game. She told you anyway. You raised your drink in toast fashion and mouthed a thank-you.

A few moments later, when you and your cousin got up to dance to one of the few upbeat songs of the night, I felt all my defenses drop like a curtain falling off a broken rod. Your curvaceous body and the rhythm of your hips would have turned a gay guy straight. It had been awhile since I had been with anyone, and so once I let that flimsy curtain down, all my physical desires were ready for high throttle, ready to slip out of neutral. The emotional pain of my past had recently stopped me from following through with cheap one-night stands. They had always left me feeling abusive and unfulfilled the next morning, and the quick shoddy release of tension would turn to remorse. I could have delivered the same result in the privacy of a long shower and with about as much emotion, depending on the fantasy involved.

Whether it was the poke of Paul's arm into my ribs to acknowledge his shared opinion of how attractive you were or my long drought with physical contact, I found you overwhelmingly erotic. And when you looked over at me and displayed those provocative dance moves, I could not help but watch. Your sweet smile sealed the deal, and I knew I would be with you that night. That is, after another couple of pitchers of beer.

The band was on their last set, and last call was fast approaching. When a particular song that was affecting me with chills running through me and raising the hair on my arms played, I took a deep breath and gathered enough nerve to walk to your table and ask you to dance. I left Paul to fend for himself as he fought to keep his eyes open. The lights on the dance floor were very dim, but strobe lights behind the drummer lit our path. The tiled floor was crowded as other couples engaged in the last dances of the night. But when I took you in my arms, everyone else seemed to vanish. I held you close, and we swayed more than stepped to the rhythm that surrounded and then entered us. I held you close, and I could feel your heartbeat and my own internal pounding that outraced your own. When I looked into your eyes, they seemed to mirror my own desire. For once, I refused to analyze nor did I care to think that I did not know you. You were now a goal, prey for the evening. There would be no later consequences, for you had come to me. Selfishness had no part of discussion with the internal part of my brain that night.

When the song we were dancing to was over, I had a difficult time letting you go. The pleasure of being so close to a woman again was rushing signals to my primordial needs. How quickly one can lose their willpower under the influence of alcohol. I wasn't ready for you, yet here I was falling into the vice of your crushing attraction. I asked if Paul and I could sit with you, and you simply nodded instead of spoke. I had to almost drag Paul to the table, but he finally relented. He sat beside your cousin, oblivious to the fact that you introduced her. He was already too far gone for coherent conversation, and I could only hope that he didn't pass out. My heart was racing as I sat beside you. My abstinence had been a novel experience, and it didn't take much to deter me from continuing such a useless exercise. That wasn't the part of me that was broken.

Last call came and sped by in a flash of surreal time. I was not surprised when you invited us back to your place, as if I had already expected it. You explained that you only lived a few blocks away, and when you mentioned going with you in your car, I thought it was a great idea. My car would stay safely parked in the bar parking lot.

Moments later we pulled into the driveway of your bungalow-style home, part of a row of old houses on a dark street that seemed more like an alley than a road. When you clicked on the light to display your open-concept floor plan, I immediately noticed the pool table on the left, and a smile spread across both my face and Paul's. Paul rose from his slouch, catching a breath of second wind when noticing this unexpected surprise. Both of our heads were swarming with memories of the pool hall days.

Your cousin offered us a beer, which we gladly accepted; and without hesitation, I asked if we could use the pool table. And so began our night in the presence of two exotic women, but also a night of living reminiscence of chasing balls around on a table of felt. I must admit that your table had much to be desired, but it was the thrill of being around one that eliminated any complaints. There was such a drift to the left side of the table that you had to adjust your aim, as if allowing for the slant of a putting green. You stood beside me as I walloped Paul into submission, who could not learn to adjust his shot to the level of the table. It also helped that your cousin was teasing him with light jabs to the ribs when he shot, in her attempt at playful fun. Paul seemed to have lost his prejudice for the night and actually showed some interest in her. This was great relief for me, for the last thing I wanted was for him to casually blurt out some racial slur that he was well-known for doing.

The novelty of discovering the pool table had worn off quickly, and we eventually moved to your living room, where your arrangement had two couches across from each other with a coffee table in between. I sat beside you, and Paul and your cousin sat across from us. It was well into the morning hours, and Paul began to get miserable and started to insist that we leave.

I paid no attention to him at first, but when he started to ignore your cousin entirely, I became concerned of what he might do or say. You sat so close to me that you were taking my breath away, your bare thighs pressing against me as the hem of your skirt rode dangerously high. The power of your appeal and the length of time since I had been with someone led me instinctively to rest my hand on your leg, and only the rest of our company stopped me from going further. Your cousin was uncomfortable and fidgety with Paul's complete disinterest. He was getting louder with his demands to go home, and now I wished he did pass out. My wish went unanswered. He continued pestering me, and my fear of what he would eventually say left me no choice but to get him out of the house. Otherwise it would have taken a pry bar for you to remove me off you that night.

I explained to you that it was best that I go, but told you I really wanted to see you again. Standing at your front door, having already watched Paul stagger out, you slipped a piece of paper into my pocket with your phone number on it. You offered several times to drive us back to the bar parking lot, but I insisted that I needed the air and that Paul definitely did. I did bother you, however, to unlock your car to let me retrieve the rose you had bought me. I was not departing without that memento, which I still have to this day somewhere stuck between the pages of a book.

After making sure that I knew the exact directions you gave me to get back to my car, you kissed me on the cheek; and I disappeared into the dark, with Paul staggering beside me. I looked back once, but you were already in the house. We did finally find our car that night. I had turned down the wrong street and tried to cross over to the next one only to find out that street was a dead end. Paul began to curse thunderously loud, and it echoed off the dark buildings around us. He began to make derogatory remarks and racial slurs, the same ones I was afraid that he would start uttering in your house. I finally had to tell him to shut up. I was so glad that it was so late that almost everyone would be asleep and the unlit houses said as much. This was your neighborhood, and Paul and I had no business walking your streets leaving a trail of unsavory remarks behind.

I spent the rest of the predawn hours driving home, with my hands clutched so hard on the steering wheel that they felt seized. This was a trick I learned to keep the car between the lines and off the shoulder. The pressure on the wheel stopped me from weaving most of the time. I drove Paul home first, not really wanting to deal with him in the morning. I had suddenly lost interest in the planned binge-drinking weekend. I wanted the day to reflect on the night, to think about you, to contemplate and consider what to do. It took a strong pull to get Paul out of my passenger seat, and I guided him to the front door to make sure he didn't end up sleeping on his lawn. He mumbled something, and although I didn't know what, I am sure it did not represent good night.

I watched the sunrise during my ride home and fell asleep on my couch a couple of hours later, dreaming about you. I did nothing else that weekend. I let my life flash before me in no cohesive manner, and I mulled over my past, my misfortunes, and failures. Not quite in deep meditation, not quite caked in the usual layers of self-pity, I did not delve into the depressing parts. By thinking in brief interludes instead of incessant thought, I avoided the pain and concentrated on the pleasantries that had been sprinkled throughout my journeys. This imagery, this odd concentration on the good parts of my past, kept leading me to my vision of you. Whether it was strictly my sex drive, the reoccurrence of feelings after such a long period of loneliness, or the simple desire to have fun, you were always popping into the top of my mind, and you were not going to go away.

I tried to avoid thinking that you were black. You were a woman, and as I had said, I was the farthest thing away from a racist as you could get. But I was influenced somewhat by my friends and their ill-reputed attempt at humor in such matters. And as proud of the fact as I was about not caring what other people thought, I could not help but wonder what the effects of an interracial relationship would have on me. The more I remembered how attractive you were, the less important my thoughts were, the less important the thoughts of others were.

And so the following Friday night, after a hard week at work and a basket of reasons to do so, I called you. You were surprised to hear from me, stating that you had not expected to ever see me again. The excitement in your voice rid me of any hesitation, and I invited you over to my house. When you said yes so quickly, I had barely enough time for a sigh of relief that hadn't come from my lungs but farther down in the solar plexus region. I thought of going to your place instead. But if I was to begin a relationship in such unchartered territory, it was better that I did it in the comforts of my own turf. After a brief conversation, the majority of it my details of exact directions for you, it was left that I would see you in two hours.

I watched you pull into my driveway precisely one hundred and twenty one minutes later. The exhilaration building up inside me had raised my heart rate, not only from the anticipation of spending the night with you, but also from the sudden recognition of your punctuality, which meant there would be no pacing of my floors tonight, no anxiety levels increasing in the same increments of a ticking clock. I had only drank three beers since my call, using the time for a shower, a trip to the liquor store for wine, and a stop at the grocery store for snacks and breakfast items. I wanted to be the perfect host, and because of that objective, I ran out of time to reach the levels of liquid courage I needed for the temerity I felt I needed when you arrived at the door. Instead, I met you at the door with my natural coating of shyness and shaky nerves.

Your pure, natural friendliness and easy flow of conversation proved to be more beneficial in relaxing me than any amount of alcohol would have. You talked and talked and talked some more. I was totally happy with what was mostly a one-sided conversation, where I would only have to interject with a nod or ask a follow-up question to allow your words to continue to smoothly flow. I had no intentions of spilling out my past to you or to struggle with explanations of my mundane life and work. I was totally enthralled and content in listening to even the most insignificant parts of what you had to say. Your stories were funny, and you had an amusing way of describing things. I was so complacent with you that time had stopped, thinking had stopped, any inner pains forgotten.

You were able to accomplish all of this before we finished our first bottle of wine. I had bought four bottles, and the gap between us on the couch shrank with each additional glass. By the middle of the third bottle, we were leg to leg. It had not been me that had moved in small advances, and my pestering timidness was aided by your boldness. We were like teenagers, slowly approaching each other in hopes of further experimentation. I would have liked to have compared it to the carefree days of my teenage years, but the scenario didn't quite fit. By the end of the third bottle, you were kissing me, the room lit only by the dim light over my kitchen stove, the living room window long painted black by a night sky.

Passion is usually left to describe the overwhelming emotions of love and adoration, but ours was pure sexual energy. Regardless, the results were the same when it came to how I felt afterward. The instinctive drive between us was so strong that I threw all precautions to the wind. My past was no longer any part of my focus as I led you down the hall. You followed with your hand grasped in mine, and even in the darkness of the hallway, I could feel the grace of your walk as if you were floating behind me. Wordlessly, I led you into my bedroom, my lair, in preparation for another notch on my bedpost. I had quickly tossed that devilish thought out, sensing it was only misplaced guilt as you did nothing to stop me, said nothing to stop our union.

I undressed you slowly, wistfully, prolonging the advancing inspiration and expectancy. In a display of tenderness, worthy of a Harlequin romance novel, we stood in the midst of feverish foreplay before finally seceding to the mattress. Whether from my recent period of abstinence or the steamy eroticism you filled my mind up with or the constant reflection of the color of your skin, the passion was next to ecstasy. I might have been subconsciously comparing you to all my past encounters, wrapping them into one complete sentient moment, almost subversively. I could feel your throes and became completely lost in our shared desire and thrills to what became the ultimate shared climax.

We quivered and trembled together, our heart palpitating at enormous speeds and then decelerating slowly, flushing the chambers with swelled rapture. This was fairy-tale sensation, and I was totally caught up in the moment. I barely felt your fingernails drilling holes into my back. The first encounter between us was never to be quite matched again, but if we had any sense of compatibility, it was between the sheets. I rolled over onto my back exhausted and perspiring, with your distinct and pleasant odor surrounding me. I held your hand and waited for my heart rate to subside into a more tranquil mode, waiting for the sting of your sharp fingernails coming from my back to ease. You wrapped your arms around my chest and whispered that you loved me.

I was so unprepared for that my moment of peace was shattered. I had not portrayed our night together as love. I had spent many years trying to separate the difference of lovemaking from feeling love, separating sex from intimacy. Although confusing them myself more often than not, I had progressed far enough along the road of understanding of how loosely those three words of proclamation could be used with such great negligence about their true meaning. I had given up on such altruistic meaning to the words, being crushed by them in the past with my own flagrant use, and had given up on finding pure love. I had lost the ability to say it, although I knew it still abided in my soul. Instead of carelessly repeating the words for you, I reached over and kissed you and fell asleep in your arms.

You were still sleeping when I woke up, the sunlight already pouring through the windows. It was very unusual for me to have slept that late. I made breakfast from the bacon and eggs I had bought, and my attempt at a decent breakfast was reasonably successful. Just as the coffee percolator was finishing its run, you came down the hallway dressed only in one of my long-sleeved shirts that you must have pulled out of my closet. It was just enough to cover you and left you looking very provocative.

You were a picture of fantasy, the kind that cements to the back of closed eyelids on lonely, restless nights. I said hello to you in such a soft tone that it was barely audible to me. You asked to use my shower, and although the thought was there, I did not ask if I could join you. My bashfulness had returned, as it always did with new encounters, especially after the effects of alcohol were diluted and relinquished its power over my inhibitions. I grabbed a double shot of vodka while you were in the shower and finished preparing the kitchen table. You came back out fully dressed, and my fantasy of having you sit across from me wrapped only in a towel was quickly suppressed for later use.

You did eat, but you only picked, and I could only hope that you were not hungry and it wasn't my cooking. I did not ask. I must have done okay with the coffee because you made short work of two cups. You were a bit melancholy, and my few attempts at humor had made you smile, but I couldn't retrieve the cute laugh I had heard from you the night before.

For some reason, I had concluded that we would be together the whole weekend while I took advantage of you in sexual overload. When you announced that you were leaving soon to pick up your son, I was dumbfounded. There had been no previous mention of a son. Had I overlooked the signs at your house? Had I been too interested in a run-down pool table to notice toys? I didn't think so. You went on to explain that he was six years old and his father had won full custody, and your only explanation for that was that your lawyer sucked. You had visiting rights every other weekend.

My lack of ability to not reign in empathy flushed me with immediate sadness, but I didn't know what to say to you. Not once did I think of asking if I could go along with you, nor did I think of inviting you back with him. The sudden shock of finding out you had a child and your failure to mention it was not registering in any form of trainable thought. When you went to leave, I merely kissed you at the door and said that I would see you later. Not soon but later, and I grappled with that for a while, wondering what Freudian slip that was rooted in.

I felt hollow inside after you left, and even though I could still feel your presence, still felt you, part of me was kicking myself in places hard to reach. I was lonely before I met you, but after learning to function with all my pains and disappointments, I was finally reaching a level where I could function on my own without the immense heartache that I used to feel when living solo. I could do this through the week now with ease, but still struggled some on the weekends. Now I was already longing for you, longing for someone to be with. I spent the rest of the morning and part of the afternoon pouting and trying to find reasoning about why I had such a difficult time adjusting to a single life, to finding self-sufficiency. It was much easier to analyze others, a better chance to look at things objectively.

Several beers later, careful to pace them in between each other, having no desire to drink but doing so out of habit, still throwing punches at myself with about as much self-control as I had with women, the phone rang. I didn't want to answer it at first, not wanting to talk to anyone, not wanting to say no to friends, telling them that I didn't want to party, only to have them twist my arm and end up spending another weekend in the land of oblivion.

I finally picked up the phone when it refused to stop ringing. I did not expect to hear your voice and was taken aback at first. Had I forgotten your proclamation of your love already, or was I too involved with a quick return trip to self-pity to disperse any feelings. It was the first time I recognized that self-pity was a potential tool. My thought patterns were becoming more twisted recently, or maybe the brain cells that I kept killing off on a weekly basis were finally eroding all logic and common sense that I so vainly believed I had.

You called to invite me over, and after briefly hesitating while I tried to sort things out in my mind, I said yes. I asked about your son, and you said you wanted me to meet him. In a flash, all my internal struggles of the morning were gone. Without thought, I was about to follow through with this relationship with you.

Late that afternoon, I pulled into your driveway; and in the daylight and with more sober eyes, I saw how run-down your neighborhood actually was. Although your house was of decent size, the wooden siding was rotting, entire boards were missing in some spots, and your yard was in shambles. When you met me at the door, I was nervous again, not in meeting you but from the eeriness of the surroundings, and that elusive mud vein of racism that I claimed did not exist in me brushed across my awareness. It was not mine but placed there by media and prejudicial friends and acquaintances. You did not live in a mixed area as that side of town was predominately black. I stepped into the safety of your house and left the dark and dirty world outside to its own prejudicial demises.

The moment I stepped in, all the influences vanished, and it was just you and I left. And your son. He was great kid, polite and articulate. Was I expecting a monster because his skin color was different? That would have been before I closed your door, away from the claws and biases of the outside world. Between the walls of your house, I was comfortable. You made me feel comfortable, just as I had felt with you in my house. It was this solitude shared between us that was the foundation of our relationship. That and some profound sex. After you put your son to bed that night, we continued to act on our physical infatuations with each other, and I let the weight of the world fall from my shoulders.

For almost two months straight, we were together almost every day, ending each day wrapped around each other. I eventually met your mother, your sisters, your brother; and although your father was divorced from your mother, I met him too. They all accepted me. The only thing close to mistrust was your father. Yet the only thing he had really said to me was to make sure that I did not hurt you. I promised him I wouldn't, but deep inside, I had nothing to base that promise on. A lifetime warranty was the farthest thing from my mind.

As you showed me your complete trust, as you introduced me to your family, you would speak in innuendos that you expected a long-term commitment. I ignored the differences of our goals. I cared for you. I enjoyed your company, and in the grand scheme of things, I did love you. But I was still sorting out my life and was old enough to start sorting out some kind of reasonable future on my own.

Whether I had begun to compare various degrees of love from past relationships, categorizing them, I cannot say. I only knew that as I got to know you better, our different backgrounds, our different experiences and the depth of our long-term goals were too varied to ever be successful together. But that did not stop my feelings for you, didn't stop the effort I made to try and make you happy. With more effort, I probably could have made it work for us. I knew you would have done anything to make it work. Maybe if I hadn't still been caught up in looking for that perfect match, that predisposed notion of a soul mate just lurking around the corner in wait, I could have given you more of a chance.

Did I use you? I would hate to admit that, but there might be grains of truth to it. It was a difficult period in my life when we met. It was a poor excuse since most of my life consisted of difficulty. And although I was convinced that I knew where I wanted my life to take me, I was still an emotional wreck. My only true guide to reality was my job and my financial goals gained by it and the concentration of savings. When I met you, your interest in me, your love and availability, was a source of stability for me, a temporary base to control my troubled mind and constant run-in with a distorted view of the world. In a sense, you were my world for a while, but I did not share that with you.

Except for the visits to your family, we never went out the whole time I was with you. I can't be sure if it was a mutual choice because neither one of us mentioned leaving our cocooned existence of the bedroom. We had begun taking turns sleeping overnight at each other's houses, agreeing that weekends would be spent at yours. I made this arrangement on the pretense that the distance made it easier for me to get to work, unconcerned about your traveling distance to your own job. But there was another agenda. I didn't want to be home on the weekends in case of unexpected visits from friends. It wasn't that I couldn't be proud of you. I just wasn't ready to make the necessary social adjustments. I was riding a roller coaster of emotions with you. Our interracial relationship was exciting for me, almost representing a continued way to balk the society that I still secretly despised. It was a statement to represent the fact that I didn't care what other people thought. Then why was I trying to hide you, subconsciously or not?

If I was so set in my rebellious ways, why was I not out there in public displaying you with pride? Was I more influenced by the way other people thought than I would ever admit? I will never know because I found other ways to guide our relationship into the sunset.

We were two giddy kids when we weren't in bed, and elementary math would easily see that more time was spent there than the totality of everything else. This simple existence and our shelter away from the world had served us well. We practically lived as a married couple, but we left outside influences to our individual needs. Those two straight months curled up in bed beside you every night were some of the most restful nights I can remember. But the demons of my past and the inner drive to find that elusive perfect mate, the one whose soul would meld with mine, ventured back to the forefront of my thoughts. They were not as buried as I thought.

It was not boredom. It was not that my affection for you had worn thin. It had nothing to do with you. If I could have shut my mind off, a feat that I have never accomplished, I could have just accepted the way things were between us and forgot about that we didn't have any great bond from the cosmics. It didn't mean we couldn't have made it as a couple. But when I kept thinking of the long-term implications, the balancing of my future that wasn't getting any longer, I couldn't place us together years down the road. God forbid me if it really was a racial matter that was really bothering me. I have to convince myself otherwise or I will have another addition to the gathering of my own abhorrent ways to add to my past.

You were beautiful, and you did fill me with desire. It wasn't enough for me, and it certainly shouldn't have been enough for you. I had to carry on with my search. This didn't stop me from hanging on to you for a while. I might have had a voided and lost soul, but you filled the void of my loneliness. If I had only known that my hunt to quench the spiritual thirst by exploring the hearts and minds of women was an act in futility, that the answers were right inside my own soul, we might still be together. I was exhausted looking for answers but still trying, and if the timing would have been later in my life, I could have settled in. You continued telling me that you loved me, and there were many nights I wanted to say it back to you. As I have stated, I have used those words loosely in the past, and sometimes it only created pain instead of what their meaning should entail. I was tired of hurting people because in doing so, I was only hurting myself.

Yes, I was selfish in my path through life, but that didn't mean I couldn't feel and understand the pain and anguish that I have caused. I did not want to put you through this. You deserved only the best, but hurting you was inevitable. The longer I waited, the harder it was going to be for the both of us. You inadvertently set my decision to back away with your repeated use of those three words that I could not get myself to say to you.

We were at my house on a dromedary day, a play on words that I used to call Wednesday. You were lying in my arms after another extraordinary exhibition of sex and passion between us when you whispered those three words again. Whether it was a change in your tone or a weak moment for me, I got chills when you said them and almost naturally repeated them. I had been so caught up in the moment, that habitual release that created my illusion of peacefulness, that I actually got the first part of it out. I stopped and hugged you instead with such force and such meaning that I was in danger of cracking your ribs. I kissed you as passionately as any actor on a movie screen and then felt the tears roll down my cheeks. I had not cried since I had met you. You didn't know it—and on the surface, neither did I—but I was kissing you good-bye.

When you left the next morning, I never saw you again. I never found the words to explain how much you meant to me, how important you were to me, but still had to let you go. I could have found the words. Maybe I was scared you would talk me out of it. So I will never really be sure if it was courage or cowardice that made me end it. I only know that you deserved more than I had to offer.

When you called me the next day, wondering where I was, the spineless part of me took care of things for me. When you called, it gave me the easy way out instead of facing you. I could feel your heart drop at the other end of the line, like the thud of my own. I kept telling you that it wasn't you, that it was me. That was far from an original line. I told you that you deserved someone better than me. I told you how sorry I was and hung up before I changed my mind. I felt part of me die.

I lay in bed awake that entire night, my tears running like brooks after a heavy rain. My pillowcase was drenched by morning. I was crying for the both of us and was totally regretful for what I had just done. I was sorry that I couldn't be there to comfort you, to return to you what you had done for me without really knowing. Twice that night, I reached over for you out of habit and found the empty side of the bed. I had just committed myself to more loneliness a few hours earlier, and I was missing you already.

I regretted not being more honest with you. Maybe if I had shared some of my past with you, it might have helped you understand me more. Please know that you were beautiful, and I cared for you very much, and I still think of you all the time. I cannot apologize enough for the hurt I know I caused you that night. If it is any consolation, I live with the same pain every day. Someday, putting aside all the internal sufferings of daily penance, I will have to answer for not just you, but for all the people I have hurt. I can only hope that for now, you have found someone, and that someone has filled you with the joy and happiness that I robbed from you.

CHAPTER 14

Jayne:

I have heard of relationships of convenience, and we definitely fit that description. It was phenomenal how we kept our relationship secret for so long, spent so much time together, and—although we had feelings for each other—were able to keep our emotional attachments at bay. We could call each other, knew each other's schedules, and were careful not to interfere with each other's lives. We had a mutual respect for each other, and our relationship did not really fit into any particular category. This was not textbook protocol, and with such unusual guidelines between us, we simply accepted it, simply enjoyed it.

I first met you at a bar during a time of complete dispossession, lost in an ocean of illusion that only patience and divine intervention would end my search for love and companionship. And when I say lost, it is in the true sense of the word as I paddled my way through foggy excursions, sometimes preying on the emotions of others. I hated myself for it, but I also condoned it, allowing it to be justified by somehow melding my actions into survival instincts. I had not yet found that path to survive on my own. So when I met you, it was just another binge weekend for me, a trip into obscurity and far away from my supposed soul-searching.

It was another weekend with my equally lost friend, Paul. I actually felt good about myself when I compared myself to him. There was probably little difference between us, except for a higher degree of tolerance for alcohol and the narrow ribbons of self-esteem I hung on to as higher intelligence. Considering myself more intelligent didn't explain the mess I had made of my life so far, but it did feed specks of hope for my future and found reasonable explanations for my past. But being smart seemed to do nothing for the present as I continued to find escape in the bottle, escape in ambiguous relationships.

You were nowhere to be found that weekend until last call in that small corner bar off the main street of Charlton. Paul and I had recently been spending many weekends in that city, both evading our small-town atmosphere. He was unusually sober that night, or at least not completely wasted as was the norm with him. In an odd act of boldness, I watched him walk up to you and your girlfriend and invite you to our table. It was so out of character for him, and I didn't believe him when he told me he was going to do it. To my amazement, you both followed him back; and in a whirlwind of jumbled memory, you were sitting next to me. Paul was soon hustling your blonde friend, and I could not remember him hustling anyone before. He saw something in her, and he was practically drooling.

I turned to get a closer look at you, and my attraction was instant, and internally, I was drooling too. You had the body of a model, and as the cliché goes, your legs stretched forever. Your smile was contagious, and if I was feeling sorry for myself that night, you evaporated most of it with one look. Our idle chat flew freely right from the start, and we soon found out that ironically, you lived in an apartment one block from my house. You and your friend had decided to come to that particular bar on a whim to go dancing and let loose. We also learned quickly from our babbling-brook conversation that we both hated living in Hilbury and that we had both been married young and had lasted about the same amount of time. You left out the part of you being recently engaged again, but you did tell me the next day.

You filled me with instant comfort, and I had no initial jitters with you. The sexual attraction was almost oozing out of my pores as if overlaid in pheromones. Your hand was on my thigh as you talked to me, sending sensuous overtones through my veins. Just before we had to clear out of the bar, Paul asked both of you to go out on his boat in the morning, and I almost jumped for joy when you agreed. Those last few moments in the bar were blurred for me, but as we reached the morning hours, things became clearer.

There is no truth behind the drink-yourself-sober theory, but my sobriety levels did appear to be greater with the approach of the sunrise. You had followed us back to my house, and I was totally enthralled by the centerfold picture of the woman sitting in my living room. You were above friendly, and I even managed to lead you down the hallway for a few moments where we had a round of necking and fondling. But your friend came to your rescue before I could attempt to get you undressed.

Back in the living room, with daylight beginning to pour through the windows and Paul still relatively sober, we all confirmed that the boat ride would happen. Paul's boat was a wooden bathtub. And although a good size at twenty-one feet, it looked like it was barely seaworthy. There were some very close calls out on the lake with him, not because of safety issues with the boat itself, but because of Paul's drinking habits out on the open water. There was no caution with him out there, and there were less chances of getting caught drunk-driving on the open water and less things to collide with. The penalties were the same if he ever got caught, but that was nothing he ever considered.

Our small fishing town of Westlake, my stomping grounds as a teenager, provided ample ways to launch a boat, and it was sparsely policed. That was a fortunate thing, for some of Paul's antics on the lake would have easily given him free lodgings in that six-by-nine cell that he was already not quite fondly familiar with. The boat was too big of a toy for a dedicated inebriate, whose passion for drinking outweighed any kind of common sense. I did have a few reservations of going out on the boat, but not only did I sometimes have the same disregard for common sense, I also could not miss an opportunity to spend the day with you.

I could also see how excited you and your friend were to go boating. And as I pictured the red-and-orange hue of the sun rising over the water, cutting a path through the velvet blue cloth of the sky and you next to me, there was no second-guessing about how great a plan this was. To the back burner went all my recollections of all the times that Paul had passed out behind the wheel while I rushed to take over the controls, all the times that he ran out of gas while we drifted for hours waiting for rescue. It never mattered before that he had no radio, no flares, no compass, and no life jackets, and that I had the swimming abilities equivalent to a rock.

You and your friend went home to change into swimwear, for the summer air was already hot. You knew the Westlake area well, so we agreed to meet you at the main launching area at the pier. Paul and I went to his place to get his truck and hitch up the boat and trailer. Not only would my clunker not have the power to pull it, I also did not have a hitch. So under the foggy film of a booze-filled night but a renewed awareness and armed with the vigor of a brand-new day, I focused only on a day on the lake with two beautiful women instead of just grumpy old Paul as company. I was being driven by pure instinct this time, without the sophisticated search for everlasting love.

Out in the open stretches of Lake Erie, the warm soft breezes blowing through our hair, the smell of bronzing skin and fresh summer air, there were overtones of romance and shared appeal. Our cast off went literally unhitched, and your timing was impeccable. At the same time that we backed the boat into the ramp and released it from the trailer, you pulled into the harbor parking lot. I was exceptionally at ease that morning, a strange sense of peace within myself with a carefree and worriless day ahead of me. In your dental-floss bikini, you were more of a vision than even the previous night, and I caught myself goggling at some of the parts that I had already had a chance to briefly fondle. A one-track mind was not something I was proud of and was fortunate enough that most of the time I wasn't consciously aware of it. I was undressing you with my eyes, my intentions hidden behind dark sunglasses, and there wasn't a lot left to disrobe.

The bow of the boat cut through the still water of the harbor, like splicing glass, leaving a perfect wake on each side of us. It flowed evenly, spreading away into small even ripples. A lone seagull followed us, and except for the mountain-shaped clouds bundled along the horizon, the sky was a deep blue globe with a bright yellow floodlight hanging from its ceiling. It was our world out there.

Paul did have one rule for his boat. It could not leave shore without multitudes of alcohol. And the beer fridge in his garage had contained the source of such provisions. We had barely left shore when he passed around the beer. Aside from my nonsensical circle of friends, most people wait until at least noon to drink; but as part of the party mode, you and your girlfriend joined us quite willingly.

The day was beyond description. You know this. You were there. The electricity between us was almost visible, like static electricity seen in the dark. Combined with the serenity and solitude of the open water, it was almost euphoric. Paul had shut the engine off and let the boat drift for a while. The shoreline was just visible, and there were no other boats in sight. When I wasn't admiring you, I focused on the tranquility and the ascending vibrations of such high volumes of water. I did not want to think of the depth below us. The wind had picked up slightly, and the flat surface had changed to small whitecaps of variable waves. The clouds that had clung to the horizon as though they were attached were now moving toward us, erupting upward and now covering half of the sky. Hues of dark gray were painted on their underbellies, blotting out where the creamy white colors had been. But there was little concern between us although we all knew how fast that lake could change.

Without breakfast, it was an easy consensus that we were all hungry. Paul suggested that we go around the point to Lexington to the tavern at the dock. That was when I first noticed the telltale signs that he was on his way to oblivion. His words were slurred, and his glasses were sliding down to where they normally sat when he was reaching the point of no return. His bloodshot eyes were magnified by the lenses of his glasses. But this was Paul, and there was nothing that was going to change him. I asked him about the sandbar that we would have to get around somehow, and he simply shrugged his shoulders. I should have known then that we were headed for trouble.

In order to get around the sandbar of the point, you had to go a long distance out into the lake; but since it was constantly shifting, you never knew how far. Way too far for comfort in the floating wooden contraption Paul called a boat, and way too far to avoid high waves. I did not want to portray myself as a coward and said nothing as Paul pointed the boat out to the middle of the lake. The weather was still gorgeous, and signs of danger were not fully registering. A half hour later, I was in water up to my chest, adrenaline at full rush, pushing the boat across the sandbar. With the aid of the waves that were licking the back of my neck and the odd one going completely over my head, I pushed the boat across. I could hear the scraping of sand, but with the propeller shut off, we avoided any damage. Several weeks later, I read about two drownings farther inland on that very sandbar, where the undertow had carried two strong swimmers into the hands of Poseidon. I shudder now at the stupidity of what I had done and the luck involved that I had not become fish food that day.

On the other side of the sandbar, the water was calm again, the bay sheltered from the winds, and we could see the Lexington dock. Moments later Paul eased off on the throttle and worked his way into the marina to dock the boat. He didn't make it. He sat back in his seat and passed out in the length of time it takes to snap two fingers together. I grabbed the controls just in time to avoid scraping the boat along the side of the pier and clumsily glided it to rest. As if on cue, you jumped out and tied up the front and back of the boat like a seasoned sailor. I could not help but smile as I watched you work the slipknots. I didn't know the difference of a proper knot from Velcrose.

Both of you were concerned about Paul, and I told you he just needed to sleep it off. The clouds had swallowed the sun, and there was only a fraction of the sky that remained blue. But the air was still warm, and although the clouds were dark, they didn't have the foreboding look of storm clouds. There was no concern when we entered the tavern. Instead, we had a wonderful time. We ate sandwiches and fries, and I ordered steady rounds of mixed drinks for us. We were giddy from lack of sleep, and whether it was the effects of the drinks or just the enjoyment of each other's company, the three of us were caught in hysterical bouts of laughter. Everything we said had a comical pivot to it, and we laughed so hard we cried. It felt good for me to have tears that did not sting with sadness, and a very rare event it was.

The food not only provided nourishment, it also helped absorb the alcohol, for none of us had a desire to join Paul. There was a jukebox in the corner, and your friend filled it with quarters, and the songs she picked were well chosen. I laughed more that afternoon than many years combined.

It was very late in the afternoon when we saw the first flash of lightning. The front of the tavern had a wall of windows overlooking the lake, but our focus had been on the triangulated comedy festival around our table. We all shared the sudden look of concern. By the time we finished our drinks, there was a clash of thunder loud enough to shake the windows, and the sky had turned very dark. Once outside the tavern, we could feel the temperature change, and the cold wind cut through us. Both of you were dressed in silk cover-ups for appropriate attire in the restaurant, but I doubted the flimsy material was made for warmth. We broke into a run down the pier, knowing that the rain and storm were inevitable now.

I only had to shake Paul a couple of times to wake him. He was groggy, but he understood that a storm was brewing, and he was able to get his bearings. There were fifty-foot commercial fishing boats on the bottom of that lake somewhere when the waves got hungry enough to devour crew and all. Paul knew the dangers. In the mode of controlled panic, we untied the boat and had to jump in before Paul took off without us. I was glad I had been able to wake him. I knew how to drive the boat, but I was far from a sailor or a navigator. In afterthought, we should have stayed tied to the pier and waited, but foolishly we set the priority to that of getting home. It had not been a clear thought, but one that had screamed demand to all of us.

I wonder now, if not for that storm, if we would have developed the same closeness, felt the same bond that exacerbates when together in traumatic situations. Most of the credit to keeping the boat afloat has to go to Paul, and maybe even more so to your friend. She had stayed huddled to his side the entire time, offering all the moral support he needed to stay focused. The Lexington side of the bay had still been relatively calm, but the waves were gathering force. We reached the sandbar in good time, but now with the waves running against us, it would be impossible for me to push the boat across this time. Paul had no choice but to go even farther out in the lake to find a way around it. The shades of the storm clouds had lost all remnants of color and were now pitch-black lit up only by irradiate bolts of lightning. The farther we went out, the higher the waves became. We still had our sense of panic concealed, but there was mounting terror.

When Paul thought the time was right, he veered the boat sharply left into the full brunt of the waves and opened to full throttle. Even over the wind and the waves, I could hear the propeller squeal as it caught the sand below and cut through to the other side. The engine shuddered for a second but remained running, and the fear of a damaged propeller subsided. But now we were at the mercy of higher waves. Paul cut back on the throttle because now speed would only endanger us in flipping over. There was only one goal now, and that was to get close to the shoreline before the pitch-black of a night storm enveloped us and we lost all sense of direction. There were running lights on the boat, but one was blown out, and the other was so dim that even on a clear night, you could only see a few feet in front of you.

As the boat cut through the waves diagonally, it rocked at perilous angles. We were knocked off our feet several times. We secured your friend to Paul's seat with a grappling strap and tied it into a knot around her waist and then wrapped it around the back of the seat. Once we knew they were both secure, I grabbed you, and together we staggered to the back well of the boat and braced ourselves into the corner. The only way that we could fall out now was if the boat flipped over, and then it wouldn't matter anyway. When the rain hit us in a torrential downpour, so did the darkness. By now the waves were six feet high, tossing the boat around like a piece of Styrofoam. I covered us with a light tarp. But the wind soon took it from my grasp, and I watched it fly out of the boat to the waiting grip of the next wave. We cuddled in the corner, like newborns in a nest, and shivered uncontrollably.

It was an eternity before we finally spotted the rocky shoreline, but there was only minimal comfort with the sight of land. The dim running light reflected off the glistening rocks, and they were more taunting than the waves. I dared not tell you that if the boat engine quit, there would be nothing left of the boat than splinters of driftwood.

I heard the engine rev up and down as Paul worked wonders with the rudder to swing us parallel to the rocks and then tone it down to a slow steady speed, just above idle but not enough to stall. He was able to throttle it back and forth with each crashing wave in such a manner as to cut through each one and keep us the same distance from shore each time. It had to have been the most tedious task of his life.

The boat was entirely in his hands, but as we were tossed around in the back of the boat with each approaching wave, never knowing if the next one would flip us over was just as excruciating as it would have been behind the wheel. Over the clamor surrounding us, we began to talk to each other, sharing our past, sharing our fear. We held each other's hands so tight that we were cutting each other's circulation off. I put my arm around you to help you stay warm, but the pelting rain had already chilled you to the bone. The warmth of the morning was a distant memory. As we kept talking to help us not focus on the tilt of the boat, the waves, the rocks, the cold, I held you even closer as if to squeeze the shivers from you. You opened up to me like I had been a lifelong friend, but with it came your honesty.

It was then that you told me you had a fiancé and you were planning to marry in the spring of next year. If not for the circumstances we faced, your confession would have shocked me. You had given me no indication you were attached to anyone. It might have been those same circumstances that also failed to stop us from developing a relationship with each other later. Whether it was the sharing of such a traumatic experience knowing our lives were in danger or our growing physical attraction that shoved us past the brink of moral implications, I am not sure. But we formed a bond that night.

What should have been a short ride home was four hours of excruciating terror instead. We huddled together, secretly praying that we would see tomorrow. The rain and waves were relentless. I left you once and worked my way to the front of the boat to give Paul encouragement, hoping I wouldn't be swept overboard. Your friend had kept him calm, and she was a courageous woman, showing no signs of her own fear. Paul had a death grip on the wheel, his fingers clamped so tight that they were white even in the dark. He would only nod when I asked him if he was all right, and as I did the walk of a drunk to return to you, I was wondering how I expected him to reply. With an intricate and detailed answer of his well-being?

You were crying when I got back to you as if you had given up on prayer. The waves had increased in their force and height, and at times the spray would go right over the boat. This roller-coaster ride had no track to follow, and with each watery hill, it became more difficult to hold on. We were in purgatory, and the strands of hope were increasingly fraying. Nothing could ever compare in our lives to the terror of not knowing whether we would survive. The incessant pounding, the perpetual erosion against the side of the boat, waiting for it to break apart at any moment. Our exhaustion blanketed some of the fear. As we nestled in the corner, braced as best as we could, I fell into a trance, not quite sleep, but in dormancy like floating through space. For a moment, I couldn't feel the waves; and I seemed to transfer this strange sense of tranquility over to you, for your crying had ceased and your body had gone limp. I was drifting above the lake, and everything was calm.

And then I was jolted back into the roughness of the water when I heard the shouts of your friend through the wind. She screamed out that they could see the harbor. I grabbed the side of the boat to look out, and between the billows of two approaching waves, I could see the revolving lighthouse light, that welcome beacon that represented our survival. My heart floated back down into a nest of pacification, as if softly plopping onto a pillow. We still had some fancy maneuvering to accomplish to get the boat into the shelter of the pier, but I felt that we were now safe.

Thirty minutes later, with the rain still pelting us like sleet, the adrenaline rushing to our feet, we guided the boat in with strenuous pushes away from the side of the dock, slowly edging our way to the ramp. Another thirty minutes later, we had it out of the water and strapped back onto the trailer. We stood in a huddle on the dock, like four drowned rats on their haunches, now oblivious to the rain still pounding on us, and shared an osmotic relief between us. I think it was joy we felt as we stood on solid ground, now understanding the refutable fact that we had not drowned and wondering who should kiss the ground first. We said nothing as if it would break the sanctity, the reality of the moment. The experience had changed us all, and it was best not to speak of it, for fear of a different result.

We did say good-bye to each other as we shivered and tried to rub away our goose bumps. You looked back at me before you got into your friend's car and gave me a reassuring smile that warmed my heart like the hearth of a fireplace. In that smile were the unspoken words that I would see you again. The fact that you were engaged didn't matter then, nor did it matter later during our summer affair.

The next day, I played hermit, trying to reflect on exactly which concoction of emotions were boiling inside my gut, simmering inside my head. Even after a solid night's sleep, void of any watery nightmares, I was restless. I buried myself in the television screen, only partially aware of what I was watching, another part of me groveling in disgust at wasting a precious summer day. At the same time, I was glad to see another day.

A week passed by, and although I thought of you constantly, I was able to offset those thoughts with my work routine. But each night after work, I pondered over whether I should find you. I knew exactly where you lived, but I didn't have a phone number or even a last name. I knew I had to see you again, but I was troubled about how to approach you. Each time the urge reached unbearable proportions and I was ready to knock on your door, your admission to me that you were engaged interfered with my decision. You had told me on the boat that your fiancé was from the city and that you didn't live together. But I had no idea when he would be at your house. I kept hoping that you would knock on my door. I had mentioned to you on that eternal boat ride that I was seeing someone off and on, but I had left out the selfish arrangement I had where only I would do the calling. No wonder I was still wrestling with moral issues that I felt corroding my soul.

I did not really expect you to knock, but I kept on hoping. By Friday night, the night when my thoughts usually found a way to start spinning around as if caught in a tornado, I couldn't stand it any longer. Primed with several beers, I walked around the block determined to talk to you. I had no other plan except that if your fiancé answered the door, I would simply apologize and say that I had the wrong house. When no one answered after several of my feeble knocks, I was almost ready to give up and leave, but then you came to the door.

I was not sure what reaction to expect from you, but when you greeted me with that warm smile, my physical attraction to you came flooding back. I wanted to kiss you right there, but instead told you that I just wanted to see if you were doing okay. You invited me in, but I had a discomforting feeling, a vibration that might have represented your fiancé's presence, either past or future, and it was disconcerting. I asked if you could come over to my house instead and added just for a coffee. I think we both knew it wasn't for coffee. You agreed, and we walked back to my place, and it was hard for me not to hold your hand.

With the trauma of the boat ride behind us and an unspoken understanding that it was best that we not talk about it, our conversation was surprisingly open. I opened up a bottle of wine, and we sat on my couch together, and you talked to me in the genre of lifetime friends. I had felt this connection between us on the boat, but I had to blame some of it on the situation. But now I knew this was genuine friendship. But with it was the power of the physical attraction that pulled me toward you, to confuse the issue, to complicate things.

I began to prod you for more information about your boyfriend, and you were quite forthcoming with a gush of details that underlined that you had nothing to hide from me. You saw each other on weekends, alternating from the city to your place. He had a great job in some life insurance company, and strangely, you added that he was always tired. I was picturing this successful business man sitting beside you with his eyes shut, telling you about his day while he offered you his love and rewards of his work before nodding off to sleep. It occurred to me to ask if you loved him, but that held no logic in finding my own justification for pursuing you. That would make me more of a fool than some of my past actions that had given me the nomenclature of nincompoop.

You asked me about my relationship, and I could only say that it was meaningless. It rang true, but it also reeked of deceitful omission. As the night went on, we delved in to each other's past by carefully chosen questions and unleashing detailed answers meant only for the dearest and trusted of friends. There was something about you that allowed me to safely bring back memories to the surface, buried bygones bubbling back without harm and shared with someone instead of them locked in storage with a dead bolt. In this case, maybe it was a combination lock that you knew of which turbines to turn. Regardless, I opened up to you in ways I never thought I could. The unhealed wounds would probably heal out in the air better than festering in the dark anyway.

I said things that night that I had trouble saying to myself. It was as if I had known you all my life. I don't know if I will ever find someone again that would allow me a path to the way I was able to talk to you. We soon discovered that our overwhelming attraction to each other would interfere with a just-friends scenario. By the time we went through a third bottle of wine, we had already graduated from holding hands and interlocking eyes to the point of no return. At two in the morning, we made love on the couch. Why the time stands out is beyond me, but when I reminisce about that evening with you, it remains somehow as a matter of importance. The hormones, the chemistry, the magnetism all pulled us to mutual seduction and had not even allowed us to make it to the bedroom. You were a bit of fantasy, maybe somewhat in a fashion to hide my feeling that you should have been taboo.

You were someone else's woman, someone already taken. It didn't seem to bother you, and I soon learned not to let it bother me. And so began a very beautiful and memorable summer for me. For an entire season, I was lifted out of the depths of depression, yet totally dependent on your company to remain that way. I relied on you. Weekends were rough for me, but we did not speak of them. The rest of the week was ours. Not a day through the week went by without us seeing each other. We were set in routine. My house became our sanctuary, our freedom from all of life's pressures. We drank copious amounts of wine, took turns cooking dinner, talked away the hours until past midnight, and then made love like clockwork. Only now it was in the solace of my bedroom.

You always went home afterward, as if that solved any issues of any further commitment to each other, as if that justified the affair. There were mornings when I would wake up just before the obnoxious ring of my alarm clock, reach over for you, and wrap my arm around thin air instead. There were feelings jostling around in my heart that represented the familiarities of true love from my past. It was difficult to keep them at bay, especially on the weekends when I would lie on my couch, wondering what you were doing. All my past loathing to the appearances of Monday mornings was replaced by the anticipation of seeing you after work.

Many would have found our relationship very strange, but in the confines of our den, we thrived on each other, and an unusual perception of happiness was shared between us. We went nowhere the entire time we spent together, almost shutting ourselves away from the outside world. Neither one of us asked or expected anything more or anything less.

Did love enter early into the picture? I am sure it did, but I had to keep shoving my feelings back into my soul before it reached my heart and mind. Those gnawing and dangerous feelings had to be kept in check, kept in their proper place for circumstance and necessity. I locked my feelings for you away in the same dungeon as I kept my hurt and pain. I had let you in to look at them, but you were not allowed to remove them.

To further label our relationship as only friends, we became sort of business partners. You had no washer and dryer. I had no vacuum cleaner. So a trade was made, where your laundry was done at my house and your roll of quarters stayed in tack, while I no longer had to pick up the lint and crumbs off the living room carpet with my fingers.

I have no regrets of that summer with you except that it eventually ended. Autumn always left me with a sense of gloom as the fading colors of summer could only mean the eventual dreaded approach of winter. Gray skies filtered through me and turned my insides the same color. As fall approached, each preceding visit with you cried for more. It had become routine for me to meet you at the door with a kiss, and we both knew but would never admit that these were more than the kisses of friends. Sometimes I would have dinner ready before you arrived, depending on my hours at work. I would always have a candle lit on the kitchen table even if it was still daylight. Were we two romantic friends?

There was never a single disagreement between us. What was there to disagree with in our fantasy existence? Everything was perfect between us. My love for you remained caged, as if it were a hungry animal that when let loose, would rip me to shreds. I cannot speak for you, but in your eyes, I thought I saw the same passion I was not allowed to feel. We were very careful never to talk about it. We had to continue to role-play and not shake the foundation of this utopian sideline existence we had created for ourselves. In reality, though, I was feeding off you, stirring the chemicals of my brain into senses of pleasure. Whether fanciful or not, I felt good about myself when I was with you. It was such a long-forgotten feeling that I bathed in it, depended on it. Too caught up in the delight of it all, I refused to think that it could end. But like everything else in my life, it did come crashing down, in an abrupt awakening that sent a chill through me as cold as an Arctic wind.

On the ninth Monday since I had met you, my time with you had reached the levels of consistent happiness, and I had started to take it for granted. This made it even worse when that inevitable day arrived when you stood at my door with that forlorn look in your eyes that was glazed in doom. Our routine kiss had the taste of sadness. I asked you what was wrong, but you wouldn't answer me. We moved to my couch, our couch, and we grabbed each other's hands almost simultaneously. I sensed dread, and you did not disappoint me. I felt my heart drop without a parachute before you even began to talk.

Your boyfriend, your fiancé, had asked you to move to the city with him. He didn't want the distance to separate the two of you anymore. The thumping beneath my rib cage had been slow beats at first until I looked at your hand and was suddenly aware of the touch of metal. Although I knew you were engaged all along, there hadn't been a ring. Now on your finger was a huge diamond shiny enough to blind me. The sight of this suddenly became a confirmation that you and I weren't real after all. My heart rate went wild at this sudden awakening that I was going to lose you. As if you were reading my mind, you answered my question about how soon before I had a chance to ask it. You were moving Saturday. Your answer devastated me. That was too soon. Something let loose inside me, and my heart dropped even further, and my stomach folded in.

I needed more time with you, and I could not fathom that four more days was even possibly enough to grasp the reality of losing you. You saw that I was upset although I tried to hide it. You tried to start a conversation to fit in words of comfort for me, words of reassurance that it would be all right. You reminded me how much you cared for me, but that we both knew that it had to end sometime. I told you that I understood, but that I had grown dependent on you, on your company. I explained how much I would miss you—fighting myself in order not to start blubbering in front of you—without telling you how truly deep my feelings for you ran.

After an unusual moment of uncomfortable silence between us, we switched the topic and talked about the weather. Not exactly about the weather, but we were able to pretend that nothing had changed. At least not for the next few days. We made love that night as we always did. I was distracted at first, but with the help of a lot of wine and your uncanny way to make me feel so comfortable with you, we became as involved as any other night, as meaningful as any other night.

Work was rough that week as I wrestled with the knowledge that you were going to disappear from my life. Through daydream after daydream, I weighed the idea of telling you how I really felt and to tell you that I did not want you to go. But an inner voice kept pushing through my thoughts and reminding me that I had already caused too much pain and suffering to others. I had no right to do the same to you. There was no choice left for me. I had to let you go. I had to do what was fair to you.

When that last Friday came, I was a bundle of nerves. The whole situation now seemed so surreal, and to believe this was my last day with you was hard to accept. When I met you at the door, the thought of never seeing you again left a lump in the back of my throat. I kissed you at the door like I had done every visit before and started to well up. Behind my closed eyes and the magic of your lips, the world started to spin. By prolonging the kiss, I was able to stop the flow of my tears and shove them back.

I had made dinner ahead of time, not wanting to use up valuable time with you. I had found a recipe for a chicken casserole, of which I doubted my capabilities of making it right. The food gods had answered my prayers, and it had turned out as quite edible. I bought champagne instead of wine, for this was to be a night of celebration instead of gloom. A single red rose sat in a vase much too big for it, flanked by matching glass candles molded into the shapes of angels. I had bought them at the only department store in town. I knew you couldn't take the rose home, but that didn't stop me from the gesture.

We had spent many romantic nights together, but that last night was of storybook variety. I can only assume that it meant as much to you. The way we made love that night was ecstatic and carried the emotional overtones of bliss. It was as if it was the last time we would ever make love on this earth. In essence it was, at least with each other. We both confirmed that last night it was more than sex we had been sharing, but we still could not say it out loud.

When midnight approached, I had you in a death grip. I was not letting you go. It was not going to be easy for me, and in a last-ditch effort, I held on. I did manage to hold on to you until two in the morning when I finally relented, either because of your pleas to let you go or a way to confirm a significance of two in the morning. I watched you get dressed in the dark, the illumination of the alarm clock the only source of light. I was numb and used that numbness to stop my emotions from escaping. Now was not the time to breakdown in front of you and turn into a puddle of sap. I had to stay true to my promise to myself, that I had to let you leave unscathed and unmarked by the ramblings of a blubbering idiot. Still, even through the barrier of numbness, I wanted to stop you from leaving, to bear my soul.

Later as I stood at the door embracing you, you whispered in my ear that you knew. I was not sure what you knew or how much you knew, but it gave me comfort. We shared our last kiss, and it was only immeasurable strength that stopped me from uttering that I loved you. You said good-bye to me, and then I stood there and watched you disappear into the night forever. I do not know how long I stood at the front door waiting for you to turn around, but I eventually moved to the backyard to watch the sunrise. I fell into a meditative trance that evoked in me a sense of peace with the world around me. My somewhat false sense of altruism, but enacted regardless, so as to not interfere with your life, cost me the one I loved.

I can tell you now that I loved you for now there are no consequences, no hindrance to your plans. Should I have tried to stop you from leaving? Should I have spilled my guts out on the floor to display my true feelings and take a chance on what you would have done? Should I have risked my heart and yours for honesty? It was an obscure idea that I was afraid of what pain might have been caused by a proclamation of truth. Was it really you I was trying to protect? Why did I let you go?

I do honestly think that I had decided that you would be happier with your fiancé, that he could do more for you than I ever could. Was that cursed inferiority complex that I dragged from my childhood still haunting me, still affecting my decisions, my actions? I had no doubt, but could never admit to it for that was a direct attack to my own survival needs. I had too many other things to abominate myself with. I only know that you remain a cherished part of my life, and the time I spent with you was very important in my growth and my search for a true purpose.

There was some regret that I never bought you anything, never gave you anything as a memento to remind you of how much you really meant to me. In essence, I did. You still own a piece of my heart.

CHAPTER 15

Bonnie:

 Three months of solitude, three months of avoiding the bar scene, avoiding people in general, afraid of what else the world had to add to my list of disappointments. I kept trying to convince myself that I could become a stronger person on my own, become a superior soul from all my hardships and the misgivings of the human race. I could learn from the bad decisions of my past.
 Except for work, I was back into a reclusive lifestyle, and easily done in the middle of a winter season. All my energies were turned to the concentration of financial gain. I jumped without looking at another chance to have savings bonds taken off my paycheck. I went overboard. My deductions were so steep that almost half of my paycheck went toward them, leaving me with thousands added to my savings after only one year, but leaving me at poverty levels for living. I managed though and still found money for wasted comforts. I had much practice in modest means. I had taken a second job for a while and was averaging three hours of sleep, with an hour of prep time each time, cyclone style. I had become a workaholic, and it numbed my incessant thinking for a while. What was one more addiction?
 As spring approached, my hours of work subsided; and I had more time to myself, more time to think. I was thinking in depth again, contemplation, reflection, self-analysis, and all the dangerous things I had kept just below the surface of a bubbling brain. I had fought with every available weapon of thought to avoid acting on my feelings of loneliness. Now with more idle time, all my past issues were flooding forward, and my inescapable desire for companionship with it. Inevitably, these feelings of loneliness would find a way around their suppression, begin to gnaw and eat at my very core. The few memories of joy, slightly more elevated than the memories of hurt and pain, shot holes through the mortar of a newly built wall, erected to keep my past in and new intentions out. The need for companionship bled through, the desire to share my life throbbing enough to feed my temples. I hated my life, but that hatred had been sheltered by my potential for a better one through my new obsession for

financial gain, for success in the material world. I had found a balancing act, so I assumed that letting the loneliness sift through again did not endanger my goals. But it reminded me of the void, an emptiness that I was quite familiar with from my muddy treadmill journey through life.

The old obsession to find answers through a woman, the yearning to obsessive levels, came rushing back with a vengeance. This time though, I felt I was dragging with me a sense of self-worth, a protective mechanism, complete with safety guards not used before. A shield had been placed around my heart, one that took years to build. I could not admit that it was built with thin materials.

I did not want to get back into the bar scene. With the lack of control over the pace of my drinking forever lurking in my background, I could not trust myself not to fall back into my binge drinking habits. Many times, I had pondered over the idea of trying to reconnect with old girlfriends. This was quickly discarded, not from pride, not from potential rejection, but from a pressing urge to get on with my life. I had spent too much time dwelling in the past.

I had heard of dating services before. Never once had I speculated or considered using one. But something kept redirecting me to the ad in the classifieds. I always read the newspaper from front to back, every report, every ad, every editorial. I wanted all the information out there so that if the world ever blew up, I would be the first to know why. It also kept my mind from wandering while occupied with the written word. In the classifieds, browsing though items for sale, help-wanted ads, and possibly finding the column that explained what to do if the world did end, I could not help but notice the repetition of one particular personal ad. Alongside a dark red picture of a cupid with its bow and arrow was the advertisement of a local dating service.

I found myself drawn to it each night, making sure it was still there, smiling at first over who would be desperate enough, and then slowly over time, debating with myself about what harm there could be. After all, it was a source of companionship that I was looking for now, not deep, profound love. So on a particular Friday afternoon, when I felt in a weakened state and loneliness was finding its way through my barrier in sieve leaking proportions, I made the call. Forgetting to avoid high vulnerability in the potentials of this quest, I listened to the sales pitch at the other end of the line; and the next Monday, my check was in the mail to pay for their services.

It was a strange setup to me. Each Thursday, I was to call, and they were to provide me with the name of someone whom they have decided is compatible with me by comparing the answers that I provided on the phone by way of a verbal survey. My requirements were generic and without huge demand. When it came to questions about myself, I realized how easy it would be for dishonesty, to portray a picture of anything. I did leave the part out about alcoholism and chronic depression. Those were mere details that could be sorted out later, as well as denial.

I skipped the first two Thursdays, still unsure of such a road, but eventually loneliness won out. Despair and that recurring self-pity played a role too. But I had no desire to recognize their destructive capabilities and pretended to leave them out of the equation. The third Thursday, I took several deep breaths, made the call to the service, and received your name and phone number. It was a city number, the one that shared the border with the States. I was relieved to find you some distance away. There would have been great embarrassment for me to deal with if it had been someone from my very town, someone who I had already scanned over at the local bar.

That Friday I made the call to you, my shyness and skeptic ways dissolved in the distance of forty miles of telephone wires. Your voice sounded sweet through the receiver, and I began to visualize how you might look. Our conversation was brief. We agreed to meet on Saturday, and I would take you out for dinner. I was surprised when you gave me the exact address to where you lived instead of meeting me somewhere. Were there not perversion and other forms of creepiness out there for you to guard against? This dating process we had entered was not exactly overlaid with screens and filters. It was practically compatibility by drawing names out of a hat. This alone should have had warning bells attached to it.

Saturday came quickly, and I was left with little time to think and rattle my nerves. I had to work overtime that day and didn't get off work until late afternoon. I had cleaned up and primed myself with a half-dozen fast beers before heading in your direction. I cannot imagine the shape I would have been in if I had the whole day to pickle my inhibitions. The days were still short at that time of the year, and it was dark before I reached the city. When I finally found the high-rise apartment you lived in, I could not find parking and ended up feeding coins into a parking meter three blocks away. A brisk walk helped revive me from the sluggishness I felt from a long day's work. I counted twenty floors from the outside as I approached the front entrance to the lobby. I pressed the button of the intercom to your apartment and heard your distorted voice from a cracked speaker inviting me up. Eighteen sequential numbers later in the confines of a small elevator, I felt the first signs of panic. My heart was racing as I now had doubts of what I was doing in such unknown territory.

I stood in front of your door for a moment, practicing deep-breathing exercises, waiting for the calming effects, and then knocked. In fashionable delay, you opened the door. And there you stood, in a low-cut black dress rising high on thighs, an innocent and apprehensive smile, anticipatory wide dark brown eyes. My heart fell into my stomach from disappointment, and I made every attempt possible to hide any signs of my chagrin.

Appearances and attraction, individual opinions of the definition of appeal and perspective of another's look, is highly subjective; but it is also affected by numerous influences and auspices, especially with the interference from peers and the statements of others. I had no attraction to you, and there was a sudden bolt of perception that absolutely nothing existed between us in commonality. I was sorry I judged you in this manner, but the discomfort to be with someone you are not attracted to is best left alone for late-night bar jokes. I was not shallow and did recognize that it was unfair to judge you by my own biased programming. I am only one alone in my judgment, and I again apologize for my lack of vision, my tumbleweed view of what is aesthetic magnetism.

I struggle now to explain how I felt, brewing in a cauldron of mixed moral values to fit my own needs. I had not considered how awkward that first moment at your door would have been for you as well. All I managed to say was hello and asked if you were ready. Your voice was as sweet as it had sounded on the phone, but without any level of physical appeal, my discomfort and the darker side of me weighed heavily. As you went to get your coat, I told you that I was parked quite a distance away and would go get my car and pick you up in front of the lobby. You agreed, and I closed the door behind me.

A thousand thoughts entered my mind, darting off my skull like fireflies in a mason jar. One evil thought kept resurfacing through the rushing mass of other reverberated thoughts. I would get in my car and leave. But if there was one thing that I had developed through all my past experiences, it was empathy, however flawed that might be for one's well-being and dangerous way for lack of self-protection. Regardless, I was stuck with it. I could not just leave you, could not just disappear while you waited in the lobby enshrouded in hurt and abashment. I had been called selfish many times, and although I really didn't consider myself that way, if I had left you standing there, there would be no more denial of such, and my overdeveloped sense of empathy would have eventually eaten a hole in my already tormented soul. So instead I pulled up to the no-parking zone in front of the main doors of your apartment, got out of my car, and opened up the passenger door for you. This was an act of chivalry I normally saved for self-indulgent impressions.

I knew of a fancy restaurant in your city of which I had read about, that provided entertainment throughout the dinner hours. I had never been there, but I had heard from others that the decorum and alluring atmosphere was wondrous. This was where I took you, for an evening of wining and dining with no hidden objective but to ensure you a pleasant evening out. The hostess frowned at me, quickly noticing my long hair and frayed jeans, and guided us to a corner table away from the main stage. There was a red velvet tablecloth, and a floating candle flickered in a heart-shaped bowl in the center of the table. There were pink petals of carnations swimming around the candle. You whispered to me how nice this place was and had only vague memories of being there before as a young girl with your parents.

After long browses over the menus and ordering stiff drinks of rum and Coke, I was able to break into conversation with you. It was not genuine interest, but I questioned you about your parents, your background, your interests. Thankfully, the questions were never quite reciprocated, for not only was I not keen on sharing information, it would soon have been very apparent that we had nothing in common. There was relief in many aspects to find that you had no qualms in lengthy explanations and could tell full-length stories in deep breaths and long runaway sentences. I was in no danger of meeting anyone I knew so far away from my hometown and in such a fancy place. So I settled in with frequent orders of double rum and Cokes, and the dim lighting helped me relax.

My nerves were still on edge, but the original sensation of my chest cavity exploding had subsided, and I realized that I could cope with the evening. We both ordered the salmon special, which certainly was a special meal for me, still coping with a steady diet of sandwiches. I ordered more drinks, only yours had switched to Coke without the rum. You explained to me that you were not much of a drinker, and I let that go. If you had only known how untrue that was for me, your opinion of me that had begun to shine in your eyes would surely have changed to one less favorable.

We had a pleasant dinner, and we watched the dinner show in between bites. It was a local comedian and certainly appropriate. I needed comic relief. By my sixth rum and Coke, I was relaxed enough to eliminate any jitters I still had felt in the pit of my stomach and had replaced it with most of the salmon. My gnawing selfish desire to end the evening and send it into the memory banks was not allowed to interfere, and I did enjoy my time with you. I had no hidden agenda except not to hurt your feelings.

After the show was over, the room became quiet and the crowd I had successfully become oblivious to, slowly parted. The night was still young and I didn't think it appropriate that I just rush you home. I suggested a movie. I had thought of taking you to a bar, a regressive thought from my past as the only reliable source of entertainment I knew, but not only had it been confirmed you weren't a drinker, I still had ridiculing voices of my past peers in the back of my head stating I shouldn't be seen with you. It was a stupid response to the turmoil inside me for one who considered himself intelligent and mature. The fact that I was still in several states of regression after recent and painfully excruciating ends to relationships escaped me. In my search to get back into social atmosphere, albeit my hermit hiatuses from time to time, left me far from mature and I carried some deep-rooted problems with me. You had only grasped me by first impressions, never getting the chance to see the litter of emotional baggage that lay just below the surface. You also did not see that the movie theatre was suggested because it would leave us in a dark and discreet environment.

There was not much choice for movies when we arrived at the theatre. I hated comedies, and the dinner entertainment was only coincidental. I preferred the special effects of science fiction or the excitement of a horror flick. We chose a comedy anyway since it seemed to be the theme of the evening. An hour into the movie, I watched your hand get closer and closer to mine. I was not insensible to your hint of wanting to hold hands, but I just couldn't find the logic in doing so. It was bad enough that I was hiding the fact that I simply wanted the night to end on a good note. Was I to falsely lead you to think more by holding your hand?

Three quarters through the movie, the long day, the boring story line, and some stiff drinks had caught up to me, and I was nodding off. Twice I had to shake my head vigorously to stop from falling asleep entirely. The movie was indeed atrocious, and to this day, I couldn't tell you what it was about. When we walked out of the theatre later and you asked me if I liked it, I could only muster an it-was-okay response.

I drove you home right after, omitting to even ask you if you were ready to. We shared a few words in the car, but I was zapped of all energy and had no strength left to continue my charade. After meandering my ways through some side streets, as you directed me after I got lost, I was finally able to pull up in front of your apartment. I had turned up the stereo the last few miles to avoid any awkward questions you might ask. I turned it down to say good night. In an almost cued response, you asked if I wanted to come in. I said to you, and somewhat lined in honesty, that I was really tired from working all day. You accepted my answer and reached over and kissed me on the cheek. I watched you get out of the car (forgetting about any acts of chivalry this time) and waved to you as you entered the building. I drove away and felt as if a huge weight had rolled off my shoulders. The night had passed, nothing wrong was said or done, and we could now both get on with our lives. We were just not meant to be.

I spent the next day alone at home, another day of seclusion on a cold spring day. There was a feeling of remorse, but I couldn't quite place it. It was different than the ones attached to hangovers. As I worked out these feelings, trying to understand them, I was able to conclude that it was not my fault that I had not been attracted to you. Most attractions have some kind of chemical inducement, something developed by our own time-constructed subjectivity. I could not be held accountable for that. It is certainly questionable, though, if some of my reactions were based on the influence of others. I wasn't interested in any psychological jargon that day and preferred to forget about it all.

You called later that Sunday night, for I had given you my phone number when I had first called you in case of any problems. You thanked me for a great time and went on to say that you would really like to get together again. I was again suddenly left in the position of not wanting to hurt you. I explained that I was working a lot of overtime hours, but I would call you at the first opportunity. As you know, I never did.

I had no regrets, and any remorse dissipated quickly. I was sure that the dating service would soon hook you up with someone else, someone more deserving than I, someone more suitable to your needs. I am sorry that our time together had ended so abruptly and that you might have been hoping for more. In all sincerity, we had nothing in common. If you had known my background, who I truly was, you would have run away faster than it took me to drink that first rum and Coke at dinner.

I am sure you have found someone really nice by now, someone that will treat you with courtesy and respect that you most certainly deserve. Someone who you can share your life with, your dreams, your goals and interests. Someone who has fallen in love with you and whose heart you hold as well. May your guardian angels guide you. Mine seem to have disappeared.

CHAPTER 16

Carrie:

It took me several weeks to call you, your name and number fading away on a crumpled piece of paper that had barely survived an adventurous ride in my washing machine in the back pocket of a pair of blue jeans. Another attempt at the dating game did not sit well with me. My first encounter was disappointing, and although I had not set any high levels of criteria, there were some standards. There had to be at least attraction and some form of appeal. I now had doubts of this new search for companionship, this new cure for loneliness. But I had nothing to lose in such a lonely journey, anyway.

When I finally did call you on a Wednesday night, you caught me off guard when you picked up on the second ring. I had no time to mull over exactly what I was going to say, although I had repeated the words a hundred times over before the initial phone call. I had expected to hear an incessant ring with plenty of time to go over the words again. When you said hello, I went blank and almost stuttered when I began to explain who I was and how I was given your name by the company referring itself as a matchmaking service. I wanted to ask you what you looked like, but even desperation didn't hold a place for such tackiness.

There were times when I wished that I was as shallow as some jocks, where character didn't matter. Maybe I was shallow. My own opinion of myself was highly subjective, and I didn't need to add to my list of established inferiorities. One needs to hold on to some kind of self-esteem and allow acknowledgement of quality traits, whether exaggerated or not. There has to be some self-worth of some kind or, when suffering from depression, you might as well follow the lemmings over the cliff.

Your voice was sweet over the phone, but our short conversation left me no clues about who you were. You asked me no questions, showed no signs of curiosity about who I was. Almost like a business transaction, we planned a meeting at your place for Saturday afternoon and said pleasant good-byes. I still could not grasp why it was so easy for someone to give up their address to a perfect stranger. If I raped you, or even worse, did you think that the dating service would be liable? They certainly had all the information about who I was, but would it not be too late if I was some demented pervert?

Nevertheless, this particular pervert was coming to visit you on Saturday. I wasn't as excited, wasn't as nervous as I should have been, as I usually was. Maybe the compounding disappointments in my life were finally numbing me, lowering my levels of anticipation. This did not stop me from drinking high quantities of alcohol that Saturday morning in preparation for our meeting. I still had to neutralize inhibitions.

This dating service covered a wide area, probably for the purpose of ensuring numbers for choice. It was over an hour drive to you, your home in a town I had only been to once before. There was an Indian reservation nearby, and the only bar that I had stopped at during my visit to your savory town was full of drunks, consisting of only two kinds—those that were passed out at their tables or very close to it, and those who wanted to fight with anyone. Neither fit my description of fun. I don't even remember what the female clientele were like, but I can imagine that if their choice in men were that limited, so were they.

My mind darted around foolish thoughts like that, more in a daydream state than actual reflections. Neutrality was finding its base in a self-induced trance to nowhere in particular. I barely thought of you until I pulled into your driveway after getting lost twice and finally asking a gas station attendant for directions. Any hopes of calmly knocking on your door vanished instantly when I studied your immaculate brick house and perfectly manicured, landscaped yard. All my insecurities flashed back like lightning bolts. My first impulse was to back up and drive home, but before I could turn cowardly and run, I got out of my car and opened up the trunk and grabbed my suitcase. Suitcase was the nickname I gave my cooler, for I seldom traveled without it. The beer bottles inside were clanging against each other as I carried it to your front door.

You could have been a recovering alcoholic for all I knew or had some deep religious faith where alcohol was taboo. I knew I should have more discretion than towing my vices around with me for everyone to see, but that devilish voice inside me was whispering that what you see is what you get. This was far from the truth, and I was a bit more complicated than that.

When I rang the doorbell, I could hear it echoing through your house like the high pitch of church chimes. And like the phone call, I had only time enough for one deep breath before you swiftly opened the door. I almost dropped my cooler, as my whole body relaxed in a huge sigh of relief. You were pretty, very pretty; and although your eyes were seasoned with distrust, they were also friendly and as blue as a velvet sky. I confirmed who I was, as if you might have lined up more than one of me in case I didn't meet approval. And in response, you gave me your name in case I had the wrong address.

Your kitchen table was the first thing I saw, and I was startled to see a rugged but handsome guy scoping me when I entered your house. You introduced me to him as your co-worker that lived directly across the road. He passed his lit cigarette from his right hand to his left and offered a handshake without standing up. I obliged and narrowly missed a face full of smoke as he exhaled at the same time of our handshake. His eyes were extremely bloodshot, and it wasn't until I noticed the roaches in the ashtray that I recognized the distinct smell of pot. You offered me a seat and a beer. I took the seat but not the beer, pointing to my cooler.

After you got a beer for you and your co-worker, you sat down to the left of me and continued a conversation with him, which was obvious to me that I had interrupted. You were talking about work and union negotiations, and it was easy for me to perceive that you did work together. Also apparent was how absorbed you were in the topic of unions. I sat there as an innocent bystander, and an ignored one as well, as your conversation became more animated. I was already digging into my cooler for a second beer, pretending to show signs of interest, when you finally apologized to me. You explained about the imminent strike vote at your plant. I quickly said I understood, and you went back to your discussions.

Your voices faded into a drone, like a low-volume static of a lost signal to a radio station. I scoured the rest of your house. Except for the kitchen table, your house was spotless, ready for snapshots to be forwarded to a *Better Homes and Gardens* magazine. Your job must have paid well, the evidence in your ceramic tile, gleaming hardwood floors, leather furniture, stainless steel appliances, and general decor of extravagant taste. It was the top of the line for you, and when I looked back at you, your confident composure matched your material world. You were attractive, very attractive; and except for the fact that you had basically ignored me so far, I did not feel that uncomfortable with you. That was more than I could say about your co-worker, and there were no disappointments when he finally left an hour later.

It wasn't until many days later when I reflected back on our initial meeting that it occurred to me that he wasn't just a co-worker but a close friend. With your obvious need for organization and order, it also dawned on me that he was there on prearrangement, as protection until it was determined that I was harmless. You had some extraordinary qualities, some of which I could only wish for. The least of all was your great sense of independence.

It wasn't until after your co-worker left that I carefully prodded you with questions. There was just too much curiosity boiling inside me to take the course of timely and discretionary inquiries. I wanted to know who you were right away, anxious to understand the mysteries I felt from you. And you did not disappoint me with lack of details. You were recently divorced after five years of marriage and had bought out your husband's share of the house. You had been left a trust fund from your grandmother and, in two more years, had access to more money than you would be able to figure out what to do with. In the meantime, you were quite comfortable with a high-paying job. Having fun was important to you, and you loved life. You took no bull from anyone, and the only reason you had joined the dating service was for fun, and you had grown tired of meeting idiots that frequented the bars prowling for the likes of you.

You wanted no strings, but you were eventually going to look for a meaningful relationship with the right guy. You enjoyed being alone, but you were also looking for someone to share parts of your life with. You poured out so much information so fast that I was overwhelmed. I had never met a woman so secure, so free of inhibitions, so self-assured. I felt small beside you, but I knew I could not let you see such weaknesses. I was a mess when I was alone and had gathered many insecurities from my turmoiled past. Instead of admitting to those, I told you about my goals and inspirations and displayed a sense of confidence that I felt you were looking for. I omitted that I could not fathom such ways on my own.

After you had put my sensory intake into overload with your honesty, your forthcomings, your beauty, you asked me why I had joined the dating service. I was blessed with a quick-witted thought and said that I joined it to find you. This struck you so funny that you laughed incessantly, and your laugh was so contagious that I had to chuckle with you. Unexpectedly, you pulled out a joint out of your purse, which had sat on the floor beside you, and asked if I smoked. The repeated paranoid effects that I had experienced lately with social use should have caused a resounding no. But then if I was going anywhere with you, I had to display perfect compatibility. So instead of saying no, I said occasionally. You lit it up and handed it to me to celebrate the start of this new occasion. Almost immediately, I felt the effects as I drew the smoke deep into my lungs, holding it in to allow the quick passage to the brain.

Whether it was because I was naturally an introvert and the drug enhanced that characteristic, I always felt like withdrawing inside myself, as my mind began to wrestle with the different aspects of my thinking processes. Same thoughts, only different angles of view, which would eventually dissipate to the original way of thinking once the effects wore off. But in the duration, the advanced spectrum set ideas in motion that didn't fit with the norm, resulting in paranoia, begging for the return to regular thought. Instead of enjoying my high with you, all my energy went into suppressing its effects so that I could at least function at a social level with you. If there was a habit that I could easily give up entirely, it was weed. For all intents and purposes, I had. Only for the benefits of being social had I joined in when asked, and for a lost cause anyway when I couldn't use it in social atmosphere and function properly.

I focused on you, trying not to think at all, and increased my visits to my cooler, hoping for the counter-effects of alcohol. It helped that you were so outgoing, and with your upbeat and friendly conversation, you were able to help me stay on track instead of trailing off to paths of musing trances. I fought to keep the philosophical outbursts from surfacing, a side effect of the marijuana that habitually opened up depth, that otherwise would remain submerged in my subconscious to be shared only by myself and my inner voice. If I started babbling about the cosmics, I might as well have grabbed my suitcase and went home. The more you talked, the more you demonstrated your carefree outlook on life. I knew that my own beliefs and mundane theories about the meaning of life would have turned you off faster than a sensitive dimmer switch.

So as I continued my efforts to fight off the effects of the weed, I secretly prayed to any guardian angels that might still be interested in listening to me and asked for them to guide me through the stone. Someone was listening, even if it was only my own schizophrenic self, and I turned the afternoon into laughter instead of panic. Somehow you had reached a tone in me, a vibratory string that led to an escape from my usual obstructed ability to have fun. Your easy way with words brought me to laughing sprees. Accompanied by your contagious laughs, we joked nonsensically, finding the simplest things hilarious. I laughed so hard at times that I was brought to tears. I just couldn't avoid those tears, but for once, they were not laced with sadness.

The moments turned into hours, and although it was difficult for me to grasp, I was as jovial as an unblemished child. I did have vague memories of that fervent rush of joy when in the middle of bouts of past laughter, but I was long overshadowed by my perpetual sadness and depression. The exuberance exhausted me in such a manner that it was more a soft euphoric mood rather than fatigue. The afternoon moved toward evening, and the soft glow of twilight filled your home. Your skin was silky smooth and white, untouched by the damaging rays of a summer sun. It left you looking sensually soft and extraordinarily beautiful. This was more than the effects of the weed, and my heart was flushed with sudden desire.

The afternoon of our frivolous ways had not stopped me from studying you. When you lit the second joint as if in commemoration to the setting sun, I was suddenly impacted by what I saw in you. Those familiar feelings came rushing in. I was in love again. How this could be happening so fast,

I didn't know from Eve. Our fun afternoon was not sufficient grounds to warrant such emotion. And for the very first time, I had a thought that although fleetingly had hit me several times in my past, had never quite registered before; and almost as powerful as an epiphany, this sudden insight frightened me. So close to truth and so harmful to my own reflections and feelings of my past, I would have to try everything imaginable to fragment the validity. It couldn't be that all those times, all the pain and suffering and dashed hopes could be summarized in such unadorned pathos. It couldn't be that all this time, all my past was based on the fact that I was simply in love with the idea of being in love.

It couldn't be that I didn't know the difference between thriving on the power of true love and had all this time been settling for the desire of it instead. There was no time to reflect on such obtruding awareness, for it would mean instant introversion, and I wasn't ready to end the exhilaration I was getting from you so quickly. Those thoughts had to be buried immediately and brought back to discovery at a more appropriate time. It had dampened my spirit though, and you recognized my slight change of mood right away. You asked me what was wrong, and I quickly replied that it was nothing except that I thought I was having a flashback. Your instant laughter over this statement assured me that you had your days in the experimentation of acid as well.

We continued with our giggle festival and our childlike display of diversion. And thankfully I was able to bury my sudden horrific awareness of how simple I might truly be. Instead I overrode all of it and let my infatuation with you determine the direction of the night. Rather, it controlled me. The more I looked at you, the stronger the desire, the more drive to express it to you physically. I had almost reached the point where I could spray out the words of how attracted I was to you when you asked me if I was hungry. I seldom ate when I was drinking, but there was a lot to be said about food cravings and increased appetite with the use of marijuana.

Half an hour later, we were sitting in a Chinese restaurant, chauffeured there by you in a brand-new Monte Carlo that had been concealed in your garage. I had sat in the passenger seat with pride and envy. To own such a set of wondrous wheels would remain in the dream stages for now.

At the restaurant, we stuck to the staples of the known. Egg rolls, wonton soup, fried rice, sweet-and-sour chicken balls. I had forgotten that food could taste so good. Recently, I ate to survive on a steady diet of countless bologna sandwiches and vitamin pills for dessert. And an overabundance of barley soup with hops in it; sometimes lager, sometimes ale.

Giddiness was still on the forefront, and even the chicken balls were funny to us. We laughed together as a couple who had known each other forever. Together, we decided that the frown we kept receiving from the waitress was not important, her display of disgust reflecting that we were disturbing the rest of the customers. Our silliness had reached ludicrous portions when behind the waitress's back you pulled your eyes apart with your fingers and said, "So solly." Under normal circumstances, I would have been discouraged by such racially profiled overtones. But I was caught up in the moment, enveloped in my brief journey, riding the clouds above depression. I found your mockery hysterical.

After a valiant attempt of eating everything in front of us, some of the rice remained; and on a mutual agreement that we didn't want to know our future, stuck our unopened fortune cookies in it. A Chinese restaurant isn't exactly the most romantic place to spend a Saturday night, but we weren't ready to leave. We were content at our little corner table, with the floating candle as a centerpiece and the framed picture of baby panda bears on the wall behind us. This poorly lit foreign food establishment became our bar for the night, and I kept ordering a steady supply of mixed drinks. Our laughter was loud, but we were not rowdy, so the scourge of the waitress seemed to diminish with each round. The dinner crowd had vanished, and there were a few times when we were the only customers. It was great to escape the pressure of trying to entertain you in some dingy bar with the music too loud to talk. This quieter environment was only further addition to the pleasures of the evening. We could have gone back to your house, but then I would have been forced to control my crushing desire to consume you. The restaurant was safe.

My need to be with you physically was inevitable, and you showed me no signs there wasn't mutual attraction, no signs that you were not interested in me the same way. And as the quantity of our drinks reached intoxicating amounts, your eyes and your innuendos led me to believe there was intimacy in the offering. It was well past midnight when we left the restaurant arm in arm, more to stabilize each other's stride than for affection. I suggested that we leave your car in the parking lot and call a taxi. You agreed.

Twenty minutes later, I was kissing you in the doorway of your kitchen, never once accepting the notion that you might be too drunk to ward off my advances. We shuffled into your living room, and somehow you turned on the stereo system without the use of any light. The only light in the entire house was a night-light that flickered from the end of your hallway, which led to your bedroom. We curled up on the couch and continued the kisses of arousal, began the dance of hormones with sensuous gropes, clothing loosened with caressing hands, and then we fell asleep almost simultaneously. But not before you whispered that you weren't prepared to go all the way with me just yet.

I woke up later with deep grogginess and, at first, was not aware of where I was. I had no idea what time it was. I only knew that dawn must be close. With the force of a tightly wound jack-in-the-box, I jumped up with the sudden recognition that I had volunteered for overtime work that Sunday. With double time and a perfect attendance record to maintain, I couldn't be late. My abrupt move woke you, and once my eyes adjusted to the darkness, I could see you were struggling to do the buttons up on your blouse that I had earlier so gracefully undone. I explained to you that I had to go to work, and in your sluggish state, you only replied with an okay. You walked me to the door, still not quite steady on your feet. I asked you about your car, and you told me not to worry about it. I kissed you on the cheek, missing my intended target when you moved your head. You agreed I could call you, and I stipulated how great of a time I had with you. You reciprocated with a soft "me too." I squeezed your hand and said good-bye.

On the drive home, I squeezed the steering wheel much tighter than I had your hand, grasping for concentration to keep my tires between the lines on the road. I was still essentially drunk, but I had become a professional at hiding it behind the wheel. The exceptions of historical mishaps with ditches did not count. I always favored the right side of the road. If I was ever to get into a serious accident, it was of great importance that I took no one with me. What a considerate inebriated driver I was!

The colors of predawn were already being brushed on the eastern horizon, and by the time I reached home, a huge orange ball was surfacing. I was running out of time to get to work on time. A very quick shower, no coffee, and taking just enough time to make sure I had my shoes on the right feet, I rushed out the door. Two hours later, in the thick of heavy work and heavy hangover, I suddenly realized that I had forgotten my suitcase. I had never forgotten my traveling companion in all the years that it had kept me company. If there was anything to vibrology, the scholars would have had a field day with the energy fields around that cooler. That is once they stripped the layers of duct tape holding it together. My leaving it behind could be nothing but an omen, nothing but a sign that I was to pursue you. It meant that I was to be with you.

I wasted no time. Winter would come fast, with autumn turning the corner, and a host of dark memoires would soon begin to flood forward if I was alone. After a good night's sleep and another day of hard work, I called you. It was not what I expected. You were friendly, but also a bit curt. It didn't matter because the results of our conversation were positive. We were having a second date on Saturday, only this time you were coming to see me. I gave you directions to my house and thanked you. It sounded awkward, and I later thought about how ridiculous it was to thank you, almost as if in a tone of accented desperation. I had to overlook it because as insecure as I was, if I started analyzing every word, every sentence spoken, I would self-destruct.

It was enough to know that I was in love with you. But when I thought of this, it didn't feel quite right. Something was off, my emotional scale not quite calibrated. The crushing weight of that incessant drive of previous devotion wasn't as heavy this time. I had almost completely forgotten the idea from the last Saturday night that maybe I was confused over my definition of love. I had to doubt it because my feelings from my past had been so genuine, so overpowering that nothing else had mattered. Lust, infatuation, affection, yearning—it didn't matter at this point. I needed you, needed a woman for insight to my own guidance. It didn't necessarily mean your guidance directed to me, and maybe that is why I was questioning this new twist in the depth of my love. That was as close to independence as I was going to get for now. I would just borrow some of your guidance and use it for my own.

The following Saturday arrived quickly, and I took another day of overtime work to speed up the process of my wait to your arrival. Not only was I not expecting you until six o'clock, but my sideline ambition for financial gain was also a far easier goal to attain than waiting patiently for you, for the perfect relationship. I had long seceded from my rebellious ways toward society. Age and reality was enough to resolve the errors of my teenage reflections. To become successful, especially in the circles of society, one has to at least live within its boundaries. The slow but attainable goal to financial freedom was therapeutic, a medicine to alleviate an unwavering depression, to fend off manic degrees. I was constantly running numbers in my head, with dollar signs attached to them, balancing future weeks of work with the desired growth of bank accounts. Saturday was no different as I waited for you to arrive. My numbers were off a little as the deduction for the cost of alcohol was a matter of fluctuation and the true cost of drinking omitted from my summations. Beer was a necessary commodity and, although not tax deductible, an essentiality just the same. As if to confirm this, by eight o'clock that night, I had already put a huge dent into a case of beer, while my patience with your tardiness slowly turned into panic.

What if you weren't coming? I was not prepared for another round of disappointment so soon. At eight thirty, after further wearing out a path from pacing back and forth from the kitchen to the living room, the phone rang. A mad dash let me catch the third ring. My heart was pumping faster than if my bloodstream had been injected intravenously with amphetamines when I heard your distraught voice. I was sure you were calling to tell me you weren't coming. When you told me that you were at the corner gas station, unable to find my street, my heart rate slowly subsided. And the irony did not escape me that I had ended up at a gas station trying to find you. You were only a few blocks from me, but I wasn't taking any chances of giving you misconstrued directions and told you to wait there. I got into my car, and moments later, you were following me back to my house. Your Monte Carlo sparkled, a beacon of luxury parked behind my Grand Prix, which was now nothing but another rust bucket; and although it should not have represented any egotistical value to me, I was proud to have your car in my driveway.

When you came close to me, I could smell your perfume, but I could also smell the marijuana smoke on you. A passing thought of how bad of a habit you actually had was quickly suppressed with my joy to see you. There was no kiss or hug because in essence, we didn't really know each other; and although we had such a great time the weekend before, I was now flushed with nervousness. You, however, seemed to be at great ease, and I silently cursed my inexhaustible supply of shyness. My alcohol levels did not have sufficient volume yet to plug the holes of my underlining insecurities.

We sat in the living room. I was ashamed of my furniture, my surroundings, when I began to compare it with your home. I wondered what deductions you were making about me. I asked you what you wanted to drink and promptly filled your order of vodka and orange juice, blessed with the availability of both. After I poured you the second one, you were already asking me if I wanted to smoke a joint. It was the last thing I wanted to do with my mind already racing around its circumference with crisscrossed radiuses. But I wasn't about to turn it down and have you think any less of me. If this was part of your lifestyle, I would have to adjust and at least give you the impression of complete compatibility.

It was a mistake to smoke weed in my state of mind, and I knew it, but I hoped for the best. I thought I could control it, but not only was your stash more potent than the weekend before, I was also too weak to fight off the introversion that I had been afraid it would cause. Conversation became awkward as I drifted inside. I felt distant from you. It was only your outgoing personality that stopped me from withdrawing entirely. When some of the initial effects began to wear off, I was able to focus on thinking of ways to entertain you. The music from my stereo seemed to be infiltrating to my very soul, and because of this, I asked you if you wanted to go dancing. And that was how we ended up at the bar.

We walked there even though it was already dark. You were as jovial as the weekend before, and I tried my best to keep up a front, all the while swatting my paranoid afflictions to the back corners of my mind and slowly exterminating them by concentrating on you. In a courageous act, I held your hand. When I entered the bar, I was flushed with pride to have you by my side. The place was crowded, and I saw familiar faces in the crowd. I did not get to know very many people in this town, but I recognized many of them with my incessant habit of studying people. Normally, I would have gone there alone, found my favorite corner bar stool, soak in the vibrations of the people, get plastered, try to avoid trouble, and stagger home.

Not only was my bar stool taken that night, it also would have been difficult for both of us to sit on it. With the walk of a strutting peacock and with you in my arm, I pressed through the crowd, looking for a place for us to sit. The only thing I could find was a pair of seats at a long table off to the side of the dance floor that was already occupied by three guys and a girl. Before I had a chance to look for alternatives, you were already asking them if the seats were taken. You immediately received a chorus of excited "No, please sit down" from all the three guys. I knew that with the big crowd, service would be slow, if not wretched, so I left you sitting there and pushed my way to the bar and ordered several vodka and orange juice. An extraordinary balancing act allowed me to get the drinks back to you without spillage. Common sense lost its prevalence or I would have stuck to beer. The effects of the weed were still putting pressure on my ability to think clearly, and I was on a mission to douse the dope with quick offerings of libation.

By the time I got back to the table, you were already thick in conversation with everyone. I should have expected it because as outgoing as you were, why would there be limitations for my benefit? The serpentine squeezes of jealousy were crushing my ribs by the time the waitress finally arrived, and I ordered us two more drinks each. You sat extremely close to the guy next to you, and I watched your hand touch his thigh as you talked. It was more than likely an innocent gesture, but it sent chills through me. The more you talked and fed them stories, the more they laughed. I was seething inside, but wore a fake smile as best as I could. At first I thought you were ignoring me because none of your conversation was directed at me, and it was not all imagination when I heard your flirtatious words. I began to think of how big of a mistake it was to have brought you there when you reached over and held my hand. It relaxed me as much as a bottle of sedatives. There were still waves of jealousy flowing in me, but now controlled by your touch and the message you were sending me. You were there with me.

We had arrived during an intermission, and the band began to play. We were so close to the speakers that conversation became screaming matches. This was a flood of relief to me, and with you shut off from the rest of our table, combined with the sensuality I felt from your hand, I settled into reposed mode. And then slowly the dangers of switching to liquor from beer took its course, and the rest of the night became a blur to me. It wasn't exactly blackouts but more of bleeps in a time machine were I lost parts of three hours. I do remember feeling comfortable most of the night, except when you accepted the offer of the guy next to you and danced with him. You did ask my permission, but it didn't stop me from cringing as I watched you in each other's arms while I tracked the placement of his hands with acute radar. It was the longest slow bar-band song in history, and the only thing appeasing about it was that it was only one dance. I went without one. That I did not forget.

We closed the place, our table of new friends and us the last ones to leave. We said our good-byes, you by their names, myself destined to never remember them. I remember putting my coat around you for the brisk walk back to my place. Fall had arrived early. You wanted to smoke another joint on the way home, and by that time, I was totally mentally challenged and helped you smoke it without an ounce of hesitation. By the time we reached my house, I was in the clouds, with only you as an anchor to hold me from floating away entirely.

I led you down the hall to my bedroom. On what was usually a hard mattress, I sank into what felt like an ocean of cotton balls. You lay beside me as part of my world. It was more than buttons that I undid this time, and as intoxicated as I was, I undressed you to the raw, as smoothly as promiscuity allowed. My normal allowance for foreplay was ascended by dire necessity. There was nothing more important than making love to you, to ultimately join with you in mutual compulsive sexual urges. As I climbed on top of you, you whispered to me and asked if I had a condom. Without missing a beat, I whispered back that you were kidding me and slipped into you as naturally as the pull of the universe. Whether it was because it had been so long since I had sex, or the psychological effects of potent pot, or my extreme desire to show you how much you meant to me, our intensity was at the top of the graphic charts. My staying power that night will never be matched again, but I have your own moans and thrusts as record to vouch that this extraordinary intensity was matched in your own pleasure.

When I finally rolled over, it took me a while to fall asleep. When I closed my eyes, the colors bouncing off my retina onto the back of my eyelids formed shapes and sizes of a mixed array of unearthly visions. They were blinding. The combination of a bucket of vodka still sloshing around in various internal organs and marijuana coating my brain cells, these visions sped around at various speeds. Sometimes it was next to nausea, but sickness was never an option; regurgitation was. Such pleasant thoughts were finally extinguished with sudden sleep, but with the vivid screen still running in front of my shuttered eyes, it continued on in an endless display of dreams

I woke up in the morning, my head a couple of sizes bigger than a soccer ball. I reached over for you, but you were gone. At first, I thought you might have slipped into town for something, cigarettes, or possibly the makings of breakfast. My last visit to the grocery store was far back on the calendar, and you would have had to have settled for dry toast and a trickle of left over orange juice. But as late morning quickly turned into noon, I knew you weren't coming back. I had dry toast by myself and spent the afternoon on the couch, unable to truly function. Too hungover to even think about disappointment to the fact that you left, it was curiosity that made me call you that night.

And again you answered so quickly that I was unprepared. I struggled with conversation for a moment and then asked you why you hadn't stayed. You said that you were cold. I could grant you that since I hadn't turned the furnace on yet, and my blankets were thin, but what kind of minced meat was I that I had no body heat? This was a thought that came much later. Then the only thing I could think of was to tell you that I was sorry. I could tell by your periods of silence that you didn't really want to talk. To alleviate the awkwardness that was developing between us, I said I wouldn't keep you, but asked if I could see you again soon. When you said yes, I asked you to call me later to set up a time. This was a subtle way for me to take the pressure off me to decide when the best time was. Your one-word answer of *sure* was your only response.

And then out of nowhere, I told you that I loved you. I heard you snicker, and it reverberated though me with discomfort and revocation. You replied with only silence. And the snicker was slowly registering to me as a sneer instead. I quickly said good-bye.

I instantly regretted using those words so loosely again. I did love you, but it wasn't from the core of my heart, that powerful sentience that was centrally driven like something pulled from the cosmos. I knew what true love was. Or did I? Had my twisted meandering paths through a multitude of relationships left me confused of the actual meaning of love? I didn't think so. It came from too far within. My past feelings were derived from the very depths of my soul; my whole existence connected to its power. But then how could I explain that just after two dates, with someone of complete opposite character to my own, that I had just professed my love to her?

That now repetitive and fleeting thought came back. Was I simply in love with being in love? And after the night before, had I carried it enough to even confuse casual sex with it as well? I have had my share of one-night stands and have had many casual sexual relations before. How confused and desperate was I to escape my loneliness, to avoid the pain it takes to develop emotional independency, to find the strength it takes for self-support? These and many other questions rolled around inside my head incessantly for the next week, almost as a source of morbid entertainment, and then I buried them along with the rest of my past. I retained only fragments of them in the forefront of my brain, only not to lose complete focus on my relentless search for stability and legitimate maturity.

I needed you. I needed someone, and you were pretty. That was the extent of my sophisticated philosophical ponderings about why I wanted to be with you. Socrates, I was not that week. At least not on the surface, at least not while I had to simplify everything to uphold my sanity. I called you the following week, after it was obvious enough for me that you were not going to. It took many rings this time, but you did answer. You were cordial, and our conversation was no deeper than your average weather report. When we wore out the details of the possibility of rain, I asked if I could see you. You said yes. I told you I would call you in a couple of days and we would plan something. Just before I hung up, I added that I promised that I wouldn't come across to you so heavy this time, sensing my swift proclamation of my love had scared you away. You snickered again, only this time it sounded polite. But I knew by the sound that love was the farthest thing from your mind. I said good-bye and repeated that I would call you. I never did.

There were many nights of regrets doing that, especially with all the lonely nights I spent afterward, waiting for some other opportunity to come along and fill the void left when I decided to give up on you. During those lonely nights, I would again reflect back to my past, my burial process obviously not deep enough. I thought of the odd times in my life where true passionate love had existed. It had been my life raft that kept me afloat on a sea of depression, and it remained my driving force to future relationships. If I hadn't set such a high standard toward deep-rooted emotion, hadn't demanded it from myself and the women I met, life for me could have been so much easier. We could have remained friends. We could have continued a casual relationship without any strings like you had requested. The sex between us certainly had potential.

Instead, I carried on with my search for the perfect soul mate, never once considering that if I ever found her, I would probably screw it up anyway. I am grateful for meeting you. Although I didn't know you very long, you gave me some insight to my difficulties. It didn't change my habits or my basic way of thinking, but you certainly gave me more to ponder. I sincerely hope that you are still happy and do envy your abilities to be so self-sufficient and to be so perceptive to ways of controlling your own destiny. I am still trying.

CHAPTER 17

Judy:

When I think of blind dates, I think of various layers of ozone in unfamiliar territory. Anticipation brews with anxiety, tossing the nervous system into a frenzy. Our mutual friend, Max, who took it upon himself to fix us up (as it is befittingly called), had given me no clue about your looks or your personality. He stated only that you were nice. Nice is in the eye of the beholder, or have I mixed that analogy up with something else?

So for an entire week until the night of our meeting, all the side effects of the uncertainty of blind dating took place. Rapid pulse, loss of appetite, daydreaming, piled on to my list of insecurities. I had joined a dating service a few months previously, and that had been no different than my present apprehensions. But I had little success with it, and this new arrangement of a blind meeting seemed to have a different twist. The whole idea of going out with someone I had never met spun rabidly through my thoughts, and I had several private debates with myself whether to follow through with it. My relentless drive for female companionship soon dissipated most of the doubt, and Friday night eventually came with internal approval to go ahead.

My palms were drenched and soaking the steering wheel of my car during my drive to your place. The fact that you lived outside the turmoil of my own town and my disturbing memories further enhanced my expectations. The privacy factor of being outside of my own environment was strangely reassuring. Reputations are hard to live down, and although I considered myself far from a womanizer, I had left a few broken hearts behind me. Empathy shrouded some of my actions, but it did nothing to alleviate some of the pain I had caused. I did not want to meet anyone else in my immediate area. For a man who walked around with his heart precariously stitched together, I could carry some of that pain with me; but with my own selfish needs, I could not prevent it from releasing and oozing out to be dispersed to carry on with my own requirements. All these jumbled thoughts were still bouncing around inside my mind when I pulled into your driveway.

"God, let this be the end of my search" had spewed out of my mouth vocally for the interior of my car to hear. I turned off the ignition and looked around at your dilapidated house but could pass no judgment. I knew, by the directions that Max had given me, that you lived in the poorer section of town, but I had no basis for any prejudice against any financially strapped existence. And then that recurring thought of why anyone would want to meet me at their home without knowing me first darted around inside my head for a moment and then became irrelevant. The power of desire wiped it out.

It was still a presumptuous act for me that wherever I went, alcohol came with me. Without any hesitation, I popped open the trunk and carried my brand-new cooler full of beer to your doorstep, as if it was the normal part of a process when ringing a doorbell. You had no doorbell, but I carried on with the necessity of the cooler as a part of knocking.

You took your time answering the door. It helped when I raised the decibels of my knuckles on wood the second time, the first knock muffled in a timidity of timber. The door opened inward, leaving you partially behind it, and the late glare of the sun behind me gave you an eerie-shaped aura around the silhouette I saw standing there. My eyes slowly adjusted to the darkness of your house, and your features began to appear like a fresh picture from an old Polaroid camera. You were nice!

Your long brown hair enveloped around a face that seemed a bit too long at the jaw, but your brown speckled eyes with the long lashes deflected my attention from that. You were slightly taller than me, but not overbearing, and our eyes did meet in parallel fashion. With a quick exchange of hellos and sweet smiles, you invited me in. With only a small hesitation, I entered your world with a clumsy but sparkling cooler being dragged behind me. I was not surprised to see Max sitting at your kitchen table even though he gave no mention of him being there that night. He was with Susan, who ironically was your friend and whom you had "fixed" him up with. It was actually a relief for me to see Max there because until I made my cooler significantly lighter, my conversation would be strained and limited. Max could talk enough for both of us, and as I soon found out, so could Susan.

Our debut went well. You showed no signs of the inhibitions that I later discovered you harbored. I began with all the basic signs of my own shyness, which after the sixth or seventh beer began to trail off to wherever shyness goes when you shower it with alcohol. It was before I reached that point that I studied you carefully, doing my best not to make it obvious. Desire, desperation, depression are all without true foresight. I saw in you what I wanted to see, perhaps more and certainly nothing less. The subconscious feed of a person's needs can literally affect the objective senses. The contents of my cooler would eventually take over my subconscious mind's job, for soon the whole evening would be placed in surreal surroundings.

As if to confirm this, not an hour into my visit, as I was slowly losing my interest in Max's rambling, the most beautiful little girl I had ever laid eyes on came strutting from around the corner of the hallway that led to your bedroom. It was your daughter. A few sunrises this side of three years old, she was a pure spectacle of innocence; and when I looked back at you, for a brief moment, I saw the same innocence in you.

But it was not you I fell in love with that night. It was your daughter. Certainly not in the pedophilic sense of the word, but in true parental instinct. Maybe in the back of my subconscious mind, I was replacing my own daughter, heartfelt sincerity in a way to make up for lost experiences.

As I listened to the clear and precise words flowing from her lips as articulate as a college graduate, I was stunned and in complete awe. And it soon became apparent who controlled your household. Just as easily understood was why you allowed it. She was the foundation of your ability to cope with your own loneliness. You weren't the first single mother to concentrate all her energies to her child. But your case was totally baffling to me. Here was the most intelligent three-year-old I had ever encountered, and yet not only was she still in diapers, but also still drinking from a baby bottle. A quick psychological assessment would have stated that you were afraid to let her grow up. The magic of our first evening together did not remotely suggest that you were restrained by laziness.

I do blame my overcompensation of my nervousness with an overabundance of alcohol to perhaps explain why you had such an initial effect on me. I could also blame my extreme need for female companionship to conquer my persistent and pestilent feeling of loneliness. Regardless, as the night went on, the more I drank, the more I became attracted to you. I did spend a significant amount of time playing with your daughter, not to impress you, but in an effort to follow the amazement she inspired in me. You had named her Farrah, and in my eyes, she would eventually put the original and famous one to shame. She was a welcome distraction for us while we searched for sources of comfortable conversation between us. She had no bedtime. She had no rules to follow that I could ascertain, and except for the occasional tantrum outbreak that matched the fury of an irate chimpanzee, the majority of the time, she was well behaved. When she finally dozed off on the corner of the couch next to you, the angelic peace of a sleeping child seemed to permeate the air around her.

Now my total attention was finally averted to you. I saw the flirtation in your eyes and was relieved to see the signs of your genuine interest.

Perhaps propelled by your own loneliness, certain chambers of your heart not able to be filled by your daughter alone, you beckoned for companionship. Why else would you agree to meet me, a total stranger? But with my own genuine intentions, could we be the same, looking for the same?

The conversation between the four of us was trivial and jovial, and the night passed quickly. It had been predetermined earlier by Max and Susan that I would sleep on Susan's couch that night, who had an apartment just around the block. I did not question this for I had no intentions of driving drunk, and if this was some source of old-fashioned proper courting where I must not spend the night with you, then I understood. Although my past normally waived such a slow process of dating maneuvers and prolonged stages of wooing, I could easily accept it. You did display a natural innocence of an inexperienced woman, and by that I only mean I didn't think that you owned a revolving door to which many men might have entered and exited.

It was four in the morning before I left you, as I haphazardly followed Max and his cohort down a dark sidewalk to her apartment. I left with only vague notions of what I had given you for first impressions and could only hope I did okay. We did exchange sweet good-byes, but I had learned very little about you. Yet I could sense that there was great potential between us. Our hidden innuendos, both spoken and not, had reflected superficial attraction, more metaphysical than direct execution. I was thrilled when you agreed that I could come back at noon. The stigma of me staying overnight on our first encounter would then be long gone in thought and potential, and I could work on the second.

I lay on Susan's couch that night with only my eyelids at rest, using the inside of them as a movie screen, manifesting live dreams that intertwined with cameo pictures of you. In that display of visuals, I had already committed to chasing you, ready to do any court dance and full of hope to properly entertaining you with the dalliances required. But I was still plagued with terminal shyness, and you would eventually find out the extent of my drinking habits. That I could not avoid.

They would lower in frequency and volume when sufficient comfort levels were reached with you. Unfortunately, that never happened when later our differences compounded, interfering with the development of our relationship. I needed the mask of alcohol-induced thinking to cope with the disappointments. This had happened to us so gradually that my dependency on you was too far ingrained to even recognize it right away or to even admit. But these thoughts were not there that night on Susan's couch as the scenes of my live dreams played out and mixed in with a picture-perfect future with you. If I had been given an honest premonition of where our paths would take us, I probably would have ignored it anyway. I chose to envision the golden road.

I did manage to fall asleep for a while after being subjected to the recognizable noises from the bedroom down the hall. At least Max enjoyed himself that night. I left the apartment around ten that morning before my hostess woke up. After a considerable walk in various directions, I found a coffee shop and used several cups of caffeine-laced mud to bring me back to alert status. I was determined that day that I would know you and had a set plan of action. A simple one, but hopefully one to a means. I would empty out the remaining balance of my cooler and then seduce you.

When I knocked on your door at precisely noon, chuckling at the thought that my car still parked in your driveway was incriminating evidence that you had overnight company. I guess the principle had been there. You met me at the door as a vision of beauty. Any notice of your flaws was to come much later. I could hear your daughter gleefully playing in the background, somewhere in the direction of your hall. We shared shy hellos and settled into a day of getting to know each other.

The three of us spent the day outside, a picnic in your small backyard instead of a park. I did not miss my favorite lake and park that day, lost in this new world with you and your daughter in the center of it. I had left briefly to find a beer store, the supply in my cooler too low to satisfy a journey to my original agenda. Any remnants of my shyness toward you were quickly vanishing, and your intentional brushes of physical contact were sending me all the right messages. By late afternoon, my intentions were set in stone. You would have to drag me out screaming if you wanted me to leave that night.

That warm sunny afternoon in your backyard was focused on me drawing pictures of your past with timed questions, and you obliged with crisp and short clear sentences. When you reciprocated the questions, I remained vague to details of my own background, knowing that sharing my past with you would only be detrimental. I told you only that I had recently ended a relationship that had not worked out. Whether it was the beer you shared with me or a progressive sense of trust, you gradually opened up to me. You had ended an abusive marriage a year ago, both physical and mental that had lasted over three years. Finally, on the advice of your parents, you moved back with them for a while and then, once social service checks started flowing your way, were able to rent a house. Your parents furnished it for you and provided money for any shortcomings arriving with such a low budget to work with. You were able to survive on your own.

I had always been commended about my listening skills, and this might have helped as I watched the quiet, nervous woman of the previous night turn to me as a trusted friend like you had known me forever. You had rubber-stamped a potential future for us that afternoon, although neither one us could have predicted how long it would last. Later that night, after finding sustenance in a delivered pizza that I ordered, we rested on your couch holding hands. The sun had already set, and the amount of fresh air in your daughter's lungs had her fast asleep on the carpet floor. I looked at her with that pure innocence still seemingly rising from her and reached over to kiss you. You turned away.

Still holding your hand, I asked what was wrong. You told me that it was just that you hadn't been with anyone for a long time, and you were nervous. In my presumptuous ways of prided seductive skills, I told you that we could be nervous together. Moments later we were necking up a storm. When I asked if I could lie down with you, you agreed, but warned me that nothing was going to happen. I carried your daughter to her bed and tucked her in, and a golden rush of adoration and underlining devotion to her well-being filled all my capillaries with such a glow of gratification that I could feel tentacles of atonement moving. There was a sudden lift from the depression that I had not experienced in a long time, taking me several levels away from its farthest depths. This innocent little child was a beacon of good fortune, and this small bundle of joy was wrapping circles around my own sense of ambition. I had fallen in love with this child and would do anything for her. Now I had to work on the rest of the package to be sure that I wasn't entering another endless archway of futile and pointless infatuation.

I lay down beside you on a very comfortable mattress, with juices flowing, probably more from recent depravity than immediate excitement. But as I curled up with you, my mind saturated with past pleasantries of spooning I could not help confuse this sensation with emotion. You felt so good as we melded together. After you allowed me to fondle you for extended periods of time, your change of posture and your constant fidgets was enough for me to know to stop. I drifted off into a light sleep comforted by the fact that you were right beside me.

I woke up early the next morning feeling more refreshed than I had in weeks. When I opened my eyes, a little angel with sparkling eyes and golden brown hair was looking at me from my side of the bed. She had a smile that would have melted the coldest of hearts. I got up with her, leaving you to sleep, and—after a short search—was able to find a supply of diapers. That was not a fun chore, but I managed to keep my gag reflexes in check. I opened up your fridge and was dismayed to see the empty shelves. There was a carton of milk among some half-used condiments. I looked in the cupboards, and among a handful of assorted canned goods and a green-tinted half loaf of bread, I found a box of sugar-coated cereal.

I sat Farrah down at the table with a bowl of cereal and a glass of milk and watched her abruptly push the milk away and run down the hallway. She came back with her baby bottle, which definitely needed a good rinse. I washed it out as best as I could and, with an apologetic look in her direction, poured the milk from the glass into the bottle. She smiled at me when I handed it to her, and I knew then that our friendship had just been sealed. It did not stop me from thinking that the intelligence that shone from this beautiful, blooming creature did not match the late development in potty training and her refusal to drink from a glass. I couldn't consciously interfere yet, knowing you for only two days. It was not my place to intervene so quickly.

You woke up a few moments later. The combination of the morning sunlight coming through the kitchen window and my vision tainted with infatuation and novelty, your appeal to me was overwhelming. I was filled with anticipation of what our future might bring. My virtue of patience allowed me thoughts of great reward, and your friendly smile of that morning gave me every indication that we would soon consummate our newfound relationship. As good as any of my altruistic intentions might have been in my aim for you to find me worthy and in my ability to help you, there was always a one-track-mind approach that gives the male section of the population the somewhat appropriate but not necessarily completely true label that we were essentially all pigs.

I did think about sex a great deal of the time, and I did thrive on it as a way of settling everything from anxiety to loneliness to actual riddance of despair. But I also used it for an expression of love. The various degrees of love balanced the various degrees of satisfaction I got from it. So you were not quarry or another mark on a bedpost as you might have been thinking when I kept hinting to such needs. I did remain in focus, and only once that morning did I whisper that I wanted to make love to you. Your innocent grin said enough that I knew my patience and persistence would eventually prevail. It would not be that afternoon, however.

That Sunday was unexpectedly devoted to the meeting of your family. Your mother and father knocked on your door that morning unannounced, which I found out later they did as a habit. I certainly had no grounds for discontentment. Your parents were extraordinary, humorous, perceptive, and an inner graciousness rounded them out. I adored them right away. They were there that day to take you out for lunch, and once formal introductions were made, I was invited along as well. Before lunch was over, I had been accepted as part of your family. It was wondrous for my own self-esteem, and I certainly had room for help in that department. They were very impressed with the interactions of your daughter and me. Farrah and I had bonded already in such a manner that she would listen and obey me. They also liked the fact that I was fully employed, and they had listened intently as I explained my future plans to buy a house, and my tight budget in order to do so. But aside from all that, I felt a general respect relating to me as the person I truly was from the inner core instead of any surface impressions that might taint their views. We read each other as fellow travelers though life, with the same trials and tribulations as everyone else.

Much later that afternoon, I met your brother and sister who dropped in, and it soon became apparent that prior announcements to visits were unnecessary in your family. There were only three years separating the three of you, with you as the oldest and your brother the youngest. Your sister had blonde hair as opposed to your dark brown, and she was every bit as attractive as you. Your brother radiated with appeal as well, and that states well coming from someone that has a limited opinion of the male species. Because you were so close in age and you all liked to drink, that Sunday and all subsequent visits were parties. I became close to your siblings, and we became good friends. Obscurely, I found out I could communicate better with them than I was ever able to with you.

Before we were even officially in a relationship, I had become a member of your family. Our mutual sense of humor had filled the room many times with laughter. Laughter was a measly part of my existence, and I welcomed it. Through you, I soaked up the levity and the easygoing lifestyle of a close-knit family. And I genuinely felt a part of it. That Sunday night, I went home even though the amount of alcohol I drank that night in celebration of my new family was well above the law's agreement of capability. I had no way of knowing that it would be the last time I would sleep in my own house for more than five months.

You gave me a quick kiss at the door, saying good-bye to your brother and sister at the same time. With the exception of you, we all had to work the next day. The chime of your wall clock, which signaled that two o'clock in the morning had been reached, was our reality check that the start of a workday was fast approaching.

Monday's work was strenuous. It was one of those days when whatever could go wrong did go wrong. Nothing some overtime didn't fix, but I was extremely tired by the end of the day. But fatigue was part of my life, and I did not hesitate to call you when I got home and asked if I could see you. When you agreed, I asked if you had eaten supper yet; and when your answer was no, I later arrived at your door armed with a bucket of chicken and a significant amount of trimmings to go with it. Your daughter brushed past you and gave me a big hug in a whirlwind of excitement. I had felt the bond, but was still surprised by this sudden show of affection. I had to ask you for a hug, and in obligatory fashion, you gave me a kiss.

After gorging ourselves with grease-covered food, we sat on your couch and played a card game with your daughter; and then well after sunset, I made my second trip to Farrah's bedroom. I read her a story and watched her drift off to sleep like some scene in a sappy sitcom. You and I drank wine that I had brought and watched television. I could not remember the last time I had watched television, and my eyes drooped quickly. Summer was for outdoors, but the comfort I received from my new surroundings, my new surrogate family, diffused any restlessness I felt from being indoors on a warm summer evening. I held your hand and could feel the physical vibrations between us and felt the flow of anticipation associated with what might follow.

It did not happen that night, and I settled sleeping with you in our curled-up positions. I had to rush off to work in the morning and had to surpass some speed records to make it there on time, underestimating the volume of morning traffic and the time it would take to get back to my own town. Tardiness was not part of my vocabulary when it came to work, and I soon adjusted to how much earlier I had to get up. I stayed overnight again Tuesday night after asking you. By Wednesday, I was no longer asking you, and this led to my permanent residence at your place.

When Friday night rolled around, your house had become a party house once again. Unknown to me was that your sister had a boyfriend, and there was a careless part of me that felt a bit of envy. I was attracted to her, but had sense and enough intelligence to never act on it. Even in passing thought, any emotional levels would grow no further than that of some idolized actress or even less to that of a centerfold. In this way, my growing affection toward you was completely localized, and I was driven in only one direction. This also allowed me to respect your sister's boyfriend even though I found him arrogant and boisterous.

They had arrived along with your brother and a supply of beer that would leave them in no danger of running out. Again, I fit right in and felt such a great connection to your siblings that I felt the bond of friendship that most times does not have to be vocalized. They did not leave until four in the morning, a festival of comedy and laughter between us mixed between levels of personal discussion that only pure trust could allow such personal details. I even found myself participating with a few verbal fragments of my past, an occurrence that usually took much prodding. The comfort I felt was not only mixed with the nostalgic memories of other relations, but it was medicinal in suppressing the depressive moods I still suffered with daily. Between your family, your daughter, and you, my overwhelming need for some sort of stability, my incessant search for it, was found right in your living room.

When we crawled into your bed at five that morning, to assume our spooning position, I had other plans in mind. My attraction had reached plateaus matching the actual physical needs and had wiped out patience. I cannot say that I was head over heels in love with you, but I was destined to follow my desire for you in loyal fashion and in a constant direction. I was a failure at being alone, next to disastrous actually. You were a chance for me to relive a family lifestyle, someone to truly care for, someone to share my life with instead of this maddening search in my cruel existence of bars and parties and strays. God, I had gone so far as to join a dating service in this search, which has its own cruel overtones.

But most of all, although she was not my own, I had a beautiful daughter to love and to nurture as well. My previous perditions of past relationships could finally be put behind me, filed away as life's learning experiences instead of the current suppressing weights attached to my heart. You had no awareness of how much I was about to relent from any sense of prudence of self-defense mechanisms and allow myself to again fall into the trap of complete reliance on a woman. You had no idea or even a slight inclination that I was dropping my shield and letting you into the vulnerability levels of my soul that allowed you the power to destroy me.

Maybe in your eyes, all I wanted was sex. That I did want, but with slightly higher degrees of meaning than I could get from the scantily clad girl standing on the street corner wondering if my money was good. I had respected your reluctance so far, but it was now time to recognize some of my needs, our needs.

When I began to fondle you through your thin negligee, you did not balk; but as I pushed toward the more sensitive areas and the caressing moves of foreplay, you tensed up and froze. Only then did I finally realize that I had overlooked how far your husband's abuse might have gone. It ran much deeper than I was able to comprehend. In soft whispers and that patience I kept commending myself for, I said that your husband must have really hurt you. You nodded your head, but said nothing else. I didn't want to think about how far this abuse had gone. Instead, with all the sincerity of a hopeless romantic that always seemed to drive my heart and soul, I blurted out but only in audible whispers that I had fallen in love with you and would never hurt you. I had said it honestly because it now registered to me that there were indeed different degrees of love, but at that point of my life, those deeper levels of past loves were tainted with sadness. My compulsion for my endless search for true love was confused in definition as a tool for survival. In an abstract way, I needed to love, not necessarily to be loved. As it turned out later, the shallowness of your thinking processes would never have allowed you to grasp how I felt anyway.

It didn't matter that night, nor did it matter for the rest of our brief time together. You were not capable of deep emotion as I gradually found out, but you were not heartless either. There were many other gratifications from sex aside from some soulful connection, least of all, pleasure. I knew that, but my obsessive strive for cosmic understanding limited my capability to fool myself into using the act as fun and relief only. I couldn't admit that my logical approaches to my past actions were of only simple diversion and frolic. But I do know that my persistence with you that night had more to do with empathy and desire to show you happiness and gratification than it had to do with my own.

With your lack of ability to truly express yourself, I cannot ever be sure why you gave in to me. The awkwardness of our first encounter did turn out to be a door to your eventual enjoyment. That first night did produce records of foreplay, but when I finally realized that you were never going to relax enough, I became forceful.

There is always a unique excitement and different sensation when with a new partner, and you were no exception. I prolonged the inevitable as long as my willpower could take me, but when the moment came where the desire could no longer be controlled, I was shivering in ecstasy. It was only after that I realized that you were crying. Afraid of what emotional damage I might have caused you, it had been an enormous relief when you told me that you always cried when having sex. I pondered over this, wondering whether it was from the memory of previous abuse or some form of joyful tears. When you mixed your tears with small outbursts of tittering, I was assured that it was a mixed reaction to your sensuality and sensations.

The ice was broken, and we made love several times that weekend, each time arousing more passion than the last. Each time you cried, but now I could hear the laughter mixed in, no longer generating a fear in me of what I might have done to you, but recognizing the signs of your pleasure peaks. If we were not to be destined to be compatible in any other way, we certainly were in bed. This was not an unusual source of complacency for me, for sex had long been an escape route. More often than not, it had become the center force of my past relationships. I did not confuse it with true love, but did mistake it for a pure form of contentment and adoration. However, it was never comparable to the love of heart and soul that I knew churned inside me, searching for that real connection.

This only mattered with my time with you in thought and reflection. What mattered was my survival, my sanity, my stability. If it took sex to do that, the trivial rewards outweighed the risks. And so began our relationship based on our physical connection, hoping the authentic emotional connection would come later.

But as my luck would have it, my search for a sound and comforting lifestyle was not to be found in your household. Ironically, in the entire five months that we were together, not once did I bring you to my place. I cannot truly say why, but I can assume that part of me wanted my memories to remain unscathed, and your presence between my walls would shake the sanctity. You never asked to go. I never volunteered. The bulk of my personal belongings and my clothes found their way to your bedroom and were stored in a dresser I bought at a yard sale next door to you.

The first month with you was somewhat blissful, as the novelty between us blossomed, and I had great expectations after each hard day's work. It soon became apparent that you didn't cook, so my trips to the grocery store consisted of many loaves of bread and the stuff of microwaves. I was certainly familiar with TV dinners, and although I could cook, it wasn't high on my agenda of things to do after a long day at work. The weekends were always spent with your brother and your sister and her boyfriend, so any hopes of quiet weekends or a break from inebriation was out of the question. A lifetime habit of my own of consistent partying had left me with no sense of deterrence. I enjoyed the feeling, but I was also at a point in my life where I was tiring of such a lifestyle. The thrill was getting old, and I wanted something else, something more. I wanted to finally find the direction that evolves maturity levels that always seemed to elude me. I did try to talk to you about it, but the blindness of my original infatuation with you had overlooked the fact that you did not have much depth. I do not attempt to insult you with this statement. Because of your need and preference for the simple things and your uncomplicated way of thinking, you were actually probably better off than I was. You needed less to be happy and would never understand my inner search for answers, my infinite drive for something better.

For me, it was the alcohol that streamlined my needs and kept things in perspective. And in my jumbled mess of a troubled mind, you were both good and bad for me. I recognized early in our relationship that we were opposites, but my love for your daughter, your convenient companionship at least gave me equilibrium to a brain without an off switch. I was trapped in your embraces, no matter how shallow.

That was why I soon stopped voicing what was bothering me and let you lead our course to wherever we were going. It was a bad decision on my part and why it was that the parties with your brother and sister were no longer limited to Friday nights. First, it stretched into Thursday nights from Friday, then Wednesday nights, and then the long summer nights soon became grounds for it to become a daily occurrence. The amount of people involved also grew. First, it was your brother's menagerie of strange friends, soon followed by your sister's representation of friends. It was not uncommon for me to come home from a twelve-hour workday to find twenty people in your backyard and still have stragglers at two in the morning. I was averaging three hours of sleep and going to work every day with a hangover. Regression into a teenage lifestyle wasn't exactly what I had signed up for. I had done that too many times in the past. Regression was something you did between relationships, not in the middle of one.

We still made love every night, but now more as a habit, and as a tranquilizer for me. Any magic we had originally felt was now a routine thrill, a customary way of saying good night. But in my polluted brain, it rounded out each day to a pleasant ending and the grounds to allow alcohol to once again rule my life.

After several months and the arrival of the colder days of fall, the parties moved indoors. I had no time for myself, no time for your daughter. She still ran around in diapers and a baby bottle in her hand. With so many people constantly in the house in the midst of a steadfast party atmosphere, I had no time to do the training that I knew she needed and thought would be so easy. By late fall, I was tiring quickly with the relentless lack of privacy, but I did not want to say anything, and it never crossed my mind to escape. Regardless of my need to step away from that lifestyle enshrouding me again, I had let it entrap me, and it had claws. My addiction to alcohol cried out as loud as ever for its taste and its effects, and there was no escaping it. Your way of sexually appeasing me every night could only be defined as more fuel to my addictions.

I kept reaching through the fog of fermented thought, however, trying to pull answers from my inner core, from my eternal soul that was much wiser than my distorted brain. With the help of some deep contemplation, a solution to a temporary escape flashed before me. I had two weeks of vacation accumulated, which I normally did not take and usually accepted a cash payout at the end of the year in lieu of time off. Winter was fast approaching. November had already been flipped over on the calendar attached to your fridge door. Before I could find reasons to change my mind, before I even discussed it with you, I booked the last two weeks of November for vacation. I was going to Florida.

You and your daughter were coming with me. You just didn't know it yet. A few days before the enchanting chore of packing a suitcase, I sprung on you the news of my plans for a Southern getaway. Your first response was that you couldn't go, but provided no valid reasons. You did tell me that you had never been anywhere before past a fifty-mile radius away from your home and family. The gloom of November had already begun to press against me, squeezing buried levels of depression back to the surface. When you remained adamant about not going with me, I thought I could tempt you by describing the Sunshine State. I explained the allure of the swaying palm trees, the white sandy beaches, the everglades, the keys, the mysteries of the blue waters of the Gulf of Mexico, and most of all, the fantasy escape of Disney World. I placed your daughter in the middle of things and asked her if she would like to see Mickey Mouse. This was an unfair tactic, but I was desperate for you to understand that I was not exaggerating about the beauty of Florida and how it would be good for us to go.

The more I described it to you in detail, the more I stirred up the pleasant memories of my times there. There had been one time when I had traveled there by myself, an adventure permanently sealed in a category of memory as extraordinary experiences, some forever to remain unspoken. There was also the memory of my first trip there, but that was a world ago, also never to be really shared with anyone but one, and she was lost to me forever.

The more I talked to you about the trip, the more important it became. It now represented the salvation of our relationship and an escape from what now had become nothing but an infinite party. I could not explain to you my gradual unhappiness with our existence, this shallow way of life that I had already spent too many years with. It was too easy to once again be swallowed with the ease of such a lifestyle. The thoughtless patterns could not be enough for me, but I had no way of demonstrating that the pit we had fallen into had ladders, and if we took one rung at a time, there were encouraging ways for us to bring together the closeness that a man and a woman should truly feel. I was beginning to feel alone, and yet still with you. This vacation to Florida became the focal point for me to grow with you. I could only hope that you had at least one iota of sensitivity to my needs, to our needs.

It was only with your parents' help that I was finally able to convince you to go. Because of the charming personality and the warm character of your mother, I was able to express my good intentions to her and was even able to go as far as sharing my worries of our current mundane and stagnant outcome of our current relationship. I could sense that she already knew that I had nothing but the best intentions for you. But it was also worrisome that she had her own passive attitude toward life. Regardless, what mother wouldn't want what was best for her daughter; and with that leverage, I made a solid case. I'll never know what your mother had said to you, but the next day, I was buying luggage for you and your daughter on the news that you had decided to come with me.

The Florida trip was wonderful and had lived up to all expectations. Although you showed the same passivity that you usually did, expressing little astonishment to the scenery of your new surroundings, I knew you well enough to know that you were enjoying it. I usually drove straight through, averaging a twenty-hour drive, but you were so uncomfortable in your first car ride surpassing sixty minutes that I stopped overnight. I did run into difficulty with your daughter. She was great at first, but either from boredom or her desire for more attention from her roost in the backseat, she had begun a series of temper tantrums. It got so distracting at times that I had to pull over, and it had been tempting to give her a good old-fashioned spanking. One look from you was enough for me to know this was not an option. So that first night in a motel on the fringes of the Georgia border, I talked to her instead.

There was an adult mind in that three-year-old body, and reasoning with her in levels well beyond her years was all it took to reach her. The rest of the trip was extraordinarily peaceful as she agreed with me that meeting Mickey Mouse was indeed reason to behave. I watched from my rearview mirror and saw the sparkling intelligent eyes of Farrah looking back at me in mutual understanding. I had thought that if I could only reach that point with you, life would be perfect. I had formed a bond with your daughter that I was afraid would be much more difficult to find with you. We did grow closer than we had ever been during our two-week trip, and there were long glimmers of hope that you were of appropriate depth to finally open up and show me signs that we could share dreams and ambitions. I had spent much of my past hidden inside a shell, and I knew that given the right opportunity, I could watch you crawl out of yours.

Our two weeks together alone provided us with the tools and experiences for a new beginning. Maybe it was the influence of my own fantasies that allowed me to see the signs of a great future with you under the blankets of normalcy. Maybe it was the opportunity of privacy that I felt us unite as a couple. Regardless of the reason, you gave me hope. My connection with your daughter reached proportions of phenomenon. Our first night in Florida, tucked way as a family in an efficiency apartment on the shores of the Atlantic Ocean, I toilet trained her. Not with the promise of reward or even sitting her on the porcelain bowl. We agreed on it verbally. Because I was so relaxed from the ocean breezes, the tranquility of paradisiacal surroundings, and the escape of daily pressures, the quickness of the process did not shock me. We had a discussion about why she wouldn't go to the toilet and, in her mature way, stated that she wasn't sure. I went on to ask her why she would want to carry a mess around with her. She did not have an answer for that either. When I asked her if she would go to the bathroom for me from now on, she said okay. The next day, the diapers disappeared. That was the complicated way your daughter was toilet trained, and I still look back at it in bewilderment.

The baby bottle was another story. Two days before we planned our trip to Disney World, she threw another of her tantrums. She had a habit of throwing her bottle during the peak of her fits. After her third fling that narrowly missed my head, I threatened to throw it in the garbage and never give it back to her if she threw it again. She tested my will, tossed it again, and lost when I caught a wicked curveball. She cried herself to sleep that night, but got up the next morning perfectly content to drink the milk I gave her in a glass. Later, I went to a souvenir store and found a sipping cup with a picture of a dolphin on the side of it, and the baby bottle was history.

You were upset with me but didn't voice it. Your day of the silent treatment said it all. I do not think majority of your reluctance to let her grow up was a ploy in keeping her a baby. It certainly played a part, but like the other aspects of your child's life, you let her have control. But it had finally become too difficult for me to sit idly by and watch you stunt her growth. Twelve hundred miles away from your home, I had control. Back at your house, the scenario would never have played out the same, and who knows how long it would have taken for her to give up the baby bottle. Of course, with the growing accuracy of her aim, I should have held out long enough to give her a shot at the major leagues. You only sulked for one day, and I was glad to see that it hadn't ruined the greatness of our vacation.

Disney World relieved any remnants of animosity that either you or Farrah had against my training techniques. It truly was the Magic Kingdom for us that day. My heart warmed like a hearth as I watched the excitement from you both, your eyes the size of silver dollars soaking in the intricacies of Disney's designs and details. When we went through the "It's a Small World" ride, your camera clicked nonstop. If we shared nothing else between us that reminds you of magical, we did share some that day. All of life's troubles vanished, and although it was only a temporary distraction, it was ours to share. I still have the picture of the two of you kneeling beside Mickey, flashing those innocent smiles.

We spent the second week on the Gulf of Mexico, each afternoon spent building sand castles, flying kites, watching extraordinary sunsets from the deck of our cottage. During that week, I had the family that I was searching for. You were the farthest thing from my search for a soul mate, but now out of your party house environment, my love grew and would suffice over any cosmic connection. I could live without some profound inner pounding that I had been lucky enough to think I had found in the past. The emotion of love would be enough. But there was something that always stopped me short from saying that I loved you after that first time.

It could have been the memory of love from my past. It could have been fear of being hurt again. It could have been that you never said it. I needed you just the same. I was finally ready to settle for your companionship and shared caring. I felt that I could find a way to overlook that the overtones of our non-proclaimed love was not of great profundity. To have you by my side would suffice for the stability and the strive for solidity and prosperity. I saw so much potential for us in those two weeks that the world had become ours alone. But like everything else in my life, reality had a way of crashing through.

I could tell toward the end of the second week that you were getting homesick. You were slowly withdrawing, our fun and frivolous conversations on the beach fading. I drank on our vacation, but not half as close to the volume I would have at home. The salty gulf air seemed to supply me with great success at moderation. I did not feel the need or the constant craving. Even when you began to withdraw from me, I did not reach for the crutch of alcohol. I did not come to Florida to get wasted.

One night as we sat and watched another spectacular sunset, I did tell you how much you meant to me, how much I appreciated that you were with me. I could feel the slide back into yourself stopping for a moment, and you gave me one of those innocent smiles and reached over and kissed me. So did Farrah.

I headed back a day early, not wanting to push your bout with homesickness out of the reach of me. I had every reason to think your time away from home had reached its limitations. It was difficult to drag me away from the beach and the warm weather, but I was ready to make sacrifices for you. We drove back in a mixture of bad weather, everything from fog to sleet to snow. You had never learned how to drive, another thing I was completely willing to overlook. But an hour's relief from the wheel would have been nice. I drove straight through, sometimes down to a crawl when visibility became next to nil. We encountered numerous accidents and very slippery roads, but I plowed on. I should have stopped somewhere and waited it out, but both you and your daughter voiced how anxious you were to get home. The hopes of a new beginning with you weighed heavily on my mind, and I did not wish to endanger these new vibrations of optimism I felt. Stuck in a motel room where none of us wanted to be would only harm our path to such. It was better to push forward, fueled with the confidence that I had found my desired family.

We pulled into your driveway at midnight, thirty hours after we had left the solace of the warm gulf waters, to step out into a foot of snow. I carried Farrah into the house, took just enough time to unpack the car before I plopped into bed and was asleep before you even made it there. The next morning, I drove to see if my own place hadn't burned down;

and by the time I got back to yours, your whole family was reunited in your living room. Your parents had brought lunch; your brother and sister and her boyfriend brought booze. Only one day back and my quiet family life was already shattered. I wanted to turn us around and head back to Florida.

Your parents left late in the afternoon, but I did not expect your siblings to do the same. They did not disappoint me. With only one day left before I had to return to work, I had wanted to laze around the house with you. When friends of your brother and sister arrived that night, all hopes of that disappeared. It was two in the morning again before we were alone. Our hopes of a new beginning were fading quickly.

The next day after I came back from work, I was extremely tired, finding it difficult fitting back into routine labor. The house was again filled with partiers. I was obligated to join in, and within days, I was back into hangover mornings, and Florida was nothing but a distant memory. Two weekends before Christmas, it all fell apart, compliments of your sister's boyfriend.

It was on a Saturday night, and the partying in your house carried on as usual. There was not a full house that night, just your brother, your sister, and her boyfriend. Her boyfriend was always boisterous and would only get louder the more he drank. I learned to ignore it, for none of his callous remarks were ever directed at me. But that night, he was extremely loud, and I was overly sensitive. Around midnight, they decided that catching last call would be a great idea, much to my relief. You and I stayed home, and we said good-bye to them at the door. I was assuming they weren't coming back. My mood was quite forlorn, and why I thought it was an appropriate time to confront you about our lack of privacy was beyond me. It did not go well. Instead of understanding my concerns and listening to me, you took offense and started shouting at me that it was your family, your friends, and they would come and go anytime they pleased. I was not expecting your reaction.

We had argued before, but mostly about trivial things. Always wanting to avoid confrontation with you, I would sidestep my pride, my hidden desire to control, and would back away from disagreements. The fact that it was your place had some influence in that. But that night I boiled over. All my frustrations I had kept trapped inside bubbled to the surface. With the sudden eruption of a dormant volcano, I attacked you verbally with such insulting and tormenting ways that neither one of us knew I was capable of.

You were cowering as I shouted at the top of my lungs. I accused you of being ungrateful and self-centered. Every piece of trivial annoyance of your past actions grew importance and rose to priority levels. In a verbal tantrum equal to insanity, I hit you with every insult imaginable. I knew I cursed you, but the mainstream of my venom was a vicious attack on everything I thought was wrong with you. Like a pent-up geyser, all my hopes and dreams with you morphed into disappointments and discontent, and to withhold them inside any longer would mean fatal ruptures.

 I had been upset in the past, but nothing could rival that night. Nor will there ever be in the future. Had I drank too much to add to the source of ignition? I had always been a pleasant drunk, usually quite melancholy unless confronted. Aggression usually came from defenses. Your constant nonchalant attitude toward me had finally made you a target. I cannot remember word for word or even the phrases you used to set me off. When one goes back to retrace an argument, we seldom do remember what was said. I only know that when I was done yelling at you, it was not a sense of relief I felt. It was emptiness, sadness, regret. When I watched you start to cry, my temper dropped at free-fall pace. I was not out to hurt you. I only wanted to make you understand. You shut down completely, your defense mechanisms drawing you deep within your shell.

 I began to apologize profusely, but you would have no part of it, incapable of recognizing my sincerity. After a long futile attempt of begging for your forgiveness, I went into your bedroom and lay down. I thanked God I hadn't woken up your daughter in my tirade. I began to sob uncontrollably. I was feeling sorry for myself, and even after swearing off self-pity many times, it always found a way to seep through. I lay there, running a video on the dark screen on the inside my forehead, the place where the third eye used to be in ancient times. All my prayers to guardian angels had not stopped my spirit from breaking, had not stopped me from bawling my eyes out in a stranger's bed. I wanted you to come in and soothe me, to make it right. I wanted you for once to come to me in a sense of mutual empathy and help me sort things out. I was doomed to think that you were never really ever there for me.

 Much later, the tears had stopped, and I had given up on you joining me and making amends. Staring up at the dark ceiling, my mind wrapped around despair and futility, trying desperately to fall asleep, I heard the front door slam shut. I heard voices from your living room and then the loud voice of your sister's boyfriend shouting out on top of everyone else. The three of them had come back from the bar to continue the party even further. I could hear them ask what was wrong, but wasn't able to hear what you had said to them. But the boyfriend's reply was unmistakable. He shouted out, "Where is the son of a bitch?"

 Those words brought me to my feet, anger mixing with an instant flow of adrenaline that did not represent flight. Any anger I had felt toward you was now focused on your sister's boyfriend. Not only from his threatening words, but also from the driving force inside me to the fact that none of this was his business.

I met him in the living room, and we quickly exchanged heated words. In his rampage that surpassed the one I had given you, he accused me of liking your sister. I was not sure where that came from. Of course, I was attracted to your sister, but always kept it hidden and would definitely have never acted on it. Maybe he sensed something, but more than likely was simply looking for a fight. Regardless, it had nothing to do with the situation at hand. I wondered how drunk he was, and then he pushed me backward without warning.

I drew the first punch, which scared me much later for I was the aggressor. Punches were exchanged, but it quickly turned into a wrestling match. I will never know if he would have taken me. He was considerably bigger and stronger than I was, so I do not know if my adrenaline would have held out. Your brother stepped in between us, and a mutual respect for him backed us away from each other. Not before the typical macho exchange of threats and curses. There was enough common sense between them to leave, knowing full well that your safety was not an issue.

I stayed on the couch that night, but we shared the bed the next night, a day separating the events to reach a calmer period. But what little communication we had before was now completely shut down. Your daughter sensed something was wrong and clung to you like glue. Three days went by, and you still weren't talking to me. I went to your parents in a desperate search for a solution and explained what had happened and, to the best of my ability, why it had happened. They already knew and had directed your brother and sister to stay away for a while.

I had always felt close to your parents, but was still amazed how casual our conversation was and how understanding they were to my predicament. They agreed with me when I told them all I wanted was to provide you with a meaningful family life and how much I loved Farrah. They had said they understood, and I had not realized before how much respect they actually held for me. Your mother had even gone so far as to say that she had talked to you about cooking me a meal once in a while. I had accepted that you didn't cook, but this fact now only added to my disappointments.

I left your parents' house that day feeling better about myself, uplifted by their trust in me. But your mother's final words said it all about my chances for their influence to make any difference. She reminded me that she was your mother, and because of that, there was an unconditional love. In no uncertain terms, her innuendos implied that you were probably not about to change and that she could not run interference to any worthy degree.

When you were still not talking to me after the fourth day, I couldn't take the heartache anymore and broke my own silence. It was a mistake for me to do so, for it then left you with a choice, a choice that you made no effort to even contemplate. I swallowed hard before I asked the question, and I swallowed harder when you gave me the answer.

My voice was choking when I asked you softly, barely audible to my own ears, if you wanted me to leave. There was no hesitation, not a single sign of misgivings. You nodded your head and stated yes at the same time. That familiar sensation of my heart dropping faster than gravity, caught in the basket of my stomach, sent my mind spiraling.

I did not want to go through the hurt and the pain of another breakup. Not this soon, as if later would make a difference. I asked you at least a dozen times if you were sure, absolutely sure, waiting for that one time when you might by chance realize that you might have given me the wrong answer. But it was very apparent that your mind had already chosen the answer before the question was even asked. In what might have been only desperation, suddenly afraid of being alone again for the second and last time, I told you that I loved you. The words were lost to you in an air of animosity that was still wrapped tightly around you. My desperation to hold on to you had wiped out my pride. Otherwise, I would have regretted using those three worn-out words. It was not the first time I had asked myself if I truly knew their meaning. Was I again caught in the social aspects of need?

Of course, there are different levels of love, but where did I fit in? From the love of a puppy to the love of life to the very core of universal heart and soul? You were somewhere in between there, but wasted on you as you had retreated deep into the protection of that thick shell. Deep within my own shell was where I should have been.

A week later, I was packing up my clothes and personal belongings into the backseat and trunk of my car, so thankful that I had not given up my own place although I hadn't lived there for the past five months. I had still made attempts to reason with you, asked for a second chance, and described what kind of prosperous future we could have together. It was to no avail. You were long gone, lost to me. For my own self-preservation, I did finally turn inward again, where it was easier to assess your faults. In defense mode, your appeal became officially tainted, and the true picture that I consistently avoided during my time with you pushed to the forefront. Even then, I still did not want to leave. But somewhere in the corner of my gut, my instincts for survival shoved through, and I finally realized I had to let you go, that there was no future with you. You would think that my packed car would have been enough to comprehend that. But I also knew that this sudden strike of inner strength to get me through our breakup was only a temporary measure to ward off another oncoming wave of depression.

Your mother was at the house the day I moved out, for the actual day of my packing had been no secret. I am not sure to whose moral support she was there for, but I was glad she was there. I checked your house one last time, under the guise that I didn't want to forget anything. What I was actually doing was visualizing our time together in a final physical presence of what had been my home for the past few months. I took a deep breath and prepared for my good-byes.

I hugged your mother first, and she asked me if I was going to be okay. I nodded and uttered that I had been through this before. When I went to give you one last kiss, you shrugged away, and I was left with nothing to say to you. I wished you good luck. And then I turned to your daughter, who was sitting at your kitchen table pretending to work on a puzzle, yet soaking in every action around her. I bent over and gave her a long hug, and she wrapped her arms around me in such a way that would have melted the most frozen hearted. Tears instantly rolled down my cheeks, and for Farrah's sake, I turned away from her before she could see me cry. I could sense a strange flow of understanding between us and felt faint from the knowledge of what this little girl had done for me, had made me feel. I would miss her for the rest of my life and would always wonder what she would become.

I said one last good-bye and left quickly before I lost all composure. A mile away from your house, the waterfalls let loose, and I could have filled buckets. By the time I pulled into my driveway, I was empty of tears, all my emotions drained with them. It was with this unusual vacancy that I intended to draw the strength to cope with the looming loneliness ahead of me. I slept on my couch that night with dream after dream of the events of my life. Some were meshed together, with confusing time lines, mixed-up settings. It reminded me of standing in front of my Maker while my karmic records scrolled in front of me in no particular order.

I woke up the next morning drenched in perspiration and sadness, yet with an astonishing feeling of hope and a lack of concern that it was only one week before Christmas Day. There was a numbness inside me alongside this hope that provided me with the strength to put you quickly into my past. So close to Christmas, I had to make fast work of desensitization.

I spent Christmas Day alone, assured of complete solitude with an unplugged phone and locked doors. The only thought that came through, the only regret that sent me to tears that day, was I had not left any presents for your daughter. Being alone that day did not bother me otherwise. All that previous practice in solitude was finally paying off. I did leave my self-imposed tomb on New Year's Eve and spent it with friends. It reminded me that I was never truly alone. But when I saw other couples at the party, it awakened that infinite yearning for the true love of a woman. There had to be someone out there for me, someone who could permanently bury my past and let me function freely.

Each forward step was bound to make me a better person. I hope I have learned something from you. I hope that in some small way, you have learned from me.

CHAPTER 18

Kathy:

Three strikes and you're out. I knew you were my last attempt at this dating game where preplanned questions were not a prerequisite. Three was enough to move onto a different game. To use baseball as an analogy was sign enough that so far, it was not working for me. Although I had myself convinced that it was just companionship I was looking for, it would be difficult to put my heart to rest. My most recent experience had raised many doubts, and my subconscious counterpart in my search kept whispering that the absence of deeper meaning leaves a hole. It had been fine with her, thrived on it actually. But to me this void of depth was pointless to the development of a solid relationship. It was becoming quite obvious that the carefree way was not the way to go.

So to delay walking away from an immediate third strike, I carried your name and number around with me for a couple of weeks before I finally called you. I was very nervous this time, apprehensive of what this final outcome would bring. You sounded sweet and sensible on the phone, but so did the last one. The primordial urge and proverbial loneliness prevailed over my worries.

We had set up a date for Friday night. You lived in the country in a part I wasn't very familiar with. Feeling foolish and giddy as a teenager, I was anxious and filled with anticipation, and I actually drove by your house the night before, perhaps looking for a glimpse of you rather than my excuse for finding exact direction for the following day. I still found it amazing that a first meeting would not take place in neutral territory. Was there not the potential of meeting someone with ill intentions? The screening process had a lot to be desired.

Whether it was the anxiety of the three-strikes-you're-out proposition I had committed to, my inhibitions, or the constant reference in my thinking process to my polluted and disgraceful background, I primed myself for my visit with you, with a fair amount of alcohol. Not inebriation, but relaxed and well within the boundaries of self-control. The laneway to your house stretched far into the farmland surrounding you. It was a shared driveway, your small bungalow on the right and a two-story wooden farmhouse with a wraparound veranda to the left. Both homes were owned by your parents, the front picture window of your parents' dwelling a huge porthole to the engagements and movements of their adult daughter. In essence, you were back to the nest, but with separate quarters to represent your independence.

I pulled behind your big blue Caprice, a huge sedan of the family kind. My exhaust leak announced my arrival. I felt the warm late-afternoon breeze of early summer though my open window, and the memories of living in the country flashed before me. I had recently moved back into a small country home, losing my place in town to the landlord's son. The crisp clear air, the quiet sanctuary, the lack of town noises had not registered during my forced move. But while parked in your driveway, it all came flooding back; and in such inappropriate timing, I found myself reminiscing about my life with my ex-wife. I shook my head and scattered these thoughts.

I shut off my engine, took a few deep breaths in an attempt to sedate my nerves naturally. After a timid knock on your door followed by my discovery of a doorbell, my attention went to the pair of kid's bicycles leaning against the porch. I was succumbing to the fact that my third decade of life meant that my odds of meeting single, child-free women were diminishing. Not that I had any problem with children, it was just the insight that package deals were the most populous in my age-group. It was fleeting thoughts like those that should have produced self-administered slaps, but at that point in my life, my mind run amok in all directions.

Your screen door creaked open, and you stood in the frame, scoping me as inconspicuously as possible. I did the same to you, and I exhaled in a silent sigh of relief. You didn't knock me over, but your contagious smile and the twinkles in your eyes won many points. You were physically proportioned, so the stigma of being with someone that was overweight would not arise. Social dirt from peers and the media spread of what is normal eats at the psyche whether you want it to or not. A part of me never cared what other people thought, but it would be fabrication to say that there is not outside influence to one's own internal judgments.

I could tell that you were as nervous as I was, so after quick introductions, I asked you if you were ready for dinner, our preplanned engagement from my initial phone call. You had me step in while you went for your purse, and I got my first view of your tiny but quaint home. Everything was in its place, a great sign for compatibility to my own need for organization.

Conversation was strained in the car, and my newest *Moody Blue* tape soothed the awkward atmosphere. I chose a restaurant in a town that I did not frequent often. With my background of a dedicated barfly and my trail of various relationships, I knew a lot of people. Whether they were friends or mere acquaintances, I had no desire to meet up with anyone and have to explain my new companion. Getting to know you first would be very appropriate.

Inside the restaurant, we had several drinks before even attempting to look at the menus, letting alcohol relax us, letting first impressions take its course without the uneasiness of portraying perfection. Through a bombardment of friendly questions and answers flowing easier with the coated effects of rum and Cokes, we had the bulk of the important parts of our past shared between us. You had been divorced for almost five years and were raising a six-year-old son and a nine-year-old daughter on your own. You moved back to your parents' farm and were renting the bungalow from them, a house that used to be your grandmother's. You collected money from social services and did housekeeping on the side without reporting the income. With your low rent, you were able to do well for yourself and your kids. You joined the dating service because you thought it was time for you to meet someone, and you hated the bar scene.

I shared my past with minute detail, avoiding the rocky parts as much as possible. I told you I was divorced and had a daughter that I didn't see. I told you about my plans of saving for a house and how I had just returned to living in an old country home after living in Hilbury for so long. I explained how I wanted to concentrate on saving one more year and then finally buy a home. I also shared some of my tumultuous teenage years and stopped there, leaving a huge gap chronologically. It seemed pointless to tell you about my checkered past with relationships, jumping from bed to bed. I was not proud of it, even though my peers seemed to be. They didn't have to live with the guilt and pain that comes from such a lifestyle.

The restaurant I chose was actually connected to a motel that catered mostly to travelers. With the tourist season only just beginning, the place was to ourselves except for one older couple on the opposite end of the restaurant, entranced in their own romance. There was always a pain in my heart when I saw other couples displaying their love for each other, further carving a bigger hole in my chest where once resided my own joy of such feelings. I looked at you with those thoughts, those memories. Your eyes met mine, the sparkles in them enhanced even further by the Tiffany-style lamp over our table. In the gleam of your brown irises, I could see the same longing that I felt. This was not the shallowness I had recently experienced and left plagued by my surmise of meaningless frolic and escapism. I have had my share of casual sex, but it all had various degrees of absurdity, which anyone with any kind of spiritual depth would recognize as totally useless. It did not take immodesty for me to know I was more than surface levels. There was a basic knowledge of the cosmos inside me, not quite understood fully, but definitely felt and experienced. But I could not share it. I could only try to explain it during weakened moments of trust and hope not to express representation of insanity instead.

All these thoughts were darting though my mind while I focused on the sincerity of your eyes. I was determined right then I was going to pursue you. You were my target to regain stability in my life, a partner to share my goals, someone to guide me and help oppress my inner turmoil. This was quite some expectant blind date, and hopefully I wasn't as myopic as the name of this first encounter. I could see just not peripherally that night. My only focus was the innocence and the past hurt you tried to conceal on your young face. We were of the same age, yet we both looked younger than described by a time table. Despite the toll that stress and tortured lives does to some, our signs of aging were slow to arrive.

I didn't exactly fall madly in love with you that night, but a sense of commitment had already formed. This fall head over heels in love at first sight had many repercussions for me before and laid doubt to the validity of it. I certainly knew what love felt like, or at least the intensity of some kind of emotion that drove me beyond the limits of self-protectionism. Something told me that night that I was finally going to be able to reach a point where I could balance my own needs and also balance my defense mechanisms with the needs of another. There was already too much corrosion of my empty shell that was once my heart. Yet also understood in that cosmic knowledge was that love was channeled through more than my heart and was only the core of its focal point. I could feel the start of a new beginning, a carefully planned process this time, calculated toward a direction of healing. You had no idea of how much I was expecting of you that night.

We ordered the salmon after a half-dozen stiff drinks. Talk was random after our mandatory background checks. The comfort levels between us increased, and there was soon a mutual understanding of each other's complexities. I had a growing sensation that I had known you all along, a coziness that whispered loudly that I would be able to share many things with you.

After our meal, I was at a loss on how to entertain you next. There was the obvious trip to a bar and dancing. Driving home drunk weighed heavily in the back of my mind, not that I didn't habitually still do it. I wanted to start off with you showing responsibility. To my surprise and relief, you suggested that we go back to your place. The sky had already been painted black when we emerged from the windowless restaurant. Time had whisked by, a good sign of our harmony. We chatted openly on the way home, the moments of awkward silences already gone.

Back at your kitchen table, with our chairs cornered at one end, we shared a bottle of wine, and then a second. Your small living room was off to the left, the open concept allowing full view of a comfortable couch that I was drawn to. It was where I would have preferred to have sat, slowly nudging closer to you in the ways of seduction. But you were the host and wisely directed my visit with you to the relative safety of the kitchen table. Your kids were staying overnight across the laneway at their grandparents, and our late return didn't allow a chance for me to meet them. You brought out a photo album at my request for pictures of your kids, and I was able to see how cute they were. One of the older pictures showed them at five and two and someone I didn't quite recognize at first. I looked at you inquisitively, and you nodded sheepishly. There beneath the plastic protector of the album page and sitting between your two kids were you, carrying an extra fifty pounds on your frame. You lowered your head and shamefully stated that you had been fat. I could only think of saying that you certainly looked good now, wondering the whole time what my reaction would have been if you had met me at the door with all that weight still in tow. This thought quickly dissipated as I looked into your eyes and saw those sparkles that entranced me.

After we drained a second bottle of wine, my attraction to you quashed any remnants of intimidation and inhibitions. I reached over the corner of the table using my elbows as a tripod to hold my head and kissed you long and passionately. Your lips were soft, and I could feel the erotic sparks of lost sensations that were stuck in long anticipation to those that matched the memories of past emotions. This was genuine sensuality, and you did not flinch but reciprocated with your own intensity. This was not rebound pleasantries to fill a void. I had spent too much time in fruitless searches to know the difference. Even with the possibility of confusing what I felt with simple desire, it was far from feeling that way. Did it really matter?

If moving on to another meant only a way of eliminating my emptiness caused by past relationships, then I would be doomed for failure the rest of my life. I could not dwell on that. You and I were individuals with separate suffusion, an outpouring of sensation and emotion to each other, not to our past memories. I let go of any doubt. It was you I wanted. We kissed forever that night, coming up only for air, to exchange incandescent glances and go back for more. My hormones raced furiously, and finally what I thought was the right moment, I whispered in your ear that I wanted to make love to you. Without missing a beat, you whispered, "Maybe, but you're not going to."

I found your statement so witty and amusing that I chuckled out loud. You were smiling mischievously, and I read "not that soon" displayed in your eyes. My respect for you came rolling in waves. You were going to be worth the wait.

I left a few moments later. The early morning hours had ticked away to very close to dawn. We shared another kiss at the door and made arrangements for me to see you again the following Saturday, sealing an unspoken pact that we were going to make a valiant effort at a growing and possibly rewarding relationship. You stood underneath the porch light while I pulled out of your driveway. The pale yellow light enveloped around you, and as you waved good-bye to me, an involuntary smile pulled at my cheeks. There had not been many smiles in my life lately, and it felt strange on my face.

As I traveled down the country road, layers of red and orange hues were already beginning to streak the eastern horizon. I rolled down the window and, in the fashion of a toddler's song, screamed out at the passing farmland and a stray cat that wandered along the ditch, "I have a girlfriend! I have a girlfriend!" I was asleep on my couch an hour later, dreaming those very words.

That Sunday I hibernated, still marinating in the night before and soaking in the fact that I had been given a genuine opportunity not to be alone anymore. It was the beginning of summer where I would usually be trying to kill my loneliness with booze and buddies, followed by a long Monday morning nursing a hangover and gut-turning acridity. Instead, I lay there thinking about you. I pondered over the comforting thoughts of a summer and a future without barhopping and picking up strays for miniscule thrills and temporary sexual release with strangers. Besides, the women seemed to be getting younger and younger in those meeting meat markets. It couldn't be that I was getting older and older.

A part of me was still decimating my own goals by denying myself the building blocks of my own responsibilities. I had to admit that even as much as I thought I could survive on my own, I was assigned to success only with the guidance I cherished from the commitment and the love of a good woman. You couldn't prove this from my past, as I managed to destroy my chances one by one, as I continued my search for God knows what. I hardly knew you, results of first impressions my only guide to my emotions. I was quickly falling back into my repetitive trap of relying on companionship for potential bliss and happiness.

I had an extra card in my hand this time in this weird poker game. Still plagued with extreme sentimentality and falling easily into the grasps of tender emotion, my past experiences had finally produced enough layers of callous hide around my heart that I had some protection against my expeditious feelings. It was a dangerous defense that could leave me looking shallow, but there were enough spear shafts broken off in various parts of my heart that one more piercing might annihilate it forever. By pulling down a cover on my endless enemy of a well full of empathy, I could defend myself from any more hurt. It seemed contradictory to my needs, but it placed me in a category that most men are anyway. But to make this a way of life would still prove more than difficult as I still sucked at being alone and got nothing from casual relationships. I still had to find balance in this new way of thinking, or rather feeling.

This is why, in spite of all my attempts to harden myself, I was already falling in love with you. Only this time, I had climbed up a few rungs on the ladder of self-preservation that would prevent you from completely devouring my heart like I had let others do in the past. So as difficult as it was, I did not call you through the week, leaving anticipation to our second date as my internal guide. But my week was filled with confusing thoughts, as I kept sliding back to the memories of the magic that I had felt at your kitchen table. I would slap these thoughts away and give my unchartered callousness a chance to intervene. It made for a strange cauldron of sufferance, an example of schizophrenia growing strange forms, like a lab experiment inside my brain.

The week lingered, but Saturday did finally come, and I was a bundle of nerves. My experiment had failed. I could only think of you. With five beers before noon running in my veins, I found myself turning into your driveway a second time. I could hear the case of beer rattling in my cooler, which sat in the trunk. You were sitting on your porch steps, puffing on a cigarette. It reminded me of how badly I wanted to quit that habit. We exchanged pleasant smiles, which represented that we both had spent the week in forethought of our second encounter.

In a flurry, much too quickly for me, was the introduction of your family. Your kids were first. They were adorable. Your son took an instant liking to me. Your daughter was more leery. It was easy to see how protective she was of you, and she had intelligence beyond her years. She was my daughter's age, and I could not help but suddenly wonder about her and what she was doing.

Two years before, I had bought Christmas presents to her, waiting patiently for her outside of her school while a winter wind cut though me and left me shivering. The animosity from her mother toward me never really dissipated, fueled consistently with her newfound husband's unsympathetic ways. There were many nights that I would spend concocting various plans of vengeance against him as he kept my daughter from me, but eventually decided to let karma take its course on him. What he was doing to me was evil, and he would have to answer to someone higher than me.

I looked at your daughter again and did see some of my own in her. I felt I could win her trust. Just as quickly as I was introduced to your children, you walked me across the driveway and introduced me to your parents. I was totally unprepared for that, but any uncertainties I had quickly vanished. Not only were they very friendly, there also seemed to be an instant acceptance of me. I wasn't sure what you had told them ahead of time, but you must have painted a pretty picture. I was good in heart, and I was normally morally inclined. I did have qualities. It was just that I carried a checkered and confusing past along with me, which I sometimes felt I carried outwardly like a huge neon sign as a warning to others. They were older than my parents or so, I thought. Without seeing my parents after countless years, my vision of them was probably distorted by my last memory of them recorded as their present looks. There were other parental figures in the past that I attached to emotionally, but in general, I looked for guidance only in the women I was with. But I took an instant liking to your parents and felt pulled in their direction as if they were a fountain of understanding.

As it turned out, we spent a good part of the evening with them outside around a campfire. The smell of burning apple wood, the comfortable lawn chairs, and the fact that your dad enjoyed a good cold beer sent me into waves of contentment. The hypnotic effects of the campfire's flames soothed me. Your parents had a way of asking questions in such a way that although some of them were personal, they didn't seem like prying. I got to know them very well that night, and as my relationship with you progressed, so did my connection to your parents.

Later that night on your living room couch, both of us tainted with the odor of burnt wood and copious amounts of stale beer fumes, we talked and we talked. Your kids had fought sleep well into midnight, curious about this new person invading their home. When I volunteered to read a bedtime story to your son, he readily agreed; and by making him laugh by purposely befuddling the words, my bond with him had already started. Your daughter was going to be more difficult, but she did say good night with tones a level higher than just politeness. When the kids finally fell asleep, we let chemistry take its course.

The same sensuous kisses I had felt at your kitchen table now in the sinking comfort of your couch sent chills through me and mixed a potion of warm desire. I stopped myself at first and then whispered the same words I had the weekend before. Only this time, there was a faint but distinct okay whispered back. You led me down the hall to the softest bed I could ever have imagined. It was like sinking into thick bundles of cotton, worthy of the thickest of white cumulus clouds. Combined with the smooth milky skin of your body, I was in ecstasy. We had undressed in the rays of a full moon, which filtered through your venetian blinds in slatted layers. It left you with zebralike patterns across your body. You took the aggressive stance and climbed on top of me.

All the recent one-night stands compounded together couldn't compare to your talents of that night. It was unspoken, but you were telling me that you hadn't made love in a long time. Neither had I in the true sense of the word. I let you and the moonlight envelop me, an exhilarating release of frustration and pent-up constraint. My whole body relaxed afterward while you curled up beside me. There was no need for conversation. We were both in rhythm with the sensations we just experienced and still felt. I lay there and thought about nothing. This was such an unusual occurrence for me that it almost scared me.

My brain almost never shut down, let alone find anything close to neutral. It was like having a stack of bricks lifted off me, and I soon found myself drifting off to sleep. I shook my head and quickly opened my eyes. I whispered to you that I should go. It wasn't so much for the benefit of your kids not to find me there in the morning, but more for holding the respect of your parents across the road. You simply said that it might be a good idea, but then added, at least this time.

I kissed you at the front door, still feeling the pulse of your body through the velvet robe you had slipped on. Lamely I asked you if we were an item now, and you replied that you would hope so. I left you that night with a skip in my heart and a skip in my step, with no conceivable idea that I had just embarked on a seven-year journey with you through life—a life of exponential success and joy.

We dated every day after that night, meeting your friends, meeting my friends, partying, and more importantly, making love. I formed a solid bond with your kids, your daughter slowly offering her love and trust. Your parents took me under their wings. I even began to help your father with projects around the farm. In my eyes, I had a family again, a family I no longer wanted to leave and return to my empty house.

There were also very practical financial reasons when I first confronted you with the idea of living together. Through my frugal ways and the savings bonds that were being deducted off every paycheck, I had gained a substantial amount for a down payment on a home. I still wanted to wait another year, allowing me another year of savings that would put me in a better price range of houses to choose from. Another year of waiting would be easy after all my previous years of living in dilapidated farmhouses and claustrophobic apartments. Winter would soon arrive again, and I did not want to live it alone.

So one night, as we lay intertwined in passion, after we were sure your kids were asleep, I mentioned to you the idea of living together. We had only been together two months, and it was probably too early to think about that. But I knew nothing about being conventional. You didn't say no, but I could tell by your tone that you were not too keen on the idea. You did not have to tell me the reasons. I had been around the block enough times to know your first priority was with your kids, and since you never talked about your ex-husband, I was assured there was still hidden pain that you dealt with. What you did share with me was that the main reason you were hesitating was you weren't sure what your parents would think. Your parents liked me, and although they were a bit too religious for me, I had grown very close to them. I explained to you that I didn't want to cope living a winter where I was, so I had two choices. Buy a house now or wait until next year and take you with me to a new abode and a life together. I almost crudely had said shack up with you.

We left the issue unresolved that night, but my persistence eventually paid off. The night before, I had told you I loved you. I had realized that for the first time, most of my past had not been dragged with me. It was time to leave the emotional safety net and take a chance again. I was truly ready for a fresh start, a new start, a new approach to a genuine growing relationship, with my baggage left at the front door. You had repeated those three words to me, and the words had honest overtones, not an obligatory echoing phrase needed to match my own declaration.

The next night, after another marathon fervor of intense sex that still matched the climatic value of our very first time, you lay beside me afterward and, in a soft chilling whisper, asked me if I still wanted to move in with you. A nod in the dark and a barely audible yes was followed by a glorious and peaceful nap in your arms. By the time we agreed to live together, I was seeing you every night anyway, rushing out of your house just before dawn each day. By moving in with you, I could share breakfast, not to mention a life.

By the next weekend, I had written a long letter to your parents, proclaiming my love for you and stating my sincere intentions in detail of my plans for a long future with you. I explained to them that I thought I would make a great father figure to their grandchildren and would treat them as my own. Every word was true. As jumbled and acrid as my past was, there was a mature and responsible individual that had developed and was looking for a way out of his obscure and troubled existence. Here was an opportunity to prove my worthiness.

I got an answer from your parents that Saturday afternoon when they approached us while we were playing with your kids in the sandbox in your backyard. It was such an unusual activity for a weekend-warrior partier. I was not totally shocked, but stunned just the same when your mother casually said in front of you and the kids that I was welcome in their family and added that it was nice of me to ask their permission, but they were in no real position to interfere with our decisions anyway. In the next breath, as slick and quick as one of my buddy's pickup lines, your mother asked me if I wanted to go to church with them on Sunday. I knew that you and your kids ritually went to the country church that was within walking distance of your house. I was not expecting to become part of that. But I wasn't about to say no after the social courteousness your parents had just offered me.

Two weeks later, I moved in with you, disregarding the longer period of time usually required for a notice to the landlord. He was quite understanding and luckily had already had someone else lined up to rent the place to. I borrowed a friend's pickup and moved my sparse belongings into your father's shed. There wasn't much. A washer and dryer, a yard-sale couch, a broken bed, an old television, an even older fridge, and a menagerie of cheap junk that sufficed for decor in my otherwise barren lodgings.

I will always remember the first morning we woke up together as an official couple. It was a combination of good feelings of what it was like to truly share a bed with a loving partner and the thrill of the sudden realization of the start of a new life. I had to get up earlier each morning now that my ride to work had increased in distance by twenty more minutes. So I missed your morning routine to get the kids off to school. You got up with me every morning and, in the fashionable way of married couples, sent me off to work with a coffee and a kiss. I felt so blessed to be given another chance at a meaningful life.

Although I had already stopped going to church with your family after my second visit, I did not need a communal building to continually thank God for another chance. My whole outlook on life had changed. Of course, I had always held on to dreams and goals, but they were always shrouded in dark clouds. I could see clearly now and poetically thought that the rain was gone.

When we form routines and are focused on regular plans and chores, time has a tendency to charge ahead with velocity. And with it, comfort. My security levels created by my new family existence gave me the long-searched ability to shut my mind off and enjoy the smaller things. I closed the doors to the seepage of my subconscious levels and the problems that stirred in there. I left those thoughts only to the dreams that filter into sleep, instead of dealing with reflection after reflection during my waking hours. By concentrating on the simplicities of day-to-day living, by finding touches of happiness in sharing your world, your world of friends and family, I was able to function at normal levels. I began to shy away from most of my old friends, further easing burdens of past experiences by disassociating from previous connections. You had many friends and relatives who had all graciously accepted me. By slowly pulling away from my old clan, I could escape my own demons, almost believing that symbolically they were some of the roots of my problems. New family, new friends, and new life were the positive route.

You had one set of friends in particular that we spent almost every weekend with. It was astonishing how close-knit the four of us became. Our camping trips together, our card games, concerts, parties, restaurants, extended family gatherings—the list went on. We shared almost everything with this couple. Our lives together were enhanced, but it was my solo time with you that was the most important.

I do not want to leisurely skip over the seven years we shared together, not once wanting to make light of how much you did for me. But it is not a mundane chronological listing of our pastimes that is important. You must hold on to some of the cherished memories we gathered together with each passing week, month, year. Maybe not as much as I do, but we did have some glorious times together.

With the comfort levels we shared came the ticking of that biological clock that speeds up time. We never discussed marriage, and although I thought of it many times, my past always seemed to throw shadows over the idea when propositioning entered my thoughts. Sometimes when we had a lot to drink, you would hint at it, but would never come out and actually say that it was what you wanted. It was as if we would rock our paradisiacal existence if we made that step. We let life do that for us.

It is very difficult to list the events of seven years, but without looking at our life in some order, it would be hard to understand where our path took us. So if it sounds like a dull tale of our history, forgive me because it was far more meaningful than that. There are files upon files of good memories and good times that thankfully overshadow the bad. We had our share of tragedy to deal with along the way, but we were able to lean on each other. There was a strong bond between us.

Our first year together went completely unblemished, a frolic dance through the fun parts of life and not a problem to be found. Although our love for each other was not of the fairy-tale variety, that of mad, passionate, blinding, ferocious heart-throbbing emotion, our wild compatibility in bed kept it close to comparison. When we partied, we never argued; and no matter how much I drank, my days of getting totally wasted seemed to be behind me. I wasn't running away from my past anymore. I finally had a focused future ahead of me. You were outgoing, and with you by my side, my own shyness seemed to dissipate as I fed from your own self-assurance. My third decade of life was becoming a turning point for actual success in ways I could only claim to imagine. The word *happiness* was allowed back into my vocabulary. After leaving a trail of wasted efforts and lessons in obscurities as my only legacy to my second decade on this planet, this new handle on life was nothing but a blessing.

I did develop internally during my past struggles down roads of destruction, but there was such a mixture of pain and confusion that it did little to develop a true sense of purpose. Now I finally fit in, and being labeled a misfit was a faded memory, remnants of murmured voices from some other life. I cannot emphasize enough how beneficial you were in helping me find a sense of direction that I could build on outwardly. Planning consists of more than thoughts and contemplations. I want to share every detail of every moment of every day again that I was with you. All of it held such great importance, especially that first year of bliss. Even the few friends I kept in contact with as I slowly switched to your network of friends and family had noticed the change in me.

There was always a cloud of depression hanging over me, almost tangible to the visual senses. It had lifted. Ben and his wife, the couple that you grew to like so much, had always been there for me and, even in the roughest of times, had put up with me. Their place on the lake was my second home many times during my bouts of wallowing in self-pity. On our second visit with them, they had told you they had never seen me so happy. Their comment enriched me even further, and I realized that life had become worth living.

Work became fun with my different frame of mind, not just a source of income. I looked forward to coming home to you every night. There was great reward in being a father to your kids, even if the title was preceded by *step*. Life had meaning, and my past sadness seeped through only in brief intervals. Our first Christmas together ripped me apart inside, with jagged memories tearing at the lining of my heart. Many Christmases alone had left the day meaningless to me. When I saw the joy on your kids faces as they unwrapped their presents that morning, I couldn't stop the tears from flowing. But they were not sad tears. They were tears of reflection, tears of recognizing some significance to the holiday season. I could finally rise above my hatred for Christmas.

For the first time, ascending out of my introverted past, I could recognize and enjoy the little details of daily life. Sure, I was attuned to nature, but the micro-picture of life itself had evaded me. It was like a sudden new insight that made my whole past existence meaningless. I knew this wasn't quite true, as my experiences had made me who I was, but this new life took sweeping precedence. All these changes in less than a year. I had spent longer periods drunk.

As we all know, life does not stop and freeze for anyone. Changes are inevitable, no matter how hard we try to prevent them. The fact that we never argued was a strange concept for me, but one we accepted as pure compatibility. It was probably me that forced the start of those inevitable changes. You were content with the way things were, and in essence, so was I. We did seem to have the perfect world. But as a new member of society, I began to feel the need to really prove myself. My wasted past ate at me, and I had only fooled myself into thinking that the material world was of little importance. Along with the maturity levels of my aging process and now stability came the recognition that no matter how much I had drilled into my head that society's ways were not for me, the truth was that it represented the center of our civilization. If I was to become an active member, I had no choice but to prove my worth. In spite of my distorted view from the use of mind-expanding drugs, my rebellious past toward society, and my hatred of its judgmental ways, I was now wrapped into demonstrating forms of material.

I was still renting after all these years, and now not even that as I was boarding at your house. You had to have understood how much that eventually bothered me. With another year of substantial savings gathered, it was time for me to buy a house, the ultimate measure of success in society's censorious eyes. When I first mentioned to you my intentions, you were not pleased. I reminded you that I had discussed it with you when I first moved in. I explained to you that it would be our house and that we could be happier in a bigger home. You told me that you didn't want to change the kid's schools, but we both knew it was you that did not want to change.

For a few weeks, I dropped the subject, not wanting to upset you. But summer was ending again, and although I liked the country, I hated country winters. Also compounding the urge to buy a house was the claustrophobia I knew was coming from being confined to the interior of your small home surrounded by snow and howling winds from the season of the dead. The long drive to work each day added to my grief. I had decided that the town I worked in made the most sense for me to live in. I was not fond of Hilbury and did not have a great list of good memories living in that town before. But it distanced me from past friends, the ones that I still wanted to break away from because of their influence on my past drinking habits. Leaving them in the past was another implementation to my new start, my new life.

So my search began for a house. I had looked at a dozen of them before putting in an offer on one in a subdivision not a mile from work. The price seemed right, and the fact that it had an inground pool only glorified it. The real estate agent I used was a friend of your parents, who was extremely helpful to me in the bargaining process. It wasn't as if I was a seasoned home buyer. I needed someone I could trust. You were by my side during my search, but your disinterest demonstrated your unwillingness for change. When I first put in my offer on the house, your name was discussed for the paperwork, but you declined to be a part of it. It was for this reason that your name was never on the deed.

The whole process happened so quickly that I had no time to let any shock sink in to the magnitude of what I had done. There had been a previous offer on the house, but since my offer had no conditions, my offer won out. With a third down on the asking price, my perseverance and determination to save was rewarded, and the bank agreed to finance me right away. The mortgage payments were much lower than anticipated, and within a week, most of the legalities were complete. I was to move in on November, the proud owner of a three-bedroom, two-bath, raised ranch with a paved driveway and a glorious backyard. It was an older home, but it was mine! My first grandiose step of long future strides to success.

You teased me about buying a house with a swimming pool when I couldn't swim. You became more humble when I said that your kids did; my subtle reminder that my actions included you. That didn't convince you to move in with me, however. We spent many nights discussing it, never raising our voices or temperament, never disrespecting each other. I did understand your unwillingness to have your kids change schools, especially when the school year had already started. I did not understand, though, why it wasn't important for us to remain together. I kept repeating how important you were to me and how much your kids had become a part of me. I begged you to change your mind, but to no avail.

One night when we had put our discussions aside and displayed our real passions in bed, with that same ferocity we had grown accustomed to, you lay there afterward beside me and came up with a compromise. With your arm wrapped tightly around my chest, your bare skin enhancing the emotions I was feeling, you promised me you would move in the following summer as soon as the kids were done with school. It was not the solution I wanted to hear, but it was one I slowly accepted. We would still be with each other in the meantime, just not under the same roof.

November came quickly. I brushed off the dust from my meager belongings stored in your father's shed and transported it to my new home. You helped me move that weekend and spent it with me. Your kids slept on sleeping blankets in the living room, quite content with this new experience. They had a blast roaming the extra space, which they did not have in your small bungalow. We christened the house after the kids fell asleep, almost completely breaking my old bed that I hadn't put together properly. We dozed off, still chuckling over the ruckus we had made.

The following Monday after work, I came home to my new dwelling. I began to reflect on the enormity of this new dimension to my life. You had left Sunday afternoon with a mixed bag of emotions, fed by my tears as I hugged you before you left. They were brief tears, stopped by the knowledge that you were still part of my life and that our separation was only temporary. Standing alone in my house the next day, I was overwhelmed by how far I had finally made it. There were times when I thought I was doomed for an entire life of drunkenness and despair. Here was solid proof that I could make something out of my life, that I did have a future.

We came up with a schedule that would help lessen the time we spent apart from each other. We alternated weekends at each other's house, and I would also visit you every Wednesday night. My nights alone felt strange at first, not because I was alone, but strange that there was no sufferance when I knew I had your next visit to look forward to. This gave me the incentive to leave the beer in the fridge and allowed me to stay away from past drinking habits. Life was good.

We spent our second Christmas together at your house, since the family gathering was at your parents' place. You had a brother and sister who had accepted me as part of the family, and you were so close-knit that I was almost envious. Your brother and his wife had three kids, and your sister and her husband had two. It made for a very noisy gathering, but festive. The only downside was that your sister's husband was sometimes abusive to your sister, and although it was no secret, no one was to talk about it. I wondered for a moment why there was so much abuse in the world.

The love of your family as a whole covered this fact in fog, and the warm atmosphere of your parents' home suppressed it entirely. I still thought of my own parents every Christmas, but only for brief moments. I still had a tendency to blame them for all my past troubles. I was an adult now, and I had to take responsibility for my own actions. I could no longer blame them, but bad memories are sometimes difficult to filter out.

With our appointed schedules and the usual way time flies by faster when you are older, summer arrived quickly. Three weeks after the kids were done with school for the year, you moved in with me. I was there to feel the tearful farewell between you and your parents and their request of me to take good care of you. Your furniture filled the barren corners, and instantly, the house had a homey atmosphere that had eluded the place before. Your kids were in their glory with their bigger bedrooms and a neighborhood full of kids to play with. They spent so much time in the pool that they looked like blue prunes at times. We were a true family once again. Life was good, indeed.

For another entire year, we were on top of the world. We were blessed with great friends, great family, great parties, and great success at pulling our happiness above and beyond any problems that had plagued our past before we met. Unlike many couples, we had found a way to leave our baggage behind. At the very least, it didn't interfere with our relationship. But as we grew more comfortable with each other, there were small bouts of bickering. It never seemed to amount to real arguments though. They were always resolved before bedtime, and just reward always followed. At first, I had difficulty recognizing the feeling, but I was truly happy, and you showed all the signs that you were too.

There are always unexpected turns and unforeseen events that can disrupt anyone's sense of contentment. Some are even tragic. Some are shocking. Over time, we found that we were no exception.

When we weren't visiting our camping friends, we were visiting with Ben and his wife. Even more often though, we had become more comfortable as homebodies, and our visits had dwindled. Instead of partying every weekend, we spent many by ourselves. We hadn't seen Ben and his wife for at least a month, and that made the phone call from Ben's sister all the more difficult to accept. In a shaky voice, she explained to me that Ben was gone. Ben was dead.

The story was nightmarish, and my heart went out to his wife, feeling her anxiety as if it happened to me. They had come home from a party at two in the morning, and Ben pulled his car into the garage, just as he had done a hundred times before. He shut the ignition off and almost immediately passed out, exhaustion and drinking a valid explanation. His wife left him there, thinking nothing of it as it wasn't the first time he had done this. He would eventually wake up and crawl to the house. Not this time. When she woke up the next morning, she went to check on him and got as far as opening the side door of the garage and froze. In front of her was their black Labrador, which they kept in there, lying motionless.

She went no farther, choking on the exhaust fumes that poured out the door. She ran back into the house and called emergency, but it was much too late. It was assumed that Ben had woken up just long enough to feel cold and had turned on the ignition for heat. He had to have fallen back asleep. Only this time, it was permanently. The carbon monoxide had overtaken him. Overtaken one of the most trusted friends I could ever have met, a friend who in his own bizarre way had kept me afloat through turbulent years. The news stunned me, and I grew numb with denial that I kept running through my thoughts. It was much later when I realized how lucky his wife had been. The garage was not attached to the house, or the fumes would have taken her as well. She went into shock, and it was awhile before she could even grasp what had happened. I could relate.

Ben was from Prince Edward Island, and that was where his family still lived. But to honor his influence and his life here, funeral services were planned here before they flew him back home. I attended, but I was in a state of dormancy trying to make sense of it all. I was so appreciative that you had come with me, helping me deal with friends and family, helping me say the right things. The whole situation was so surreal, and everything was in slow motion when I watched mutual friends pay their respects. Ben was always a practical joker, and I kept looking at his casket, expecting him at any moment to sit up from inside his coffin and shout out that he was just kidding. I kept waiting for him to at least say something inside my head, but it never came. I did not stick around for the customary gathering after the service. I wanted to be alone. I wanted to be alone with you.

We had an extremely quiet weekend after the funeral service. You kindly gave me the space to reflect on my friendship with him and to muse that like many other aspects of my life, I had taken him for granted. I would miss him terribly. Time passed, and life went on as it always does. But it seemed that once tragedy struck, there was a train of it to follow. Several months later, one of the few people at work who I considered a friend had a massive heart attack right at work. Al had taken me under his wing when I first started, and if not for him, I probably wouldn't have developed the skills I needed for the job.

It happened in the warehouse, right in front of me. As I came around the corner, he crashed the forklift into the wall at full throttle. He was hanging off to the side, his foot caught between the clutch and the brake. Both the foreman and I ran and got him down to the floor, and I could see that he was not breathing. Not two weeks before, we all had taken a first-aid course, and although I had little problem blowing into a plastic dummy, to suddenly put my lips on to another man was an entirely different situation.

Whether it was hidden instinct or panic, I did. I had no idea if I was doing it right, but the air did go in as I watched his chest move. My foreman synchronized the chest thrusts with me, and I can only assume the combined adrenaline between us gave us the ability to save him. The janitor who came upon us was sent to call emergency. After what was probably ten minutes later but seemed like hours, the paramedics arrived. Miraculously, he left breathing. I was shaking uncontrollably afterward, my nerves kicking in with a vengeance. I finished the day's work, but in a daze.

Just before I left for the hospital to visit him, my nerves calmed from the time frame that had passed and the alcohol, I got the call that told me Allan had passed away in the hospital. A dozen more beers later and your patience of your futile consolations wearing thin, you went to bed and left me to fall asleep on the couch. It was the first time since you had moved in with me that we had slept apart.

Another funeral for another friend left me with an unusual episode of reflection on my own mortality. To try and comfort his wife, Debbie, and to find the right things to say was devastating for me. We cried in each other's arms for a moment, and then I was shoved down the receiving line never to speak to her again.

But as we all know, the passage of time and the pressures and routines of daily life takes over our reflections, and any philosophical insights we gather at the loss of a loved one is pushed back to subconscious levels, and we carry on.

In the fourth year of our relationship, which was now labeled as common-law marriage, our comfort levels with each other had reached the stages of taking each other for granted. Our love for each other was still there, but there was a restless feeling. I wanted to confront you with it, explain how I felt so that we could act on it and turn it into something positive. Before I could find the right moment, the dreaded theory that death comes in threes was proven correct.

Paul, my longtime partner in crime of alcoholic binges and society balking antics, my friend since my pool hall days, had succumbed to lung cancer. In an obscure way, we related to each other. We were so similar with our alcohol addictions, our attitudes enveloped in self-pity and the risk-taking actions of someone who lacked the drive and ambitions to change themselves. I had not seen him in over a year. He was not susceptible to change, and I had outgrown him in the sense that I needed a better path. He did not care for you that much, for you represented the changes in me. He was stuck in the same lifestyle that you had so graciously pulled me from. To make matters worse between us, he hated kids. It was simple to see why we had pulled apart.

I had heard he was diagnosed with the disease and was told that he had made no effort to help himself. He had given up completely. When I got the call that he had been hospitalized, I wasn't expecting it, not having heard anything in some time. From the distance and out of sight, his cancer was only a rumor and did not bear authentic fact. Against my better judgment but under your advisement, I went to see him the day before he died, when Chad had called to tell me he was on his deathbed.

He had wilted away to nothing, a look of complete emaciation sunk into the folds of a hospital cot. His frail body of skin and bone and hollow face still haunts me. I think he knew I was there, for he had slowly nodded his head when I touched his hand and told him that I was with him. His eyes had been focused on something else, something on the ceiling that I couldn't see. He had started to gag and couldn't catch his breath. The nurse rushed past me to comfort him. I left without saying good-bye.

You didn't know Paul that well. You only remember him as the staggering drunk that dropped by the year before. When he started to torment your kids, you asked him to leave. I had to back you, not only on moral grounds, but also to make him understand that I could no longer accept him acting that way. One of my very first drinking partners had taken the path that I had almost followed, but I was lucky enough for the guidance not to accept it as destiny. The alcohol had fried Paul; his tolerance levels had become practically nonexistent. He had died a lonely man, and I could never stop thinking how easily it would have been for me to end up that way.

I went to his funeral alone. I told you it would be all right. You had just started a brand-new housekeeping job the week before, and we thought it best that you not jeopardize it by taking time off so soon. I made it halfway to the funeral home and turned my car around. I panicked. I did not want to face old friends and acquaintances. I did not want to face Paul's family. I became overwhelmed with the feeling that I had abandoned him somehow. By not going to the funeral, I could keep him alive. In my twisted thoughts, I was able to justify my reasoning. I drove back to the Hilbury town bar and celebrated his life by myself.

With my suit on, I looked like a businessman stopping for a liquid lunch. I sat on my favorite bar stool and silently toasted Paul with shot after shot of tequila and eventually toasted myself instead. I helped him drink his way to heaven. My job as a tour guide to his transition became a blur, and my vantage point from my bar stool soon lost track of him to see if he had made it to the pearly gates. That same bar stool was where you found me that night, talking to some pretty blonde that had sat down beside me. I am not sure how you tracked me down. I don't know who the blonde was. I only remember how close she was sitting to me. I remember talking to her, but I do not remember about what. I do remember some attraction.

The only real memory I have of that night was of you dragging me off the bar stool with the flimsy style of a rag doll in your hands and out of the dismal bar. You yelled at me for an unbearable amount of time. We did not speak to each other the next day, and your face was still distorted with infuriation the next morning. I was full of remorse for many reasons, but I could not find the words to apologize. There was a part of me that was denying I had done anything wrong, but that didn't explain the remorse. I lost some of your trust that night, and I think now with reflection that I never really did gain it back.

I began to wonder why my friends were dropping like flies. After you finally forgave me, I began to hold you every night, tighter than ever before. But now it seemed that part of the magic was missing. Eventually, things did return to normal, but somehow the purity of our relationship had been shaken.

Another summer, another colorful display of fallen leaves, another Christmas, and another year of hard work with multitudes of hours of overtime put most of our past into perspective. There was still a planned future for us. I was determined to pay the house off as soon as possible. Then I could continue on to another goal. Whether it was a pipe dream or not, I would concentrate on saving and reach financial independence.

That was many years down the road, but these envisions of such a future kept me focused on the importance of not sliding back into a life filled with depression. Even though I was happy with our existence, there was always that unsettled feeling in the pit of my stomach for more. Was it that adulterated, philandering seed planted in me years ago taking root again? I prayed to God that it wasn't, not after all this time taken to eliminate it. I was resolved to the contentment and commitment of our simple but stable life.

Outside influences alleviated the constant pressure for my need of a perfect relationship. Sharing our time with friends and family was part of our bond. We had spent enough years together now that we could take our comfort levels for granted and get away with it. Most of the time, we were a team in resolving issues and in planning things.

When your sister came to us, it was not difficult for us to agree to help her. Her husband had finally gone too far and beat her to the point of hospitalization. A police report and a restraining order finally gave her enough courage to leave him. There was no discussion needed between us when we took her in for a few weeks while the separation and other legalities took their course. There were many things for her to finalize, including a new place to live. With her two kids, it made for some cramped living quarters for a while, but we managed, and we were just so glad to finally get her out of such an abusive situation. Her kids seemed to adjust well, almost as if they could sense the release of pressure escaping from their mother, who no longer had to live in constant fear. Your kids were something to be proud of as they treated their cousins as royal guests during their stay with us.

Your sister's new boyfriend, Andrew, had entered the picture too quickly for you. She met him only a month after she moved in with us. You never voiced your opinion to her, but you did discuss it with me frequently. I tried to share your concerns about how they had grown attached to each other so swiftly, but couldn't honestly agree with you. I thought that she deserved happiness in her life, and there was no set time frame that I was aware of. My opinion was somewhat biased for her new boyfriend, and we had become good friends from the very first meeting. During the times that we shared our past in private, some of our experiences had parallel roads. There were many things that the two of us could relate to. I also liked the way he treated your sister, and his love for her was genuine and readable. Three months after they met, they were living together.

We spent a great deal of time with them, even after your sister moved out of our house. You slowly warmed to the fact that they were very happy together and accepted that it was meant to be. Weekend after weekend, we drank with them, sharing laughs, discussing life as close couples do. You found a new attachment to your sister. You were always close, but now you shared some life that wasn't possible when she was with her husband. And I had found a new close friend. Life was great once more, but six months later, the grim reaper found me again. He would not stop following me. Only this time, he did more damage than take another friend.

Andrew was a hard worker, and he also liked his beer. Your sister worked a job that consisted of steady afternoons. It became a habit for Andrew to come to our house with your sister's kids and spend the evening with us while waiting for her to finish her shift. He enjoyed our company, and I certainly had a lot in common with him. You and I always enjoyed entertaining together. It kept us from the deeper conversations that I would attempt sometimes. You were far from shallow, but my philosophies had to remain buried from you. Not only were most of them against your religious beliefs, you also preferred the simplicities of daily life. This was precisely what had helped you steer me right in the first place, and I didn't want to rock it. So entertaining company was like a distraction to my underlining need to probe your soul.

That night started out like any other Friday. He would arrive around six, and we would sit around the table drinking. Sometimes we would play cards or board games. Usually, we just talked. But there was something different going on as that night progressed. Something wasn't right. It was only something I sensed, and I don't know if you did as well. We never discussed it later.

The kids were busy playing downstairs. We were drinking beer as usual. And then Andrew got up and went to his car and brought back a bottle of whiskey. It was unusual for him to drink hard liquor, but it was not out of the question. What was more unusual was the change in depth of his conversation. His words were as habit, simple yet concise. That night he began to ramble about the meaning of life. I refrained from joining in, preferring to be amazed by this sudden change in him. Someone else was sitting at our kitchen table, or at the very least, his normal plane of thought had temporarily been overtaken by some cosmic insight. I watched him take your sister's kids aside when they had come upstairs for a drink, and he talked to them like I had never seen before. He lectured them about respecting their mother and loving her every day. He told them to be thankful for every moment of every day. It was so out of character for him to demonstrate the high levels of emotions that were in his words. It was in him, but mostly unspoken. It was not until after that it really bothered me when I went over the night in my head a thousand times.

Each time our conversation changed to simpler levels, he wanted to go back to talks of spirituality. It was becoming dangerous for me, for I was full of my own beliefs, my own insights that would perturb most religious people, even if it was equivalent to their own beliefs once you removed the dogma. I regret now that I hadn't voiced my opinion, for it might have helped me explain where his mind was. Your few interjections in an attempt to argue your own religious beliefs did nothing to help the conversation. I was glad when your sister arrived to permanently deter me from joining in. She helped me in my effort to change the subject. The jovial mood of your sister raised us above the deep discussion, and her presence put us back to our normal levels of frivolity. Even Andrew had dropped his attempt to explain what was really bothering him. He showed no signs of drunkenness as was usually the case. But I was getting concerned at the pace he drank the whiskey. At two in the morning when they went to leave, he still looked okay though. The only broken routine was that he asked your sister to put the kids in her vehicle. They always went with him, preferring his convertible sports car over their mother's van.

We waved good-bye to them from the driveway and then went to bed like any other Friday night. An hour later, the phone rang. I watched you turn from a sleepy calm demeanor to hysterics. All I could get from you at first was that he didn't make it. That alone was enough to send terror through me. Without a single detail, my heart dropped. When I was finally able to get you to stop from sobbing, you were able to tell me what happened. A living nightmare formed in my mind that I still see whenever I hear of any related events.

Andrew and your sister lived just outside of town, but to get to their road, there was a sharp curve that followed a creek. It meandered though the county, eventually emptying out into the lake. There were no barriers or reflectors to warn drivers of this sharp turn, only a lone caution sign that stood too close to the embankment. Your sister had been following in her van and watched in horror as Andrew did not turn the corner and drove straight into the creek instead. It plays over and over in my mind like a recurring dream that you can't wake up from and in such vivid detail. It was as if I had been in the car with him that night.

His car had flipped over, and the soft top sank in the muddy bottom, turning the car instantly into a watery casket. Andrew drowned while your sister frantically tried to get him out. The water was only a few feet deep, but with the oozing mud surrounding the doors, it was impossible for her to get them open. She ran to a neighboring house, but it was much too late. By the grace of a higher power, or possibly just luck, the kids had fallen asleep and were oblivious to the nightmare unfolding around them. Except to fathom later the explanation that Andrew had passed away, they were saved from the details and left unscathed from the trauma of witnessing the accident.

Surprisingly, your sister seemed to be only moderately affected by everything. She remained stoic and soon carried on with her life as if it had been just a passing incident in the grand scheme of things. I did not. For the longest time, I blamed myself. I ripped myself to shreds looking for answers, looking for things I could have done differently that night, looking for something I could have done to prevent it.

He drove that same road every Friday, every day for that matter. He had not seemed drunk when he left. Had I missed something? Should I have told him not to drive even though he was perfectly capable of driving just like any other Friday night? It was an acceptable routine that had never once entertained the idea of danger. Why that night? My esoteric thoughts ran amok. His unusual behavior that night, talking about spirituality, instilling in your sister's kids things I had never seen him say before, could have been a sign. Had he somehow been aware of his own fate?

My sanity was crumbling away from guilt as I convinced myself that there was something I could have done. I couldn't get myself to talk to you about it, and we never mentioned that night between us. It was if we had made some secret pact, some vow of silence. I was being eaten from the inside and drew back into the introversions of my past. There were times when I considered getting professional help, but that would mean weakness and defeat. I had to carry on by myself, just as I had done all my life.

Slowly, very slowly, I was able to put it behind me, but it had profoundly affected me. I do not think that my inability to talk about it was the turning point in our relationship. It was more a gradual recognition through time that we never really did talk to each other, not on the deep personal levels I craved for. I began to think we simply existed. The longing for some cosmic soul connection, which I had spent so many years trying to suppress, were finding holes through the barriers I had set up. It was a reverse shield that instead of protecting things from entering from the outside, it protected the inside from filtering out. By burying my cosmic connections to my subconscious, I had been able to think clearly and function within the boundaries of society's rules. Now they were escaping again and throwing me off balance. I ached for more.

I did not let the return of the ethereal nature of my thoughts influence my actions as I had done in my teenage years. With a substantial amount of maturity developing in the frontal lobes of my brain, I knew that focusing on the cosmics was only a recipe for disaster. It was for this reason that I was able to salvage our relationship, realizing that my own withdrawal was turning you cold to me. We regained our way of life, returning to the entertaining of friends, partying. We returned to the task of a household and raising a family. Our compatibility in bed returned. Both our interest had wavered over Andrew's tragedy. We talked again and were content with weather reports and grocery lists. The only thought I allowed to seep through at any great length was how deep our love was for each other. Regardless of its lack of profundity, we did have some form of love between us, and I again succumbed to processing a simple life. In reality, my life had always been simple. It was my brain that complicated it. So we carried on still relatively happy with our relationship.

That winter we used some of my accumulated vacation time to go to Florida and to Disney World. When I watched the excitement of your kids, it was extremely rewarding and kept my mind off my own memories of the place—a time when I believed in soul mates, but a time when I was also lost. This family atmosphere was good therapy for me. But always lingering just below the surface was that pulsing ache for more. I could not rid myself of it entirely.

It was the following year when I combined that relentless drive with my selfishness to later justify resolution to take a chance on jeopardizing our relationship. It began when a new policy came out at work where vacation time could no longer be accumulated and had to be used up to the present calendar date of seniority. When my boss first confronted me with the fact that I had to take three weeks of vacation that summer to comply with these new rules of no more accumulation, I asked if I could simply be paid up to date in lieu of time off. He insisted that the new company policy was to take time off. When I told you that night, you didn't seem to understand until I explained that I couldn't just sit around the house for three weeks. I wouldn't want to waste vacation time by not going anywhere. You reminded me that you couldn't take time off from your housekeeping jobs.

We had many lengthy discussions about my vacation. I told you of my desire to go to Prince Edward Island and honor the memory of my friend Ben by visiting his gravesite and exploring his home province. You were dead set against it, stating how wrong it was for me to go on vacation by myself. I told you that I needed some sense of closure on the loss of my friend and repeated over and over how I did not want to sit around for three weeks and do nothing. I begged you to find a way to come with me, but you kept reiterating how you couldn't. I was wrapped in the idea that all the losses in my life could be solved by this journey to the East Coast, like a sabbatical away from all life's problems and an enlightenment to find the meaning of it all. It was a far-fetched theory, but one I had already convinced myself of. Whether I was able to persuade you of my sincerity or it was your decision to show some trust in me, you finally agreed that I should go.

The following week, just at the break of a beautiful crimson summer sunrise, I threw a suitcase (actually two if you include the cooler) in the trunk of my car, excited, but also anxious about leaving you behind. I gave your kids huge hugs and promised to bring them back something. I looked at you standing in the driveway in the path of the rising sun and saw a beautiful aura around you. Your eyes were not warm however, and they were void of any deep emotion. You were hiding your disappointment, but it was thinly veiled by your glazed look. I gave you a hug and kissed you with great meaning, but I could not feel the reciprocation. I wanted to spout out words of comfort, but your indifference labored any vocalization. You must have seen the sincerity in my eyes, the signs of regret that you weren't coming with me. I told you that I loved you and choked out a good-bye and could feel the tears start to run down my cheeks. I turned away before you could see them and drove out the driveway without looking back. I had an odd sensation that things between us would never be the same.

I have been on many excursions by myself, but never for the length of time ahead of me. I had even traveled to Florida alone once, and those ten days were enough for me to enter into strange situations that to this day I have never shared the details with anyone. I could not predict the events of the next three weeks, but I wanted to make the very best of it. I would pay attention to every detail, the landscape, the people, every small item of my travels. Instead of a vacation, I wanted to find some aesthetic value, to absorb every experience of my journey into the depths of my soul. I wanted to come back a changed man, even more so than I had already become with your help. I had so much potential trapped inside, but still many issues to deal with. I wanted to let it unfold outward, to give it a chance to blossom.

I had come a long way from my street urchin days, but those years of lack of proper guidance had left me following a path of self-destruction. Although neutralized now, that part of my existence still lurked just below the surface. It was not an easy chore for me to eliminate how my past had affected me. My life with you was certainly a good start in doing so. My life with you was good. Sure, we had our moments of bickering, and our love might not be of fairy-tale variety, but any problems we had were trivial and easily forgotten. You had brought stability in my life, given me prospects of a great future. But there was always that inexorable zeal for something more, an internal drive as powerful as any physical addiction. I wanted this trip for soul-searching where I could finally cast out any demons I had inside and rip out any corruptive thoughts that still lingered. Then I could come back and truly dedicate my life to you and your kids. That is what I sincerely set out to do. That was not what happened

The first two days were uplifting with nothing but the open road and that aforementioned aesthetic appreciation for the scenery that passed by like the slow progression on a clear movie screen. The East Coast was beautiful, and for a few fleeting moments, I felt the parts of my soul I was trying to reach. Whether it was because of the stunning landscape so new to me or if I could actually feel the magnetic pull of the Earth from the rolling hills, I was completely at peace.

Late the second day, that tranquility was rudely interrupted. I was only a few miles away from where I could catch the ferry to Prince Edward Island, cruising at a comfortable speed, gawking endlessly like a typical tourist. The lady at the information booth I had left an hour ago had informed me that I had just enough time to catch the last ferry of the day. If I missed it, I would have to wait until morning. My concentration on getting to the island that day and watching the countryside slide by at the same time could have been the reason I noticed nothing wrong with the front end of my car. With no warning at all, the front left tire came completely off the car. I held on tight to the steering wheel as the car tilted to the left and dug into the warm asphalt. I looked in my rearview mirror and saw a colorful display of sparks as the hub dug into the road. My tire bounced playfully along and then fell slowly to rest, like a spinning coin losing its final momentum.

Traffic was very light, and only two cars coming from the opposite direction witnessed what happened. They slowed down, watched in amazement, and went on their merry way. My car came to an abrupt stop, rutted into the asphalt. I was unable to get it off the road. It was only a two-lane highway, so I had the road blocked on my side. If I hadn't been so astonished, I would have found the situation funny. One car behind me went around after narrowly missing the dead tire lying in the middle of the road, slowed down, and then sped away, probably quite apprehensive of the bizarre sight.

I stayed in my car for a moment, still stirring around in my mind what exactly had just occurred. I gathered my wits and got out to access the situation and the damage. All the lug nuts had fallen off, and when the last one let go, so did the tire. I retrieved the tire that was a considerable distance back. With the lane blocked, I was subjected to gawkers who would slow down to a crawl for a look and decide I either didn't need help or I was beyond help. I removed my carjack from the trunk, and working in the middle of the road in constant danger of getting an inch or two shaved off my butt, I was able to lift the car high enough to put the wheel back on. I took two lug nuts off the tire from the other side, and it was enough to hold it on and pull the car off to the side of the road. Three of the studs had been bent, and I knew that it would be highly unsafe to continue driving.

I sat on the trunk of my car watching the sky turn to the darker shades of twilight. There was not a house around anywhere behind me, and I doubted there were any ahead of me within walking distance. This was a desolate stretch, which the only purpose was to connect to the ferry. No one opted to stop, and I flagged no one down. I lay back, at ease, like a man on vacation with not a worry in the world. My assumption was that a cop would eventually drive by, and I was proven right much quicker than anticipated. A Royal Canadian Mounted Police officer pulled up behind my car, and after I explained what happened and where I was going, he went into rescue mode for me. He called a tow truck for me and stayed with me until it arrived. He told me which gas station it was going and drove me into the next town, the only town. He drove me to the motel only a few blocks from the gas station and wished me luck with the rest of my vacation. This was a welcome change from my past memories of police officers. I thought their only function when it came to me was impaired-driving charges. I gained new respect, but was also glad I hadn't been drinking. That came later.

The tow-truck driver had told me that the gas station would not be open the following day. There were no others, which meant I was stuck for at least two days, and I was only five minutes from where I needed to catch the ferry. My disappointment was minimal when I considered the amount of time I still had left for vacation. I had favorable lodgings, and I discovered there was a bar next door. Once I settled into the motel room, my intentions were to get something to eat, wash it down with a couple of beers, and lie back and see what Maritime television had to offer. I should have known better. The combination of new surroundings, no responsibilities, and new varieties of beers to try was a recipe for old habits.

For a small town, the bar was crowded; and with me as a total stranger, there was a whole building of untried minds to play with, and my undying belief in telepathy was going to get a workout in new territory. At first it was fun, but the more I drank, the more pieces of paranoia entered my thought processes. I was entirely alone, over a thousand miles away from home, and the feedback I was getting did not represent that of the friendly kind. They recognized me as a stranger, and I soon recognized how close-knit this community was. The more I drank, the more of an outcast I felt I was. This was not the way I wanted to feel. I was in a new land, one supposedly waiting for me, filled with abundances of new discoveries and new people. Instead, I found myself retreating within, something I had done very seldom since I had met you. The connections of this group and the shared adornments of friends, neighbors, and lovers around me, I was not meant to be part of. But the displacement and the unwanted feelings did not stop me from further analyzing those around me.

There was one couple in particular that sat at the table next to me who at first warmed my heart and then filled me with envy. I watched the way they held each other's hands as tender and sensuous as any dreams or memories of my own past. I was silently sighing when I noticed the depth and the longing they shared as they stared into each other's eyes. I had periods in my past where the feeling of loneliness was overwhelming, but nothing like it did that night. It flooded over me, and I could not escape the sudden distress. I kept wondering what you were doing right then, and I felt so desolate. I felt abandonment and an inexplicable rush of solitude burrowed right to the marrow of my bones. I kept wishing you were with me, but as my thoughts began to ferment, disappointment turned to resentment. I lost all my original perspective with the copious amounts of alcohol. I had spotted what appeared to be two single women flirting with the bartender, and there was something tempting about them. But not only was I afraid to approach anyone in what was very apparent to me as an everyone-knows-everyone atmosphere, I was also hanging on to threads of decency and fidelity. These were terms that took me a long time to learn. I might have resented you that night, but you still had all my respect. I staggered back to my motel room and almost called you. I didn't want you to know how drunk I was, so I stopped myself and planned to call you later. Later never came.

I woke up with a hangover the next day, with my head pounding, and the morning sun was excruciatingly painful on the eyes. After a greasy breakfast at a small diner that was situated a couple of doors down from the bar, I bought a pair of cheap dark sunglasses at the convenience store next to it. I could only assume mine were still in my car. I spotted the sign on the light post at the four corners of town that read that the Atlantic Ocean was only two miles. I walked in the direction of the sign's arrow, and the fresh morning air was invigorating. Once more, in spite of my hangover, I felt the vibrations that resonated from nature, and I could feel them tickle my spirit. Standing on the shore of such a powerful body of water and sensing the life beneath its surface guided me back to the purpose of my trip. Not only to find Ben's final resting place, but more importantly, also to find myself.

I could feel the pull of the ebb tide, and I stood astonished about how fast the water receded, leaving pockets of saltwater in the sand, stranding crabs and small fish. I felt the force of the planet in the center of my being, and the lost memories of the magnetic pull of Lake Erie and the spot by my favorite boardwalk during my earlier years came flooding back faster than the high tide I witnessed later. Trust me when I tell you that there is a cosmic connection to be found right here on Earth, and I am sorry we were never able to experience it together. The esoteric journey of that day was the whole purpose of my travels, a long sabbatical resulting in the true discovery to the core of existence. If I hadn't let alcohol interfere with the rest of my trip, I might have been able to accomplish it completely.

That day on the Atlantic Coast eventually was labeled as a distraction to the loneliness I felt the night before. The magic disappeared the moment I walked back into my motel room. I was plagued with a massive buildup of memory of all the days I had spent alone. My mind was racing back to all the difficult times in my life. My cosmic connection of that day was short-lived.

I did sleep that night, not without a string of bizarre dreams of the incomprehensible kind. Late the next morning, my car was repaired, with minimal damage to my wallet; and that afternoon, I was on the ferry to Prince Edward Island. I did not want to admit it to myself, but as I breathed in the ocean air, trying to recapture the euphoric feelings of the day before, I knew my original plans were washed up. I was not going to have stories of new discoveries to take back with me. I knew I was headed for a long drinking binge instead, which would only result in disappointment, heavy remorse, and a completely failed attempt at finding whatever answers I was looking for.

When I drove my car off the ferry onto the solid ground of the island, I grabbed a free map from the tourist booth. No matter what the rest of the trip would bring me, there would be no losing focus on finding Ben. I knew he was from Summerside, and that was where my new home would be for the next two weeks. I found an efficiency apartment right on the beach and was glad to discover that the town of Summerside was not inland. Except for some days of exploration of the island and some detective work tracking down Ben, my car would be resting most of the time, enjoying its own vacation.

I did not leave the apartment the first day except to stroll through town and find where everything was and to buy some supplies. My map brought my attention to the military base outside of town, and a jolting memory from the past flabbergasted me for a moment. I had met someone from there years ago and wondered how they were doing. Not enough to consider finding out if they were still there. I went back to my apartment to behave myself. It did not stop me from drinking though, and with the outside patios of each apartment adjoining each other, I had many idle conversations with other tourists. Conversation with strangers meant drinking.

The following day, I put my Dick Tracey hat on, and my game of private investigation began. Summerside was a small town, and I didn't think it would be difficult to find the cemetery. What I didn't know was how sprawled out the rural community surrounding the town was. There were churches everywhere. They seemed to outnumber the farmhouses. Dirt roads wound in every direction. The red soil and the rolling green hills did the glossy pictures of geographical magazines no justice. Hypnotized by the meandering roads, a cloudless deep blue sky, and the tranquility of the countryside, I found myself traveling too far in every direction. There were small cemeteries everywhere, and I stopped and read each tombstone. The hidden history I discovered from the inscriptions and the dates were mind-boggling. But none of them were inscribed with my buddy's name. I would head back toward town each time, and after two days of fruitless hours of searching and countless cemeteries, I decided to go to the closest Catholic Church to see if they had records.

You would never have known Ben to have been Catholic, but it is not like people carry painted signs professing their religion. There was a rectory beside the church as monstrous as the church itself. I parked in the driveway and sat there for quite some time before mustering up the courage to knock on the door. A priest the size of a bear answered the door, and when I explained my purpose, he invited me in. He asked me if I had visited Ben's family yet, and I told him I did not wish to bother them. I had never met his parents. They had not come to the service in Westlake. A second service had been held on the island. I did not want the discomfort of forced conversation. I had not even bothered to tell his widow that I was coming although we had remained close friends.

The priest offered me tea. I asked for water instead. He went through his record books and found the date of the service and then tried to find the plot on the schematic drawing of the cemetery behind the church. When he couldn't find it, he uttered how strange that was, and I couldn't help but think what I was doing there was strange. He had me walk with him through the grounds where he appeared to think Ben should be. He could not find him, and I had a thought of comic relief that I almost voiced out loud, but I was stopped by the serious demeanor of this huge and intimidating priest. I had thought it was just like Ben to hide his casket!

We went back to his rectory, this profound abode with the cathedral ceilings and polished maple wood that gleamed with layers of varnish and reflected various radiant colors from the sunlight filtering through the stained-glass windows. I could not even imagine what the inside of the church looked like if his home was any indication to its beauty. I felt small. This man lived by himself and was completely at peace with it. Why then had my own loneliness been such a burden? No such thoughts had passed then but later in reflection. Then I was very uncomfortable, especially when he suggested that we should call Ben's family and find out where he was buried. I told him that I didn't want to bother them, but he quickly rebutted me stating that he was sure they would be glad to help me. They were members of his congregation, so I relented to him. He was graceful on the phone, and I could tell it was Ben's mother he was talking to by the drift of the conversation. He explained to her that I was from out of town and a good friend of Ben's and was there to pay respects. And this was how I found out that although Ben was given a Catholic service, he had been buried in a Protestant cemetery. I did not ask why. I thanked him for the information, now wanting to make a run for the door. He gave me directions, not only to the cemetery, but also to Ben's parents, who now wanted me to stop in and visit with them. He stood at the door, waving a final good-bye to me as I backed out of the driveway to visit my vertically challenged friend.

I did not visit Ben's parents, but I did drive by their house so that I could envision my friend as a child. There was a wooden swing set in front of their sprawling wooden ranch, and I could almost see Ben in it. But it was only his grave that now represents my current memory of him. The cemetery was a good size, and it was a while before I found his name etched on a plain cement square set flat in the ground. I went back to my car and got two bottles of beers out of my trunk and sat on the ground beside him.

The countryside was so eerily quiet that afternoon. There was no wind, no birds, not even a recollection of an insect. The grass was warm beneath me, and I began a one-sided conversation with my dear friend. I opened up his beer for him and then mine, and I toasted him. I conjured up all my abilities for deep meditation, dug into all my past experiences with transcendental thinking, and waited for divine intervention. I sincerely thought that I could reach him, for we had spent many nights delving into the very topic of afterlife. We were usually stoned out of our gourd, but we both believed in life after death. When he first passed away, he did reach me in a dream, but that isn't real proof. I sat there having a drink with him one last time, begging for him to talk to me, to show me any ethereal connection that existed between heaven and earth once and for all. I was expecting some flash of epiphany, some conclusion and final substantiation that could solidify the foundations of my beliefs. It was the least he could do for dying on me.

He left me empty. If he was there, he had decided he wasn't in a talkative mood. I did not stay for long. For me to have traveled across the country to see him, to feel his presence, to depend on him to help sort out my confused mind, only to have him spurn me with silence, was grounds enough for me to leave him to finish his beer on his own. I cried on the way back into town, but I couldn't be sure if the tears were for him or for me. I was more lost than I had ever given myself credit for, and without you by my side, it was magnified. I know you didn't nor would you ever accept my stories for what I did with the rest of my time on the island. I can tell you the truth now since it can't change what already happened to us. It is pointless to hide the details now that our connection is so severely severed.

Enveloped in sudden fatigue when I returned from my visit with Ben, I lay down and actually did drift in and out of sleep a couple of times. But by sunset, the walls were caving in on me. By dark, I was out the door and opening up the oak door to the Summerside Tavern, my car keys left underneath my mattress. It hurts me to say that you were not in my thoughts that night, but if it is any consolation, I was not in my thoughts either. I left myself somewhere that night and didn't return until my ride home to you. The freedom of vacation in a land where no other soul knew me allowed me such a surreal existence that it was easy to forget myself. I lost all control. I spent the next two weeks in a fog, drenched in alcohol, pretending to be someone else. I did have the best of intentions originally, and not to remain faithful to you was the farthest thing away from anything I wanted to do. If escaping the planet for a while was my new intentions, it did not require the use of company. Maybe the company found me.

My first mistake was taking amphetamines with me on the trip, my excuse being that they would help me stay alert while driving. Instead, I began to pop them recreationally that night and used them to counter-effect the alcohol, a wide-awake drunk in other words. There was another bar in town, and it still haunts me not knowing that if I had gone to that bar instead, or if I had chosen to wait one more night to paint the town red, or if I had actually stopped and spent some time with Ben's parents, I wouldn't have met one of the natives, and you and I would still be together. Have you heard of the butterfly effect? There is great truth in that. Of course, if you had not been so quick to judge me, so quick in your determination to believe my infidelity, had not shut your ears to my pleas of how much I cared for you, we would still be together. You must have had some inclination how much you meant to me even through your hurt and disgust.

I will be brief, even though now I can be honest with you, instead of continuing to vehemently deny that anything had happened. I can only say I wished it hadn't. I can only say that I lied for us.

She came up to me late that night and asked me to dance. If it had been just the one night, I wouldn't even be able to tell you what she looked like. You have seen me drunk before, but there was always some flow representing tolerance levels that kept me on level ground. It was a combination of comfort, respect, love, and responsibility. It was the stability that you made me feel. I had none of these to work with a thousand miles away from home, resolute to not a care in the world that particular night. Instead of evolving into progression, which had fed my original purpose of my trip, I was already at the start of a full-blown regression. And without any tools to balance my tolerance levels, I was doomed. In other words, I was wasted, and my world back home forgotten.

I danced with her, and it was a slow dance she had chosen. There was a soothing rhythm, and I could feel my heart beat when she embraced me like she had known me forever. It is painful for me to share this with you, but I have committed myself to honesty. Please understand that it does not diminish the respect and admiration I still feel for you and will forever remain untarnished in my eyes. Yes, I brought her back with me and slept with her that night. When I woke up in the morning, she was gone. Yes, she left me a phone number on the nightstand, which I used that afternoon. When she answered, she denied knowing me stating that I had the wrong number. That was a rejection that made me think the karmic wheels were rolling and would certainly have given you satisfaction in any pain you felt necessary for me to have thrown my way. You can imagine the thoughts floating around in my head. My emotions might have been numb from gallons of alcohol, but the fact that I had so trivially become unfaithful to you had filled me with enormous guilt.

When she knocked on my door that afternoon, I was already on my way to the return of intoxicated levels. It turned out that she was married but extremely unhappy. The fact that I was not from here had appealed to her, and she had never came close to ever fooling around on him before. I asked her why she left me her phone number, and she had no decisive answer except that she knew she wanted to see me again. Her husband had been standing beside her when I called. I told you I would be brief, so let me simply say that I spent the next two weeks with her. I lived with her from mid-evening until early morning. Each night we would get drunk together, sometimes at the bar, sometimes in my apartment. How she explained her absence to her husband, I never asked. Each passing day, I was drunk, functioning but living in a fog of bare existence, falling farther and farther into my reliance for alcohol. I was even replacing it with my morning coffee. By the middle of the second week, my memories of sobriety were vague, my memories of anything for that matter. I was a complete wreck, but I had no way of being aware of it.

Each afternoon I would pace the floor, waiting for my evening fix with this island woman. She was nothing more than another form of addiction, and if I would have had any clear thoughts left, I would have recognized myself, would have recognized my past. The routine sex between us was meaningless, but it was also foolhardily known to us as not only necessary but also required duty. I know this probably doesn't help you. But now that I have finally admitted to you what happened, after all my denials, I hope somewhere among the pain and hatred you hold, there might be room for you to understand that I would do anything to have changed the events.

In my mind, I had. I was coming home to you, putting all of it behind me like a bad dream. I was coming back to you to carry on with a prosperous future for you and your kids. I had done my escaping of the world, now understood myself better, and I wanted to let time forget. It was part of what I set out to do, but although the circumstances turned into a state of the bizarre, the results were the same. There were no profound cosmic connections found, but I was at least finally able to bury my past. I would carry on with my life a completely changed man. I was yours forever.

I know this sounds obscure to you, but during my long ride home, I had convinced myself I no longer needed a life of spiritual journey and could find happiness in an uncomplicated life with you. If you hadn't found that letter in the glove compartment of my car, I would wager that this would have happened. I know I would have made every attempt to make you happy, to make us happy.

Was it carelessness or that selfishness that seems to linger inside me like a disease? It is like a thorn picking at my morals. The night before I left Prince Edward Island to go home, I passed out without saying good-bye to my island friend. I woke up in the morning to find a letter on the nightstand stuck in a pink envelope. You know what was written. She had professed her love for me and would leave her husband in a heartbeat to be with me. She went on to describe her emotional attachments as if we had proclaimed a commitment of lifetime devotion to each other. I had not mentioned you to her, and I should have. As I have explained, I was totally lost from reality during those two weeks.

Whether her words lifted my spirit or my ego was raised a few notches or that I was not immune to some emotional attachment, I could not get myself to throw out the letter. I foolishly stuck it in my glove compartment as if it was some souvenir of my trip. Not only was I oblivious to the fact that you might find it, I had actually forgotten about it. And now you have forgotten me.

Not at first. When I first returned from the trip, I was suffering from sheer exhaustion. I was also suffering from withdrawal. I tried my best to hide my shakes from you, but you could tell something was wrong. You were infuriated that I had not called you once, and my excuses for not doing so was far more than lame. The kids were excited to see me, but were disappointed that all I brought back for them were T-shirts. You let me curl up to you my first night back, but it was another week before you let me make love to you. It felt so good to be back with you, and although it took some time, you finally warmed back up to me, and I could feel your love again. I went back to work, returned to a more conservative drinking habit, weaning myself back to health, and my life with you found its comforting routine that we had before I left. My journey to the Maritimes was history, a distant memory, or at least the parts I could remember. Life was good again.

A month later, my comfortable world came crashing down. Mondays were always the roughest day of the week, not only because of the extensive workload, but also because of the fatigue of the long weekend nights that we were accustomed to. I always looked forward to coming home on Monday nights for a peaceful night curled up on the couch with you. But that Monday, you met me at the door screaming for me to get out, waving a pink envelope at me in a fit of rage. A quick flash of memory saw you going to my car that morning just before I left for work to look for your wallet you thought you left in it. Suddenly I felt like I had been hit with a cement block. My heart dropped to levels I didn't think possible. I was caught, and no intricate explanation in the world would find me a way to escape this seine. But I still vehemently denied that anything had happened.

There was fire in your eyes that was more than just hate. If you were hurting, it was covered by your sheer hostility. I flashed back to long ago when I watched my ex-wife melt away in front of me when I admitted my infidelity. I remember feeling the part of her that died. Even though it was my doing, part of me was destroyed that day too. There was none of that this time as if the intensity of your anger doused any feeling of remorse or empathy I should have felt. The fact that you were adamant about kicking me out of my own house did not help. It was my house in all aspects, including in legal terms. My house was proof of my place in society, evidence that I was no longer the burned-out social outcast previously labeled, and I now held a legitimate place in this world. After all my struggles from such a turbulent past, there was not a chance in Hades that I was leaving my house. It now defined me.

I pushed my way past you when you refused to stop blocking my entrance. You had sent the kids to the neighbors beforehand, and I was grateful for that. They had no place in your uncontrollable display of abhorrence. I had no idea how evil I was until you told me that day. I had seen bits of your temper before, during some of our disagreements. But we were always able to resolve our differences before the start of overheated and inappropriate words. This time you had lost it, and I sat on the couch helplessly as you bombarded me with cursive venom. I was sure that if I had provided you with a lethal weapon, you would have used it. There was little I could do or say. I just kept repeating over and over again, between your fire-breathing exhalations that seemed to scorch the very room around me; that it wasn't what you thought, that nothing happened. It didn't matter. Even if I could have placed some doubt in your mind, even enough to calm you down enough for hopes of reasoning, it was too late. Your mind was made-up. We were through.

After what seemed like hours, you finally realized that I was not leaving no matter the extent of your ravings, and you went into silent mode. Needless to say, I slept on the couch that night. I went to work the next day and came back to a house so full of tension that the walls were bulging. The kids were extremely quiet, and I could only hope you had not involved them.

The following night, you wanted to know how much I was going to give you for your share of the house. I reminded you that it wasn't your house, and you immediately threatened me with a lawyer. Instead of arguing with you, I tried to tell you calmly that we should be able to work this out. I told you I loved you, and we had spent too much time together just to throw all of it away. But there was no hope in getting through to you. I even attempted to get your sister to intervene and pleaded with her to help me get you to change your mind. This was how I found out that your ex-husband had cheated on you many times, and to have it happen to you again would mean that there was no room for forgiveness. I told your sister that nothing happened, and she bluntly told me it didn't matter. If you suspected it, it happened. Your sister told me there was nothing she could do. I was defeated.

When I finally accepted that we were beyond salvation, I went into protective mode. I could only assume your threats about the lawyer were idle. I reminded you that you were still collecting social service checks by not changing your mailing address and not letting them know you were with me; you were in a fraudulent situation. You also had income you did not claim. I did not want to use this for ammunition, but if it meant stopping you from trying to take my house, I was prepared to use it. We had no joint bank accounts, but I moved all my money to a different bank anyway, all the while still hoping for some miracle that we could stay together. Your kids were growing more distant from me, and it became obvious that you had said something to them about me. I watched the bond I had with then deteriorate at an alarming rate. I wish you hadn't done that because I loved your kids.

Two weeks later, I came home to an empty house. Not only were you and the kids gone, but so was everything else, save for a mattress and the old beer fridge I kept in the garage. Instead of the pain and hurt I thought I would feel, I felt relief. Your consistent torment of abusive words, your relentless spew of hatred, and your constant reminders of how despicable of a human being I was had begun to wear me to an empty shell. The stability, the security, and the contentment I had gained from you had already departed ahead of you. You added a final dig and used your camping friends to help you move. They had become my friends too. But you took them as well.

I did not pursue you, and the empty house became a monument of my independence. At first, I thought it might become a mausoleum of regret. When you left me, I swore that I would not fall apart, but I had no guarantees I could do that. But my cycle had to be broken. I had to prove to myself that once and for all, I could survive on my own and did not need a woman to depend on. One day I will find true love, but with a sense of security that comes from me and not require the dependency of that relationship. I must continue to dream and to hope.

I never saw you again. I did bump into your sister a few times, and I could not help but give her a hug each time. This was how I found out that you had moved in with an old boyfriend you had still carried a torch for, someone from before your failed marriage. But she also told me that you were not happy. It bothered me to hear that. Despite what you think of me, I always wanted you to be happy. Although we were far from soul mates, you did have a huge piece of my heart, and you had become my future. I have many regrets in my life, but losing you was a big one. I am sorry that I hurt you and would have done anything for you. I have spent too much time in the past, trapped in self-pity, following paths to self-destruction, wallowing in my misgivings and mistakes that I can no longer dwell on them. I had to get over you quickly.

I know that I have the strength to continue on my own, but in a different light this time. I have my time with you to thank for that. I sincerely hope that you find happiness. You certainly deserve it. And maybe someday by forgiving me, you will be able to thrive in a beautiful relationship with someone, without your past to interfere with it. I can only hope for the same.

CHAPTER 19

Lana:

When I walked into Brown's Tavern that Saturday afternoon, it had been a whole two weeks since Kathy had left me. Primed with three beers before I left my house and an internal promise not to get drunk, I pondered over the reason I was hitting the bar scene so soon. Desperation, desolation, depression did not fit the description this time. I spent the entire forty-five-minute drive adding up all the possible pathos buried in my subconscious and came up with no reason. It was actually uplifting to feel shallow, that no other purpose existed except for sheer entertainment. Or maybe while I was picking from the vast depths of my soul, I missed finding the primitive part of me, that recurring urge, that natural instinct to procreate.

That internal promise not to let the influence of alcohol affect my wandering out for adventure was ludicrous, for only it would rid me of my inhibitions for such a primitive development in the first place. But I had forgotten which bar I was going to, where instigation on my part was not really necessary. The reputation of the women there was so well-known that it was practically posted in the lobby.

The rain outside, the dark gray sky pushed down a surreal fog, not only over the terrain but also over my thoughts. It did not deter my goal to completely avoid any forms of depression to interfere with my day. The idea of using the bar scene in lieu of a good movie was not a unique one in my past. That day, I was convinced that the picture show I was about to enter would be a comedy, and so I laughed at the rain. It was a vengeful rain, however, and it drenched me during my brisk walk from the parking lot to the bar's rear door.

My fake wet smile had the taste of salt when I swung open the dark wooden door that led me into the gloomy dungeon. How quickly the mind's perception of reality is distorted when relying on old memories rather than directly through the optical nerve. I hated this place, yet I was drawn back to it with a weird sense of past pleasures. Maybe I did thrive on my own depression. That taste of salt on my lips was not from fresh tears but those of reminiscence. They ominously flowed in my memory bank and mixed with the pungent smell of an atmosphere with such social disgrace that the paneled walls seemed to be caked with it. The weather outside was a tropical paradise compared to the stale air inside, which had already reached the capillaries of my lungs and was quickly spreading to my autonomous nervous system. Part of me wanted to turn and run, but the brief panic was not strong enough for me to escape the claws of the prospective offerings of potential pleasures.

It didn't matter that the envelope of depression had quickly come back to choke me, the precise thing I was trying to avoid. Distortion had already set in the second I closed that dark wooden door behind me, leaving the gray and the real fog behind me and entering this world of brown. I am quite sure that it was not called Brown's Tavern because of the brown decor, but everywhere you looked, there were tints of it—chestnut, walnut, mahogany. There were shades of cocoa, coffee, Kahlúa; tan, ocher, beaver-pelt ceilings; umber ground-bay bar stools; corroded bronze table legs. But I do not need to describe the place to you. I found out later it was your second home.

I let my eyes slowly adjust to the darkness. As overcast as it was outside, it was still darker inside, not a window to be found. Small wall lamps enshrouded in frosted glass hid dark yellow bulbs that were covered with insect droppings and layers of cigarette smoke. Rays of dim light cut through the shadows between the mismatched and scarred tables. I cut a serrated path toward the bar, bumping into a couple of antiquated chairs that were scattered in no conformity, as if they had never been moved back in place from their shuffle of the night before. The gray skies outside beckoned to me once, but I was already trapped.

The bartender ignored me at first, his attention directed to the four bikers dressed in full leather gear at the far end of the bar. It was not until I noticed them that I realized I was the only other one in the place. A wall clock behind the bar with a broken glass face read one o'clock. I had twelve hours of steady drinking ahead of me, and with the true dedication of an addict, I would not leave this place until they stopped serving, my vow of sobriety supposedly intact. A grand feat, but one that I had committed to countless times with limited success by simply changing the definition of sober to an appropriate standard of cognition and proper standing abilities.

A nervous cough that came from the pit of my stomach was all I needed to get the bartender's attention. I ordered two bottles of beer, not wanting to bother him again in probably what would be less than ten minutes, and paid him with exact change. Any tips would be saved for waitresses later on. Both hands held tightly to the golden nectar that would be my prime source of company and, once more, without the embodiment of a relationship intertwining its effects. So many future brews to brew in while I avoided contemplating my past, at least for one night.

I made my way back through the maze of chairs and tables and headed for the back wall, toward what I referred to as the stalking table. Safely tucked away from the rest of the room, it overlooked the entire area and had a clear view of the dance floor. It gave me a sense of security and comfort with my back against the wall, a feeling I needed to accomplish my mission, a refresher course in social studies. I had convinced myself that these studies would be synonymous with looking for prey, if that was where my lessons would take me. Defense mechanisms, even those set up to defeat my own remorse or lost sense of morals, could twist the meaning of anything to fit the images accordingly. I watched from my territorial perch as I prepared myself for the bar scene to unravel before me, planning to label myself as a victim of circumstance and not responsible for anything that would occur that day. I would leave out the possible influence of a roving alcohol-soaked mind talking to itself.

I was so busy amusing myself, interrupted only by constant trips to the bartender and various detours to the cigarette-butt-filled urinals, that five hours went by before I was aware that the bar was beginning to fill up with people. I had to have been in a deep trance. This was unusual for me because one of my favorite pastimes was watching and studying faces, a blunt description of the very social studies that I had come here to do. A quick overall view showed me the strange mix I had remembered of this bar. I was relieved that I recognized no one. I had no real pleasant memories of this place and still wondered why I had chosen it. I was a frequent client in my earlier days, and there were several individuals I did not want to meet up with in here, but that was the risk I took when I had decided that this would be my dwelling for the evening. Even the two waitresses that had begun their shifts and meanderings had gone unnoticed by me until I had snapped out of my trance.

I had drank quite a bit the night before, but my tolerance level for alcohol ruled out that I was already suffering from sporadic memory loss. I wondered if my vow to block out all the thoughts of the woman I had just spent the last seven years with had affected other processes. I stopped thinking about my blackout and motioned to one of the waitresses instead. She either did not notice me or ignored me. I began to study the crowd, but I could not focus. Any telepathic abilities that night became a jumbled mass of vibrations. Instead of individual wavelengths, it was a cornucopia of different frequencies that served no purpose. I abandoned this exercise immediately. I could not allow something as vain as trouble with my sixth sense to interrupt the flow of surrealism flowing through my veins. The alcohol had indeed taken control already, and the importance became to immerse in this golden bath of impassivity.

It was this toxic potion of lack of remorse and get-on-with-my-life attitude that distorted my vision and memory of that day. I had been so used to the steady diet from my past of depression and self-pity stinging from the broken arrows still stuck in my heart that this new carefree posture was shocking my system. It was unchartered territory, friction rubbing against the grain of my true personality. I wanted this newfound ability, but it was like stepping into traffic with no sense of direction. My inner soul was fighting any attachment to this fervor for apathy. I might as well have thrown a shot of whiskey into my beer glass and watched the same boilermaker stimulated into physical form to visualize what was happening to me inside.

I finally waved down one of the waitresses, the one who had originally ignored me, and ordered two more beers. The cold flow of liquid down my throat continued to lessen the tangibility of the reality of the night. It also added to faded memory even though I had vehemently denied I would allow that to happen. Suffice to say, the rest of that evening was of kaleidoscopic effect.

I vaguely remember being passed a joint on one of my trips to the bathroom from someone I had no idea about who they were. Giving into this substance so quickly after many years of abstinence was a bit shocking, if not fearful. I had no cause for deterrence that night in the frame of mind I was in, and I filled my lungs to capacity with it. I remember talking to the providers and held a contorted picture of what they looked like, but would never be able to pick them out of a photo album, let alone out of the crowd later on that night.

I remembered the sounds of drums starting, followed by the distinct sounds of a keyboard and the word *testing* repeated over a microphone. The maze to get back to my stalking table was more of a floating process than a walk, interrupted by a near collision with a serving tray and my waitress. She was no longer ignoring me. She gave me an understanding smile of a seasoned waitress when I apologized. I cannot remember if I reciprocated the smile, but hers was enough for a surge of confidence compounded with some serious potent pot. I had not seen her as pretty before, but the rest of the night she was, although I never saw that smile again.

Back in the comforts of my acclaimed territory, the beer continued to flow, now at an even more accelerated rate as I tried to wash the weed out of my system. It wasn't the paranoid effects that I had expected to stream in, but it was the discomfort of such immediate and heightened awareness in a room full of strangers. I was long out of practice.

The band had set up on the stage to the far left of me, and the dance floor angled in front of it. They had just started their set, and the music flowed through my polluted veins. My chest was thumping with the vibrations of the monstrous speakers to the point I could feel it against my ribs. From the soles of my feet to the nape of my neck, my entire nervous system was surrendering to the concoction of outside influences I was subjecting it to.

This was my frame of mind when halfway through the band's first set, I could feel your presence. You were standing to my right, but I wasn't sure for how long. This was a great contradiction to what my heightened awareness should have been, but I do not wish to get into philosophical discussions of different planes of reality.

You were beautiful. There was a golden aura around you, and it wasn't from the dust-laden light bulb several feet behind you. Your auburn hair sparkled with vitality and encircled a face of sheer anticipation and longing, yet with brush strokes of innocence. Dark brown eyes pooled with reflections of assurance bore through me, but only as far as my post-acid glazed pupils would allow. Your eyes erased my fear and protectionism and awoke natural cravings and sent my wheel of desire into overdrive. That innocent yet provocative wink you gave me put the steering on automatic, and we were instantly destined for some history between us. As simple a process as it seemed to be, you had me possessed before my mind could filter through what was happening. Inevitably, I could not change my soul, only add to its karma.

I cannot admit this openly, for I derive strength from thinking otherwise, but I had deceived my own reverie of sensibilities that night. There are times I envy those whose existence borders on callous and are impervious to their actions. That type of existence was a swim upstream for me, and I couldn't swim.

The rest of the night at the bar was oblivion, fragmented only with faded apparitions of my time with you. I vaguely remember dancing with you, and there are only two pieces of conversation I can grasp. One was from you when you stated that you were probably older than me, and I remember correcting you. The other voice that had pierced through my fog was that of the waitress. Sometime through the night, she had whispered into my ear, "Be careful of that one." The words registered to memory, but I had been well beyond any deep cogitation. Her candor had been wasted on me, although it might have inadvertently given her better tips. It was not until much later that her tip to me became apparent and in a jolt of recognition to the legitimacy of her warning.

We left that bar that night holding hands, the sensation of touching new flesh stirring primal passions. I know without the aid of recollection that it was well past last call when we left. This was conventional practice, and even my seven-year hiatus wouldn't leave room for negotiation. You lived only a few blocks away, yet I still drove us to your home anyway. Impaired driving means nothing to the impaired, even with past experiences. I was missing the stability of family life already. It was not registering in thought, but I could feel it churning inside. My actions that night was part of a lifestyle left behind, detesting its waste and insignificance. How I could have fallen back into its traps so fast was beyond my understanding. It certainly didn't matter that night, anyway, as you led me into your house and directly down the hall to your bedroom.

You undressed so quickly that I was suspecting that I would have to leave you money. I had always used sex as an escape of some form or another, and my day had begun with the mission to escape. Your softness, your aggression only escalated my desire and was also intensified by a dose of cannabis that had been missing from my bloodstream for many years. You were better than what money could pay for, but my recent abstinence had left me without stamina. You had brought me to a peak quickly as the combination of your unexpected offensive moves and the touch of new flesh sent me over the edge. I was fast asleep only moments later.

When I woke up the next morning, the remorse came flooding in like tidal waves. Why I had fallen back into such meaningless play so rapidly was eating away at all my common senses, the ones I had spent so much time developing. I needed meaning now, a life of caring and responsibility. I wasn't giving you much credit in that department even though I didn't know you. That morning you were just an object, a way of thinking that added to my regret. I practically ran out the door that morning. I promised to call you, and you informed me that you had no phone. I told you I would see you later then, and you only nodded.

I drove home with my head throbbing, my temples looking for a way out of my forehead. I was relieved to have escaped and put the whole night behind me. But then the dreaded empathy that had plagued me all my life came rushing back with a vengeance. Once back in my house, sprawled out on my couch, nursing a huge glass of vodka and tomato juice, I was finally able to focus. I remembered how innocent and confused you looked as I made my quick flight out your front door. In the solitude of my house, I was able to realize that you really had done nothing wrong; and for the first time, I saw your face in a vision of retrospect that needed recognition. You were definitely beautiful and probably as lonely as I was. And of course, I could not shake away the extraordinary talents you showed me in the sack.

As I sat in my empty house, the feelings of loneliness that I had managed to keep at bay for the past two weeks enveloped me and squeezed me with serpentine pains. The drive for companionship was shoving me forward again and past the gates of caution. By the time I finished several morning cocktails, all my thoughts were wrapped around the idea of seeing you again. I wanted to spend some time with you to find out who you really were. This was how you found me at your doorstep that same Sunday afternoon with a cooler full of beer.

In just one night, I had regressed back into the land of irresponsibility, acting as if I was eighteen again. It was not easy work for one who commended himself for his complexities. When you answered the door and I actually really looked at you for the first time, the urge for companionship combined with your good looks gave me the ability to explain to myself why I was there. It didn't matter that I wasn't experiencing some profound emotion and had not fell madly in love with you. I decided I did not want to be alone, and that absolved me from my dedication to the last seven years of a normal life. I was back in a world where only today mattered, at least for now. Your smile removed any doubt that this regressive behavior down promiscuity lane was dangerous and that being alone was not in the best interest of my well-being. If I had known your background ahead of time, how different my reasoning would have been.

We drank at your kitchen table all afternoon where with some prying questions I was able to delve into your past. You had recently split up from a highly abusive marriage and had just applied for a restraining order. It was only then I noticed the telltale signs—the faded bruises on your arms and the small one just below your left eye. My pride for attentively gathering detail hurt for a moment, upset that I had not noticed this before. You were married for many years, constantly splitting up temporarily and then reuniting for another vicious circle of punishment. I could only decipher it as a love-hate relationship. I felt relief that I didn't have to live with the regret of hitting a woman.

I listened to you ramble on further about your past, but I couldn't concentrate on the details. I was completely attracted to you physically, and I kept thinking about you leading me down the hallway again. It wasn't that what you were telling me did not interest me. It was the simplicity in which you said it. You were not deep, and I could tell right away that you floated through life. And as I watched you drink, I saw the signs of alcoholism. This was confirmed later, but that day, it didn't matter at all. That day nothing mattered, my concentration toward my own future put on hold. The only concern of importance was to get to work the next day. Even that didn't seem to matter that afternoon as we poured back the beer. I was lost in the moment with you, trapped once again in the tranquilizing effect of female companionship.

You had informed me that you had a sixteen-year-old daughter only minutes before she walked in trailing a boyfriend that was much older than her. She was beautiful as well, but as I learned quickly, very misguided. It was easy to see that she had complete free will and reign of her own life. You were incapable of steering her in any right direction, letting her fly on her own much too soon. There was no discipline whatsoever, and she no longer answered to you. My life at that age flashed briefly before me and then vanished as a matter of unimportance.

But I also briefly woke out of my stupor and realized that I had no business being with you. I suddenly noticed the shabbiness and the uncleanliness of your place, but then when I looked at you, the rashness of not caring about anything rushed back in and reflected away rational thought. I was back to the obsession of bedding you again. Not before I allowed troubling rumination as I thought of my own daughter when I looked at yours. She would have been the same age by then. I was saying a silent prayer that she had turned out okay.

You introduced me to your daughter and her boyfriend, and we exchanged friendly hellos as I watched them grab a beer out of your fridge, walk down the hall, and disappear into the bedroom across from yours. She had just returned from being gone all weekend with not so much as an inquiry from you where they had been. It was not my place to say anything and instead grabbed another beer from my cooler to enforce my new sense of irresponsibility.

Later that day, the four of us went out for supper at the Chinese restaurant directly across the road from you. There was a sense of déjà vu as we closed the place with an extremely large beer tab. Partying at a Chinese restaurant is not normal, but I had left normality behind two days ago. Besides, that déjà vu feeling was bogus and was the result of a fleeting memory of another Chinese restaurant in another town in another time.

It was clear that you and your daughter were drinking buddies, and the fact that she was only sixteen did not bother you in the slightest. I had left my morals and maturity levels at home and was simply along for the ride. There were thorns of despair though, but uncannily, I was able to suppress it with my desire for a temporary ride in this bizarre existence. It was the only explanation I could live with when later that night, I lay on top of you with the silk sheets below you, thrusting deep inside you, releasing a universe of frustration, and feeling no regrets. It was the only explanation to understand that the noises coming from across the hall in your daughter's bedroom had not bothered me. We had sex again an hour later and then again in the morning before I rushed off to work.

I had compiled all my anxieties into a night in the hay, and the ferocity between us only added to its need and allowed the poisons in my mind to escape. It was as if every event from my circumvented past relied on the intensity of our passion, and if it wasn't passion we were feeling, it was certainly extremely magnified desire.

I did not see you again until the following Friday night. I could still feel you until then. It didn't matter to me that the emotion of love was elusive this time. My reasoning was that there would be no danger of pain that way, one less layer of distressful malaise to carry with me if things did not work out between us.

That Friday night, we continued where we left off Sunday. We drank a bottle of rum at an alarming rate. Your drinking pace offered great competition. Your daughter had already left for the weekend, off to her own path of self-destruction. By two in the morning, we had reached an inebriated state high enough to head for your bed to replace our alcohol addiction with our sexual one. I could not understand how I could get such gratification from such casual sex when I had spent so much of my past trying to parallel it with a search in profound feelings of love.

I had no idea where our relationship was going, but did recognize that we had little room for growth. We were feeding off each other, escaping into this fantasy world of alcohol and sex. It soon became apparent that we had nothing serious to offer each other and we were eventually doomed to failure. In the meantime, I was not looking for anything, and even though I knew I had to be extremely careful not to fall back into the traps of my youth, the instant gratification I received from you overrode my caution.

The next weekend, I asked you why you had no telephone. You told me that your husband had cut the service out of spite, and you did not have good-enough credit to get it under your name. So the kindhearted fool that I was waived precautions and safeguards, and I gave you several pieces of my identification and told you to go get a phone. I did not think once about trust. I was only thinking that this way, I could talk to you throughout the week; for regardless of how much I was willing to let myself regress back into the land of immaturity and irresponsibility, I had to keep some control. I could never allow myself to jeopardize my job. I tried seeing you through the week a couple of times, but your drinking habits were too influential on my own. They put mine to shame. When I was almost late for work one morning from not only a hangover but also because I couldn't resist when you climbed on top of me, I knew I could not risk seeing you through the week. A phone call would suffice.

I could have brought you to my place, but something from the depths of my subconscious wouldn't allow it. Not only was most of my house essentially void of furniture, I still felt in my heart that my loyalty to Kathy had never really been broken. It would take some doing before I could break the shrinelike qualities I felt between the walls of my house. In her honor, I was keeping it empty of furniture and of people. You never asked to see my house. I never volunteered.

That was why our relationship consisted of only weekends and only at your place. We did go out from time to time, and it was always your desire to go to Brown's Tavern. It didn't help the frequency of our outings when each time you would get completely wasted. One of the turning points that made me decide to restrict our drinking to your house was the time you fell down in the parking lot and couldn't get back up. It woke me to the fact of how much of a problem you really had. You kept repeating that I didn't love you. I had no idea where that had come from, unless it was the fact that I had never said it. You had no way of knowing that I couldn't say it. Certainly, I had feelings of love for you, but they were not deep. They were not feelings that represented the depths of love I had felt in my past and still longed for. You had whispered frequently in my ear in the confines of your bedroom that you loved me as you showed me your constant heated passion, your flesh wrapped around me.

My recognition of the seriousness of your drinking problem was gradual, but then I was noticing that every time that you drank, you words were slurred and your balance would be off. Your tolerance levels had gone haywire, and it was taking you less each time to reach inebriation. It was only in afterthought, lying on my couch in the middle of the week, that I realized that you were getting drunk every day. Why that had escaped me for so long could only be explained by my hope that there was a slim chance that you weren't. There were many things I was overlooking about you. You didn't work. You didn't do housework. You didn't cook. I had no idea what you did for income. I could only assume government checks of some kind. On top of it all, evidence pointed to the fact that you were definitely an alcoholic.

This was not a good match for me, especially with my own past battle with the bottle. I knew all these things, and they all pointed to a futile future with you. I knew you were detrimental to me, but I kept going back for more. Whether I was still plagued with empathy that my own well-being was secondary in importance or whether you had become another addictive habit and an obscure source of comfort, it didn't matter. I held on to the hope that you could change. No matter how drunk you got, you always knew how to appease me. Different positions, softer kisses, tantalizing caresses. There is no truth to the old saying that the way to a man's heart is through his stomach. It is lower. At the very least, it promotes tolerance, allows oversight of faults, maybe even creates blindness. Especially to a man who has always relied on sex in a variety of emotional ways and, even on occasion, found it as the truest form to express his love.

I did lose myself with you. I did lose sight of the direction I had spent so much time finding. But eventually, the little intelligence I was able to hold on to at conscious levels, the few brain cells that I hadn't destroyed yet and were still clumped together enough for significant thought, let me slowly lift out of the fog. You had surrounded me in a thick mist with whatever incantation you used on me.

One Saturday night, halfway between inebriation and another evening of fantasy escape to the talents you produced between your silk sheets, the telephone rang. At first, you weren't going to answer it; and then after innumerable rings, you changed your mind. It wasn't long into your conversation that I was able to deduce that it was your husband you were talking to. I immediately wondered what restraining order did not include phone calls. While my mind was still trying to grasp why he was calling you, in a bizarre turn of events, you handed the phone to me. I took the receiver from you and, in a state of confusion, said hello. I could not figure out how he knew I was there and, secondly, what he could possibly want from me.

He asked me who I was, and I told him I was a friend of yours. I felt I was stating the truth because I could not remember any discussion that represented further commitment. When he asked me where I lived, my demeanor changed, and I abruptly told him that I didn't think that was any of his business. I accomplished nothing by that except to raise his ire. He quickly announced that you were his wife and it was very much his business and instructed me that I better leave. His voice was strange, almost demented. And I had visions that I was dealing with someone walking on a tightrope, and the slightest breeze would drop him into insanity. His next sentence confirmed it.

He calmly told me that if I didn't leave within the hour, he would come over and pour gasoline all over me and light me on fire. I was aghast. It was not said in a threatening tone, not set in motion by anger, but in a nonchalant, matter-of-fact statement of truth. Your husband was obviously not playing with a full deck. I looked at you and could not help but wonder how many cards you were missing. I said okay, lacking any bold statement to confront him with, but in a weird sense of defiance, waited until he hung up before I cradled the phone. I looked at you again in wonderment, but you would not meet my eyes. I asked you how he could have possibly found out your phone number and was completely bewildered when you said that you had given it to him. The only answer to my why was that you had seen him in town that week, and he asked for it when you told him you had a new phone. I guzzled an entire beer, unable to grasp what was happening. None of it made sense.

I knew that my life had become a giant mist of disorder and delusion, but this was even beyond the boundaries of surrealism. I had been in threatening positions before, faced altercations, held my own to situations with obnoxious drunks whose claims to manhood was to create any reason to fight. Most of the time, I could talk my way out of fights. I was not a scrapper, but when confronted and pinned into a corner, I could defend myself. No one can forget the rush of adrenaline and its effects. The threat sounded real, but a part of me couldn't take it seriously. Yet the fact that you can't fight a gasoline fire with a fist was quite daunting, and I was very uneasy.

I asked you about the restraining order, and you assured me that there was one, but could not come up with an answer when I asked then why you had talked to him in town. I poured back another beer and drowned any fear that I felt. The hours passed, and just before dawn, like a heroin junkie needing a fix, I let you lead me to your bed again. In a full mating ritual, you held me down by the wrists and aggressively took care of me. I fell asleep afterward, waking up a couple of hours later with full recognition that your magic over me was wearing thin.

I spent the next week juggling ways in my mind to end it with you, my subconscious mind feeding me pieces of reality that this was becoming a situation that was not right, a situation that had the potential for snowballing. My thoughts were short-lived.

After a full week of sleeping on my couch, after a week of gathering loneliness, hearing the ghostly noises of Kathy and her kids that used to roam the rooms of my house, the pit in my stomach groaned with misery. I missed them, and you had become a distraction to keep my mind off things. I knew I had reached the full circle of regression but refused to think about it. I was back to alcohol-fueled weekends to escape my cluttered mind and again relying on the cheap thrills of sex for quick pleasure. You had me hooked, and I became totally oblivious that there was a whole world of other people out there waiting to be discovered.

I didn't have the energy or the ambition to continue to strive for the perfect relationship, my drive waned from so many past experiences gone awry. You were convenient. I would worry about my future later. I was still on track with my financial goals, and with the exception of the increased alcohol expenses, my frugal ways had laid a course for me to have my house paid off soon. My days of poverty still affected my thinking. So did my days of failed relationships, but I could not focus on them in the same positive way. They would give rise to thoughts of despair, and it was simpler at that point in my life to go back to floating directionless to cope with matters of the heart. I had convinced myself that it was only temporary. I had great faith I would change back to the right direction, but right then, I needed the easy way. It seemed to me, aside from your passionate proclamations of love conveniently uttered only in the confines of your bedroom lair, that you didn't want much more either.

So we continued our relationship, never straying from our routine. But as the weeks passed, your continued drunkenness was getting old, and it became more difficult to fool my false sense of contentment. The turning point came one Friday night when I had arrived later than usual. I was given a chance to work overtime that afternoon, and realizing that we were going to spend the whole weekend together as we normally did, I didn't think a few hours would matter to you. I guess it did, for when I looked through your screen door when you didn't answer my knock, I could see that you were slouched over in your chair, one hand hanging on to a whiskey bottle that was almost drained.

I walked in, and instead of a cordial hello, you slurred over and over again, and I was able to decipher enough of it to understand your claim that I didn't care about you and I didn't love you. When I asked you why you were drinking whiskey, you simply repeated over and over again that I didn't love you. You were so drunk that you were vaguely aware of your surroundings. I picked up a smoldering cigarette off your linoleum floor, too late not to decorate it with a charcoal mark. It matched the fan of other burn marks encircling your chair.

There was no talking to you. Your mind was incapacitated, and I was surprised that you were functioning at all. The fact that I didn't love you was embedded in your head like a groove of a scratched album, and after hearing it a hundred times, I was in a desperate search for your off switch. You guzzled the last few drops remaining in the whiskey bottle, and I watched helplessly as you and the bottle went crashing to the floor in different directions. Neither you nor the bottle broke. You weren't out cold, and you were still mumbling about me not caring for you anymore.

You were not heavy, but you were not of small frame either. I picked you up from underneath your arms and dragged you down the hall, careful not to careen you into a wall. I lifted you into your bed, where after a few moments you eventually stopped mumbling your pitiful excuse for a mantra and replaced it with snoring. I did not ponder over what happened, but I did feel disappointment. I had been looking forward to seeing you. I cleaned up your kitchen as best as I could and then checked on you to see if you were okay. I covered you with a blanket from your daughter's bed, not wanting to disturb you by removing the one underneath you. She wouldn't need hers for I had yet to see her home on a weekend before Sunday afternoon.

I thought of leaving you a note, but then thought of it as pointless. I drove home, not once tempted to go anywhere else. I spent my first Friday night since I had met you alone and sober. And the breath of pure health I felt Saturday morning was message enough for me to understand that the two of us were probably never going to make it together. That didn't stop me from calling you around noon that Saturday, for regardless of what happened the night before, you had become an unshakable weekend habit, another new addiction.

There was no answer, and I tried every half hour after that for the rest of the afternoon. I drank beer and enjoyed my backyard for the first time since Kathy had left me. I kept visualizing her kids frolicking in the pool and was flushed with a new round of sadness, the very sadness that I had sworn to stand off. You had been such a distraction for me that I had forgotten the real me, the depressed one. The very person that I vowed to not let return, the one that carried around entire bricks of depression on his shoulders and in his heart most of his life.

My simple way of thinking ended that afternoon, and although the reminiscing was kept to a minimum, my mind was swirling regardless. I decided that if I was to remain with you any longer, then I had to talk to you, had to finally surmise if there was any depth to you at all. Hope had always driven me, and I had hope that you could change. I had hope that I could find some kind of dreams and inspirations in that troubled soul of yours. I had hope that we could help each other in more meaningful ways. Ours paths, as they existed, were heading nowhere, but my fondness still held with it some confidence in you. But we had to change directions, and we had to do it soon.

I called one last time, any meditative thoughts of the afternoon now turned into obsession with you. I had to see you and perhaps better explain where my heart was, what I really wanted for us. The sun was already setting when I started my car to go find you. If you weren't home, I thought I could find you at your favorite tavern. Your complexities were not of full web. You did not drive. You did not own a car. You did not steer from habit.

As I got closer to your house, I became nervous. At first, I couldn't explain it, and then resolved that I was afraid I would find you drunk somewhere and my need to talk to you would dissipate into thin air. When I finally pulled into your driveway, it was dark enough that if you were home, some lights should have been on. I saw none, your windows dark as the sky now was. I could see that the kitchen door was wide open. At first, I was uncomfortable with the idea of entering your house unannounced;

but with all the time we had spent together, I concluded that there was nothing wrong with it. I called your name from the screen door, anyway. It was not loud, but firm enough that you should have been able to hear me.

The door squeaked on its hinges, and once inside, I flicked on the kitchen light. There were beer bottles everywhere, and the ashtray overflowed with a massive pile of accordion-shaped butts. An empty vodka bottle sat in the midst of the array, like a centerpiece accentuating the brown bottles encircling it. I walked down the hall to your bedroom, now assured I would find you passed out. Your bedroom door was ajar just a crack, and I pushed it open. The outside streetlight filtered through your curtains enough for me to see your bed.

You were lying on your side completely naked with your back to me. I started to walk over to you and froze in my tracks. Something wasn't right, and at first I thought the low light was playing tricks with my eyes. And then an astonishing rush of horror flushed through my veins, running ice through my blood. There was a man's leg wrapped around yours, the rest of his body hidden behind you. As my eyes adjusted from the brightness of the kitchen light to the darkness of your bedroom, I could see his head resting on the pillow that not that long ago held my own. I was frozen solid, my skin feeling like it had just been touched by Arctic winds. My heart was pounding hard enough that I was in fear of it jumping out of my chest. My first impulse was to shout out your name in the loudest form of screeching and screaming I could muster. I wanted to startle you so badly that you would fall out of bed, dragging your new lover with you. Was I mad? Yes, but it was only to cover up the severe pain that throbbed not from the center of my heart but from my solar plexus. Getting kicked in the stomach by a shoed horse couldn't have hurt worse.

You stirred a bit when I began to slowly back out of the room, but you did not awaken. I had no interest in who he was, what my replacement was named. My anger turned internally, wondering how I could have been so stupid. As I retreated down the hall, tears started to well up in my eyes. It wasn't so much from sadness but from disappointment in myself. A sudden flash of my past scrolled across the screen inside my forehead, where dreams are normally displayed. The visions were as bright as neon signs, followed by huge capital letters pulsating the word *fool* over and over again. I could barely concentrate on the drive home. My whole life was flashing in front of me, like the scrolling effects of hallucinogenics.

My tears didn't make it out of my eye sockets. They dried up at the corners, forced away by the anger I felt toward myself. I had brought this situation on so I could not find a way to blame you. I was only sorry that I was so blinded by my own selfish needs, my clueless entrapment of instant gratification, that I had not seen from the beginning how messed up you really were. Was I any different? Was I so desperate for love and companionship that I didn't even bother to take the time to figure out who you were? Obviously, but if I wanted this love and companionship so badly, how had I steered off the path so far in my search for it? Why had I sabotaged so many relationships, destroying the good ones, following the wrong ones. There would be no more.

You changed me that night more than any other woman had. Was it the shock of finding you the way I did? I tried to think otherwise. I felt that I had finally awakened the person inside me that had never been able to totally emerge. There were a thousand reasons for that, a thousand things to blame it on. Like an epiphany from the heavens, I finally found myself that night. There would be no more futile searches. I would concentrate on finding myself through me, something I always understood was needed but could not do when it was so much easier to drown in my sorrows and to flood my thoughts and feelings with outside influences.

I parked my car in my driveway that night and sat there staring into space for an immeasurable amount of time, lost in some other dimension. My new insight was too much for me to handle all at once, and I did walk to my town bar and then stagger home after last call.

But you had given me the tools to finally start a new life. I knew it would be a slow process. The shock treatment you gave me had sprouted ventilation systems throughout my mind, and a lifetime of poisonous existence was about to spew out and finally leave me cleansed. No religious experience could ever match how I now felt about my future. It seemed ridiculous to me that I had not found the means before to like myself. This was a basic summation to what this all amounted to. All the philosophy and psychology books could explain it in a dozen other intricate ways. But this was a concrete and uncomplicated way to finally find the strength to independency. And once I have perfected it, then maybe I could be good to someone in the truest sense of love. Overnight, all my pains were now instruments for future prosperity in all aspects of my life. I state no lie when I tell you that I was profoundly changed that night.

Over two months later, when you were nothing but a bad dream, the reality of my time with you came back to haunt me like an unfinished penance. I came home from work one night to find my phone not working. From a phone booth, I called the telephone company to find out it was out of service, disconnected for lack of payment. I have always paid my bills on time, except for that rough period of time in my early twenties when my finances fell apart. As I tried to have the customer representative explain to me what bill hadn't been paid, a gnawing pain in my gut was causing internal organs to flip-flop. Almost simultaneously, the memory of putting a phone number under your name flashed back to the surface as the woman's voice at the other end of the line asked me if I did not have another telephone with a Lexington address.

Honesty had always created a problem in my past, and there were circumstances where a couple of well-placed lies could have changed my whole life. This time, I was able to find the power of deceit some others could probably find naturally. With a swallow of air, I denied any knowledge of that phone, your phone. At first, I couldn't even do that right, a loose moral fiber slapping me around over my lie. Instead of a firm no, I had said I didn't think so. When she went on to say the bill was up to sixteen hundred dollars, my heart skipped a beat; I became more adamant, and there was a strong denial based on the foundation of self-protectionism.

After a firm proclamation of "definitely not," she explained that all my personal information was in their records indicating that the phone was registered under my name. Reiterating my denial, I asked what I could possibly do to rectify this obvious mistake. My anger with you was no longer turned inside, and I moved it all outward and pointed it directly at you. I was able to fuel my prevarications with confidence and convinced myself that my own lies were the truth. It was my first insight on how perpetual liars functioned and could operate within the boundaries of their own conscience. But I was glad this was one habit I would never claim to fame. I only had to maneuver out of this one trap and go back to riding the ropes of moral fibers.

She explained to me that if I thought I was a victim of fraud, I should contact the police, and they could then contact the phone company's fraud investigation department, and they would work together on my case. I thanked her for her advice, and before I hung up, I asked her why I wouldn't have been contacted before with such an astronomical bill. She told me it was not normally their policy to call the customer, and before I headed off in any other wrong direction of foolish questions, I thanked her and said good-bye in a manner you would end the conversation of a friend.

I stood in the phone booth and stewed for a while. Because of your phone bill reaching such monumental numbers and your phone under my name, they had cut off my service too. I had spent many years regaining my credit, managing my finances better than some accountants. It was one of the few pieces of pride I had ascertained. The fact that you would take such advantage of me stirred my blood, and I couldn't focus at first while I boiled over. I was beyond enraged, and various thoughts were tossed around aimlessly about what to do. I could go to the police, but it would have to be the Lexington police since it was their district. This was the very same police force that many, many moons ago had arrested me for standing in the middle of the street, which they thought was inappropriate fashion. Would they remember me after all these years, or was I simply panicking over how well I could carry a consistent story of fabrication needed to make you responsible for this phone bill. I kept convincing myself that I could on the grounds that it should not be my responsibility, and I had been punished enough for past mistakes. I was willing to accept all emotional punishment for I had spent a lifetime consenting to the karmic results of that. But driven by memories of my days in poverty, I could not accept the penalty of such a potent blow to my finances.

If someone had told me the day before that I would step a foot anywhere near your place again, I would have asked them what they had been smoking. I had no desire whatsoever to see you again, but this was one of the few times where I had let anger seethe through and dictate my actions. If I could not bring reason to you and have you admit that this was your responsibility and make you tell the phone company as much, then I would go to the police to release any dormant acting abilities I had.

The ride to your house was not comfortable. I did not arm myself with liquid courage. The anger still boiling inside me, questioning how you could possibly have done this to me, carried enough kinetic energy with it to push me forward with unbending determination. Even then, I hesitated before I knocked on your kitchen door. It was wide open as usual. I knocked timidly at first, but then followed with a series of bangs loud enough to scare the sparrows out of the spruce tree in the neighbor's yard. I thought about just opening the door and walking in, but I already knew before I knocked that I would not be stepping into your house. If you had been home, the conversation would have been from your porch.

Convinced that you weren't home or were hiding from me somewhere, I drove straight to the police station without a moment's hesitation. The long ride to your house had given me plenty of time to plan my statement and what would be my unwavering story. I had absolutely no knowledge to how your phone ended up in my name. This was self-preservation by any means necessary, and if it meant stomping the last remnants of empathy from my system, then it would be done.

It was with this combination of anger that was borderlining on hatred, protectionism, and the determined drive to fix the wrongdoing you inflicted on me that gave me the extraordinary character change I needed to get the job done. In any other circumstances, the police officer that helped that day would have been intimidating. He towered over me by at least a half a foot, and the uniform always daunted me. I found it surprisingly easy to explain my situation to him with the credibility of a lawyer's statement. I merely left out that one piece of incriminating information, that I had given you permission to put the phone under my name.

The feeling that I had never been transgressed as badly by anyone allowed my own mind to believe that I had not permitted such a thing and made it all that much easier to sound convincing. I had convinced myself. I was fast on the draw to any of his questions. He was thorough. He wanted to know where I met you, how long I had been seeing you, and the extent of our relationship. I think it was the only time I had ever used the phrase *friends with benefits*. It still sounded inappropriate to me, but mostly because I wondered if we had ever been friends.

When he asked me how I thought you got my personal information, I told him that you must have taken it out of my wallet while I was sleeping. He found this quite feasible. After he read over the finished report he had written based on my answers, he had me sign it. He put it in a folder and said he would investigate. When I told him I was worried about the high bill and my reputation, he assured me that everything would be taken care of. It was what he said afterward when walking me out of his office that sent such a relief through me that the push of gravity seemed to lose its hold and I felt like I was floating off the ground. He said that you were well-known to the police and that you had a record, and he was not surprised by my accusations. I knew he wasn't about to share the details, so I shook his hand instead of asking and thanked him with enough sincerity that it forever fractured the wall of intimidation I held for police officers.

A week later, I got a call at work from the same officer. It was the only way I could think of for him to get in contact with me since your creation of my own dead phone. You can only imagine the grand sense of relief I felt when he informed me that you had admitted to fraud. As confident as I was in the outcome, I still had spent the week frantically fretting, trying to avoid the fact that all you had to say was that I had given you permission to put the phone under my name. I would have vehemently denied it, but what a mess the whole situation would have become. I am not sure why you accepted total responsibility. Maybe you had more of a conscience than I gave you credit for. Maybe you were just so totally lost that you weren't even aware of the phone bill. I will lose no sleep about why, but will lose a few hours from time to time living with the fact that I had to lie to stop you from burning me. As you know and as the officer explained to me later, the representative from the phone company and the police confronted you right at your house and explained to you the penalties for fraud. You agreed to pay the bill in lieu of being charged. I can only assume your previous record scared you into admittance. I can only thank you for doing the right thing.

The whole situation was something I had to bury quickly, for it had brought unexpected interference to my new beginning, to my new direction in life. I am grateful that you took responsibility and ended the whole matter. For that I give you respect, and I can assure you I had none left.

Before the officer hung up on me that day, he went on to say that the original bill that I had been quoted did not include the final month before the service was cut. It had risen to over twenty-five hundred dollars. I asked with the tone of shock in my voice how it could possibly become so high. I couldn't have talked on the phone that long in several decades. He informed me that your daughter's boyfriend had been charged and found guilty of armed robbery and had been shipped to a penitentiary far up north. From there was an extraordinary amount of collect phone calls all accepted by your daughter. At the same time I was thanking the officer for all his help, I couldn't help but silently pray for your daughter. What kind of future was ahead of her? What was mine doing?

My phone was reconnected the following week, and the whole mess became part of my history. My anger for you has long dissipated, but more importantly, so was the anger to myself. You were a learning experience soon not to be forgotten, and although the whole experience had nightmarish overtones, you did save me from what could have been an entire lifetime of regression.

I often wonder if I had tried harder, I might have been able to change your path of self-destruction. But I also wonder how thin the line was that I had walked most of my life to a path of my own demise. I hope somehow you have found yourself, that there might be some powerful intervention to help you. I could not. But in the deep roots of your existence, you helped me find my own way; and for that, not only do I offer you my forgiveness, but also my gratitude.

CHAPTER 20

Dear Soul Mate:

I know you are still out there. I just can't be sure when or where I will find you. The bar scene is now far behind me, not only from the age factor creeping its way to the development of maturity levels that I couldn't quite comprehend before, but also to keep in balance a newly discovered respect for the detriments of alcohol. Moderation has finally reached compatibility with my need for accountability and my reach for common sense. Moderation was not part of my vocabulary through my struggles through life. For the first time, I have surpassed the network of my attempts and endeavors of a wandering mind and feel that I have control over my own destiny.

I am not ashamed to admit that I finally found the courage to seek professional help. Once I got past the hurdle of disagreeing with someone with a master's degree in the workings of the mind and convinced her that my childhood should be left out of any discussions and that I alone was responsible for my actions, then progress was made. I had no intentions of blaming anyone else, including my parents. Once that was established, we began the right path for her to help me and to warrant the eighty bucks an hour I was forking over to her. It ended after only a few sessions, however, when it became apparent that I was having too much fun analyzing her. But it was not a complete waste. I was able to bring a few buried feelings out to thrash over, hearing them out loud instead of whispering them in the privacy of the cavities of my skull.

I have caused a lot of pain and suffering during my journey through life, and for that I will eventually have to answer for. I have many regrets that in my strive to become a better person, in my lost searches, my wrong paths, I had fallen into so many pitfalls. Always plagued with the bindings of depression, any optimism or periods of happiness became bogged down with feelings of futility and hopelessness. It was like walking through swamp water laden with entangled vines, making the trek uphill difficult. Each time I tripped, it was harder to move ahead, harder to get back up. But at the same time, each time I fell, in spite of the mounting despair and forlorn outlook, there was always some celestial beacon coming from the core of my soul that would give me the strength to push forward.

When I look back now, I realize that my depression was not necessarily all detrimental in my quest for inner growth. Without the struggles and disappointments, there was a possibility that vanity and pride would have suffocated the true nature of my universal love, that unwavering drive of mine to the notion of cosmic connection. My natural shyness controlled what could have become a runaway ego, enough to endanger my ability to find the real answers from my inner voice. We all have the answers right inside us to our endless quest for meaning. Few of us ever listen.

I now carry with me the rest of my days an enlightened soul, ready to call my search complete. I am far from spouting religious dogma or that of any new age spiritualism, but I am stating that I am finally at peace within myself and am ready for all atonements. I have been blessed with ethereal knowledge well beyond the planet's limitations and perhaps beyond the efforts of decipher from the best of philosophers.

Do not perceive that I dwell on this knowledge. I am now content with what life has to offer and have found solace from my past. It is time for me to move forward and utilize the rest of my time enjoying the simple things that life offers. Too much of my time has already been wasted in my endless search for understanding the most trivial of things. There were needless complications. The understanding of it was there all along.

There are those who still portray me as a selfish human being, and that does bother me some. I know compassion, and the deepest part of my soul is filled with empathy for others almost to a fault. If it does not show in my actions, it does dictate my every thought. If I have somehow intertwined selfishness with survival, then I might have been guilty for some self-serving ways. For that I will find ways to make amends to everyone I have hurt, even if it is as minuscule as praying for them and offering willing guidance for their success and happiness.

There is a woman out there for me. I can feel you. I will continue to search for you and, if my destiny allows it, will spend the rest of my years on earth in blissful harmony with you, my true soul mate. You have eluded me so far, but there is still time. The scars of my heart have healed, and I am ready to share the rapture of true endearment. I have a world to give you.

If I do not find you, rest assured you still own my heart. Take it and carry it with you as infinite love. Use its strength to guide you for all eternity, for I will always be a part of you.

CONCLUSION

Dear Reader:

I am Melissa's daughter. I am my father's daughter. My father passed away recently, one day before his fortieth birthday.

Although I did not know my father, I always thought I could feel his presence throughout my childhood. I have vague visions of him holding me on his knee when I must have been very, very young. The only clear memory I have of him was on a cold, wintry day. He was standing in the street, looking very tired. He was waiting just outside the school yard, where I would exit for my short walk home. My memories of him at that time were only cloudy recollections, but they provided enough source for me to know who he was. He knelt down in front of me and handed me a huge shopping bag of Christmas presents and told me how much he loved me. He kept saying he was sorry for everything. I was not sure exactly what he was sorry for. I was still too young to distinguish the difference between my real father and my stepfather, so the fact that he had abandoned my mother and me did not register yet.

Later when I was older, as I began to ask more questions and began to pressure my mother to explain things to me, she opened up to me. It was not unbiased words that she used. In her eyes, and hence in mine for the longest time afterward, I pictured him as a selfish man, a shallow man whose own self-interest came before all others. My mother drilled incessantly, in vile words, how useless he was. I had been sorry I asked. But that day in the cold street, any notion that he might have been reaching out for me was quashed by the actions of my stepfather.

When I got home from school, practically dragging my bag of gifts down the sidewalk, my stepfather met me at the door. When he found out where the gifts had come from, he yanked them out of my hands and tossed them into the garbage pail, crushing them with his foot to make them all fit. I did not cry out of fear.

In retrospect, I did not need my mother's loathing to influence my view of my father. My stepfather's view was quite sufficient. He had cursed at me and, in a long spew of disgusting remarks, placed my father in the garbage pail along with my gifts. I wouldn't exactly describe it as complete brainwashing, but I was certainly led to believe that my father could care less about me. The loud rambling of my stepfather's voice that day echoed throughout the house, and I remember his spittle nearly hitting me as he sprayed his venomous words in front of my face. They were powerful enough, intimidating enough, that they fogged over my very last appearance of my father. I never saw him again.

He had said little on that cold day in front of the school yard. I had said even less. I cannot even remember saying thank you to him. I do remember telling him I had to go, straight home from school drilled into my head. When I turned to walk away, he had given me a hug and repeated how much he loved me. It carried a warm breeze through the chilling winter wind that caught my heart for a second, only to be annihilated shortly after. Until now.

When I strain really hard and force the shadowed memories above the evil words of my stepfather, I remember looking back and watching those huge tears running down the sides of my father's cheeks, so plentiful that they seemed to puddle on the sidewalk. I watched him wave to me, and only now do I recognize the love in his eyes that day. This was not the face of a selfish man.

When my mother first broke the news to me, she did it in a sensitive manner. With the reality of death smacking her in the face, I think she finally understood that she had been wrong in depriving me of my father's love. She has since apologized for leading me to believe that he had wanted nothing to do with me. I might have found out on my own eventually, for I had spent the last year gathering enough courage to go and see him. As I grew closer to womanhood, I wanted to hear it from him. I wanted to hear his side of the story, whether his words would devastate me or not. It is too late now.

My father lived alone before his passing. He was alone the night it happened. Sometime during the night, he had driven his car off the cliff of a campground and directly into Lake Erie, only a quarter of a mile from where I was told he had first met my mother. Some campers had taken a stroll across the boardwalk that morning and spotted the silhouette of his car just below the surface of the water. The medical examiner listed the cause of death as drowning. There was an assumption that he died at two in the morning for that was when the clock on the dash of my dad's car had stopped. Rumors had it that he had been drunk, but no blood tests were ever taken. So to respect his life, I will forever believe that he was not.

But I also have to contend with the fact that he might have taken his own life. That is more difficult to deal with. The few of his friends I managed to track down after my mission to discover my true father had said that he was often depressed. They had not seen him in a while before his death, so they could not vouch for his frame of mind at the time. They all agreed that he deserved happiness, but he had always struggled to find it.

They went on to say how hard of a worker he was, yet lived quite modestly. There were also plenty of testaments that he was a good, caring man, who was known for helping others, and one friend's wife went as far as to call him altruistic. What was the most heartwarming for me was that every one of his friends and acquaintances that I was able to find all said that he had mentioned me to them. Most of them also had a humorous story about drinking with him. These I do not wish to comment on.

I do not have a long eulogy to honor my father with. What I do have is information that makes me state that he was a good man, human and allowed mistakes.

My father had written a will, and in that will, he had left everything to me, including his house. No one contested it, and that is how I came to live under my father's roof once more. He also left me a substantial amount of money in various bank accounts, mutual funds, and other high-interest investments. There was no mortgage left on the house. No one knew.

After my father's funeral, I wanted to find some way to commemorate his memory and his life, some way to preserve his time on earth. I probed my mind at night trying to think of something more meaningful than an expensive headstone to mark his bones. It was several weeks after when I was making preparations to move into his home that I made a startling discovery.

I had begun the morbid chore of packing his clothes and personal belongings (there weren't many). Impulsively, I decided to look underneath his bed. Against the back wall, I found a tattered elongated cardboard box with stacks and stacks of handwritten pages. There were thousands and thousands, all in tidy cursive writing. No one I spoke to had known my father to write, yet here were several manuscripts, many with such philosophical dribble and theories of the universe and afterlife that he had me lost in the meaning of it all.

But set aside from the rest, wrapped in a thick elastic band, was the *Memoirs to My Women*, which I can assume you have just read. I could think of no better honor to my father than to have these writings published, these words of my father. I do this as a display of respect to the women that were a part of his life and to also hopefully disclose his true heart and his longing for love. I do this to honor anyone that he might have affected or might have affected him. I did my best to edit his work, but without truly knowing him, I can only surmise that he was trying to make an ingenuous attempt at making amends.

My lawyer advised me against publishing, remarking on privacy rights and a whole list of other legal implications. The memory of my father is more important to me, and for all intents and purposes, this is a work of fiction. Except for the parts relating to my mother, I am regarding all other characters as his fantasies, fictional medicinal doses of his own imagination to ease his loneliness. It is the underlining message that is of importance. I am reminded of a disclaimer at the end of some television shows where any similarities to real characters are purely coincidental. You have just read mine.

I hope that his story gives some small piece of recognition in each and every one of you, in your own trek through a mean world where the lonely can be left behind. If my father's words can reach or touch someone's heart to help them go through life in their own search for love and happiness and let them not lose focus on what they might already have, then my father's life will not have been in vain.

I love you, Dad.

Get Published, Inc!
Thorofare, NJ 08086
12 April, 2010
BA2010102